SHE BEGAN TO WRITHE....

And he came down on her, his arms going around her, steel bands, unyielding, and he felt the heat of her against the stiffness of his groin. He pressed against her, grunting with pleasure. Her sobs mingled with his labored breathing. But that was not what stopped him. It was the sound of galloping destriers. One more moment and he would be deep, so deep inside her. He was on his feet, his sword battle-ready in hand, in the next scant second.

"Rolfe, my lord, stop!"

Guy reined in, and Rolfe, standing there with blade upraised, was a hair's breadth from killing his best vassal. Guy knew it, for he shouted, "She's Mercia's sister! Good God, she's Mercia's sister!"

"What?"

"She's Edwin's sister, Rolfe. Edwin and Morcar's sister."

Rolfe turned, stunned, to look at the wench who lay curled up on the ground, the wench he had been an instant from raping. *His intended.*

Also by Brenda Joyce

THE DARKEST HEART

LOVERS AND LIARS

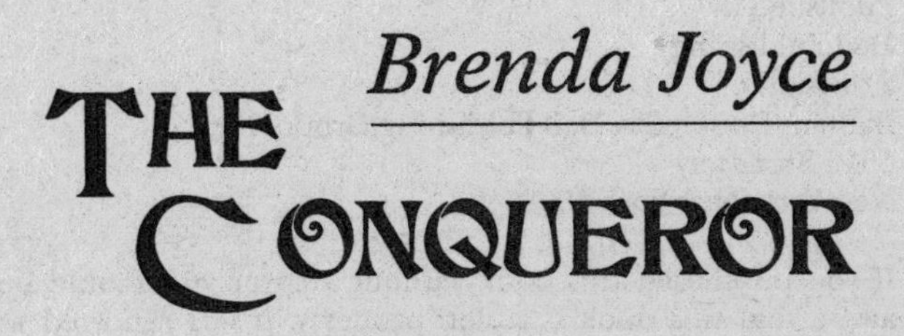

A DELL BOOK

Published by
Dell Publishing
a division of
Bantam Doubleday Dell Publishing Group, Inc.
1540 Broadway
New York, New York 10036

ISBN: 0-440-20609-X

First Dell Edition Published September 1990

Printed in the United States of America

Published simultaneously in Canada

October 1996

10 9 8 7 6 5 4 3

RAD

The Conqueror is dedicated to:

My mom, truly special and even more wonderful

And my dad, one of those guys who move
mountains

Friends always said that one day it had to happen,
because of my constant creative visualization,
a man just like one of my heroes
would sweep me away,
and finally, it did!

For Eli—a real hero

With a special thank you to Maggie Lichota

CHAPTER 1

Near York,
June 1069

"My lord?"

"Rouse out all the villagers."

Rolfe of Warenne watched expressionlessly as his vassal Guy Le Chante wheeled his destrier around, calling to his knights. He sat motionless on his massive gray stallion in the middle of the road. He had removed his helmut; it lay in the crook of his left arm. His hair, flaxen and curly, was dark and damp with sweat. His mail hauberk clung to his broad frame, and his right hand rested casually on the hilt of his sword.

He watched his men rousing the remaining villagers. He had only to turn his head slightly to the left to see the dozen slain Saxon rebels, their bodies already giving off that peculiar stink of death in the warm June sun. His blood still coursed from the recent battle, his muscles were still thick with it. Another nest of Saxon rebels, yet the king would not be pleased. Far from it. The war in these savage northern climes looked to be endless. It had been a fortnight since William's iron fist had come down hard enough to shake the entire table as he sat with his vassals at York. They had just turned the Danish invaders back, retaken York, and sent the Saxons fleeing into the Welsh marches. This was the second uprising in as many years, and King William had been furious, especially as the Saxon lords Edwin and Morcar had escaped. Again. "No mercy," he had roared. "We will burn out every croft and every cranny until these barbarians learn who their holy and anointed king is!"

The orders stood.

Rolfe saw his men herding a dozen villagers, male and female, away from the village. Like most of these hamlets, it consisted of a dozen small thatched huts, a watermill, a few common pastures for sheep, a cornfield, and vegetable patches. A cry of outrage made him turn his head.

"No!" The young woman had hold of Guy's arm as he lifted his sword to sever the head from a sow. She screamed again; Guy decapitated the creature effortlessly. Blood sprayed her gown and Guy's horse.

Rolfe watched with a twinge of interest. He wasn't sure if his interest was due to her daring and foolishness in opposing Guy, or to her hair, the most magnificent and unusual mane he had ever seen. The color of the richest bronze, in the sunlight it sparkled as if seeded with gold flakes. The braid was as thick as his destrier's tail.

She stood in shock, clutching herself. Guy came trotting up the road. For a moment Rolfe did not take his eyes off her; he felt the stirring in his groin and made another decision. Guy reined in as the wench was led to the group of pale, stricken villagers by one of the peasants. He wondered what she looked like up close, then dismissed the question as needless. It didn't matter; she would serve. "My lord?" Guy asked.

Two oxen and a dozen sheep had been slaughtered, enough to feed his men for a sennight. He waited a beat, until one of the knights had dragged the slaughtered sow aside, then pierced Guy with cold blue eyes. "Burn everything."

"The cornfield?"

Rolfe's jaw clenched. Without their livestock and without their corn, the peasants would starve this winter. But they would not harbor any more rebels. "Everything."

Guy turned with a cry. No war cry, but a shallow, lacking rendition. His men were not looters, not like many of the mercenaries come to England. Rather, his men were highly trained, the most elite Norman fighting force there was, the king's personal household troops. They had been honed by years of war to establish William in the duchy of Normandy, in resisting invasion in France and Anjou, in conquering and holding Maine. Hastings had been a lark in comparison; and three years later the Saxons had proved they were no threat on the battlefield. Only in the hills and vales and forests of the borderlands, Rolfe thought. Then they were very skilled warriors, indeed.

He did not have to look to feel the agitation coming from the peasants, for his senses were keen. But look he did. He saw an old woman and a man holding the honey-haired girl, who was struggling to break free. He watched keenly. She slipped their grasp and, with her skirts lifted, giving him a glimpse of bare, dirty feet and slim, shapely calves, she ran up the road to him.

Bloodlust, thick and hot, filled his sac, tightened it, weighted it. He watched her approaching. "My lord, please," she cried, panting, her hands clasped to her bosom. "Please, stop them, it's not too late!"

For an instant, Rolfe couldn't answer. She was dirty—dirt smudged her face, her gown and tunic, her hands. But he barely saw her filth. He was looking at her perfectly oval face, at the high, aristocratic cheekbones, the straight, slightly tilted nose, big, wide purple eyes. And that mouth. Too full, the only imperfection, a mouth made for a man's pleasure. Some Saxon lord's by-blow, he thought, and knowing what was to come, there was the slightest easing of the hard line of his lips. His friends would know he was pleased.

He ignored her plea, of course, and turned his head slightly to watch one hut go up in flames. It was instantaneous, because of the thatched, straw roof. Another followed. He did not feel satisfaction. There was no satisfaction to feel. He was the king's man, he was his sworn vassal, he was doing his duty. And as a warrior and William's most trusted knight, he knew the soundness of this policy. It would, eventually, break the back of the rebellion.

She grabbed his foot.

Shocked, Rolfe twisted, as his steed pranced furiously and then lashed out. She jumped back as Rolfe fought to control the maddened stallion, who was meanly humored and as likely to kill men as not. When he had his mount under control he pierced her with a look that combined anger and incredulity.

"Please spare the corn," she cried. Tears streaked her grimy cheeks. "Please, my lord, please."

She would starve along with her village, he thought, and a muscle ticked in his jaw. He looked away again and watched as the corn went up in a blaze of flames. He heard her gasp out a choked sob, then knew she was leaving. He was compelled to gaze after her, running, stumbling, not back to the villagers but into the forest. He watched her hips. The heaviness in his groin grew. Smoke billowed over the village; the old women were sobbing. His knights had finished their job, and Rolfe saw two of them turn and set chase after the girl, no doubt with the same intention of bedding her that he had. Instantly adrenaline tightened every fiber of his being and reflex had him leaning over his stallion's neck, spurring him on.

Guy and Beltain were ahead of him, pursuing her at an easy canter, and he heard Beltain laugh. Rolfe smiled. Beneath him, his destrier stretched out into a gallop. The two men heard him and looked back, startled. Ahead of them Rolfe saw the girl disappear into a copse. She knew she was being chased and her feet had wings. Rolfe reached his men and surged between them. He was vaguely aware that they had dropped out of the chase, as he had known they would. The girl came into sight again.

Every muscle of Rolfe's body was taut with tension and expectation. He was hard and throbbing beneath his undertunic. He could almost feel her soft woman's body beneath his, the sticky heat of her sheath around him. She screamed as she fell, looked back, saw him. She was up and running again. He was behind her. Alongside her. He easily drew her into his arms and up onto his thigh. She screamed again, clinging, though, not struggling, as his destrier was in a battle gallop, and one fall would be her last. He pushed her completely over his lap, facedown, and felt soft breasts on his thigh, her ribs against his stiff groin. He brought the stallion immediately to a blowing halt.

She was twisting wildly, and her elbow almost caught his manhood as she tried to right herself and slip off, but Rolfe was too fast and too strong. He slid to his feet with her in his arms, went down on his knees, and pushed her flat on her back.

For an instant, their eyes met.

Hers terrified and furious, his hot and bright.

He had to have her, and now. He caught her braid by the nape, and even as he leaned over to claim her lips he was shoving her gown and tunic up to her waist. She writhed but his one hold was enough to pin her.

He kneed her thighs wide apart. "My brothers," she said, gasping. "My brothers will—"

His mouth closed on hers, his tongue delving deep into the space she had provided. He ran one hand over her breasts, full and lush. His hand didn't stop. He tore his mouth away and reached down to clasp her woman's mound; she arched in panic beneath his touch. "They'll kill you," she screamed, her body coming up off the ground to try to escape his touch. But he still had her nape and her head remained a firm anchor; she wasn't going anywhere. Not until he allowed it.

She lay spread before him, and the sight of her pink woman's flesh drove him to the edge. He released her wrists, violently ripping open her bodice, exposing full, lush breasts and a small pouch she wore on a thin chain. The sight momentarily froze him. With a shriek, her nails flew at his face, but Rolfe's reflexes were honed by years of battle, and he caught her hands again, the grip cruel, causing her to cry out. Already his shaft was huge and thick, straining his hose, ready to burst. Rolfe transferred her hands to one of his, yanking them high over her head, hard, effortlessly, even though she still fought him. And then he was taking a nipple into his mouth.

She began to writhe again. He came down on her, his arms going around her, steel bands, unyielding, and he felt the heat of her against the stiffness of his groin. He pressed against her, grunting with pleasure. Her sobs mingled with his labored breathing. But that was not what stopped him. It was the sound of galloping destriers. One more moment and he would be deep, so deep, inside her. He was on his feet, his sword battle-ready in hand, in the next scant second.

"Rolfe, my lord, stop!"

Guy reined in, and Rolfe, standing there with blade

upraised, was a hair's breadth from killing his best vassal. Guy knew it, for he shouted, "She's Mercia's sister! Good God, she's Mercia's sister!"

"What?"

"She's Edwin's sister, Rolfe. Edwin and Morcar's sister."

Rolfe turned, stunned, to look at the wench who lay curled up on the ground, the wench he had been an instant from raping. *His intended.*

CHAPTER 2

Ceidre crouched panting and shaking in the dirt.

She could still hear the rumble of thunder that was the massive destrier's hoofbeats as the Norman knight had ridden her down. She could still feel the steed's hot breath, and her own terror. She had been inches from being trampled to death, and she had seen these Normans run down hapless peasants before. This knight, like the others, would have probably done the same to her out of sheer perverted amusement. Sweet Saint Cuthbert!

She could still feel his arms around her, arms of steel, holding her hard and fast to the moist brown earth. And his hands on her womanhood, his mouth on her breast, defiling her. And the heat of his manhood . . . Mother of God!

She understood the Norman language fairly well, but had been too shaken to comprehend the rapidly fired conversation now occurring. Yet she could not miss her brothers' names, could not miss "Mercia." She fought to still her trembling, straining to listen, with her face still pressed to the ground.

"God's blood," Rolfe said, and she knew he was looking at her. "She can't be."

She could feel the heat of his stare, feel the shock of whatever news had been imparted, in the silence now held between him and his man. Sweet Mary, how she hated him!

"I heard it from the villagers," his man said. " 'Tis well known. And Aelfgar is not that far from here."

Ceidre tensed at the name of her home. They must know who she was. She slowly sat up, clutching her torn gown together. She fixed him with a stare of intense hatred.

His gaze, cold and vividly blue, held hers. His look darkened and warred with hers. A nerve in his jaw ticked. She could feel his anger now and knew it was directed at her. For what? For her insolence in hating him? For what he had been denied—the rape of her body? Or because he knew who she was?

He moved. He came to her swiftly. Ceidre started to shrink away, then caught herself and held her ground, raising her chin with defiance. She could feel the thick, unnatural beat of her heart, the cloying terror. He could rape her and then beat her before killing her, but she would not show fear of this man. But he had seen her initial reaction, and this too displeased him. His anger was a visible thing, darkening his eyes again, and his face.

And then his expression changed. He stopped abruptly, staring.

Ceidre had seen many people look at her the same way, when they first noticed her eye. Surprise, usually, was the initial reaction, then puzzlement, then comprehension and horror. Behind him, she saw Guy draw back. "I'd heard it but I didn't believe it," he whispered nervously, unable to tear his glance from Ceidre. " 'Tis the evil eye."

Rolfe's gaze was riveted upon hers. Ceidre hated the deformity that had haunted her her entire life: Her right eye sometimes wandered away at will. It was not a frequent occurrence; usually it happened only when she was extremely tired, and was only noticeable by those in close proximity. People thought she could gaze in two opposite directions at once—'twasn't true. Strangers who did notice this defect crossed themselves for protection when they saw her "evil" eye and kept well away from her. It had been that way her entire life, since she was a tiny toddler in swaddling. The villagers at Aelfgar, her own people, many her own kin on her mother's side, were long used to her, knew she wasn't evil. Yet that she could heal the sick as her granny did only confirmed their belief that she was a witch. So even her kin were overly aware of her, in awe. Only her brothers, well used to her, seemed entirely indifferent, and Ceidre had long since said prayers of thanks for this blessing. Yet even they were not beyond begging a boon—Morcar had once asked her to bewitch a lass who had been leading him on a merry chase! Now Ceidre flushed, hating this deformity more than she ever had in her entire life—hating being exposed before this man.

His cool blue gaze swept her features one by one, returning finally to her eye. Then he spoke. "She is no witch. She is flesh and blood. That is enough."

"My lord," Guy protested nervously. "Be careful."

He was standing above her, his sword sheathed, hands curled into angry fists on his lean hips. "Are you the lady Alice?"

She blinked in surprise. And then she understood his misconception; he was confusing her with her half sister. Ceidre was no fool. Alice was not a by-blow. Being nobly born, she was of more import than Ceidre herself was. Depending, of course, on circumstance—on which game of war this Norman pig chose to play. For now she would go along with the false belief, to save herself from a certain rape, or worse. Ceidre said, "Yes."

Her answer seemed to please him, for suddenly he smiled. Ceidre was momentarily stunned. Not by his response, or by the fact that he actually could smile. She remembered how he had looked charging after her on his destrier, like a golden pagan god. How he had looked, sitting there so impassively as she had pleaded with him to spare the corn. Now she realized he was devastatingly handsome with his short golden curls, his blue eyes, straight white even teeth, and features that were sensually, ruthlessly chiseled. She stared at his proudly sculpted face, unable to stop herself.

"What do you think, Guy?" He was grinning, not tearing his gaze from her as he asked his knight the question. For a moment their gazes held.

Guy didn't answer. His dismay was answer enough.

Ceidre didn't like the possessive way the Norman's eyes were stroking her body, and her anger returned in full force. Anger and something else, uneasiness. She started to get up, and he was there. His touch infuriated her, and she wrenched away; she did not need his help, would never need it. But why wasn't he afraid of her now that he knew the truth? Instead, he was angry at her response, but he was obviously a man of discipline for he held himself carefully in check. Gone, though, was the beautiful smile. "My lady," he said stiffly. "What are you doing away from Aelfgar? Dressed as you are? It is not safe in these times."

He would show concern for her safety? It was a mockery! "And what affair is it of yours? Am I your prisoner?" she demanded, chin high, eyes flashing. Yet inside she was quaking.

His own jaw came up. His mouth was tightly compressed. A few moments passed before he spoke—before, Ceidre thought, he trusted himself to speak. "You are not my prisoner, my lady. I will escort you back to Aelfgar to ensure no harm comes to your person."

"I don't need an escort," Ceidre managed. " 'Tis not far, just six kilometers or so."

"Have you never learned respect for your men?"

"For *my* men—yes."

He stared. "I will escort you to Aelfgar. We will camp here for the night."

"You are keeping me prisoner!" Ceidre cried.

"You are my guest," he said, very firmly. "And Guy will see to your welfare." Rolfe gave Guy a hard look. "But you still have not answered my question."

She was a prisoner and she knew it, a prisoner of her hated enemy, maybe even one of those who, for all she knew, had captured, hurt, or killed her brothers! "Spying," she said, oh-so-sweetly. "Whatever else would I be doing so far afield?"

"Do not test my charity of spirit," he breathed.

"I am good with herbs." She glared at him, remembering the sow. "I came to heal the sow."

He stared. "To heal a pig?"

Her chin lifted. Was he dumb or deaf? Both, of course, being the Norman pig he was and no pun intended. "Yes," she said through gritted teeth. "After all, I am a witch—or have you already forgotten?"

His lips might have curled up in the slightest of smiles. "You did not cast your spell through the air?" he asked.

Ceidre gritted—now he was making fun of her. "She was a prized breeder and suffering with congestion. Newly bred too. Of course, it no longer matters."

"You traveled six kilometers to heal a sow?"

"Six and a half."

Rolfe turned to Guy. *"C'est incroyable!* Do you believe this?" He had automatically reverted back to French.

"Perhaps we should let her go," Guy said, low. "Lest she cast a spell on us."

Rolfe's gaze was like a lance. "Perhaps she needs to be wedded and bedded. To learn a *woman's* true place."

Momentarily distracted, his eyes brightened at some vivid imagery. Then they narrowed. "Guy—she is here, the rebels were here. Who better to pass along a message? Look at her clothes! To heal a sow? I think she came disguised as a peasant to pass a message to her traitorous brothers! I think she is very smart—thinking to fool me by so openly admitting such a thing."

"Jésus," Guy breathed. As one they turned to look at her.

Ceidre hastily looked away, pretending she hadn't understood. But she had. Oh, why hadn't she kept her mouth shut! How, in this time of war, could she have declared herself a spy in her fit of temper? Now what would they do? She was already a valuable hostage, and that would keep her alive and safe, as long as they did think she was Alice. But if they thought she was a spy . . . And what was all this reference to wedding and bedding? She was struck with foreboding.

"No wife of mine will spy against my king," Rolfe stated savagely. And he seared Ceidre with a blazing look.

Stunned, Ceidre stared back. No, it could not be. He could not mean . . . "I don't understand."

Rolfe's face darkened at the lack of respect in her address. "Soon you will have to call me my lord," he said. "Whether you like it or no."

"No!" Ceidre cried.

"Oh, yes," Rolfe said. "We are to be wedded, my lady. You are to be my wife." And he smiled.

CHAPTER 3

The lady Alice and Aelfgar were the attainment of his every fierce ambition after a dozen years of serving William, and serving him well.

Less than a sennight ago, William had been pacing his tent furiously when Rolfe had arrived. Like Rolfe, he was still sweaty from the recent battle that had freed York from the Saxons and sent the Danes back to the coast and their ships. His bearded face was fierce with frustration, and Rolfe knew exactly why. "What news?" William the Conqueror demanded.

"The Saxons are routed, Your Grace."

Their eyes met, William's darkening with what was not being said. "Those bloody traitors?"

"There is no sign of Edwin or Morcar," Rolfe informed him.

William's brother, Bishop Odo, and one of his most powerful nobles, Roger of Montgomery, were the only others present. They sat relaxed, although alert, with refreshments. "I hope, Your Grace," Odo said smoothly, "that there will be no clemency this time?"

Rolfe and Roger both winced at Odo's blunt referral to the past. Edwin and Morcar had not taken up arms against William at Hastings (fortunately for William, Rolfe knew), for they had been weakened in the years prior by an attack from the king of Norway. Both had sworn allegiance to William at his coronation, and had followed William and his court back to Normandy when the south of England was secured. Edwin had been given what amounted to one third of England, including most of his lands in Mercia, and Morcar's Northumbrian holdings. He had also been promised William's daughter, the lovely Isolda, as a bride. Any other Norman bride would not have been controversial, but even Rolfe was leery of the magnitude of power that this would give the dangerous Saxon eaorl. In the end, William had reneged, and Edwin and Morcar had gone home furious.

A year later they had almost taken York, having roused the entire north to arms against the king. Although Rolfe had participated in the battle for York, abruptly thereafter he was sent to quell disturbances in Wales. Edwin and Morcar had repledged their allegiance, but this time William had left loyal vassals in their territory, to build and garrison and man royal castles.

And now it had happened again. The two northern lords had again led a rebellion, this time with a concurrent (coincidental? Rolfe thought not) invasion by the Danes. This time they had escaped, and there would be no royal forgiveness for their treason. For York had been demolished. A hundred Normans had been slain.

"Never again," William was roaring. "Those two Saxon traitors will hang if it's the last thing I ever do!" He turned abruptly to Rolfe. "Your place is here, it's clear," he said.

Rolfe stared but did not let any of his consternation show. What of his estates in Sussex and Kent, awarded to him after Hastings for his valor and loyalty? As the fourth and youngest son of the Comte de Warenne, Rolfe had become a mercenary soldier, the only recourse left to him. His eldest brother, Jean, was the Comte de Warenne in Normandy. The second brother was a priest. His other brother, William, had small holdings in Normandy, but had also followed the Conqueror to England. After Hastings he had been given Lewes, just as Rolfe was awarded with Bramber, Montgomery with Arundel, Odo with Dover, William fitz Osbern with the Isle of Wight. This handful of powerful vassals immediately secured Sussex and Kent. Rolfe had not returned to Normandy that year, for he was busy with fortifying his position. For now, for the first time in his twenty-eight years, he had his own land, a patrimony for his unborn son. And he knew, as did all the vassals who had followed William to England, whether from loyalty or greed or land hunger, that the possibilities were limitless.

"I am giving Bramber to Braose," William continued forcefully.

Rolfe's expression did not change.

William smiled at him. "I give you castellanship of the new castle you will build at York."

Rolfe's jaw tightened.

William's smile broadened. "And Aelfgar."

Roger of Montgomery gasped.

Rolfe smiled. Aelfgar was a huge fief, and with castellanship of York . . . he would be one of the most powerful lords of the north. Aelfgar had been the seat of Edwin's honor. He realized that this meant the two Saxon rebels were dispossessed. He also knew it would not be easy to secure his new fief, yet still, his pleasure with this vast reward was huge.

"Your borders are uncertain. You may extend them north as far as you can go," William said, smiling. "And to cement things nicely, you may also have their sister, Alice. After all, she is now sole heir."

Rolfe was grinning. The possibilities were limitless! The sister to secure his position!

"A fine move," Odo told his brother. "Holding

these border countries is no easy task. If anyone can do it, Rolfe can."

"Yes, with Rolfe in the north, and Roger in the marches—I have given Shrewsbury to Roger," William said. "I have high hopes these rebellions will become fruitless, quickly."

Rolfe remembered himself and dropped to one knee. "Thank you, Your Grace."

William smiled. "Up, Rolfe the Relentless, up. Bring me the heads of Edwin and Morcar and I'll give you Durham too."

That stunned everyone, including Rolfe, who doubted that the king meant it. For if such should happen, his power would rival the king's, and William was no fool.

He had been on his way to inspect Aelfgar and claim his land and his bride a few days later when he had encountered the Saxon rebels. Now it looked as if his own bride might be a Saxon spy and was apparently thought to be a witch. He smiled. Rolfe was not a superstitious man. He supposed it was possible that such a thing as witches existed—but he had never met one, and doubted he ever would. Most so-called sorceresses were frauds, hoodwinking others for their own prosperity. A witch? She was no witch, but a flesh-and-blood woman. And even if she were a witch, she was first and foremost a woman. *His* woman.

But she might be a Saxon spy. Just the mere thought infuriated Rolfe—and worried him. He was taking over his fief, an alien invader, surrounded by enemies. Morcar and Edwin were still alive, as far as anyone knew, obviously in hiding, but they would not take the granting of Aelfgar to a Norman lightly—they would fight for what had been theirs. Rolfe knew it without a doubt, just as he knew the two rebels, knew the quality of men that they were. It would be a tough battle, but

Rolfe was confident that he would emerge the victor. His name was not Rolfe the Relentless for nothing. He was always victorious in his quests, and this time, with Aelfgar and with the woman, would be no different.

She would be a difficult one to tame, and until she was tamed, a dangerous thorn in his side. But he couldn't help it, he liked the sound of that—he liked the thought of that. Taming his bride. He felt the surge of his lust again. Her place was at his side, taking care of him and his needs. Her place was in his home, in his bed. She would learn this, maybe not quickly, but she would learn. And of course she hadn't known, until he had told her, that the king had given her to him. He recalled clearly her shock. She would get over that too. He tried to imagine her reaction when she found out he was now the lord of Aelfgar. Unfortunately, he knew exactly how she would look. A woman enraged.

His bride—his enemy.

He must remind himself never to forget it.

CHAPTER 4

Alice was to marry the Norman.

Ceidre realized she was pacing the confines of the tent. What did this mean? How had it happened? Ceidre feared the worst. If William had given the Norman Alice . . . Panic, icy cold, rose up to shrink her guts. If only there were news of her brothers! They had to be all right! But there had been nothing, no word, since the fall of York, and that had been a sennight ago.

She would not think the worst.

Maybe, just maybe, there had been another conciliation between the Norman invader and her brothers. It had happened a year ago. William had taken both Edwin and Morcar back, had forgiven them, and they had resworn allegiance. If it had happened again, maybe Edwin had given this Norman Alice, and maybe a Norman bride had been given in return to him. Ceidre desperately hoped so. For the alternative was too unbearable: dispossession . . . death . . .

She imagined her half sister and the Norman standing side by side in the village church. He so golden, so tall and broad, she so petite and dark. Something tensed inside her. There was, unfortunately, no love lost between herself and her younger sister. But Ceidre would never, ever wish the Norman on Alice. She shuddered just to think about it, and, unbidden, a hot image of the Norman straining between her thighs taunted her. She pushed it grimly away, only to imagine him in the same position with her younger sister. Her body became so taut it felt like it might snap.

Well, the marriage hadn't occurred yet, and although Alice was desperate for a husband, ever since Bill had died at Hastings, Ceidre would help her avoid this suit. There was no way she could let her little sister walk to the altar with this beast—their sworn enemy!

She paced. The tent was only a thin hide stretched over saplings, with a separate leather flap for a door, now closed. It was big enough to accommodate a few paces in either direction and the pallet—consisting of blankets and hides. It was *his* tent, she knew, just as she was certain it was *his* pallet. She would never lie on it.

It was still light out, the days being long in summer, and Ceidre could see the shadow under the hide door that hadn't yet moved—Guy.

Her protector.

She wanted to laugh. Oh, she was a prisoner all right, even if *he* thought she was his bride. Somehow she had to escape. Get back to Aelfgar, warn Alice of her dire circumstances, then maybe the two of them could flee together, to find her brothers. Surely, if Edwin had arranged the marriage he could unarrange it, surely he would protect them. And then, knowing the vast burden he carried on his shoulders for all of their safety, and for all their people, for the entire north of England, for Aelfgar, Ceidre's hopes sank. She could not add to Edwin's vast responsibilities. She would have to resolve this situation and help Alice herself. And there was no time like the present.

Earlier they had brought her food, and thread, which Ceidre had used to mend her clothes. Now she eyed the cheese, bread, and ale. Then, in a rapid movement, she reached into the bodice of her gown, to the pouch she carried. Ceidre didn't hesitate, but extracted some herbs finely ground into a powder and sprinkled them into the ale. She replaced the leather thong in her dress, smoothed back her hair, and calmly lifted the flap of the tent.

Guy Le Chante straightened and turned immediately. "My lady?"

Ceidre was well aware of Guy's unease. He was tense, shifting slightly. She smiled at him. "Aren't you tired, standing out here after riding all day?"

Guy flushed. He was her own age, she suspected, a year or two past twenty. "No, my lady, I'm fine."

"I was about to eat," Ceidre said, as gracious as any of full noble blood. "Please, join me in repast and conversation."

Guy's eyes widened. "I don't know . . ."

" 'Tis only for a few morsels and a few words," Ceidre said. Then her eyes darkened. "Or is he such an ogre he denies you those rights as well?"

Guy stiffened. "My lord is no ogre, my lady. He is the finest of men, the finest of warriors. He is the king's best man, and all the world knows it."

Ceidre bit back a retort. "Am I allowed, then, to sit here in the fresh air with you?"

"Of course."

Ceidre fetched the ale and food and sat delicately beside Guy, who, standing, shifted uncomfortably. The rest of the Norman's men were scattered about, a good stone's throw from her tent, for the sake of her privacy, she guessed. A large cookfire was going, one of the lambs spitted and roasting, bread baking in rock ovens. She saw the Norman instantly, sitting apart on a boulder, papers at hand. He was staring at her.

Ceidre went hot and jerked her glance away. "Please sit," she invited Guy, her breath catching. The

Norman's regard was always like scorching embers—and she didn't like it. Ceidre was no fool. She had witnessed lust most of her life—it was as natural as the wind and the rain. But never had she felt such intensity from a man before. It unnerved her.

She dared another glance his way. His bold gaze met hers instantly. Ceidre folded her arms across her breast and quickly gave him her back. She was trembling.

Her father, before his death five years past, had tried to arrange a marriage for her. Ceidre had been fifteen when he began, seventeen when he had died. The old, powerful eaorl's first choice had been the second son of a northern lord, John of Landower. They had met once, at a joust. He was dark and lean and so very handsome, and there was also a softness to his brow that told of kindness. Knowing her father had picked this man to be her husband had overwhelmed her with unbearable joy—and Ceidre's days and nights were soon filled with dreams of her wedding, her marriage, and a family replete with love and babes.

John had refused.

No amount of land or gold would entice him. No dowry could be large enough. He would not wed a witch.

Oh, her father had told her he had changed his mind, that the boy wasn't good enough for her, but Ceidre heard the truth—gossip ran rampant around the manor. She would never let her father or her brothers see her hurt, but alone, she had grieved, cried hot, miserable tears, and finally asked God why He should give her such a deformity that the world thought her a witch.

The eaorl had chosen other suitors, but Ceidre, afraid they would refuse her just as John had, rejected them, outwardly pretending that they did not appeal to her. She knew her father would never force her into a marriage she said she did not want. She could not face such a rejection again. She knew no one wanted her—no one ever would. Somehow Ceidre feigned indifference as she casually refused each man her father brought to her attention. And she stopped dreaming her dreams.

But *he,* he looked at her with burning eyes, his hot lust bright and bold, for all to see.

He wanted her.

Guy was flustered by her invitation to sit and sup. "My lady . . ."

Ceidre poured the ale into a beaker and handed it to him. She felt a twinge of guilt. "Are you allowed to drink?"

"Of course," Guy said. "Thank you." He drained the cup.

She knew he was approaching. She would not look at him. Yet she felt his continuing stare, and it must have compelled her, for she raised her gaze to his. His face was expressionless, his strides long, determined. She met his gaze as boldly as she could. 'Twas not easy, yet though she might be his prisoner, never must she show fear.

"Enjoying the air, my lady?" he asked politely, his blue eyes raking her.

Ceidre rose to her feet. As she did so, both men automatically held out a hand to assist her. Ceidre took Guy's. "I was," she said coolly. "But I fear it's stifling oppressive now." She turned and slipped back into the tent.

Rolfe stared at the flap door, rigid, nostrils flared. Then he looked at Guy, who immediately glanced at a distant tree. "Oh, relax," Rolfe snapped. "I'm not going to smite you where you stand."

"She only offered me some food and drink," Guy said.

"So I see," Rolfe said, turning abruptly.

Ceidre waited for the potion to take effect. Some fifteen minutes later she peeked out of the tent's flap door. Guy sat now fighting to hold his eyes open. Another quick glance showed most of the Normans eating and drinking; one was strumming a viol. There was no sign of her captor, and that made Ceidre both grateful and wary. Where could he be?

It didn't matter. She would have to take her chance.

Ceidre pulled the flap closed and moved to the other side of the tent. It was well secured, and she had to work the edge up to make enough room to crawl through. She managed to slither out on her stomach, then snake across the dirt and into the trees. There she paused, listening to the sound of the Normans' talk and laughter, wishing it were dark.

She got to her feet cautiously, and keeping to the trees, with many frequent glances over her shoulder, she began to steal away from the camp and to the village. Once she was on the other side of Kesop she would feel safer. She hoped none of the Normans had decided to take their pleasure in the village, assuming any of the folk had stayed. And again, she wondered where *he* was.

The cornfield, now blackened grotesquely, offered no protection, and Ceidre hurried to the shelter of the burned-out huts. She saw no one. As she had thought, the peasants had fled north to Aelfgar for protection, or maybe east to the neighboring village of Latham. She started to cut between the partial walls of two adjoining cottages, but before she got to the scorched gardens at the back, she knew she wasn't alone.

It was a moan.

Ceidre's reaction was instinctive. She began to rush

forward. She was a healer, and someone was hurt and in need of her. It didn't matter who it was, or even if it was an animal. As she rounded the corner, she heard it again—but too late did she realize her error. That it wasn't a moan of pain, but of pleasure.

She gasped the instant she realized, which was the same instant she saw them.

Ceidre knew the woman, Beth, dark and voluptuous and a widow. Her white, fleshy thighs were spread wide, her hands grasping wildly at the broad straining shoulders of the man above her. She was pumping rhythmically. So was he.

The Norman. She was mesmerized, she couldn't move. He was clad in his undertunic and hose, moving like a stallion, covering her, his power immense, yet restrained. He poised over her, his organ huge and red and slick. Then he plunged into her. Beth thrashed violently in pleasure, crying out, again and again. He gasped. She could see his face clearly, dark with passion, with ecstasy. He collapsed on top of her.

Ceidre's heart was slamming in her ears. She realized they could both see her, they would both see her, the instant they became cognizant of their surroundings again. She started to back away. Her eyes stayed glued on the two of them. And then he turned his head.

Their gazes locked.

Ceidre was frozen for one instant, then she began to run.

She knew he was chasing her, chasing her again. His presence behind her was as tangible as imminent thunder. She had taken ten steps when he knocked her flat and hard to the ground, landing on top of her, causing her to cry out. His arms were around her rib cage, tight, pressing into her full breasts. His mouth was on her neck, just below her ear. His breath was warm, still coming hard and fast from his romp with Beth. "Spying again?" he murmured.

Ceidre wanted to scream, she wanted to cry. She wanted to turn around and claw him. Furious, frustrated, she began to struggle. He loosened his hold to let her twist around, but then he was straddling her. She poised her fingers like talons and aimed for his eyes. He caught both her hands in his and pulled her hard upright—into the hot strength of his groin.

Ceidre instantly twisted to bite his wrist. He realized her intent before her teeth could touch his flesh, and he cursed, pulling her hands behind her back and pressing her more intimately against him. She shrieked in outrage. She felt him hardening against her navel. She tried to bite his shoulder. He caught her braid and yanked her head back, pinning her in a precarious position, twisted, braced against his unmistakably powerful male body, anchored by her own braid. She let out a sob of frustration.

"Stop twisting," he growled, "or by God, I'll take you here and now!"

Ceidre froze.

He was panting. "How did you get past Guy?"

She found her breath. "He fell asleep."

His blue eyes were bright, suspicious. "Guy? Guy does not fall asleep when he has duty to me."

"He fell asleep," she retorted, eyes blazing.

He stared back.

Ceidre hated him. Then she watched his eyes move to her mouth. She went rigid. "No." She remembered, vividly, the feel of his tongue, hot, wet, in her mouth.

His look was sardonic. "And will you say no when you are my wife?"

"Always!"

He laughed, without mirth, released her, and rose

to his feet. Standing above her, he was immensely tall. "I think not."

"Think whatever you like."

"You have the tongue of a witch—or a viper."

"My tongue is honeyed for some."

His blue eyes blazed. "For whom?"

"For those I respect—and love."

"For whom?"

Her chin lifted. "It is not your affair!"

"No matter," he said, after a moment. "For soon it will be my affair, and then it will be ended." His look was unyielding in its purpose. Ceidre decided not to respond. But when he rudely dragged her to her feet, she cursed and twisted away.

"A viper," he muttered.

"Go back to your leman," she hissed.

"I have no more use for her," he said.

Ceidre folded her arms and leered. "No?"

He started to smile. "The only use I have," he said, "now, is for you." His tone, amazingly, had softened. Now it cajoled. "Come here, Alice."

Ceidre was incredulous.

"We are going to be wed, you and I, and there is nothing you can do to change that. Reconcile yourself to your fate. Come here." Silky soft.

"No."

"Show me your goodwill." Softer still.

"I have none!"

"Think again. I know you are not dumb."

"I have none!"

"So you will fight me to the end."

"Yes," Ceidre said stubbornly, desperately.

His eyes glinted. "We shall see."

CHAPTER 5

"What did you do to him?"

Ceidre stood behind Rolfe as he bent over Guy, now sound asleep. Rolfe straightened and turned, grim and angry. "Answer me, wench."

She stepped back, her heart starting to slam.

He took a step toward her.

"Nothing." She gasped.

He grabbed her before she could react. "You put something in the ale! What?"

He was shrewd, and she would remember it well. "Just a sleeping potion," Ceidre cried. "He will awaken shortly!"

Rolfe released her. "Are there any other effects?"

"He will be sleepy for a while, but then he will be fine."

Rolfe's flashing look told her she was very, very lucky she had not truly harmed his man. "Where did you get this potion?"

Her heart picked up its thick beat. Ceidre flushed. She took another pace back. That was when she became aware of all his men, standing behind them tensely. She heard someone whisper the word witch and another said something about the evil eye and a curse. Her color deepened.

"The potion, Alice," Rolfe said. "Let me have it."

"It's all gone," Ceidre lied.

He stared at her, then took her arm and led her, ungently, to the tent. He raised the flap. Ceidre knew an immense relief and she scurried into the safety of the hide shelter, wanting nothing more than to put as much distance as possible between him and herself. She was barely inside when she heard him ordering his men to disperse, and then, suddenly, his huge frame dwarfed her, seeming to fill the entire space of the tent. Ceidre inhaled in alarm.

He dropped the door flap closed behind them.

"What are you doing?" Ceidre cried, shrinking back against the far wall—as far from him as she could get. In truth, it wasn't far at all, a bit more than an arm's span.

He didn't answer. It was dim inside now, yet she could make him out well enough as he lighted a torch. He carefully placed the rushlight upright in the ground, then turned fully to face her. "Need I ask again?"

If only there were somewhere to go—somewhere to run too.

"Alice."

There was so much warning in that one word. "I lied! 'Twas a curse. You are pressing me too far! I will curse you too!"

He smiled then, the first genuine sign of amusement she had ever seen from him. He did not believe her. He truly did not believe she was a witch. She was disappointed—she was thrilled.

"Mayhap," he said slowly, eyes sparkling. "You have already cursed me—or was it a blessing?"

"I don't understand."

"Did you smite me with this unnatural and ungodly desire I have for you?"

She moved completely against the hide wall, seeing the sparkle turn hot, glimmering. "No."

"No? You did not bewitch me?"

"No, I swear."

"I don't believe you." His hands snaked out. She had known he would grab her, but still, he was too fast for her, and even if she could have been swifter, there was nowhere to go, nowhere to escape to. He pulled her so close she could feel the softness of his breath—feel the heat of his body. "The potion," he murmured. "Give it to me."

"I don't have it," she whispered, his hands, on her waist, like hot irons. So large, so strong. She attempted once to twist free, and realizing it was hopeless, she went still. She tried to brace herself away from him with her hands on his chest. He was as hard as a rock, but warm, alive, beneath her fingertips.

"Your waist is so small," Rolfe said, low.

Ceidre looked into his gaze and could not look away.

"My fingers almost touch one another."

She could not breathe.

"You are too beautiful to be mortal," he said huskily.

His hands, on her waist, tightened. Her own body was throbbing, her blood racing madly. "Let me go," she said weakly.

"Mayhap," he said, and his mouth was closer, his lower lip fuller than its mate, beautifully carved, "you are a witch."

"No," she heard herself say fiercely. *I am not a witch* — she wanted to tell him the truth—she wanted, desperately, that he should know this and believe it.

One of his hands moved up to her rib cage. Ceidre shuddered at the gentle—impossibly gentle—caress. She tried to push herself away but could not. He was unyielding. His hand paused beneath the full weight of her breast. Surely he could feel her heartbeat vibrating throughout her body. Surely he would not dare touch her more intimately—or would he?

No man had ever dared to touch her like this.

His hand swept up with the delicacy of a hummingbird's wings, barely brushing the full, aching globe of her breast, the flesh of his palm grazing her erect, swollen nipple. A tiny gasp, half shock, half pleasure, escaped Ceidre. And then his hand slid over her back and he leaned down, his lips closing over hers.

She forgot that he was the enemy. There was only his mouth on hers, slightly open, soft, seductive, this time, and his hand gently stroking her shoulder. So this was kissing—so this was the pleasure of the flesh. When he drew away she blinked at him, dazed.

He was staring at her. He smiled, ever so slightly. Ever so smugly.

She struck him.

The blow was furious and reflexive, and all of her anger and desperation were behind it. He ducked to avoid her palm, so she only grazed his jaw. Her heart was thundering right out of her breast, and she froze, stunned with what she had done.

For one split instant, he froze too, shock and disbelief and incredulity written all over his face. And then his lips tightened grimly and her offending hand was seized by his—and he jerked her hard up against the steel wall that was his body. His reaction had been instantaneous.

"No!"

His other arm imprisoned her and his mouth found hers, and this time there was nothing soft or seductive about his kiss. He was the conqueror, she the vanquished. His mouth bruised hers. His mastery was total, his domination complete. Ceidre felt his teeth actually grating hers as he forced her mouth open. She struggled like a wild, snared fox, but her movements were impossibly futile. When he released her she choked on what was a sob and a gasp for air, her breasts heaving.

"No one," the Norman said, his face flushed, his breathing harsh, "has ever dared what you have dared."

"The devil take your soul!" Ceidre cried, fists clenched. "Damn you, damn you to hell!"

He stared, his own fists clenched and trembling at his sides.

Ceidre took a step back and felt the wall of the tent. Trapped. She was trapped. And although she would never show it, she was afraid, oh-so-afraid.

Their gazes locked, warred. She would not look away, no matter what, despite her pounding terror. His lips seemed to curl up at the corners.

And then, like lightning, his hand delved into her bodice.

"What is this?" He held up the leather pouch.

Rage swept her. "Give it back!"

He pulled it from her before she could respond and slipped it over his own head, tucking it into his tunic.

"Bastard!" Never, in her life, had she flung that most vile epithet at anyone. "Rotten bastard!"

"I do not want my men poisoned," he said grimly.

She was panting, furious. "You tricked me!"

"Tricked?" He grinned. "Call a scythe a scythe, sweetheart. I am a man. You, only a woman. I took what I wanted. Would you rather I'd beaten you?"

She gritted her teeth, fists clenched.

"Do not fight me, Alice. As you have seen, we shall do well together, very well." His glance swept down, lingering over her heaving bosom, her pointed nipples.

"Never!" Ceidre meant it.

He smiled broadly, his ruthless features exquisitely

transformed into a picture of pagan beauty. "Deny it now, while you still can, for very shortly you will no longer be able to deny it."

He paused at the door of the tent. "Or me."

CHAPTER 6

She always had the dream when she was anxious or afraid. And it came to torment her again that night.

She was a child of seven, standing on the steps of the manor, blinking in the bright morning summer sunlight. She could hear the sounds of childish laughter, squealing, shrieking, and Ceidre smiled at the happy tones, turning to locate their source. She saw a group of boys and girls, from her own age to twelve or so, all her familiars, children from the village whom she had grown up with. Her half sister, Alice, two years her junior, played tag with them.

Ceidre lifted her skirts and ran down the hill, skipping in her eagerness. She quickly darted into the game among the milling, racing children. A boy named Redric was the catcher, and Ceidre just dodged his outstretched hands, squealing with laughter.

In the confusion, she knocked into Alice and sent the little dark-haired girl tumbling into the grass. Alice cried out, and at the sound, everyone stopped to gather around and see that she had skinned her knee.

Ceidre was instantly remorseful. "I'm sorry, Alice, I—"

"You pushed me!"

"I didn't mean to."

"She pushed me!"

"Alice," Redric said, being the oldest, almost thirteen, " 'twas an accident. Let me help you up."

Tears filled Alice's eyes. "Who asked her to play anyway?"

Ceidre felt a familiar stabbing and backed up a step. "I'll go get Granny," she offered, wanting to help Alice, wishing with all her heart that she hadn't hurt her sister, wanting desperately to make everything all right. The only problem was that it would never be all right, for Alice seemed to hate her.

"No!" Alice screamed. "Mama says she's a witch, and I won't have that witch touch me!"

It was a hated word, and Ceidre felt herself tensing up inside. It was a word she had been hearing whispered around her for her entire life. In confusion and dread, she had always shut her ears and turned away. "She is not," Ceidre managed.

"Mama says so, everyone says so," Alice cried, glaring at her. The children ringing them began shifting uncomfortably, and there was a murmur of agreement. "My mama said so too," blond Jocelyn said quickly.

Alice stood up. "Go away, Ceidre. You can't play with us."

Ceidre didn't move, but she felt a slow flush creeping up her face. She darted a glance at the others. "She can play," Redric said. "C'mon, let's start."

The children dispersed.

"I won't play with a witch!" Alice shouted.

Ceidre froze, confusion rearing up, dread ballooning. She blinked at her sister, not understanding, sure she had misheard. Alice sneered. "Witch!"

Ceidre folded her arms, shrinking up inside. "I am not."

"Witch! Everyone says so! Witch!"

She was going to cry. Alice didn't mean it. It wasn't

true. She fought the tears. The children were staring at her, the little ones with curiosity, but Redric and Beth with unease. A long silence descended, then Redric broke it. "It's not true," he decided.

Beth, also twelve, looked at him. "I've heard it too. Maybe we shouldn't let her play with us."

Ceidre looked at the ground. "I'm not," she managed. Hot tears burned her eyes. But she could hear the echoes of Alice's words, a familiar haunting echo, so familiar it was frightening. She was frightened. She looked up, wiping her eyes.

And then it happened.

"Look," Alice screamed. "Look! Look! She is a witch!"

Ceidre backed up, truly afraid. The children were staring at her in horror. "It's the evil eye." Beth gasped. "I've never seen it afore!"

They were all staring, staring. . . .

Ceidre woke up.

Her heart was pounding, and she felt the heat of a crimson blush. As always, there were tears in her eyes, tears, she supposed, for a little girl's first brush with ugly reality. For the dream was not just a nightmare. It had happened, exactly as she dreamed it.

And after that, the children veered away from her. They would not let her join their games, and if she tried, they would stop playing and disperse. And then there was Alice, always hurling that vile epithet, flinging it in her face. "Witch!"

Ceidre sat up. She wished, this once, her father were still alive. She could remember running to him in tears, and when he had picked her up, swinging her into his arms, she had begged to know the truth. "Am I a witch, Papa? Am I?"

He had hesitated. Ceidre had clung to him, waiting for the worst, suddenly knowing it was true, so confused. "No, sweet one," he had said, lifting her chin. "You are not, and don't ever let anyone make you think otherwise."

A child's instincts are perhaps more accurate than an adult's, unfettered with preconceived notions, and Ceidre sensed his own turmoil, his own lack of sureness. She was not soothed. She was not reassured. She was more confused than ever, and now, now there was no turning her back on the whispers that followed in her wake. It was a harsh reality for a child to face, but everyone believed her a witch.

She did not know if it was true or not. She clung stubbornly to her father's denial, and she began avoiding the other children, who, quick to follow Alice's lead, too young to be afraid, also called her vile names. She spent more time with her granny, helping her prepare her concoctions for healing, and much time alone, in the woods or the stables, always with Thor, Edwin's favorite new wolfhound, who became her constant companion.

Time heals all wounds, and Ceidre adjusted to her status. The persecution of her peers ceased as they became young adults, marrying, making families, taking on a serf's responsibilties. Ceidre became as adept as her grandmother in the arts of healing, and was much sought after. She was treated with a combination of awe, nervousness, and familiarity that was friendly as well. And then her father decided it was time she marry, and he began to seek a groom for her.

So life had dealt her another blow, another ugly reality to face. Ceidre had survived that one too, just as she would now survive this. She got up and folded back the door to the tent, letting in the first pink rays of dawn. She performed her ablutions with the urn of water left her, then stepped outside.

The man guarding her instantly stepped aside, with

a hasty glance in her direction. Ceidre ignored it but, having withstood his kind of behavior her entire life and fresh on the heels of her dream, she was pierced with hurt. She looked out at the Normans breaking camp. And, as if metal drawn by a magnet, or the eye seeking the sun, she found herself gazing at him.

The Norman stood in deep discussion with Guy, the knight she had used the potion on last evening. But his gaze was on her.

Ceidre felt the instant flood of memories. How he had imprisoned her in his embrace, with his superior strength proving his mastery over her, her punishment his hot, hard kiss. Good God, she had reacted as pitifully as a helpless, ensnared hare. She stiffened at the very remembrance, anger and agitation making her blood pound. If he dared to touch her so again she would rake his eyes out. This time she would not miss! She shuddered, glancing at him again. And she would not wonder at his daring—at his complete lack of fear of her and her "evil" eye.

He didn't smile, but he suddenly, abruptly, began striding toward her. Ceidre felt herself freeze. She did not want him to approach. She did not want to talk to him, even see him. Yet she could not move away. And now she was assailed with worries.

They were close to Aelfgar, which was normally her sanctuary. Alice would greet them, and the Norman would find out her deception. She knew he was, like any man, proud, thus he would not take kindly to having been deceived by a mere woman. He would be humiliated and angry at being made the fool. Of course, she knew his anger would recede, for he would be relieved to be wed to Alice, and not one such as she. But until it did recede, was she in jeopardy?

And how, oh how, could she help her sister to avoid wedlock to this man?

And what of her brothers? Did this Norman know something? Ceidre realized he would know more than anyone, being so close to the Bastard Conquerer, but how could she win his goodwill to ask and receive the truth? He was so shrewd, surely when he realized she was desperate for news he would use his position as a source of power over her. Yet she had to ask—she was dying to know something—anything.

He paused in front of her, his steely blue eyes riveted upon her face. "Have you passed a good night, my lady?"

And she could feel her cheeks flushing. "Y-yes."

"You hesitate. Perhaps"—and he smiled—"you did not sleep well. Perhaps your dreams were filled with me?"

She would never ask him anything! "I slept unusually well."

He studied her. His gaze drifted to her mouth. "Then I envy you."

His meaning was clear. She went scarlet.

He turned abruptly. "We leave in half an hour's time."

She watched his back, broad at the shoulder, small and narrow at the hip. It was not what she thought, he did not mean what it seemed he meant. Did it?

CHAPTER 7

He eyed her as she rode alongside him on a mule, as haughty and proud as any queen astride a blooded Arabian. And beautiful. Her profile stole his breath away, and once again Rolfe blessed Dame Fortune.

For it was rare, so unbelievably rare, for a man to want the woman who was his wife. Last night, after escorting Alice back to the tent, he had lain awake unable to sleep. Even having slaked his lust with the peasant, he was hot and uncomfortable again. He should never have touched her as he had, but he could no more stop himself than he could stop a summer storm. What a boon! Aelfgar and its lady, the most bewitching, seductive woman he had ever met. William had ordered the marriage performed as soon as his convenience allowed, and now Rolfe smiled, thinking that immediately would be at his utmost convenience!

It was early morning, the sun now pale and champagne-hued, the day still cool with the evening's chill. The terrain was hilly and rocky, good for sheep raising, which was no surprise to Rolfe, for he already knew that the crux of Aelfgar's prosperity was lamb and wool.

He could not stop himself from glancing at Alice again, just as he could not stop the sun from rising and setting. She had not looked at him, not once in the past hour. This irked him. He knew she was not indifferent to him. Yet she would pretend to be so. He was a soldier, not a poet, not a priest, so polite conversation did not come readily or easily to his lips. Yet Rolfe resolved to try.

" 'Tis still cool. Are you warm enough, my lady?"

She cautiously glanced at him. "Yes." She hesitated. "Thank you."

He was aware instantly, of course, that she refused to address him properly. No man would dare to show him such lack of respect by failing to call him "my lord." Yet she dared. Last night, given the circumstances, he could let it pass. Today 'twas incredible. Today he could not allow it. His blue eyes scored her. "Say it, Alice."

Her gaze flew to his. "Say what?"

"Do not play the confused idiot with me," he commanded. "Say it: my lord."

She stiffened. "You are not my lord."

He could not believe his ears. His hands, on his reins, were so very white. She would defy him? Openly? She, his intended, a lady, a woman? He did not know which fact of her being made it worse!

He turned his furious gaze upon her, about to stop the column. He saw her eyes, wide, purple, he saw the fear there. It flashed through his mind to go softly, he who knew only how to wield his sword boldly. And then a locust of arrows swept down from the trees.

"Ambush!" Rolfe roared, wheeling his destrier in that same instant between Ceidre and the hail of arrows. A stone, shot from a sling, bounced off his helmut. From the corner of his eye he had already spotted one perpetrator, and he was swinging his mace, standing high in his stirrups. The Saxon in the tree above met his gaze, saw his ruthless intent, and opened his mouth to scream. Rolfe's studded weapon hit him flush in the chest, ripping him open and knocking him out of his perch. He saw another archer, arrow leveled, bow twisted with tension. At the same time he knew the wench was right behind him, her frightened palfrey pressed against his right knee. "Do not move from me," he roared without ever taking his gaze from the Saxon. He threw his mace as the Saxon released his bow. The arrow missed, Rolfe did not.

Rolfe had been a soldier his entire life; he had lived through a thousand battles. In one quick glance he saw the fighting around him, saw his men were in control, knew there were five dead or dying Saxons, knew a nearly equal number were fleeing, a few still in the process of being routed. He was reaching for the bridle of the palfrey as the animal bolted. Instinct made him whip around to see a huge Saxon with his broadsword charging toward him, on foot, from the woods. With a war cry, Rolfe raised his own sword, as long as he was tall, and faster than the eye could see, much swifter than the Saxon with the heavy broadsword, Rolfe cleaved the man in two, decapitating him.

The battle had ended. The glade was starkly quiet, except for the harsh blowing of their mounts and the panting of his men. Rolfe immediately noted that seven Saxons lay dead and that all of his men remained mounted. He was still holding the little palfrey, and scanning the area once more, he turned to the lady at his side. " 'Tis finished," he said gruffly. "Are you all right?"

Her beautiful purple eyes were wide, frightened. She was panting, her hand on her bosom. Rolfe clenched his jaw, furious now. He was enraged that she had been in the midst of this attack. His scouts had said no danger lay ahead. "Alice . . ."

With a cry, she slid off the far side of the palfrey and

leaned against a tree, trying not to retch. Rolfe was stricken with the urge to go to her and somehow help her, yet he had not the slightest idea of what to do, and he was even embarrassed with his own desire. Fortunately, Guy rode up. "Two wounded, my lord: Pierre Le Stac and Sir de Stacy, but not badly."

"Prisoners?"

"None."

"How many have escaped?"

"Six, I think, my lord."

"Send me Charles." His tone was ominous.

Rolfe turned to Alice, who had straightened and was facing him, pale and shaking, visibly upset. Rolfe slipped to the ground, wiped his dripping sword upon the grass, and sheathed it. He strode to her. There he hesitated. "Come, we do not dwell here."

She backed away. She blinked tears. "Have you no remorse?"

He stared.

Ceidre knew what she had witnessed. She had seen him effortlessly, efficiently, slaughter three men. In the back of her mind she also knew he had been attacked, that he had fought to defend himself, his men, and *her,* yet she refused to listen to this nagging voice. He was the invader, the enemy, the Norman. "You have killed three men," she whispered. "Have you no remorse?"

"None," he said. "For had I remorse, Lady Alice, you would now be sporting an arrow in your pretty chest." He turned abruptly away.

'Twas true, yet . . . Ceidre chased him, grabbed his sleeve. "They were my people, my people you have killed." She felt the tears, and she wanted to weep, weep for the dead, the serfs and peasants she knew, and weep with the waste of it and with her hatred of war.

He looked at her but said nothing.

Guy approached with another soldier. Charles's face was drawn, his eyes anxious. He dropped to one knee, head bowed.

"You have failed in your duty," Rolfe said. "Because you failed in the task I gave you, we were ambushed. Fortunately, only two of my men have suffered casualties. Stand up."

Charles stood.

Rolfe stared at him and saw that his eyes were red. He glanced at Guy for confirmation. Guy nodded. Rolfe's mouth went tight. "You overimbibed last night, did you not? Your lust for women and wine makes you weak, not fit to be one of my soldiers. Take your sword and go. You are discharged from service to me."

"But, Lord Rolfe! I followed you from Normandy. I have been faithful to you, ever faithful—"

"No man fails in his duty to me, not once, not ever. Get you gone, I care not where." Rolfe turned away and the matter was ended.

Ceidre watched, stunned and horrified. Charles slumped, then proudly turned away. How could he be so cruel, to his own man? He truly was not human! She turned a wide gaze back to him and found him regarding her expressionlessly. "Can you not show mercy?" she asked, unable to stop herself. She was too overwhelmed to be frightened at her own audacity.

She watched a muscle spasm in his cheek. "You question me?"

She wet her lips but stood her ground. What had she done? She would never have questioned her father or her brothers, yet she was questioning the Norman! "He is your man—a Norman."

He stood over her, crowding her. "You openly defy me, question me, disapprove of me?"

She bit her lip, panting slightly, and managed not to flinch when he took another hard step to her.

"Lady Alice," he said, furious. "I am a soldier—only a soldier. And you, you are only a woman." He paused for effect.

He was a bastard! Ceidre felt a rush of fear and knew she should capitulate. "At least," she said, and there was the slightest tremor in her voice, "I am not a Norman." *A Norman pig,* she wanted to add, but wisely refrained.

His voice was low, hard. "True. I am the Norman, you the Saxon. And"—his voice roughened—"because you are to be my wife, I will explain something to you. We escaped lightly only because my men *are the best in the land.* My men know what is expected of them, and they do not fail me. Ever. Should they fail, they are not the best. When they are not the best, I cease to be King William's best. Should I fail my king, I fail myself. And I am Rolfe de Warenne."

She looked at him as he stood there blazing in his glorious anger.

"Do you understand?"

"Yes."

"I am no ogre," he said, and his look penetrated. She went red.

"After you, my lady," he said stiffly.

CHAPTER 8

Aelfgar.

Rolfe sat very still. Beneath him, his huge gray destrier shifted restlessly. The blood was pounding in Rolfe's ears. For the first time that day, he wasn't even aware of the beautiful woman mounted beside him. He was aware of only one thing.

Aelfgar.

Aelfgar itself was a vast fief, and they had been on its land all morning. But now, this was the heart of the honor. They had paused on a ridge. Below them ran a thick river, an estuary from the sea, and nestled in the hilly terrain was the village and the manor.

Truly it was not impressive, but Rolfe was unconcerned. The village boasted a dozen wattle huts, a mill, a cornfield, orchards, and vegetable gardens. Sheep were on the hills everywhere. The village was only slightly lower than the manor, which, compared to Norman keeps, was nothing more than a rectangular wood building, its roof timbered, boasting upper-level windows, open now to the summer breezes. There was not even a palisade. But Rolfe saw more, much more.

He saw a keep, three stories, set high on a mound, with a moat around it. In stone, of course. High, fortified walls. Below, another palisade, enclosing the bailey where his men and their women would live. Then, below that, finally, the village.

He smiled. Construction would begin immediately. And with his practiced eye, he made instant decisions of where he would place each structure, pleased with the natural lay of the land. When he was finished, Aelfgar would be very defensible.

It was the Norman way, to crush the Saxons, destroy their homes, and erect timbered keeps in their stead in the Norman style, with motte and bailey. When time allowed, the fortifications were replaced with stone, first the palisade, then the keep, and so on. Rolfe himself had overseen this process a dozen times since coming to England four years past; he was sure he would oversee it another dozen times before he died.

He urged his stallion forward. Coming out of his reverie, he turned to smile at his bride. "We are home," he said, his tone rich.

"This will never be your home," she returned coolly.

His glance was lightning, filled with warning. She ducked her head. Not even her defiance could dispel his pleasure and his purpose.

They had entered the village. Rolfe reined in, his retinue halting. The villagers paused in their work in the fields and gardens, children, curious, approached the one road where they stood. "Rouse everyone, Guy," Rolfe said quietly.

"No!" Ceidre cried, stunned, recalling only too well that these had been his exact words yesterday before razing Kesop to the ground.

Rolfe did not look at her.

"You can't." She grabbed his sleeve. "Please, my lord!"

The men came in from the fields, the women from their homes, children tugging at their skirts, babies at their breasts. Rolfe was pleased. They were a well-fed, healthy lot. Ignoring Ceidre, he turned to Guy. "I want a precise head count this afternoon. Listed by family. Every name, even a day-old babe."

"Yes, my lord."

"And possessions, be it scythe or sow."

Guy nodded. " 'Tis done."

"Good." Rolfe smiled, then stood in his stirrups. "Here now," he said, raising his voice so it boomed. "In the name of the king, William of Normandy, you have before you your new lord, the eaorl of Aelfgar, Rolfe de Warenne."

A collective gasp went up.

"No!" Ceidre cried. " 'Tis not true!"

Rolfe turned a hard stare on her. "Keep your tongue," he warned.

"How can it be?" Ceidre cried, hysterical. "Are they dead? Are Ed and Morcar dead?"

"Your brothers are alive," he said coldly. "Aelfgar is mine, just as you are mine. Your brothers are traitors, enemies of the crown. Their lands have been forfeit, and they will be lucky if their lives are not."

Dispossessed. Ceidre thought she might faint. Edwin and Morcar had been dispossessed, and this man —this Norman—was the new lord of Aelfgar. She wanted to weep. She wanted to kill.

"I am your lord and master, Alice," Rolfe said. "And the sooner you accustom yourself to this, the better 'twill be."

"You will never be my lord and master, never!"

"I am tired of your foolishness." He addressed the crowd again. "As you can see, I have the lady Alice with me—she is my betrothed. There is nothing you can do to prevent what has been done. Treason to your new lord will be punishable by flogging and the stocks, or even hanging. There will be no mercy." Rolfe signaled to his men, and they moved forward.

The villagers murmured openly, shocked despite all

these years of warfare. "Lady Alice?" someone said. " 'Tis Ceidre!" And her name was echoed again and again.

Rolfe heard, of course. "Who is this Ceidre they are referring to?"

Ceidre's anger fled in the face of an icy-cold panic. "I do not know!"

He stared at her.

They arrived at the manor, fifty of William's fiercest troops, a mass of barely contained horseflesh, stomping, blowing, nostrils bugled, manes tossing. The knights' chain mail, shields, and swords were glinting riotously, dazzling the eye, while above the royal blue, red, and black penants were flying, proud and sinister. Ceidre was certain that the half-dozen men-at-arms left behind by her brothers would not resist the Norman with his forces. They were greeted at the front of the manor by Athelstan, the eldest of the housecarls, left in charge of the six men by Edwin. With him were the other five.

Rolfe rode his mount ahead of the column, then reined in. His black cloak, lined in red, flew about his broad shoulders. "Lay down your weapons, Saxon. I am the eaorl of Aelfgar, Rolfe de Warenne, your new lord and master. To raise bow and arrow is only to die. Especially as I have with me my bride, and no man raises arms against the lady Alice."

Ceidre felt sick.

"I know you," Athelstan said grimly. "Rolfe the Relentless. Your name flies ahead of you on a falcon's wings. But if you think you can take Lord Edwin's patrimony from him, you are wrong."

"Time shall tell. At present, I am only taking it from you."

"We have laid down our weapons." Athelstan indicated the ground at their feet, where their quivers and shields lay. "But when Edwin and Morcar return, we shall raise them up again."

"Fair warning," Rolfe said, and he smiled. "I believe you to be honest, old man, and I like that well."

"I am honest, so heed me with care. What is this foolishness? The lady Alice? That is not the lady Alice."

Rolfe's smile disappeared. "Do not jest."

"This is no riddle. That is certainly not the lady Alice."

Rolfe whipped his head around, furious, eyes blazing. "Just who are you?" he demanded.

She could barely get the words out. *"Not your intended."*

Their gazes locked, his strong and enraged, holding her frightened, valiant one.

From behind Athelstan, a small, dark-haired woman stepped forward. "I am the lady Alice."

Rolfe stared in disbelief at his bride. He recovered. "You are the old eoarl of Aelfgar's daughter? Edwin's sister?"

Alice, petite and slim, nodded, her dark eyes huge and wary. "And you, sir, are our new lord?"

"Yes," Rolfe said stiffly, and Ceidre could actually feel his fury—it was murderous. "Who, may I ask, is this woman besides me?"

Alice smiled—it was a sneer. "Oh, her? No one, my lord, just one of the dairymaid's brats."

Ceidre flushed. "Father loved Annie and you know it."

Alice laughed. "Love? Come now, Ceidre, we've been through this before. 'Twas my mother he loved, not that whore who raised her skirts for every cock about town!"

Alice had never openly talked this way before, although in private she had always insisted Annie a whore and her mother, Jane, their father's love. Ceidre was furious. "How dare you!"

" 'Tis the truth." She turned to Rolfe. "My lord, you must be tired. Come. Let me take you to your bath."

Rolfe turned to look at Ceidre, a spasm in his jaw ticking. "So you are old Aelfgar's bastard?"

She raised her chin high. "Yes."

"I will deal with you later," he warned.

Ceidre's breast rose and fell and she fought to contain real tears. She watched Rolfe dismount, saw Alice smile up at his dark visage and place her delicate white hand on his sleeve. "Do not bother yourself with her, my lord," Alice said. "As you remarked, she is just one of many by-blows, and of no import. Tell me, 'tis true? We are to be wed?" Her tone was bright and eager.

"Yes."

They walked inside, arm in arm, Ceidre unable to look away, stunned with Alice's enthusiasm. As they disappeared from her view, Ceidre heard her sister laugh, charmingly, coquettishly. Her hand found the mule's neck, and she began to stroke its soft fur blindly.

"I am sorry, Ceidre," Athelstan said sympathetically.

"See to these men," Ceidre said, her voice high. "They need refreshment. Their mounts need feed, and the dun has lost a shoe."

"Yes, mistress."

Ceidre slid off the mule and only then did tears start to slip down her face. But she would let no one see. Just as she had never let anyone see her hurt and disappointment, not when strangers recoiled from her, nor when her father failed to find her a husband. Especially this time would she hide her feelings, for there was no reason for her to be hurt and disappointed.

CHAPTER 9

Rolfe was rigid with restrained fury.

That witch had lied. She had deceived him. She was not the lady Alice, not his bride. She would pay dearly for her deception.

And he was to marry another.

"My lord? Your bath grows cold."

Rolfe had been scowling, nostrils flared, gazing at the tub in front of the hearth without seeing it. He was in the Lord's Chamber, which had been hastily prepared for him. Now, at the sound of his bride's hesitant voice, he lifted his gaze and pinned her. For the first time, he studied her.

Alice was pretty, but it was a hard fact to discern after being in her sister's presence for the past day. She was very pale, her skin a foil to her dark, curling hair. She was short and petite, with none of Ceidre's lushness. She could not compare to her sister, and Rolfe recognized the deep, yawning pit of disappointment for what it was.

He also knew, had he never met the witch, he would have been satisfied with Alice and not given it a second thought. This, however, was not now the case.

Alice smiled tremulously. "My lord? You brood so. Perhaps some ale would lighten your soul."

"Why do you not ask about your brothers?"

Alice hesitated. "Your arrival has completely fogged my mind." She laughed nervously.

"Will you resist this marriage?"

"Oh, no!" She was clearly pleased with him for a husband.

"You find me to your liking?"

She blushed. "I am in need of a husband, my lord. My betrothed died shortly after Hastings, and in the past few years, with all the rebellions, Edwin has not had time to arrange another match. And I am getting old."

He nodded, she made perfect sense. "You are younger than your sister."

Briefly Alice's face tightened, then the look vanished. "I am twenty, she is two years more." Her nose went in the air. "Why do you concern yourself with her? She is just one of countless brats my father sired. Why, he did not even see fit to arrange a marriage for her! And now"—she smirked—"no one will have her, because of her evil eye! She is a witch, you know."

Rolfe's jaw tensed. He was no fool. Alice clearly despised her sister, but he found it hard to believe that she actually thought her a witch. "There will be no more talk like that of your sister," he commanded. "She is no witch."

Alice bit her lip, then lowered her head in obedience. Rolfe stripped off his mail hauberk, tossing it onto the floor. Alice rushed to his side. She helped him remove his vast sword, then his undertunic. She stared at the pouch hanging around his neck. "Why, 'tis hers!"

"And now 'tis mine," Rolfe said calmly, piercing her with a look. He removed it and placed it carefully with his things. Alice began removing his garters. Rolfe looked down on the top of her bent head and wished it were Ceidre performing the task. When he was naked, he turned his back to her and stepped into the steaming water. Alice hastily averted her eyes from his hard, powerful body with a shudder.

"Would you like your back soaped, my lord?"

Yes, I would like to be soaped, by that bronze-haired witch. "What I would like," he said, "is some wine. Is there any wine on this manor, Lady?"

"I think so," Alice said.

Rolfe grunted and she hurried away, leaving him alone in the great chamber. His thoughts grew dark, more ominous than a hurricane. She had deceived him. To gain what? Respite, he guessed, from his intentions to rape her. Damn her. He was more than furious. She could not defy his authority, could not continue to do so—and it seemed she did so at every turn! And this, to withhold her identity, have him believe she was his bride, this was very serious indeed. But . . . what penance?

He was so angry he forced his thoughts from her, to deal with more pleasant matters. He leaned back and began to plan his afternoon. There were still hours of light left—he would inspect the eastern side of his holdings as far as the coast. And tomorrow, first thing in the morning, construction of a modern Aelfgar would begin. He smiled at the thought.

His pleasure died. And what of the marriage? When would it be? A fortnight, he decided, would be soon enough. After all, he had much to do in the next days, and wouldn't it be better to have most of the new construction under way before wedding?

He snorted derisively. Had it been Ceidre, he would wed her tomorrow and bed her soundly tomorrow eve!

A flash of gilt caught his eye. He straightened, eyes locked on the open doorway. Ceidre stood in the frame.

Rolfe smiled slightly, his eyes never leaving her. He was struck again with her beauty, her bold coloring, her seductive form. Maybe she is a witch, he thought, momentarily and slightly amused, for already he was responding, just to the sight of her. He was thickening, swelling . . . "You seek me—Ceidre?"

"I beg for the return of my potions—my lord."

Rolfe did not look at the chest where her herbs lay atop his garments. "They are not here," he said silkily.

She fidgeted. "My lord, please, I truly have need—"

"Come here, Ceidre."

At his sensual tone, she froze.

His smile, predatory, grew. "Come here." A beat passed and she did not move, frozen like the netted lark. "And I will give it to you."

Ceidre hesitated, then boldly came into the room, and Rolfe watched the swing of her hips. His pleasure was so vast it was more like pain. She paused an arm's length from the foot of the tub, eyeing him warily, a hunted doe. "I will have it now."

"Will you? First, penance."

"Penance?"

"For your lies." His tone was silky soft.

"What would you have me do?"

"Come here."

Her gaze widened. She only looked at his face.

"There is no one to wash my back."

Her breath expelled.

"Here, Ceidre."

Slowly she inched toward him, then, in a burst of desperation, she was suddenly behind him, dipping the cloth in the water. "I expect my amulet back," she warned, touching his back with the wash rag so lightly it was like a feather's tickling.

"Not if that is the best you can do," he purred. And

he leaned forward, exposing the long length of his hard, muscled back from shoulder to hip.

Ceidre stared at the superb, glistening flesh. His back was flawless; his torso had one long diagonal scar running from hip to nipple, and half a dozen smaller ones. Her heart, of course, was slamming wildly in her chest. She took a breath, grimly, and touched the rag to his nape.

His body stiffened under her hand. Her own chest grew tight. "Finish," Rolfe said.

"Yes, my lord," she muttered bitterly. "But are you sure you don't want the good lady Alice to do this?" She put all her strength into the task and began scrubbing his shoulder.

He winced, but she did not see. "She is not here," he said calmly. "And you are."

She scrubbed harder. She hoped to tear the flesh from his body—'twould serve him right!

"Ceidre," he warned.

She was panting from her exertions. And then she spied the pouch on the pile of his tunics. In a flash she was on her feet and at the chest, packet already in hand. She made two more steps to the door. His hand, large and powerful, closed over her wrist, yanking her around to face him, and his other arm came around her waist like the jaws of a trap. She was pressed, immobile, against his wet, naked body.

"You play with fire, Ceidre."

She stared wildly into his bright, triumphant blue eyes. She could feel the dampness of his body. Her own gown and even her undertunic were becoming wet. Her breasts were crushed against the rock-hardness of his chest, achingly so. But mostly she was aware of his shaft, throbbing and hard and pressed against her hip. She tried to move away from it, he jerked her tighter against him. She gasped.

"Fire," he said harshly. "Now, penance." And then he claimed her mouth with his.

His kiss was fierce, hard, utterly uncompromising—but not hurtful. Ceidre gasped as her hands came up to resist, bracing away. Yet that too was a mistake. Instead, they spread against warm flesh, softly furred. He growled, the sound animal, warning. His teeth clashed against hers. With a cry, she wrenched away, only to be caught again and yanked back against his body.

"No!"

"Oh, yes," he purred, the light in his eyes brilliant, momentarily stunning her already stunned senses.

For one instant it was a standoff: she braced to fight yet held hard against him, as their gazes warred. "And what of Alice!" she cried, desperate and furious. "What of your bride!"

His expression became cruel, even ugly. "You should be my bride."

Ceidre's mouth opened to protest, but she made nothing more than a choked sound. For his palm anchored her head and his lips claimed hers, his tongue thrusting deep into her mouth. One of his hands closed over her buttock and lifted her groin completely against his erection.

His mouth left hers. "No," Ceidre managed again, but it was weak, a lie—she was on fire, trembling with wet heat, aching unbearably, unable to stand. His mouth moved voraciously against her throat, nipping, tugging, kissing her skin. And then he bent to bite a puckered nipple through her gown.

Ceidre cried out, clinging to his broad shoulders in a feeble attempt to push him away. Then, abruptly, he pushed her from him. Panting, stunned, shaking, Ceidre tried to recover. Rolfe was holding his undertunic, shielding his blatantly aroused manhood. He pierced her with a look—a warning—and then Alice and a servant entered the room with refreshments.

Alice stopped short, looking from Rolfe to Ceidre. Ceidre knew everything must show—her lips had to be bruised, her face flushed, her gown wet, her hair escaping from its thick braid. Oh, Saint Edward! Realization of what had just happened cut her like a knife. She was horrified.

"Thank you, my lady," Rolfe was saying smoothly. He stood casually, the tunic draped over a forearm, still covering him. With his other hand he took the beaker of wine and drained it. The cup shook.

Alice seared Ceidre with a look of hatred. Then, angelically, innocently, she said to Rolfe, "Another, my lord?"

"No, 'tis enough."

"You are finished already?"

"Yes."

Alice handed the bag-beaker to the servant, picked up a towel, and began rubbing his shoulders dry. Ceidre felt a sick stabbing at the sight—and she hated him. She forgot the herbs—she fled.

He did not call her back.

CHAPTER 10

Ceidre was angry.

She stomped through the bracken, swishing her skirts. Every now and then she paused, face flushed, to inspect a cluster of yellow flowers and to pick a few delicate tiny green leaves, placing them in her basket. Then, stomp-swish-stomp. All because of him. Had he given her the pouch she would not have to be doing this now, when she was so very weary and so very hungry. When all she wanted to do was lay her head down on her pallet and sleep a dreamless sleep.

She thought of Thor and grimly continued her quest. Thor was Edwin's oldest wolfhound—why, he was almost as old as she was. He had been badly hurt in a dogfight that Athelstan said had happened yesterday. The sleeping potion she had given Guy, when mixed with mandrake and valerian, would numb him sufficiently as well as help him sleep. Now he was suffering greatly, and it hurt Ceidre unbearably, not just because he was Ed's but because he was her old, trusting playmate as well. She had barely enough of the weed, and it was already approaching dusk. She thought of how much of the potion was left in her pouch and she cursed, wishing for once she were truly a witch. Oh, then she would make him suffer!

A penance indeed!

Why need she pay such a perverse penance to satisfy

his perverse lusts? She flushed with fury—and dismay—just to recollect it. And he was to wed Alice. Her heart leapt at the fact. She would not dwell on it yet she could not ignore it. She was upset, but surely 'twas only because of the thought of bringing her worst enemy into the bosom of her own home. Yet she had a vivid image of Alice toweling him dry. She imagined him kissing Alice—the way he had kissed her. Her sickness was so overwhelming she had to stop and gather her wits.

She was not jealous. She hated the Norman and all he stood for. He was the enemy, the invader, the conqueror. He was dispossessing her two brothers, whom she adored and worshiped. He was cruel and cold—he had razed Kesop to the ground without a twinge of conscience. She was not jealous—but, oh, what a mockery of Fate, that finally a man should not fear her, should so greatly desire her—and he be the Norman whom she could only hate!

Tonight she must talk to Alice. Alice could not truly want this marriage, and Ceidre would move heaven and earth to help her evade it—even if it meant poisoning the groom.

No. She had never hurt another soul, not man, not beast. It would have to be a very grave situation indeed before she would use her powers, so carefully studied from her grandmother, to harm instead of heal. No, there must surely be another way.

In the single hall of the manor, Rolfe sat at the head of the long table with Alice by his side. He was clad only in cross-gartered woolen hose, shoes, an undertunic, and his scabbard and sword. His men sat clustered around the table eating heartily, with those who had not managed to find a seat standing. Guy was on his right, Athelstan on Alice's left. His bride touched his hand with her tiny white one. "My lord? You do not like the wine?"

Truly, it was atrocious, even though he was verily sick of the Saxon ale. " 'Tis passable."

"But you do not eat," Alice persisted. "The fare does not please you?"

"It pleases me," he responded automatically, although in truth he did not know—he had yet to take a bite. Again his gaze raked the hall. Where was she?

He hadn't meant to go so far. He had been angry, he was still angry. Ceidre could not deceive him so on some capricious whim. Yet it was she who had dared to invade his chamber while he bathed, and he had not been able to contain his wicked impulses—and to soap him was surely the softest penance she could possibly pay. Yet when she had grabbed the leather pouch, he had responded not with rational thought but with a soldier's instinct. He had seized her. If Alice had not returned he would have taken her, right there, as she stood.

His need for her was out of hand and he knew it. He also realized it could not continue, for he was to marry the sister. Many lords would not blink twice at taking Ceidre while wed to Alice. After all, she was just Aelfgar's by-blow. Yet he could not—it was not right. Before it had been different, when he had thought her just a passing peasant wench, and he intended to rape her. Now she was his bride's sister. He wished sorely that he were a different man, that he could have the one for wife and the other for mistress. But it could not be.

Therefore, he would have to control himself. And this, he vowed to God, he would do.

But where was she?

"My lord, shall I have something else prepared, more to your satisfaction?"

Her concern would soon become annoying. He sensed it was because she feared greatly to lose him as a husband, that she was desperate to be wed. He understood her difficult position well, for soon she would be too old to turn any heads. He should reassure her, even though he was not in the mood. After all, the lady was his bride. "Lady Alice, the fare is fine, it seems only that I have no appetite. Why is your sister not here?"

Alice stiffened. "Ceidre does as she pleases, she always has. Often she eats with the maids in the kitchen, as, in truth, she should. Sometimes she spends days away, the saints only know where, practicing her witchcrafts."

Rolfe was furious. He rose abruptly. "You dare to openly defy me?"

Alice gasped, her hand covering her mouth. "I am sorry! I had forgotten you forbade me to talk of it! But 'tis only the truth!"

"Your tongue drips with jealousy, and 'tis most unseemly."

She straightened. "I am not jealous of her, some whore's brat."

"Leave me," he said. "I am displeased."

Alice, white, angry, fled upstairs. Rolfe turned to Athelstan. "Why does she hate her sister so?" His tone was low, so only those closest to him could hear.

"You have remarked it, my lord," Athelstan said. "Jealousy, of course."

"Were she not so mean she would be passably fair."

" 'Tis not her fault, 'twas her mother's."

"Tell me." Rolfe sat back down.

"Aelfgar loved his first wife greatly—the lady Maude. He worshiped her doubly for the gift of two fine, proud sons. Yet she grew weak and feeble before her time, and many years passed that she could not receive her lord as a wife should."

Rolfe shrugged. " 'Tis not unusual."

"But Aelfgar loved her, truly. He did not seek out others—ever."

Rolfe laughed skeptically. "No? Ceidre is not his get?"

"After many years, he finally, being human, dallied with a pretty dairymaid, Annie, Ceidre's mother. Maude was dying. Aelfgar was sick with despair—yet Annie was beauty, light, laughter—joy. Maude died—and Annie gifted him with Ceidre. She surpassed even her mother with her beauty and her laughter—Aelfgar worshiped the tiny babe. He offered Annie the hand of his reeve, the finest of the peasants, but she loved him and so refused. Thus Annie stayed in the kitchens here, and Ceidre grew up underfoot—everywhere. In the kitchens, in the hall, in the stables, in the woods. All knew, of course, she was the eaorl's daughter, yet not being nobly born, she was left free to do as she pleased. Yet her father loved her, her brothers adored her, and all would have been well save that Aelfgar had married Alice's mother, the Lady Jane."

"Yes?"

"When Aelfgar realized that he was falling in love with Annie, a lowborn serf, he was determined to correct the situation. Jane brought him a small manor on his northern borders. It was just a year after Ceidre's birth. Yet Jane was the opposite of Annie—dark, cold, spiteful, and very, very bitter to find her husband wanting another. Finally Aelfgar turned to Annie again. He never returned to Jane, who bore him Alice, but he treated her with respect. Yet Jane knew of his leman, and hated her and her daughter with all of her passion. Alice too grew up feeding on this poisonous hate. She has hated her sister from the day she could feel the emotion, before she could even talk."

"There were no others?"

"Aelfgar was an unusual man, not needing more than one good woman. No, there was only Annie after Maude died, and Ceidre is his only by-blow."

"Lady Alice would have me believe Ceidre is one of many brats."

"Mayhap she believes it herself—mayhap not."

"You are as wise as your years, Saxon."

"You are wiser than yours, Norman."

Rolfe found himself smiling slightly—and Athelstan finally did so too. "Is it true that Ceidre disappears for days at a time?" He didn't like the thought, not one bit. Nor did he like the way it made his innards cramp with tension.

" 'Tis rare." Athelstan stared at him. "You ask many questions of the sister, my lord."

Rolfe met his gaze directly. "She is a beautiful woman—and I had thought her to be my promised wife. 'Tis normal, given these circumstances."

"You do not fear the eye?"

Rolfe laughed, without mirth. "You think she is a witch too?"

"Oh, she is a witch, all right," Athelstan said gravely. "Even her father knew it. But a good witch."

"She is flesh and blood, a woman—made for a man." And his traitorous thoughts sped ahead: *My woman—made for me.* He grew grim, not liking his own treachery.

"Of course, my lord. But tonight she practices her witch's arts."

"What in God's name do you mean?" It was almost a roar, accompanied by a slap on the table, which nearly made the wood crack.

"She has gone far afield to find a special herb for Thor."

"Explain, old man."

Athelstan dryly told him, and Rolfe was furious and incredulous all at once. "She goes off into the night, alone, unescorted, to fetch herbs to heal an old dog!" He was on his feet, ordering his men to rise. "We shall end this foolishness once and for all."

CHAPTER 11

Alice's face was a mask of rage. In her anger, she was taut and ugly, older than her years. She listened to her lord and his men as they rode out into the night, by torchlight, their massive steeds' hooves rumbling like thunder. To find Ceidre.

It was impossible—but true. Her betrothed wanted her sister. Ceidre had cast a spell on him, she was certain. Why else would he look at her the way he did—when no other mortal man dared? Or was he himself unnatural, maybe not flesh and blood, but Satan's creation—the devil? Alice shuddered.

No, he was man, of flesh and blood. She had seen his male body, hard, muscular, battle-scarred—so ugly. For some reason he was not afraid of Ceidre's eye, and thus he was overwhelmed by her vivid, unnatural beauty.

Alice hated her sister so much she felt as if she were choking.

Alice had never been afraid of her sister, ever—her hate was too strong. And with the passing of time, she grew bolder, for Ceidre had never cast a spell upon her. Alice was sure it was because they were sisters—because it would have enraged their father. Or maybe Ceidre had no power where Alice was concerned. That thought pleased Alice greatly.

Now Rolfe was riding out at night to search for her.

Alice wished she could kill Ceidre. Rolfe, like her father, was not afraid of her and hence was bewitched by her unusual coloring, her beauty, her form. Thinking about her father made Alice ill. The way he had adored Ceidre, adored that whore, Annie, openly—while barely giving a smile to her own mother, since remarried, or to herself. Her brothers too had always favored Ceidre, oblivious to her eye, entranced by her smile and her laughter. Everyone who counted in Alice's life had always preferred her sister to her—it was only those who didn't count, like that young, pimply faced fool, Bill, her betrothed, who didn't. Alice wished, just once, she could see Rolfe recoil in horror from her sister. She knew how much revulsion dismayed Ceidre.

Ceidre was not going to ruin what was surely her last chance at marriage, Alice swore.

And a plan began to form in her mind.

An hour had passed at least—the moon had risen. Full and yellow, it glowed in the night. Rolfe reined in, listening to the silence. There was no sound, not even of crickets, owls, not even the wind. He raised himself in his stirrups. On an adjacent ridge, and in a dale, and across on another hill, he could see the flickering lights of the torches his men carried as they combed the countryside. His body was as taut as a bow string. Never would she roam afar again! "Ceidre! Ceidre!"

There was no answer. Now he was truly worried, sure a terrible fate had befallen her—wolves, brigands. Then he heard a noise and whipped his head around. He knew instant disappointment, as he saw the light approaching—'twas one of his men. And then his heart leapt as he heard, "My lord! I have her, I found her!"

His expression changed, worry evaporating, his

mouth settling into a hard, ruthless line. He spurred his steed forward to meet Beltain. "Well done," he said, low.

"Put me down, you oaf," Ceidre said through gritted teeth, a bundle squirming upon Beltain's lap.

"My lord?" Beltain asked.

Rolfe's fingers itched to spank her until she could not sit. "Put her down."

Beltain let her go, and she slid to the ground, panting. "What is the meaning of this!"

Rolfe reached down and swung her up in front of him. "Do not test me," he warned, and at the deadly sound of his voice, Ceidre ceased to protest. She went very still, sitting sidesaddle on his hard thighs. "Signal the others," Rolfe said. And he spurred his mount back toward Aelfgar.

Ceidre clutched her basket, anger fading in the face of his powerful presence. Tension reared, her heart began thundering. He was angry, very, very angry—which made no sense. And why were his men out looking for her? What she did, 'twas not his affair. She did not understand, not at all. And she did not like being treated like his property—which, if she accepted him as the new eaorl, she was.

He said not one word and the ride was swift. At the manor he dismounted, dragging her quite rudely down with him. He handed his destrier to one of the pages, his grip on her elbow so firm it hurt. He yanked her into the hall.

Alice looked up from her embroidery. She sat with her maid, a plump woman named Mary. A few of the men had returned already and were drinking ale and dicing. Alice regarded them steadily but said nothing.

"Everyone leave," Rolfe said, releasing Ceidre. She took one step. "Not you," he said.

She froze.

"You stay."

She turned to look at him. He stared, only at her, unsmiling, his gaze dangerous. Everyone left.

Ceidre fought to control the pace of her breathing, which had become shallow. No man had ever made her a coward before, and he, the Norman enemy, the usurper of Aelfgar, would not either. It was a valiant battle, which she won. Bravely she managed, "Do you have another penance for me to pay, my lord?" She spread her hands. "Perhaps right here, upon the floor? After all, we are alone, you have ordered it so."

His fine nostrils flared. "Do not test my good humor."

"Good humor?"

"You are forbidden the right to leave the village or the manor," he said shortly, eyes piercing her.

Ceidre gasped.

"Do you understand?"

"You can't!"

"I can, and I do. I am the lord here, this is my law. You may, however, ask me for permission, and I might, if generous, grant it. But there will be no more wandering afield at night!"

"You are still angry," Ceidre cried, dismayed, "because I deceived you with my identity!"

"Oh, yes," he said softly. "I am still very, very angry. You are lucky to have escaped my wrath so lightly, Ceidre." It was the first time he had addressed her by name, and the word on his tongue dripped like thick honey.

She did not like the tone. "Lightly?" She choked. "I do not think this persecution light."

"Persecution." His tone was heavy. "I do not persecute you, Ceidre."

"No? Then have you a better name for your actions?"

"As your lord, I may chastise where I will."

"Had you not stolen my herbs, I would not have had to wander this eve!"

"Had you not poisoned my man, I would not have had to seize your amulet."

"Had I not been prisoner, I would not have given Guy the draught!"

"Had you been a true lady, there would have been no need to have Guy guard you."

Ceidre quivered, not sure if the slur was cast upon her origins or her eye. "Do you taunt me now with the name bastard or witch?" she said bitterly.

"Neither," he said, moving swiftly. He shook her. "I am a man who has no need to throw names. You misunderstand—I refer to your very nature—not that of a meek, boring lady, but as fierce and unpredictable as battle. And as exciting."

His words struck her and she could not move. *Fierce . . . unpredictable . . . exciting.* She was pinned by his bold regard. He released her, and she felt the lack of his touch. He looked at her mouth, his gaze lingering, hungry and wistful. Then he turned very abruptly and strode up the stairs, leaving her alone and bewildered. And feeling the desperate urge to cry.

CHAPTER 12

"Wake up."

Ceidre had fallen asleep before she could sneak upstairs to discuss with Alice her imminent marriage. It was a heavy sleep, dreamless, the oblivion she so badly needed.

"Wake up!"

Ceidre was rudely awakened as Alice pulled mercilessly upon her hair. She gasped, rising up on one elbow. She slept on a pallet on the floor of the hall with all the others. "What? Alice, what is it?"

"Get up," Alice hissed. "We are going to talk, you and I."

It was the middle of the night. The snore of the Norman's men and Aelfgar's own surrounded them. Ceidre got to her feet, reaching for a mantle to cover her long undertunic. "Couldn't it have waited?"

Alice took her hand and pulled her, until they were outside near the kitchens. The light of the moon was just enough to see by, and as sleep left, Ceidre saw that Alice was angry.

"I am warning you, Ceidre, I am going to marry him and nothing you can do will stop me!"

Ceidre stared.

"You stay away from him with your whore's tricks," Alice whispered. "Do you understand?"

"You can't want to marry him!"

"I do! He is mine! He might dally with you—as our father did with your mother—but he will never make you his true wife!"

It hurt. It shouldn't, but it was God's truth, and for that reason the pain was overwhelming. "I hate him," Ceidre said. "He is a killer, the enemy, a Norman. He is stealing our brothers' land. I would not marry him if I were truly you, or even if he wanted me."

"Good."

"Alice, are you mad? How can you even think to marry him—the enemy—the usurper of Edwin's patrimony?"

"William is now king," Alice said. "And I do not care. Nor do I care if Edwin be eaorl or not. In all, 'tis better this way, with the Norman lord of Aelfgar and me the lady." She smiled, triumphant.

"I would help you," Ceidre offered. "To run away. We could go together—find Edwin. He would protect us from the Norman!"

"No! Did you not hear? I am marrying him—gladly! But you—you stay away from him. You flaunt your witch's unholy beauty in front of him and he pants after you like a stud. I will not have you enticing him into your bed. I will not have you his leman, as your mother was our father's. I mean it, Ceidre, I warn you!"

"I would never be his mistress," Ceidre snapped.

"Good." Alice drew herself up straight. "Now, the next matter. Your place here."

"What?"

"I am the lady here of Aelfgar. I am tired of your ways. With our father dead, our brothers gone, many men lost, 'tis time you did your share."

"What are you talking about?"

"At dawn you will go to the kitchens," Alice ordered. "You will work as cook's assistant to replace

Jess. And, Ceidre, you will take your meals with the rest of the serfs as well."

Ceidre stared. Alice was the lady of Aelfgar and had been since the widowed Jane remarried last year. Never had she ordered her to a station. In the past she would not have dared—Edwin would not have allowed it. Yet she had the authority to do so. "Surely you jest."

"No. The Norman agrees, there shall be no slack hands here."

Shock assaulted her. "He agrees to this?"

"Yes, of course. You are his serf, Ceidre, just like any other."

"I am a free woman," Ceidre said, "and you know it. You know Father gave me and my mother our freedom."

Alice grinned. "Can you prove it?"

"Everyone knows."

"Do you have the papers?"

"There were never any papers."

"Then you cannot prove it."

She could not believe the wicked intention of Alice's game. "Everyone knows!"

"Who will swear on the Bible—or in the shire court? You? Your witch-grandmother? The villagers? Athelstan? You are a bastard brat, Ceidre, nothing more. Whose word will the lord accept, yours, a commoner's, or mine?"

"Our brothers know the truth!"

"Do they? But, Ceidre—they are not here!"

"What are you trying to do?"

"It does not matter. You live in this household, Aelfgar is your master, whether you are serf or no. If you leave, I will have you hunted down as serf. If you stay, you do as I command. Is that clear?"

Alice knew she would never leave her home, it was

in her blood. Had she convinced the Norman Ceidre was his serf? She was stunned. "You are very clear, Alice."

"Good." Alice smiled.

While one crew felled timber for the new palisade, another was given the task of digging the huge ditch that would surround the keep. There was a natural mound Rolfe would build upon, and this pleased him greatly. Unfortunately, the village would have to be razed to make room for the bailey, but once reconstructed, it would be in a more defensible position just south of the bailey's palisade. Rolfe himself, once certain all the tasks were being carried out correctly, stripped off his hauberk and joined those digging the ditch. He relished the use of his powerful muscles, sweat streaming down his body.

The villagers had been recruited for labor as well, their usual seasonal tasks of mowing the fields of hay postponed until after the keep was erected. At noon everyone halted for repast, the villagers fed bread, cheese, and ale on the site, and Rolfe and his men returning to the hall for mutton pies. He washed briefly outside, then took his place beside Alice. Instantly he found himself looking for Ceidre, but she was nowhere to be seen. This annoyed him.

"Why does your sister not join us?"

Alice smiled sweetly. "She has undertaken the supervision of the kitchens, my lord. And as you can see, the fare is already vastly improved."

Rolfe had not noticed, but he was satisfied that she had not defied his edict of the night before, and he commenced his meal.

Because of the fear of fire, the kitchens were outside in a separate building behind the manor. The huge stone hearths, large enough for Ceidre to stand in, emitted vast heat, for they were constantly kept fired, day and night. Here all meats were spitted and roasted, turned by hand by a young serf, who stood naked, sweating. Here too vast cauldrons of stew simmered. Adjacent were the ovens, mostly used for baking bread, but also for baking cakes and even poultry and pheasant. In a small, separate enclosure were the pantries, where the butter was churned, and the alehouse, where the beverage was brewed. There were no windows, just one open doorway. The smoke escaped through a hole in the roof.

Everyone worked in their undertunics because of the heat, barefoot, hair pinned up. Ceidre was no exception. As she shoveled yet another loaf of dough into an oven, the heat scorching her red, flushed face, which was shining with perspiration, she wished she could go naked like Teddy, who was young enough not to care. Her undertunic, the thinnest wool because of the season, clung from her shoulders to her ankles like a second skin. In addition to the heat there was the problem of the smoke, which billowed inside in huge, thick clouds. For the hundredth time that morning, Ceidre was seized with a fit of coughing.

If only it would rain.

She fantasized a sudden downpour. She would run outside and let herself become drenched. It would be heaven.

She was no longer angry at Alice. She decided she could not blame her sister. Alice felt threatened, and Ceidre understood. The Norman did lust after her. Ceidre still found it unbelievable, and a frisson swept her, a combination of fear and something else unidentifiable. She felt the charge of some powerful emotion that she refused to comprehend. Yet Alice should have been reassured when Ceidre told her she absolutely did not want the Norman and would not have him, much less seduce him. And although Ceidre was rightly upset that Alice would try to regulate her as a serf, Alice was her sister. Ceidre forgave her.

The Norman was another matter.

She could not shake his golden pagan image out of her thoughts. He dismayed her—he angered her. His confining her to manor and village infuriated her. She would not obey. She certainly would not ask his permission when, in truth, she was free and could go as she pleased! And if he chose to beat her, she would bear it without a tear, without a cry. He was not her master, and he never would be. Just as he never would be lord of Aelfgar.

She knew, of course, that his agreeing to her new station in the kitchen was punishment for the deception of her identity. This was *his* punishment, thus she would pull her weight in the kitchens along with Tildie and Teddy and the others. This was the strongest reason she had for working hard, without complaint, head held high. Working harder than everyone. And after all, she was no better than any of them. In fact, Teddy was her cousin. And her mother had worked here after Ceidre was born until she had become sick. It didn't matter that it was in a supervisory capacity.

No, she would work harder than anyone. If he thought he could make her beg for forgiveness, beg for mercy, then he was wrong. She would die before she begged him for anything. She would show the Norman she was as relentless as he. As relentless an enemy.

CHAPTER 13

'Twas so hot.

Ceidre paused, feeling light-headed and weak. It was dim and smoky in the kitchen, and it became even darker. She gripped the bowl of peeled potatoes, taking a breath, fighting the need to faint.

"Get a goin'," cried Tildie. "No time to play slug-a-bug now, girl, the lord's already coming in from the village!"

The bowl went crashing out of her hand, shattering, the potatoes flying everywhere, into the dirt.

"You fool!" hissed Tildie. "You stupid fool! Now what will we put in the pie?"

The world became clear again and Ceidre focused on Tildie just as the woman delivered a sharp, hysterical slap to her cheek. Shocked, Ceidre drew back. Even more stunned, Tildie, realizing what she had done, gasped, her hand covering her mouth, her eyes widening into O's of horror. The two women stared at each other through the smoke. Tildie's full bosom, heavy with her fifth pregnancy, heaved over the mound of her belly.

" 'Tis all right." Ceidre spoke first. Her face hurt now. "I know you did not mean it."

Tildie stepped back, and tears flooded her eyes. "I didn't!" She started to cry. "Oh, Ceidre, how could you spill the spuds? Now what will we do! Mayhap he'll whip us all, and me so gone with the babe!"

Ceidre put her arm around the weeping woman. "Shh, Tildie, he will not harm you. I promise."

Ceidre was well aware that Tildie's sentiments were not unusual. In the past few days since she had been working in the kitchens, she had realized very quickly that the serfs were wary and afraid of their new master. He was so big, and he never smiled. His eyes were so cold—mean. They had heard all the stories of Rolfe the Relentless. He was William the Bastard's top commander. He was ruthless. At Hastings his men had slaughtered a hundred Saxon archers before they could break for the forest. He had been awarded Bramber, in Sussex. A rebellion had been stopped before it had begun, its leaders publicly hanged. Just recently he had burned York to the ground, every cottage, every shop, every tree, and every garden, after they had finally routed the Saxon rebels. And on his way to Aelfgar he had razed Kesop, not even sparing the cornfields. This was their new lord and master.

"We will bake extra bread and 'twill suffice," Ceidre said firmly. "Hush, now, Tildie. Go and sit down outside. I'll make the bread."

Rolfe was smiling broadly. The ditch had been completed, the dirt removed tossed within, and now a small hill sat in the center, the foundation for the keep. Already half the palisade had been erected, the thick, stout timbered walls over twice his height—and he was very tall. In no time the new great hall of Aelfgar would be finished and the bailey would be begun.

Rolfe was only wearing his undertunic and chausses. The tunic was the thinnest wool, a rich beige that, wet with sweat, molded every rippling sinew it contained. His dark gold curls clung thickly to his head. Wiping perspiration from his eyes, damning the day for the unusual heat, he mounted and rode back to the manor, approaching from the back because that was the side where he had been working.

Ahead of him were the kitchen and pantries. Smoke drifted in incessant puffs from the outbuildings. He could smell the pungent aroma of mutton, and his stomach growled. A maid was carrying butter from the pantry, another trenchers from the kitchen, both converging upon the manor. A boy drew water from the well, then he too disappeared. The area was momentarily deserted, and Rolfe was about to ride past the yard. Then another serf stepped outside from the kitchens, heading toward the alehouse.

Rolfe's heart broke its rhythm.

Unconsciously he halted his mount. There was no mistaking who it was. It was Ceidre.

He hadn't seen her in days. This did not mean he hadn't thought of her—often. He had tried grimly and unsuccessfully not to think of the wench, but 'twas impossible. Every time a woman entered his line of vision, he had looked, to see if it was her. It never was.

His mood these past few days had been abrupt and even foul. He had been quick to find fault with his men and equally quick to demand new, faultless effort. Guy had openly remarked upon it. Rolfe had said nothing. Guy, trying not to laugh, had suggested that he ease himself with Lettie, a peasant wench his men were most fond of. Rolfe had ignored him, although he had considered the suggestion. He usually slaked his lust at will. However, his lust had not arisen upon the sight of any of these village women in the past few days, hence he had not bothered with a tumble. But now—oh, now there was no problem!

She had not seen him. He couldn't breathe, he was so strangled with thick, hot need at the sight of her.

She was practically naked. Her wet undertunic clung to her full breasts and her lush derriere, leaving little to his imagination. 'Twas white, and opaque. He could just see a hint of her skin's color—that unusual creamy gold. Rolfe forgot all his vows and started his mount forward.

Ceidre suddenly paused in the center of the yard and had a fit of coughing, bent over double. Rolfe leapt from the stallion and seized her, holding her upright until the spasm had passed. She was trembling and weak, leaning heavily against him. His lust had vanished; in its place was abject fear.

"I'm all right," she said hoarsely, still allowing him to support her. She looked up. Her eyes went wide. So did his.

Her face was flushed crimson and gleaming with perspiration. There was a bruise on her jaw. He could see circles of fatigue beneath her beautiful eyes. Her hair was soaking wet, pinned in coils atop her head. She drew away from him as if repulsed. He let her go. She paled and swayed precariously.

He caught her. "You are ill!"

"Let me go." She gasped. "I am fine." She was panting from the slight exertion of trying to remove herself from his grasp. She was so weak, like a newborn kitten. He kept one arm around her. "Let me help you, Ceidre. You must sit down."

Her chin lifted. " 'Tis only from the smoke."

"The smoke?"

"Within."

Rolfe did not believe her. He was appalled at her condition, but, certain she could stand on her own, he left her and entered the kitchen. There were four serfs inside, including a naked boy stirring a cauldron. He had thought it hot outside. Here it was unbearable, dim and dark, and the smoke was so thick it was a miracle anyone could breathe at all. He returned to Ceidre grimly. " 'Tis abominable in there."

She shrugged. " 'Tis how it is, how it always has been. Where there is fire there is smoke, every fool knows so." She brushed damp wisps of hair away from her face.

Rolfe had never entered a kitchen before, and he wondered if the kitchens on the estates he had possessed in Sussex were as badly ventilated. "The smoke can be lessened."

Ceidre regarded him warily.

"With windows and a fitting on the roof."

"There is no such thing as windows in a kitchen."

"There is now." His gaze swept her. He noted the flour on her nose, the stains on her gown. And that darkening bruise on her face. "What happened to your jaw?"

" 'Twas an accident."

"You look like any kitchen wench."

"What do you expect? I am any kitchen wench. I work in the kitchens, after all, 'twas your decree."

Rolfe stared, his anger increasing, roiling, like a storm. "You do not supervise?"

"Supervise?" She laughed. "Do I look like I'm supervising?" She gestured down at her soaking body. Her hand trembled slightly.

"You are exhausted."

She raked him with her own contemptuous gaze. "I am not tired, and I've forgotten, dallying here with you so. I still have much to do." She turned her back abruptly on him and began to march away.

That she would do so, leave him before he had ordered it, and in such a manner, was unbelievable. Yet this was less significant than the issue at hand—and her well-being. He caught her wrist, jerking her to a halt. "You will not go in there. And what is this nonsense—I decreed your place here?"

"My penance—my lord."

"I have decreed no such thing," Rolfe said furiously. "But I decree this. You are to rest for what remains of this day—and you are never to work in the kitchens again. Do you understand?"

Ceidre stared.

"I see that you do," Rolfe said. "Then understand this as well. You do not turn your back on me, Ceidre. You are not nobly born."

She bit her lip. Her flush increased. He saw the defiance in her eyes, and the mingling of apprehension before she lowered her head. She mumbled an affirmative. "Yes."

He stared at her. Her anger was arousing—she was arousing. She would fight him regardless of her fear—and he knew she feared him. He felt the soaring of some emotion like respect, which could not be, of course, for she was only a woman, and another he understood well, annoyance. He did not like her afraid of him. He touched her chin, lifting it with one forefinger. He saw the startled light in her eyes and felt the impact of their touching just as, he knew, she had.

"My lord," he said softly.

Her bosom rose and fell. She was ensnared, unable to withdraw her gaze.

"You cannot beat me, Ceidre," Rolfe warned softly.

Defiance flared. "Yes—my lord."

He smiled, satisfied, but did not drop his hand. His finger stroked her jaw. "Was it so hard?"

She winced and pulled away.

Rolfe cursed, furious with himself for catering to his own base, male instincts, and forgetting her bruise.

"Go to your grandmother," he said harshly. "Have her make a poultice before it swells further."

She was gone before he had finished, holding up the hem of her gown and running—from him.

CHAPTER 14

"Lady, I would have a word with you."

Alice stood near their two chairs at the head of the table within the hall, waiting for Rolfe before seating herself. His men had already come in, sat, and were busily eating. Rolfe's eyes were bright blue and cold—like the sky in January. She glanced around to see who had heard his tone. His man, Guy Le Chante, was studiously watching every mouthful he ate, but old Athelstan was slow (and insolent) to withdraw his regard. Alice seethed, but hid it behind a pretty smile. "Can it not wait, my lord? The food is hot."

"No." He took her elbow rudely and propelled her up the stairs.

Alice would not show her anger at being treated this way—like some field wench. She kept her lashes demurely lowered. And she reined in the little knot of fear he inspired.

"How is it," Rolfe growled, "that you told me Ceidre supervises, when in truth she is reduced to the task of any common serf?"

Alice's lashes flew up. "But she is any common serf!"

"She is your sister."

"My half sister—some serf's brat."

"She is still the eaorl's daughter, Lady, and that

raises her above the place you would have her. She will not work like a common peasant in the kitchens."

"Yes, my lord." Alice waited a beat, until he had relaxed slightly. "My lord?"

He waited, impatiently now.

"What tasks should she perform, then? She is a mouth to be fed. Every serf at Aelfgar works for his fare, this you know."

"I will find her other duties. Enough of this topic." He started down the stairs.

Alice touched his sleeve. "My lord?"

He made no effort to hide his annoyance. "What now?"

"You have not said"—she took a breath—"when we will be wed."

A frown flitted across his features. "I have not? I thought I had. In a fortnight, if it suits you."

Relief brought a wide, happy smile to Alice's face. "Oh, yes," she cried. "It suits me well!"

Ceidre did not appear for the noon meal, but Rolfe assumed she was resting, and was satisfied. However, at supper there was no sign of her either, and he began to worry. He knew she was not well. Anger rose in him again at the thought of his bride's little scheme, for he was certain she had abused her power over her sister in her jealousy. He wondered if it had always been this way, Alice ordering Ceidre to unpleasant tasks, the girl, being low-born, having no choice but to obey. It was only natural that she obey, but it bothered Rolfe—and he had never in his life questioned the natural order of things, nor sympathized with a serf's plight.

He had not been aware of the fact that she was a serf until Alice had mentioned it. Now he felt pleased with the thought—she belonged to him. Before, when he had erroneously assumed her to be just another member of his household, she also had to obey his authority, but this was entirely different. She could not travel without his permission, not one foot off his land. To do so would be considered running away, a severe breach of the law. She could not leave Aelfgar without his permission, to reside elsewhere. She could not marry without his permission, and she owed him a certain amount of services each year—services he had not yet determined the nature of. She was his complete responsibility. Legally she belonged to him.

Perhaps the reason she had not come to sup with them was because she was ill, even with fever. Rolfe lost his appetite. He knew he should send someone to check on her, but he decided to do so himself. He left his wife at the harp, his men dicing. He knew she often spent time with her grandmother, who lived in the village, and guessed she was probably there. However, first he would inquire of the servants.

For the second time in his life, Rolfe entered the kitchens, now lighted with oil lamps. He would not have been more shocked if he had seen a ghost. For there she was, hard at work. Ceidre sensed his presence, and from where she was cleaning up, she half turned.

He was so stunned at her complete defiance he gaped.

Ceidre, already flushed, went crimson.

He found his voice. "You dare," he managed, livid, "you dare to defy me this openly."

She clutched the cutting table. "I can explain."

It was beyond belief. "My men do not defy me."

"Truly, there is a reason."

"My men fear just chastisement." He was actually shaking.

"My lord—"

"But you—you do not fear me?" He stepped forward.

Ceidre stepped back, holding her hands up as if to ward him off. She was too exhausted for a fight, and had dearly hoped he would not find out she had continued in the kitchens. "My lord! 'Tis Tildie—she has begun her labor. We are short of hands here, I had to help!"

The anger was replaced with puzzlement. "You would work yourself to death in another's place?"

"She is about to have a babe, my lord," Ceidre said softly. "She is my friend."

He shook his head. "Enough! You cannot disobey my commands, Ceidre. I cannot countenance it."

"Will you beat me?"

He clenched his jaw. "I would dearly like to! This time, Ceidre, only this time, do you escape punishment. But harken well. The next time you disobey me 'tis at your own risk—for the price you pay will be most severe."

Her mouth trembled, and she consciously straightened her spine.

"Enough. You are finished here. If ever aught like this happens again, you come to me—do not take it upon yourself to decide whether to continue or no, especially if it means defying me. I will see you to your bed."

She felt relief and was angry for feeling so. "To it—or in it?"

"Are you suggesting the latter?" His tone was mocking.

"No."

"You have only to invite me. You know I am willing." Silky, now.

"Well, I am not!"

He almost smiled, and his gaze stroked over her

breasts. "Your mind, perhaps—but your body is most willing."

Ceidre folded her arms. "Not true."

"Do not think you can ever spar with me and win," Rolfe said softly. "What you begin, I will finish. Always."

"I hate you," she said, low. "Norman!"

" 'Tis what I am. Where do you sleep?"

"In the hall," Ceidre said, dodging his proffered hand. When, in truth, she would have liked nothing more than to lean upon his solid, powerful frame.

They stepped outside into the night, bright with stars and a three-quarter moon. Ceidre lifted her face to the air and sighed. Rolfe could not take his eyes away from her uplifted profile. He was mesmerized, ensnared. She caught him staring, and she blushed.

"Come," he said gruffly, taking her elbow.

She trembled, but she came.

Ceidre was in that strange state of exhaustion that makes sleep difficult to come by. She had just, finally, managed to drift off when loud voices and strange hands awakened her. "Ceidre, Ceidre, awaken! You must awaken!"

Ceidre blinked and became aware of Athelstan and another man, a serf from his attire, bending over her, a rushlight in one hand. "What is it?"

One of the hounds began to bark. The men began to stir. Someone called out angrily for quiet, and another dog yelped.

" 'Tis my wife," the serf said, and Ceidre recognized him. "She is in a bad way, Ceidre! The babe won't come! 'Tis her fifth and all the others came so easily, but this one won't! Please, help her!"

Ceidre was standing, her mantle already around her shoulders. "Of course I will come, John," she said soothingly. But her mind was racing. She undoubtedly needed her herbs.

"What is the meaning of this?"

Ceidre whipped her head around at the sound of his voice. Rolfe was poised halfway down the stairs, clad only in woolen hose, but he held a sword. Athelstan answered. " 'Tis the woman, Tildie. She's birthing a babe and it's not going well."

Ceidre was already pushing past the men, sprawled on pallets everywhere, to confront the Norman. Rolfe said, "Send someone else. The wench is overtired."

Ceidre felt a rush of anger, and paused before the stairwell to face him. "There is no one else, my lord," she said very firmly. "I need my pouch."

Rolfe stared, then barked a command at Athelstan. The Saxon hurried upstairs to fetch the herbs while Ceidre waited, meeting his gaze unflinchingly. If he would order her to remain abed and not tend Tildie, she would disobey, but he said nothing—he only stared. Athelstan returned and handed her the pouch. Ceidre grabbed it and hurried out into the night.

They were at the cottage five minutes later, Tildie's moans carrying outside. Her four children, ranging from three to ten, sat huddled in the single room, the five-year-old crying. "Hush, sweeting," Ceidre said, placing a hand on the boy's head. "Your mama will be fine. Hush now."

She looked at John. "Comfort them."

Tildie was drenched with sweat. Her waters had already broken. She thrashed and moaned, her contractions close together, but the baby would not come. Ceidre saw instantly what the problem was. The babe was a breech, turned completely around, trying to leave the womb feet first. 'Twas not good.

"I will have to turn the babe around," she said to John, without looking at him.

"Have you ever done such a thing before?" Rolfe asked.

Ceidre gasped, stunned that the Norman had followed them. He stood in the middle of the small cottage, seeming to take up every inch of its entire space. He had thrown his sinister black mantle over his bare torso, but had only slipped shoes, not chausses, on. Now Ceidre understood why the hut had become so very quiet. The children were gaping, bug-eyed. Even John was stunned, immobile.

"Once," she answered, turning back to Tildie and stroking her brow. "If you are here, fetch me fresh water and clean rags and soap." Tildie had fainted.

"I will get them," John said, clearly relieved to flee.

"How is she?" Rolfe asked, not moving from where he stood.

"She has fainted. She is better off. Now she can rest a bit before the real work begins." Ceidre kept stroking her brow.

The five-year-old redhead began to cry again, pitifully, calling "Mama, Mama."

Ceidre, kneeling by the pallet, twisted to soothe the little boy. She stopped, amazed, to see Rolfe stroke his big hand through the child's curls. She had never seen him gentle before, had never even thought he could be gentle—but he was. "*Viens à moi, petit,*" he said, his voice low, comforting. "Do you know who I am?"

The boy blinked, staring. "N-no."

" 'Tis our lord," hissed the eldest, a girl of ten.

Rolfe rewarded the girl with a smile, then lifted the redhead into his arms. "She is right, I am your lord, Rolfe of Warenne. Do you know where Warenne is?"

The little boy shook his head, staring, awed, into Rolfe's face, so close to his.

" 'Tis far away, across the sea. Would you like to

know how I came to be here, how I crossed the sea on a big boat with all my men?"

He nodded.

Relieved, and still amazed, Ceidre turned back to Tildie, listening to Rolfe as he began the story, thankfully omitting all political details, his voice low and rich and soothing. John entered and handed her the items she had requested. Ceidre washed her hands and began wiping Tildie's brow. The woman started to revive.

"Tildie?" Ceidre leaned forward. " 'Tis Ceidre. I am going to try and turn the babe. He's facing the wrong way, and it must be done."

Tildie opened her eyes.

Ceidre smiled. She reached out to stroke her temple again. Tildie cried out and shrank away. Ceidre froze. Rolfe halted in midsentence, and John and the children all stared.

"No!"

"Tildie—"

"No! Don't touch me! Please, don't!" She began to weep.

Ceidre hesitated only for a fraction. "She's overwrought. I'll give her a potion."

"No! I won't take your witch's brew!"

Ceidre felt as if she had been punched in the stomach. She recovered, with effort. "Tildie, 'tis me. 'Tis Ceidre. Your friend. I—"

"This is all your fault," Tildie hissed. "You cursed me and the babe because I slapped you! Get away from me! Get this witch away from me!"

Rolfe handed the redhead to John and was at Ceidre's side. "Listen to me, mistress. I am your lord."

Tildie stared, tears streaking her face.

"She is no witch. She is going to give you a potion to

calm you, then she will turn the babe. 'Tis my command."

Tildie began to weep. "I'm sorry." She sobbed. "Sorry. It's just that I'm so afraid . . ."

"Give her the potion," Rolfe said tersely, his gaze riveted not on Tildie but upon Ceidre's face. Her expression, sick and stunned, twisted his gut into knots. He wished he could curse the foul wench for doing this to Ceidre, when she meant only good.

Ceidre recovered and, murmuring words of comfort, she administered the potion. Tildie was soon in a state of lethargy. Rolfe regarded her brisk efficiency, despite her being clearly upset. She did not shrink but boldly delved into the other's body, yet her touch was gentle. Tildie gasped in pain. Ceidre began to turn the babe, perspiration filming on her brow. Rolfe admired her in that moment greatly—she had immense courage. He reached out to blot a drop of sweat on her forehead before it interfered with her vision.

"There," Ceidre cried, relieved. "The babe is turned, it should not be long now."

"Well done," Rolfe said quietly.

She glanced at him. His gaze was warm, unwavering. She flushed and concentrated on the task at hand. Tildie's contractions were now strong enough to pop the babe out easily. Ceidre reached for the infant and knew instantly that it was dead.

It had strangled in the womb, its birth cord wrapped around its neck.

Ceidre blinked back tears and wrapped the infant in its swaddling. Rolfe reached down and took it from her. "I will bury it," John said, resigned. He considered himself lucky to have four healthy children as it was.

Tildie opened her eyes. "My baby?"

Ceidre hesitated. Rolfe stepped into the breach.

"The babe could not survive. 'Twas not meant to be. He died in the womb."

"No!"

"I am sorry, but 'tis so. You are young and strong. God has gifted you with four healthy children, and if it is His will, He will gift you with many more."

"No!"

Rolfe touched Ceidre's stiff shoulders. "It is time to go. There is nothing more you can do. She must grieve herself."

"I will give her a sleeping potion."

"No!" Tildie screamed, somehow raising herself up to a sitting position. "No! I want my baby! Give me my babe!"

Ceidre took Tildie's hand as she wept. "I'm sorry. Oh, Tildie, I tried . . ." She broke off, unable to continue, thinking that if she'd come sooner maybe she could have saved the baby. Her heart ached for her friend.

"Oh, my baby," Tildie moaned.

John came to his wife and Ceidre rose to her feet, brushing at tears. She really couldn't see, everything was a blur. She had tried, she knew that, she had done the best she could, yet . . . If only she had thought to check on Tildie that afternoon, if only she had come sooner. She escaped the dark, dank hut and gulped in the fresh night air. She realized she was running. She didn't care.

CHAPTER 15

She ran into the half-mown hayfield.

"Ceidre—stop!"

Him! He was the last person in this world she wished to see. Ceidre kept running. She stumbled on the furrowed earth but did not fall. She heard him calling again. Stalks of hay tore strands of hair free from her braid and whipped her cheek. She reached the far side of the field and paused, gasping for breath, at the edge of the dark, looming forest. Would he never leave her alone?

She rested a shoulder against the rough bark of an ancient oak, and her knees gave way. She curled her fingers into the dirt and swallowed a sob. Her world was spinning. Her breathing was still ragged and uncontrolled.

"Ceidre."

She turned her head slightly and saw his foot. She forced herself up, into a sitting position. "Leave me be." To her dismay, her voice was husky with unshed tears and not fierce at all.

Rolfe stood, tense and uncertain. He ached as if he were the one wounded. He wanted to reach down and touch her, stroke the dirt from her face and the tendrils of hair away from the corners of her mouth. Damn that peasant wench!

"Come," he said, the sound gruff even to his own ears, and he reached down to assist her up.

She shrank away. "Leave me be!" she cried shrilly. "I do not want your concern!"

His hands fell to his sides. "You have it whether you want it or not. All of Aelfgar is my concern."

She turned her face away, wishing he would leave, staring at her hands, white against the black earth.

Rolfe had never suggested anything to anyone, but now, awkwardly, he said, "Let us go back."

"You go. Just leave me alone."

He could order her, of course, but for some reason he was loath to do so. "You wish to spend the night here?" It was inane, his remark, but he did not know what to say.

"No," she spat, "I don't wish to spend the night here. Oh—God's blood!" She started to weep.

For the first time in his life he felt helpless. Ceidre wept at his feet. His urge to touch her was strong, yet he had never touched a woman merely to comfort, without lust—he did not know how. He clenched his fists and just stood there, unsure, feeling weaker than the weakest of boys.

She shoved herself abruptly to her feet, pushing past him. Rolfe was overwhelmed with relief. He followed. They said not a word. She held herself proud and straight, when he knew she was utterly exhausted. She had more courage and determination than most men. At the manor door, she nodded stiffly to him without meeting his gaze. He said nothing, going to the stairs. But there he turned, his gaze automatically seeking her out. He saw her shed the mantle, pause, almost ethereal in the thin white nightgown, and then she collapsed upon her pallet. He hesitated, thinking she would become cold, but he did not move to go to her.

And then a form rose at Ceidre's side. Rolfe went stiff, murderous. He held up his lamp—Athelstan gazed directly at him. Rolfe watched the old man pull the blanket up over her, murmuring something soft and unintelligible. Rolfe was seared with jealousy—and it was only Athelstan.

Alice ran from the window in Rolfe's chamber to the solar across the hall where she slept. She had barely dived onto her own bed when she saw his shadow passing her doorway and entering his chamber. She lay rigid, seething. She had known it—hadn't she? She had known he was going to meet that whore when he had left earlier. Seeing them return together confirmed it. Alice had never hated Ceidre more—or Rolfe.

She would pay. Alice would make sure of it. But first, more important, she had somehow to keep Ceidre out of her way—and out of her lord's bed. Until after the marriage. Once Alice was securely wed, she would find a way to deal with Ceidre—to remove her permanently from Rolfe's lusting perversions. Even if it meant marrying her off to some serf in a village at the far end of Aelfgar's borders. Better yet—have her abducted by Scots! Then they would never see hide nor hair of her again!

Alice, soothed by her fantasies, fell into the deep embrace of sleep.

"A fortnight?" Ceidre echoed.

"Yes. The banns have already been posted," Athelstan said.

Ceidre turned away. Her mind was racing. She could not allow the viper into their nest! She could not! But how, how to stop the marriage when her sister was willing? And was it even fair to do so, when

Alice so desperately wanted to wed? Ah, but surely there were others—she did not have to wed the Norman! Not the Norman!

"We must stop them," she muttered to herself.

"You will not stop that one," Athelstan said. "He is not called the Relentless for nothing. What he wants, he pursues until 'tis his. 'Tis well known, Ceidre. And he wants Aelfgar and its lady."

"Yes," Ceidre said bitterly. She couldn't help it, she remembered the warmth in his eyes and his voice when, after she had turned the babe, he had said "Well done." Then she recalled the feel of his mouth on hers in his chamber, his body wet from the bath, hard, sleek, thrusting against hers. Something coiled tight within her. Would he be so ready to bed Alice? Why did that thought upset her? She had no place even concerning herself with such an affair, unless it was to feel sorry for her sister.

She had been given no duties. With resolution, Ceidre went to check on Tildie. The events of the night before were fresh, so very fresh, in her mind. Had her own friend shown her truest, deepest feelings —that she too was reviled and repulsed by Ceidre's "evil" eye? Ceidre knew that Tildie had been hysterical, but still, it had hurt, it did hurt. And then there was her own sense of failure. Most of all, Ceidre wanted to help her friend through her grief.

Tildie was not, surprisingly, in the kitchens. According to the servants, she had been given a day of rest by the lord. Bemused at such unheard-of charity, Ceidre walked down the slope to the village. The sun was high and warm, shedding its strength, burning away the finest spun clouds. There was a faint breeze, carrying with it the familiar odor of sheep and the fragrance of baking bread and hyacinth. Somewhere just to her right a lark sang, and a mockingbird responded.

The palisade of the Norman's new keep would be completed today, Ceidre thought as she came closer. The first floor of the tower had been framed as well. A drawbridge lay open, its wood pale and fresh. A knot of men stood there, working on the portcullis. Ceidre saw the Norman.

He was stripped to his hose and chausses, his torso, golden brown, glinting in the sun. His hair glimmered, its soft, thick curls threaded riotously with gold and flaxen and even spun silver. It was, she thought, becoming overly long for the Norman style. In the back, where it had been shaved, as was the mode, it was growing in. Unlike his fellows, he would never be able to sport the popular style with a neat fringe of bangs because his hair was so unruly, untamable; even close-cropped, it would not lie flat upon his brow.

He turned to stare.

Ceidre realized she had paused to study him, and she flushed. Whatever had possessed her to do so openly, in front of half of Aelfgar! He did not smile, but wiped his hands upon his muscular thighs and approached her. Ceidre wished she had not halted, but it was too late. She raised her chin a notch, tensing.

"Good morning," he said.

She couldn't help it—something fierce swept her. He was near naked before her, his body sculpted with muscle, his chest broad, darkly furred, his waist narrow, hips small. His thighs bulged. His hose was damp, clinging—cupping his sex, conspicuous even now, when at ease. Ceidre forced herself to meet his gaze. His eyes were hot.

"Do not look at me that way, mistress," he said, low. " 'Tis unholy provocation."

She knew she was coloring again. "You flaunt yourself and know very well every wench who passes will eye your form."

"Do I flaunt myself?" He was smiling now, the transformation in his visage startling. "You think all the wenches look?"

Ceidre stared at the portcullis so as not to regard him. "You know they do."

"So I am comely?"

She took a breath. "Nay, merely—different."

"Different?"

"An oddity!" she shot, eyes flashing. "Taller than a tree, thicker than a mountain, gold and white—a most strange sight!"

He laughed. It was the first time she had ever heard him laugh, and she was stunned by the richness and the warmth of the sound. "We cannot all be dark and short and Saxon," he said, eyes sparkling.

" 'Tis too bad."

"Nay, 'tis good." He reached out a hand, and one strong forefinger touched her chin, raising it. "I am glad you are not short and dark, Ceidre."

"Like Alice?"

"Like Alice."

"Your gladness means nothing to me," she gasped. "I must go."

"Where do you go? I purposefully ordered your day to be free. You need rest."

She eyed him warily, reluctant to answer. "And why does my well-being interest you?"

His eyes glinted. "Everything about you interests me, Ceidre."

She inhaled.

"You belong to me," he said, soft. "I guard well what is mine."

Ceidre understood the reference to her status as

serf. So Alice had spread the lie, and why should he doubt it? "I am no serf."

"You deny you were born to your mother?"

"Of course not!"

"Then you belong to Aelfgar and thus to me. I repeat—where do you go this morning?"

She clenched her fists, controlling her frustration and the urge to make him comprehend the truth. Yet why should she care what he believed? It did not matter what he thought of her, for she had no intention of leaving. He would not remain lord anyway, of this she was sure. Her brothers would die before willingly relinquishing Aelfgar to the Norman. No, she would be patient, until this mess was untangled. Until the Norman was defeated—and retreated or died.

A chill swept her.

"I go to visit Tildie. Mayhap she has need of me."

"After what she did last night? Her accusations? You have the goodness to go to her again?" He was incredulous.

"She was overwrought and grief-stricken. 'Tis always easiest to blame someone other than oneself or God."

"Your heart is overly large."

"You would stop me?"

"No. Go. But do not let anything she says upset you, Ceidre." There was warning in his tone. "We both know the truth, you and I. 'Tis enough."

"And you are so sure of the truth?" Ceidre heard herself ask.

He smiled. His blue gaze went from her eyes to her mouth, lingered, then raked her from breast to hip. "The only power you have, wench, is that of seductress, not witch. Your power is as old as the gods, the power of woman over man."

She could not look away, spellbound by the low,

sensual note in his tone. Something strangely uplifting like elation swept her from head to toe. Finally she found her voice. "I am no temptress."

"No?" He laughed. "Then you are a witch—for you have bewitched me—as well you know."

She folded her arms, tight. "No," she cried. "No! You are a slave to your own lusts—when you are to marry my sister!"

His smile faded. His eyes were hard. "If I were a slave to my own lusts, I would toss you now, here, in the dirt, like any common wench, for all to see."

Ceidre flushed.

"But I wed your sister in less than a fortnight."

" 'Twill never be!" Ceidre hissed. Her vision had blurred.

"Do not think you can stop me," he said. "Your powers are not that strong."

Tears, of anger, of hurt, came into her eyes. "I will stop you, Norman! But not as you suggest, with my temptress's powers. You mistake it if you think I want you for myself! 'Tis Aelfgar I protect—from you! And I will gladly die before I see the day when you are truly lord here!"

"You are alive, Ceidre," he said coldly. "And I am truly lord here. So put any thoughts of treason from your head. I warn you here and now."

"May I take my leave—my lord?" she asked, blinking furiously, the effect of her sarcasm ruined.

He was fighting down his anger. "Go, before I act like a boy, not a man, and give in to my needs. But remember my words."

She bit down a retort and, hands clenched at her sides, whirled away. He gazed after her for a long time.

CHAPTER 16

"How are you feeling, Tildie?"

Tildie paused in the act of scattering feed to three hens and a cock. The two women looked at each other.

"I'm sorry, Tildie. I tried," Ceidre said uncertainly.

Tears welled in Tildie's eyes. "I know. I'm sorry too, for saying such awful nonsense. I didn't mean it, Ceidre, I didn't."

You didn't mean it, Ceidre thought, but you said it—how could you have said such things to me? Yet she did not voice her thoughts, instead managing a smile. There was a time when the two women would have embraced in their apology, but an invisible wall had come between them. "How are you feeling?" Ceidre asked.

"A little tired is all."

They exchanged a few more words. What had happened created a tension between them that had never existed before. Then Ceidre said good-bye and turned away. She walked aimlessly, trying not to think.

"Ceidre?"

At the sound of Albie's voice, Edwin's most trusted man, Ceidre almost fainted. She whipped around, eyes widening at the sight of him. He was dressed as a simple serf, not as a thane's son. She restrained the impulse to jump into his arms. "Albie! You have news?" Her voice was low and urgent.

"Let's walk," Albie suggested. He was her own age, sent to foster at Aelfgar when he was six. They had grown up together—he was practically a brother.

Ceidre twisted the sash of her girdle nervously as they strolled into the apple orchard. "They are fine?"

"Yes. Edwin took an arrow in his thigh, but he is healing well."

Relief swept her, and sorrow that she hadn't been there to see to his wound. "You are sure there is no infection?"

"You know Ed. Strong as an ox."

Ceidre smiled, torn with missing both him and Morcar. Edwin was as strong as an ox, of average height, with her father's strong, hawklike features and his raven hair. Morcar was taller, leaner, his hair brown and unruly, his eyes a dancing blue. Yet his quick smile hid as fierce a will and intelligence as Edwin's. The brothers seemed opposite, the one brooding and intense, not one for excess words, the other quick to laugh and smile and shout, yet they were really of the same stuff. And loyal, the one unto the other.

"Where are they?" She glanced around again, but they were alone, the villagers going about their normal activity, the Norman still with his men at the drawbridge, now a good kilometer away.

"In the fens. Ceidre, Morcar is coming as soon as he can. Edwin will not allow this dispossession to occur. You must watch every move Rolfe de Warrenne makes. And listen as well. Anything of import that you see or hear you must relay."

"I understand," Ceidre said. "The Norman has fifty men, all seasoned knights. I've seen them in battle." She shuddered, remembering how the Norman and his men had slain the Saxons at Kesop, effortlessly. "He may have more."

"Of course he does, but they've been left at York. He's the new castellan there, did you not know?"

"No, I did not."

"William the Bastard still stays at York, with royal troops, to oversee the rebuilding of the castle. Rolfe must be in close correspondence with him. Ceidre, we need to know their plans. If they have written messages, you must find them, and you must try to overhear their conversations. . . ." Albie looked at her.

Ceidre thought of the price of treason: public flogging and the stocks, or even hanging. "I will try, Albie, but 'twill not be easy. The Norman is very smart."

"Do your best."

"You know he is to marry Alice?"

"No, I did not. I will relate the news to your brothers. When is the wedding?"

"A bit more than a sennight now. The time flies, Albie."

" 'Tis not good, I think. Morcar will come before, I am sure. Until then, watch and listen. I had better go."

Ceidre took his hand. "God speed you, Albie. I was so afraid."

"Your brothers are near immortal." Albie grinned.

"Do not joke upon such matters, no one but God is immortal," Ceidre said sharply. He shrugged, and she watched him trot off into the forest. A glance at the construction site told her the Norman and his men were still hard at work. Now was as good a time as any to hunt for royal missives. She started back to the manor.

Alice was in the kitchens, dictating the day's fare. Ceidre slipped past the open doorway without being seen and entered the manor by the front of the house. At this time of day there was no one in the hall, save a serf wiping down the long trestle table. Ceidre hurried up the stairs.

She felt a tinge of apprehension as she pushed open the massive cedar door to the great chamber. She slipped inside, then thought the better of closing the door all the way—she left it slightly ajar so as not to look too suspicious should she be caught. She glanced around.

The room boasted a large bed, the bed her father had slept on, the bed that had been Edwin's—and was now the Norman's. There were several chests along the walls, where the Norman's things were stored, also used to sit upon. They were not chests that belonged to Aelfgar—he had brought them with him. This seemed as good a place as any to start.

It struck her that he might not be able to read, as most men did not. She had not considered this sooner, because he was so shrewd it seemed unlikely he would not possess such a power. It occurred to Ceidre, then, that a man like the Norman would destroy any written missives—and that many could be verbal. Yet she must look. And, even if he couldn't read, there would be the village priest to decipher anything written—if he could. Ceidre almost smiled. Father Green was drunk most of the time and wenching the rest. She supposed a monk could be sent for. Or—he could ask her to read a message to him.

Her heart sped. She must find out whether he could read or no. If not, she must make him aware of her usefulness to him. The situation would be ideal!

The first chest contained tunics and hose and mantles, brooches, a bag-beaker, shoes, an extra pair of garters. Another, fine silks from the Orient in the most beautiful colors Ceidre had ever seen, rich velvets in gold and red and a cape of tawny, cream, and red-streaked fur. But no missives. The last trunk contained

Oriental rugs and an old, broken sword in its jewel-studded scabbard. She replaced it carefully. The Norman had brought his most valued possessions with him, she thought bitterly, but little did he know—he was not staying at Aelfgar. Aelfgar belonged to Edwin.

There was no other place for messages to be stored unless they were truly hidden.

"What are you doing in here?"

Ceidre, absorbed in her speculation, whirled at the sound of Alice's harsh voice, immensely relieved to have finished her search and closed the chests. "I was looking for my herbs," she replied smoothly. It was a lie, of course; she had retrieved it the other night for Tildie's sake.

"Does he know you are in here?" Alice demanded. "Did he give you permission?"

"No," Ceidre said carefully. "Alice, he would be very angry to know I was looking for my amulet."

"Yes, he would be, wouldn't he?" Alice sneered.

"Are you going to tell him?"

"Have you disclaimed your serfhood?"

"He did not believe me."

Alice was triumphant. "Why should he? After all, you were born to that whore who was a serf. Did you find your witch's potions?"

"No."

"What did you do last night, Ceidre?"

She knew, Ceidre thought. She knew she had been with Tildie and had had her herbs with her. Ceidre fumbled for a response.

"Whore," Alice cried, and slapped her hard across the face.

Ceidre drew back, shocked.

"I saw him sneak out after you," Alice hissed. "You spread your white thighs for him—didn't you? You are just like your mother, Ceidre, a rutting whore!"

She knew it was better to have Alice believe she had been with Rolfe than to know she had been healing Tildie last night. For Ceidre did not want Alice to know that now she was spying, not searching for her herbs. Still, she could not let Alice think the worst if she could help it, and Alice had no right to slur her mother so. "I only went for a walk," she said, flushing. "Truly."

"He followed you!"

"Yes. He thought I was running away," she lied hastily. "He has forbidden my leaving Aelfgar. But, Alice, he did not touch me, this I swear. You have no right to call me names. I am not a whore—my mother was not a whore. She loved Father so much she sickened after he died and died herself—you know this to be true! Why do you have to persist with such foul lies?"

"Your mother was a leman, Ceidre—that makes her a whore. Of course she loved your father—he was her lord and master and she dared not. But he only loved her on her back! What did Rolfe do when he followed you?"

"He demanded of me where I was going."

"You liar! You were gone two hours—the two of you! Ceidre—you will regret this, I promise you! I will make your life unbearable if you do not stay away from him."

Ceidre knew she meant it, her passion was evident. "I hate him," she urged. "Truly I hate him, I did not lie with him!"

"Just remember," Alice said with a snarl. "All you can ever be is his whore, being nothing more than our father's bastard get. But I, I shall be his wife."

Something stabbed through her, a pain of the heart. "Alice, one last time, do not turn your back on your family. I will help you to evade this marriage and to find another."

"I am marrying the Norman," Alice spat. "And when I am his lady, you will be dealt with—have no fear. For I shall not be made a fool of like my mother."

CHAPTER 17

"My lord, more wine?" Alice asked gaily.

Rolfe, in the act of knifing a leg of mutton, nodded curtly. His bride's knee touched his. So did her arm. She was a bony thing. Did she truly think to seduce him? He was highly annoyed. She had been overly garrulous and attentive throughout supper.

Alice poured the wine, knowing the lout would not thank her, he was such a brute. Still, she could live without manners. She flashed him another charming smile, fluttering her lashes, but he did not see—for he was not looking. His gaze was on the low end of the table. On Ceidre. Alice felt like overturning the table and dumping the entire contents on her damned bastard sister.

Rolfe watched Ceidre eating, with a real appetite, but with utter feminine deportment. He was glad to see her at his table. It was a vivid reminder that she was a part of his household, and this thought was heady and provocative indeed.

She wore a simple tunic of rust wool, over another of deep blue. The two colors were perfect for her, complementing the rich bronze of her hair, the dark purple of her eyes. She nibbled a joint. She was too far away for him to see the whiteness of her teeth, but her lush lips opening upon the meat were fascinating, mesmerizing. He could not look away, did not want to look away; in truth, he wanted much, much more than to look. He was already thick with aching lust. He shifted and adjusted his hose.

"My lord," Alice said sweetly, once again trying to gain his attention.

Rolfe sighed, not regarding her, draining his wine. She, of course, ever dutiful, promptly refilled his cup. "My lord, I found *her* in your chamber today."

Rolfe was all ears. "Ceidre?"

Alice saw that she had his instant, complete attention—now that the topic was her hateful sister. "Yes."

"What do you have to say to me, Alice?"

"She was in your chamber. Searching for her amulet," Alice said, watching him closely.

Rolfe shot Ceidre a hard glance. Now what was the wench up to? He knew very well she was in possession of her herbs. She is your enemy, he reminded himself. No longer your bride, yet still your enemy. Do not ever forget it.

"Will you punish her?" Alice asked.

"I do not punish lightly," he said, reaching for a hunk of bread. The topic was ended. Alice gripped the table, hard.

Ceidre was trying to ignore Rolfe's impertinent, and so very hot, stares. But she was embarrassed—and flustered, uncomfortable. There was not a person in the hall, she was sure, who did not see the way the Norman lusted after her, so openly, with his bride seated at his elbow. Ceidre would not look at them. She had seen enough. Alice's gentle trills had sounded all night, were even now ringing. Rolfe listened courteously to whatever she kept spouting—once he had almost smiled. And Alice, Ceidre had seen her flirt many times, but tonight she went so far as to brush her small breast against his arm. Ceidre felt sick, and wished it was because of the food. She knew it was not.

She told herself it was because of the upcoming marriage—because he was cementing his position at Aelfgar at her brothers' expense. Not for any other reason.

But this logic was starting to sound, and feel, feeble, even to herself. Ceidre wished she could escape the table. Of course, she could not, not until the "lord" and lady had risen first. How she preferred the sweltering kitchens to this!

From outside a horn sounded, warning of the arrival of a stranger. Another blast sounded, indicating there was no call to arms. One of Rolfe's men, who was on guard duty, entered, followed by a royal messenger. Ceidre went stock-still.

He was obviously sent from William, for he wore the Bastard Conqueror's colors. He was coated thickly in dust, indicating a long, hard ride. He dropped to one knee before Rolfe, who impatiently waved him up and dismissed the company in the midst of their meal. Ceidre's heart fell. How could she find out what was going on if she had to leave?

She was slow to exit, letting everyone wander out of the hall ahead of her. A glance over her shoulder showed Rolfe holding a sealed missive in his hand—but making no move to open it. So he did receive written messages! Oh, could he read or not? If only she could read it to him! His glance swept the room impatiently and pinned her as she loitered. Ceidre quickly turned and left.

Ceidre stood outside restlessly, knowing there was no way for her to find out what was going on inside the manor. Rolfe could be reading the document, or he could be listening to a verbal report. Whatever the message was, it was brief, because the assembly was soon allowed to return. Rolfe was leaning back in his chair, sipping the red wine that was becoming tolerable, staring at the hearth. The messenger took a seat at

Ceidre's end of the table, across from her. Ceidre was no longer hungry, but could not let this situation pass. She smiled at him. He was blond like the Norman, but slight and of average face. He looked at her, startled.

"You look tired, sir," she said. "I would not relish having to ride so hard and so far."

" 'Tis not easy," he said, flattered at her interest. He tore off a hunk of mutton and began to eat. "But I am young and strong, and the most trusted of the king's messengers," he boasted.

" 'Tis true?" Ceidre asked, awe in her tone.

"God's truth," he said, grinning, mouth full. "What is your name, wench? I have never seen so fair a damsel, not in all of France and England combined."

"I am Ceidre. And you?"

"Paul." He drained a beaker of wine. "Mayhap you will walk with me after I sup?"

She had only a moment to make her answer known, and thinking only of her goal, she said, "Yes, how nice." She would deal with the problem of his expectations later, she decided.

Rolfe watched this interchange with growing irritation. When Ceidre first graced the boy with her smile, he was stabbed instantly with an emotion suspiciously like jealousy—something he had never in his entire life entertained. Distrust arose also—what was the little witch up to with her flirting manner? Then, as their dialogue progressed, the messenger as proud as any strutting, puffed-out cock around a hen, Ceidre coy, admiring, his irritation became vast annoyance. Did the wench think to provoke him, test him? Or was she so foolish to think to learn of the royal business at hand? Or did she truly like the mealy-mouthed boy, barely out of his swaddling?

It was as if Alice had read his thoughts. Her voice was undisguised in its pleasure, and in its spite. "You see, my lord, how she carries on with the king's man? 'Tis disgusting. Why, she is no different from her mother! No different at all!"

Her words burned, fueling his jealousy. Was she like her mother, who had been no more than the old eoarl's mistress—his whore? Did she tease and tempt others as well? His tone was harsh. "I care not, my lady, what you think. If I want your opinion I shall request it. Otherwise, keep your malice to yourself."

Alice went red.

Rolfe stood abruptly, his chair scraping the floor, and, face grim and angry, he strode from the hall. Immediately his men jumped up. Ceidre's heart was pounding in both elation and anxiety. Now she must seduce this messenger into revealing what he knew!

Everyone had adjourned except for the Norman across from her and Alice, fuming as she sat on the raised dais. The messenger was grinning, sprawled comfortably, his back against the wall. His gaze was lewd.

Ceidre felt her heart take a nosedive. How was she going to do it? A lump of despair rose in her breast. With sheer will, she leaned forward and smiled enticingly. "The nightingale sings, can you hear?"

His grin widened. "Then we must not miss the tune." He stood, waiting expectantly.

Alice's chair made a grinding noise as she rose, and then she was passing her sister with a hateful yet triumphant look. "Have you acquired a taste for Norman meat, Ceidre? Was last night only the beginning?" she hissed.

Ceidre wanted to smack her, hard, but she refrained because of her goal, and the lout waiting for her hadn't understood Alice's whisper anyway. Grimly she extended her hand. To her shock, he pulled her abruptly forward and began kissing her wetly, fondling her breasts. Reflexively Ceidre tried to twist free, but only succeeded in maneuvering her back up against the table—and he pushed her resoundingly down upon it.

"Stop!" She cried furiously, all thoughts of spying gone. He had her skirts up to her knees as he pinned her down, his mouth smacking her neck, one hand on her breast. She fought to pull down her gown, remove his hand from her chest, and heave him off at the same time. Panic started to set in as she realized he was much stronger than she and not more than a mere moment from actually raping her.

The sound of Guy's voice was the most welcome thing Ceidre had ever heard. "Hear, hear! What's this?"

The messenger ceased wrestling with her, turning with irritation, although not quite releasing her. Ceidre pushed away from him and out from under his arm as if she were leaping off hot coals. "Sir Guy!"

"Rolfe wants you, Ceidre," Guy said, his expression grim and fixed upon William's man. "Is this how you abuse Lord Rolfe's hospitality?"

Never had Ceidre thought she would welcome the Norman's summons, but she did so now. She fled up the stairs, leaving the messenger sullenly defending his actions—and blaming her for enticing him in the first place. Once in front of the Norman's door she paused to push at stray tendrils of hair and sweep a hand down her gown. She was damp from the lusty encounter, flushed, and still a bit out of breath. But before she could regain more of her composure, the door swung open and the Norman stood there, scowling.

His gaze swept her so thoroughly Ceidre's relief was forgotten and in its stead rose bristles. His tone was abrupt. "I want a potion."

Ceidre knew what she looked like and was both dismayed and furious. Did he think she'd actually been fornicating? "For what?"

He smiled unpleasantly. "It seems I have the devil's hooves pounding right here." He touched his temple.

He had a headache? He had summoned her for a headache? Suspicion came swift and hard. "I believe," she said, quite sarcastically, "more red wine will ease your suffering."

"Are you upset, Ceidre?" His tone equaled hers. "Disturbed? Have I disturbed you?"

"You are my lord and master," she said, too sweetly. "How could you disturb me?"

"That's right," he said, leaning close, his gaze riveted upon her bruised mouth. "Your lord and master." He smiled again, and Ceidre felt a frisson almost like fear. "I do not want red wine. I want a potion. Some of your witch's brew. For my head."

Witch's brew. His words stabbed, so she turned away haughtily. He was so fast she didn't take even a step, for his hand gripped her arm and he whipped her back around to face him. "And no loitering, Ceidre," he snarled. "No *dallying.*"

Her eyes went wide with understanding and surprise. He was telling her in no uncertain words that she was not to rendezvous with the messenger! Something hot rushed along her veins, something like elation. She found herself smiling. "I will not *dally,* my lord."

His ill humor increased. "Good! Go, then!"

Ceidre left to fetch his potion and was not at the top of the stairs when she heard his door slamming like thunder. She began to hum.

CHAPTER 18

"He has ordered the village destroyed!"

Ceidre stared at her cousin Teddy. "Surely you jest!"

"No, 'tis true, the entire village, Ceidre, 'twill be burned!"

Two days earlier Ceidre had given Rolfe the potion he'd requested and then been promptly dismissed. Rolfe had taken a score of men and disappeared the morning after and had not returned until late last night. There was no way that Ceidre could find out where he had gone, nor for what purpose. She had once again been free to do as she pleased. She decided to stay out of Alice's way, and had spent time with her grandmother, gathering herbs, crushing them, blending them carefully into potions for numbing pain, for curing sores, for inducing sleep, for fertility and impotence. It was early morning.

Teddy, clad in a tunic and wool hose, clung to her wrist. "Can you not curse him?" he begged. "I know you are a good witch, Ceidre, but can you not, this once, strike him dead? He is destroying all our homes!"

The Norman had not one human bone in his entire body, Ceidre thought furiously. She strode past the manor, staring at the keep, three stories high, square and ugly, its only windows tiny slits, gracing the barren hill above the village. A huge, deep ditch had been dug around its entire perimeter, excluding the orchard and the hayfield and the corn. Then she saw a cottage go up in flames.

She lifted her skirt and began to run. It was a terrible moment: déjà-vu. The Norman sat his big, ugly stallion, watching, surrounded by three of his men. At the sound of her hard, fast footsteps, he shifted his horse and regarded her.

"You must stop at once!"

A hint of a smile appeared on his stern features. Ceidre was panting, bosom heaving. His gaze roamed from her face to her breasts. It was distinctly greedy, like a wolf in winter. "Did you hear me?" Ceidre cried.

"Do not interfere," he said, turning away from her. Another cottage went up in flames. The sound of women weeping drifted to them.

"You have no soul," Ceidre hissed. "And no heart. How sorry I am for you!" Tears stung her eyes. His men were efficiently setting the huts on fire, and now half the village was burning.

He turned a dark look upon her. "The village must be moved."

"Why? 'Tis their homes. Their lives. Their livelihood!"

"Everything will be rebuilt, Ceidre," he said, warning in his tone. "Do not interfere in what you do not understand."

She ignored the threat. "You get perverse pleasure, do you not, using your power so? Frightening the ignorant with fear of a Norman death?"

"Ceidre, cease."

"You terrorize the helpless—women, children, serfs. Yes, that takes a lot of courage. I am surprised they do not call you Rolfe the Brave for all the courage you show!"

He was red-faced. Mounted next to him, Guy Le Chante was incredulous, and also crimson. The other two men pretended not to have heard. Ceidre did not care, she was frantic and furious, beyond fear. "Yes, from now on, that is your name—Rolfe the Brave!"

It happened so fast, she could not react. The words were not out of her mouth before he had jerked her roughly up onto his mount, slamming her facedown across his thighs. And the stallion was in a hard gallop, almost simultaneously. Ceidre could not have moved if she wanted to—which she did not. The breath had been knocked out of her, and she could see two things —his foot in the heavy stirrup and the ground, speeding beneath them. She was in terror of being dropped beneath the great destrier's thick, shod hooves.

And in terror of what he was going to do.

Oh, why, why could she not keep her unruly mouth shut?

The beast stopped. She was pulled down even as he dismounted, in a most undignified way, like a sack, hanging over his arm from her waist. She began to writhe. For one scant second. Her pelvis was jammed hard onto one braced thigh, the movement nearly shoving her nose in the dirt. Then, at the feel of her skirts being tossed over her head, realization took hold, and she screamed, trying to wrench free.

"You have tried me again and again," he said through gritted teeth as he bared lush white buttocks. He was so determined, the sight did not deter him. "A child deserves a child's chastisement."

"If you hit me!" Ceidre shouted, furious, disbelieving that he would dare to spank her.

"You will what?" he taunted, and he smacked her hard across her buttocks.

It hurt. It also stunned her into immobility—but not for long. "How dare you!" She was enraged.

He held her easily although she struggled to get free with all of her strength. "I dare anything I please." He hit her again, harder.

"How *brave* you are!" She gasped, writhing across his lap.

A third slap followed. "No one, not man or woman, talks to me the way you do," he said harshly, staring at her white flesh. She was impossibly shapely. Her legs were long and curved, her buttocks high, round, and lush.

"I will never forgive you." Ceidre choked, more humiliated than hurt.

"I need not your forgiveness, but you need sense," he said hoarsely, unable to tear his eyes away from her derriere. His hand settled of its own accord upon one firm buttock.

Ceidre jerked as if burned. His hand closed upon her, squeezing. Her breath caught in her throat and she could not breathe. Nor could she move.

"You try my vows," he said harshly, sliding his hand down to the back of her thigh. His fingers splayed, slipping intimately between her legs, a hair's breadth from the moist heat of her womanhood.

Wildfire, hot, electric, raced through her. His hand moved, so slightly, but it was enough to press against the soft curls guarding her femininity. And against her hip, his maleness thrust boldly, hotly. "Do not," Ceidre managed hoarsely. "Please."

He suddenly pushed her to her knees, his hands holding her hips, hard. "I care not for my vows," he said, gasping, his tone strangled. He groaned, long and low and so very male. "God, Ceidre, I cannot . . ." His groin pressed against her buttocks, hot and full, and she felt his mouth on the side of her neck. In another moment her virginity would be lost. There was despair—and there was elation.

And then he released her.

With a cry, Ceidre scrambled away on hands and knees, then turned, crouching, her back against a thick, ancient oak. She was panting, her gaze riveted upon him. Her heart thundered in her ears.

He was on his knees, staring at the ground, sweat standing out upon his face, his arms and back corded beneath his tunic. She both sensed and saw the battle he was waging, his mind against his lust. Passion and arousal darkened his features, strained them. His body looked as if it might snap. Ceidre whimpered, in abject fear—or in abject need? He lifted his head and impaled her with his hot blue eyes.

She shrank back.

"I will not hurt you," he said harshly.

"I hate you!"

He got slowly to his feet. "I will not hurt you."

Tears rose, hot and bitter. "You will not?" She laughed, with a little hysteria. "You beat me and try to rape me and tell me you *will* not hurt me?"

His jaw hardened. "I did not beat you, I did not rape you. *You provoke me, Ceidre.*"

"Blame me! Blame me when it are you who are at fault!"

His blue eyes blackened.

Ceidre choked on a sob and cursed herself for her vicious tongue. She slowly got to her feet, her back pressed hard into the bark of the tree. He watched her. She watched him.

"If you were not Alice's sister," he said, piercing her, "were you any common wench, I would take you as I willed. You would be my mistress until I could exorcise you from my soul and from my blood. I am only a man, Ceidre, and you try me beyond belief."

" 'Tis not my fault!"

"Oh, 'tis your fault," he said, silkily now. "Your

beauty defies earthly description. And you, you defy me at every turn, arousing my most extreme humors. Do you not think my manhood does not arouse itself as well, in the tempest you create?"

"Should I watch you burn the homes of my kin and say nothing?"

Remembrance brought darkness to his blue eyes. "And in front of my men! I warn you again, Ceidre—do not provoke me. If you do, you will find yourself flat on your back!"

"You would rape your bride's sister!"

"When you are spread beneath me, do you think I know who you are? You are only Ceidre, a beautiful bronze-haired, purple-eyed witch."

She knew he did not mean the word, yet she flushed. Or was her coloring due to something else, perhaps his graphic imagery? Feeling a potent desperation, she clung to the topic of import. "What will happen to the villagers?"

"We are rebuilding," he said. "The village is being moved, Ceidre, and 'tis not a fancy whim. I am a commander, and I have seen more wars than you can imagine. The village will be better defended beneath the walls of the bailey. This suits everyone, not just myself. 'Twould even suit your brother, were he here."

Had she been wrong? Impetuous?

"Come, Ceidre," he said, his tone strangely grim. "I will take you back."

"Do not ask me to come with you," she hissed. "I will walk."

Now his face was expressionless, his blue gaze shuttered. "Come. I will not leave you here."

"Why not?" she cried.

"Because I will not," he said, hard.

They stared at each other.

And she knew she could not win. She felt the sudden

wave of tears rising, and defeat was bitter. She stumbled forward. He had held out his hand to assist her in mounting, and now bewilderment and a strange softness crossed his expression. He dropped his hand. She met his gaze, and before he could guard it, she saw the confusion and what looked like pity—or compassion. But surely she was hallucinating!

"If you wish to walk you may," he said abruptly.

Immediately she stopped in her tracks and folded her arms tightly. His face closed, tightened. He nodded, turned the gray, and trotted away. Ceidre watched him go. She stared after him, for a very long time.

CHAPTER 19

The message was relayed to her before the noonday meal, by Teddy. Ceidre wanted to leap with joy. Morcar had come home, and he was waiting for her in the woods not far from the orchard.

He was just in time—for the Norman was to wed Alice on the morrow.

She had to appear at dinner, for not to do so might arouse the Norman's suspicions. Also, he might think that she was sulking—or hiding. In fact, she was angry over his treatment of her, although equally relieved he had not taken her as he almost had. She would have to tread carefully around him in the future. She had not realized when she aroused his ire she also aroused his desire; she would be certain to do neither from now on.

The meal was interminable, but Ceidre did not fidget. She refused to look at Rolfe, seated with his bride, although she knew he watched her often. When he and his men returned to the field, Ceidre escaped to the orchards, basket in hand, careful not to be followed. The Norman, she saw, was so involved in his task that he did not even remark her going.

Morcar's tall frame became visible in the glade by the stream as she approached, crying out with joy. He beamed, blue eyes sparkling, and swept her into his hard, familiar embrace.

"Are you all right?" she asked, holding his face in her hands, when he had released her.

"Me?" He laughed, removing her hands and clasping them. His smile faded. "Ceidre—how have you fared?"

"I am fine."

"You have not been harmed by these pigs?"

She felt color creeping into her face. "No."

His grip tightened, his handsome features darkening. "What happened? Have you been touched?"

She was flaming, and she knew Morcar's quick, hot temper. "It's all right," she cried. "Truly it is! 'Twas before he knew who I was—but he found out in time and did not harm me."

"Who?"

"The Norman."

"Rolfe de Warenne? The Relentless?" At her nod he scowled. "Explain, quickly."

"There is nothing to explain. I was at Kesop, to heal a sow. He thought me a peasant. His men had just slain a band of Saxons, and he chased me down on his horse. But his men called out my identity before he could—before he could do as he would. In truth—" Suddenly she smiled. "He thought me Alice, and thus I was saved from his embrace."

Morcar swore, foully. "I wish I had been there," he cried, blue eyes flashing as he paced. "I would have killed him for the mere impudence of his desire!"

" 'Tis finished now, Morcar," she lied. "How is Ed?"

"Near healed. We will not let this pass, Ceidre," he said, hard. "We nurture our wounds now, and when we are strong, we will chase the Normans to the sea and beyond."

"There was a royal messenger here four days past. I could not find out what was said. The next day, at dawn, the Norman and a score of men rode out. They returned two days later. I know not where they went."

"William the Bastard had a scrape in the north with the Scots." Morcar shrugged. "We know he sent for Rolfe to turn them back. He is highly trusted and very able." He scowled then fiercely. "Too able!"

Ceidre touched his sleeve. "You did not come alone?"

"I left two men beyond yon ridge, Ceidre. I have no wish to encounter the Norman now. What is this news of Alice wedding with him?"

"Tomorrow, Morcar, 'twill be done."

"Alice is willing?"

"Yes." At his frown, Ceidre found herself defending her sister. "Try to understand, Morcar. She is afraid to grow old, a spinster. And he is very handsome." She realized what she had said, and her eyes widened. She pictured his Adonis-like visage, his powerful body, and knew she had not lied.

"I wish there were a way to prevent this marriage. If only Alice would refuse, become sick upon her wedding day!"

"You would have to abduct her to stop her from marrying him," Ceidre said.

"I would," Morcar said with a growl, "if I had the men and thought I could do so without risking a single life. But I know 'twould be suicide."

"Do not," Ceidre said. "Mayhap her shrewish ways will keep him soft in her bed, and they will not be married in truth under God's eyes." Ceidre frowned, for it was most unlikely such a man would rest soft near any woman!

"Ceidre, you may have an idea," Morcar exclaimed. "Could you not give him a potion to make him deathly ill?"

"You want me to kill him?" She gasped, appalled.

"Of course not," he said. "I am no murderer—nor are you. I mean," he said impatiently, "a potion to make him sick so that the wedding is postponed."

"Morcar—do you intend for me to keep him sick from now until the day you and Edwin are victorious?"

"Damn," he said. "That would probably kill him, would it not?"

"Most certainly, and 'tis not right, not godly. I cannot. I have never harmed anyone."

He cupped her face tenderly, his tone urgent. "Ceidre, a potion then to make him impotent? If the marriage is not consummated when we retake Aelfgar it can be annulled, and he has less legitimacy as lord here, now and when 'tis done. A simple potion, Ceidre?"

"Oh, Morcar," she said reluctantly, yet . . . What harm could it do? The man had more potency than a stud stallion, surely it could not harm him? Just something simple, to take away his desire. . . . To take away his desire for Alice.

Morcar saw her capitulation, and he laughed, sweeping her into his arms. "I love you, Ceidre," he said. "You have more loyalty in your little finger than Alice has in her entire heart."

Still unsure, yet strangely elated too, at the thought of keeping the Norman away from her sister, Ceidre hugged Morcar fiercely back, burying her face in his chest.

Rolfe had eyed Ceidre as she carried the basket, heading toward the orchards, every so often glancing over her shoulder. She was up to something, but what? Although immersed in the final stages of the destruction of the village, he kept one eye on her—and watched her disappear into the forest. He had a suspicious feeling, and he did not like her wandering alone.

She was too enticing a wench for any passing stranger or brigand. Rolfe spurred his destrier after her.

From a distance, he watched her rendezvous with a tall, dark man. It was a reunion, this he could see, and see well. He was stunned as she leapt into her lover's arms, stunned, and furious. But the embrace was short, fortunately, for Rolfe would have killed the man then and there. Instead they spoke quickly, seriously, urgently. His anger seeped and seethed and he edged his mount as close as he dared without their hearing him—but neither could he hear them, as he desperately wanted to. And then the man laughed and swept her up into his embrace again, and this time Ceidre clung, burying her face in the folds of his mantle. The man rocked her.

Rolfe drew his sword and, with a war cry, galloped into the glade.

Ceidre screamed as Morcar threw her aside, drawing his sword to meet his attacker. He was of fast reflex, but could barely get his sword up before Rolfe swung his own weapon, blade crashing against blade. Yet Morcar did not release his sword. He was knocked by the force of Rolfe's charge to the ground, but nimble as a cat, he jumped to his feet and was poised to fight.

Rolfe reined in and leapt to the ground, weapon held high. His eyes went wide. "Morcar!"

Morcar smiled grimly. "I shall enjoy this, Norman," he said. "I have dreamed of this day!"

"Stop!" Ceidre screamed, frantic, knowing that two such powerful men could not both survive this encounter—one would die. "Stop, please, God, stop!"

"Come to me, Saxon," Rolfe said softly.

Morcar thrust; Rolfe parried. The two men's blades clashed again and again, echoing in the forest, as they lunged and feinted, thrust and withdrew. Rolfe's tip sliced open the sleeve of Morcar's tunic, and his forearm, trailing blood. Morcar opened a gash above Rolfe's right eye. Again and again they danced around each other, their blades ringing. Rolfe scored again, upon Morcar's thigh. Morcar responded with a vicious thrust that forced Rolfe backward, until the Norman feinted, pretended to fall, and then reversed the process, relentlessly driving his foe backward.

The minutes stretched away. The glade was silent except for the sound of their harsh, heavy breathing. Sweat drenched both men, causing their tunics to stick damply to their frames. Blood trickled into Rolfe's eye, but he did not wipe at it. Their movements became slower, like a dream, heavy with the sustained effort. Morcar swung his blade, Rolfe's turned it back. At least fifteen very long minutes had passed, and it was apparent that the two men were evenly matched.

Ceidre watched, mesmerized, terrified. She could not go for help—'twould be the end of Morcar. Her brother had to win—so he could escape. And then the Norman's strength proved superior.

Morcar tripped on a root. As he lost his balance, the Norman lunged for his heart. Ceidre screamed, loudly, shrilly. Morcar, one knee on the ground, froze, as Rolfe's blade pressed against his breast. But the Norman did not break his flesh.

"Why do you hesitate, Norman?" Morcar gasped. He was still holding his sword, but at an angle impossible to lift to defend himself. "I am not afraid of death."

"Drop your blade, Saxon," Rolfe said, panting. "Drop it now, or you will be at her pearly gates."

"No, don't," Ceidre cried, running to him. "Please, my lord, do not run him through."

Rolfe ignored her. "Drop it now, if you wish to live. If not, I will send you on your way."

Morcar stared boldly back at Rolfe, fearless and unflinching.

"Please drop it," Ceidre cried. "Please, Morcar, please!"

Morcar dropped the sword.

Rolfe, without removing his own blade from his enemy's heart, kicked it away. Then, exerting pressure, he forced Morcar onto both knees. "In the name of King William," he said, "you are my prisoner."

Ceidre was standing almost directly behind Rolfe. She did not think. She picked up the heaviest stone she could find and raised it, to send it crashing down upon his head.

Rolfe whirled and grabbed her wrist, almost breaking it. The stone tumbled from her grasp, and he sent her sprawling to the earth. Morcar was on his feet, but before he could pick up his sword, Rolfe's blade jabbed his abdomen. The two men stared. And at that precise moment, Guy and five knights came charging into the woods, alerted by Ceidre's screams.

Rolfe smiled coldly, his eyes never leaving Morcar's. "Place him in the dungeons, Guy," he said. And without looking at Ceidre, he added, "I will deal with you later."

CHAPTER 20

Ceidre was escorted by Guy back to the manor and into the hall. He did not leave her side. Alice, amusing herself with her two lapdogs, looked up, startled. Guy turned to Ceidre. "Await him here."

Ceidre looked away, desperation cloying. Morcar was at this very moment being thrown into the dungeons below the manor—and he was hurt. He must be cared for, and he must, somehow, escape.

Alice, her hand in one terrier's long white fur, said shrilly, "What passes? Why does my lord wish you to await him here?"

"Morcar has returned, Alice," Ceidre said. "And the Norman has taken him prisoner."

Alice gasped. "And Edwin?"

Ceidre shot Guy a dark look. "At this very moment, Edwin rides with a hundred men to chase the Norman into the sea!"

Rolfe's spurs clinked as he entered and strode to her. His face was rigid, his eyes blazed. "Tell me more, mistress," he said softly.

Ceidre whirled, taken by surprise. "You heard well enough!"

"Is it true?" Alice cried, standing, hands clasped tightly.

Ceidre turned to her. "You sicken me! You are

afraid our brothers' return will ruin your wedding! Have you no thought for anyone other than yourself?"

"Whom shall I think of, Ceidre? You? You who play the whore with my groom? You think I do not know? You wish to stop this marriage for yourself! Not for Edwin's sake!"

"Enough," Rolfe said with a growl. "Lady Alice, leave us. And you, Guy."

Alice went pink with anger, then, snapping her fingers at her dogs, she stalked away. Guy exited more gracefully. Ceidre, her heart picking up a quick, frantic beat, wondered what the Norman would do now.

His look was ice. "My scouts have seen nothing of a hundred Saxons, Ceidre. The truth!"

Ceidre swallowed a lump of fear. "They are in hiding, I know not where."

He said nothing, just stared. Ceidre's hands were shaking. She tried to hide them in the skirt of her gown.

"You should be afraid," Rolfe said grimly. "Very, very afraid."

She should beg his mercy, even if it meant getting down upon her knees. But she would not—she could not. So she watched him, her eyes huge and purple and frightened.

"I fear greatly," Rolfe finally said, "that your presence here shall always be that of a serpent in the garden."

She did not respond, she could not respond.

"You understood," Rolfe said heavily, "as well as the next, the punishment for treason."

Her heart leapt up to choke her. He would have her whipped? Or hanged? She wet her lips. Somehow she managed to speak, her voice trembling. "Yes."

Rolf turned away to pace. He was like a caged lion, barely contained. The silence and the anticipation stretched endlessly, torturing her. He finally turned, piercing her with his gaze. " 'Tis not treason to stumble upon one's brother by chance in the woods."

Relief, vast, vast relief, swept her.

"Ceidre."

"Yes, my lord?"

"You have surely bewitched me, but I warn you, do not test my clemency again. If you commit treason, you will suffer the same as anyone. Do you understand?"

She could hear her own heartbeat. She swallowed. She said the word yes, but it was so low as to be inaudible.

"Do you understand?" he repeated harshly. A vein throbbed in his temple.

"Yes," she whispered.

"Then get you from my sight, before I come to my senses."

Ceidre clutched her hands to her bosom. "My lord?"

His eyes were blue fury. "Ceidre . . ."

"Please—may I attend my brother?"

"*No!* Now get!"

Ceidre turned, took a step, then with a breath ran from the hall. Once outside in the fresh air, she leaned against a trough, shaking. She had come so very close to a severe punishment, but had somehow—and she thanked God, St. Edward in shrine at Westminster, and St. Cuthbert—evaded it. Yet there was still the awful reality to face: Morcar was the Norman's prisoner.

And it was up to her to do something about it.

Immediately Ceidre began to plan Morcar's escape. She would slip a potion into the guard's food. When he was asleep, she herself would unlock the dungeon and free Morcar. She would have a horse ready and waiting. And then it would be up to him.

And she would not think of the Norman's threat.

But when she left the manor to gather more of the herb, she was startled to find Guy at her side. He glanced at her sideways, but stopped as she had. "Sir," Ceidre said, spirits sinking, "why do you play the shadow?"

"Lord Rolfe has commanded I be your escort," Guy said.

Ceidre turned her face away before he could see her consternation. Then she continued on. She would gather what she needed, and worry later about how to shake Guy this night to free her brother. Yet that evening, to her utter dismay, Guy pulled a pallet next to hers and stretched out beside her. Ceidre could not believe that she was to be guarded so, day and night. Amulet around her neck, she got up. Guy followed.

"Nature calls," she hissed furiously.

"I am sorry, mistress," he said, "but where you go I go as well."

She would test him. She stomped outside, he was on her heels. He would not leave her to seek any privacy other than to turn politely away. Ceidre stormed back into the manor, and careless of the hour—past midnight—she stomped up the stairs and crashed her fist down hard on the Norman's door.

It opened immediately. The Norman stood there, stark naked, keen alertness fading and being replaced with a flicker of amusement. Ceidre blushed and looked at his shoulder. Behind her, Guy coughed.

Rolfe grinned, unable to prevent himself, and then he chuckled. " 'Tis my lucky night," he said. "The lady of my dreams seeks me out—just when I need her most."

'Twas not funny, not at all. Ceidre lifted her gaze to

his, red-faced. "Have you no shame? Or are you flaunting now for me?"

Rolfe threw back his head and laughed. "I gladly flaunt myself for you, Ceidre—any time, any place."

His tone was so seductive, her heart tripped.

Rolfe grinned at Guy. "Await her downstairs."

"No, stay!" Ceidre cried. Of course, Guy didn't hesitate, he was already trotting away. Ceidre, looking from Guy to Rolfe, managed to glimpse a goodly portion of naked flesh—and to her dismay, she noted he was becoming aroused. "Can you not clothe yourself?"

"But you seek me out," he teased.

"Not for the reason you think," she managed, staring at his shoulder again.

He gave her a last look, then turned and went to retrieve his hose. Ceidre could not help it, she studied his back, taut and ridged with muscle, and his backside, high and hard. She realized she had almost forgotten why she had sought him out in his chamber.

Rolfe turned to her, shrugging on a thin undertunic. He gestured to the hearth. Ceidre stepped inside the room, but hovered near the door, for safety. Now that her senses had returned, she realized he was in rare good humor, and seeing the near-empty bag of wine, she wondered if this was the cause. He noted her gaze and grinned.

"Some wine, Ceidre?"

"I detest your Norman grapes," she said haughtily.

He grinned. "Do you? Truly?"

"Yes."

"But the Norman fruit bears seed more potent—did you not know?"

"Do not play with my words, you know what I mean."

His blue eyes sparkled. "I think that there is Norman fruit you like very well."

She went scarlet. "You are drunk!"

"I have good cause to celebrate."

"Oh, yes," she said bitterly. "You may now deliver my brother's head to your bastard king!"

His easy humor vanished. " 'Tis correct."

"I demand you free Guy of his guarding me."

"You demand, Ceidre?" His brow lifted. He was amused, indeed in a rare spirit.

"I request," she amended, flushing.

He leaned against the hearth indolently, yet his aura was unmistakably sensual. He crooked a finger. "You may demand whatever you like."

She blinked.

"Come here and demand of me, Ceidre, that which you want. I am most amenable tonight." He smiled again.

It was like the brightest of suns, when he smiled, perhaps because true mirth, from him, was so rare. Ceidre realized her heart was fluttering madly and that her limbs were taut. "You are not serious."

"Oh," he said softly, "I am most serious. Do you not know you can get anything you wish of me?"

She stared.

"Especially"—his nostrils flared as his gaze shifted —"when you are clad in such a thin gown, your eyes so dark with righteous anger, your mouth so full and slightly parted, mayhap for me . . ."

Ceidre trembled.

"Take down your hair," he said softly.

"What?"

"I have never seen it loose. I wish to see it now." His tone was still easy. "Please me, Ceidre."

"I did not come here to please you," Ceidre managed. "I came to insist—to request—that your man leave me be. I cannot even seek a private spot for my body's needs without him there, on my heels. 'Tis most unjust."

He smiled his beautiful smile, his gaze wandering over her again, slowly, with languid enjoyment. "I do not trust you," he said mildly.

She flushed.

"Take down your hair," he coaxed, his tone distinctly sensual. "Please."

Startled, she realized that he had asked her, not ordered her, to free her hair. The word please rolled like honey from his tongue, yet she was sure he had rarely used it. Of course, she would not do as he asked.

He smiled, and before she knew it he was in front of her, his hands gentle in her hair, pulling the binding off. Ceidre could not move, she could not even breathe, as with his fingers he loosened the strands until a cloud of bronze tresses whirled around her shoulders and breasts, down her back, and past her hips.

She could not look away from his gaze, now turning even brighter than the brightest sun.

He stared at her and a small sound, much like a groan, escaped him. She knew she must retreat, now, while she could. Her back found the door; he approached. His hands again delved into her tresses, his expression strained and awed. "I am beyond all hope," he murmured, low, so low Ceidre wasn't sure she had heard him at all correctly.

His hands, wrapped up in strands of thick hair, cupped the back of her head. "You make me weak, Ceidre."

In truth, Ceidre thought, he made her weak too. His hands were so warm, so large. She wondered if he would kiss her. Her gaze found his lips, closer now. She wanted him to kiss her. And with the perversity of chance, she thought of two people at once, Alice in the solar across the hall, and Morcar, in the dank dungeons below. She twisted away.

"Leave me be, please!"

"One kiss," he breathed. "Just one, Ceidre. Just one."

He was the strongest man she had ever met, and he used his strength now, to pull her close. In truth, she did not want to resist, it was only a token. He ignored the feebleness of her struggles and claimed her lips with a harsh, guttural cry. In his drunken state, he was fierce and greedy, like a newborn babe, his mouth hot, insistent, frantic. She was open and pliant beneath him. Her bracing away became a kind of soft clinging.

His lips found her throat, and she arched for him. He nibbled and teased with his tongue, making soft sounds of unfettered pleasure. His mouth found her ear. "I want you, Ceidre," he whispered urgently. "Tonight, now, 'tis like a dream." His arms tightened around her and he pressed her against the wall. His body shifted until he had pressed his huge maleness into her warm recesses. "Say yes, welcome me gladly," he urged, kissing her neck. "Tonight is our night, Ceidre, sweetheart. Tonight belongs to us." He lifted her into his arms.

She was spinning away with pleasure, hot and potent, as he carried her to the bed. Never had he asked, nor cajoled like this, even begged. It had always been to threaten and to take, as if they were in the midst of battle. Now he was a gentle lover, and she was succumbing to his seduction. She knew it; she wanted it.

And, ever a warrior with a killer's unerring instinct, he knew it too. He laid her upon the soft mattress. "Please," he said throatily, nuzzling her breasts, his body covering hers.

But again, perversity raised her ugly head. Morcar's

image flashed. He was a prisoner, and he would surely hang, because of this Norman. Sanity returned and, with it, her own will. As weak as it was, it was also desperate. She pushed up at him, protesting. "No! No, never! I hate you for how you use me, Norman! My brother rots below, my sister sleeps next door. Tomorrow you will wed and bed her; in how many days will Morcar hang? And you expect me to pleasure you of my own free will?"

He had not released her, but he had stopped his assault, his breathing harsh, and he heard every word. "You come here to tempt me, then you turn me away." He was angry. " 'Tis a very dangerous game, Ceidre. I am a scant instant from impaling you." He rocked his thick erection against her.

She went very still, all pleasure gone, fear in its place. "Alice can probably hear every word."

"She is asleep."

"I doubt it. I will scream. Your bride will not be happy to see her groom raping her sister."

"A moment ago it would not have been rape."

She was bitter because the truth was foul. "I lost my head, 'twill not occur again." She meant it. "Let me up!"

"You test my very soul," he cried, with real despair, drunken or no. He pressed his face into her neck, his body hard against hers, throbbing with its own male need. " 'Tis torture," he growled. "True torture."

She rested very still, so as not to provoke him further. Now that she was sane again, she was sure her sister had been a spy to the entire interlude, for the door was open and Alice's chamber was but a few paces away. She felt dismay. This coil was beyond her. If only she could remain strong and use the Norman's lust against him! But she wasn't strong; in matters of the flesh, she was realizing, she was very weak indeed.

His body was rigid on hers, and she was still imprisoned in his arms. She felt him relaxing, felt his embrace loosening. Ceidre attempted to roll free; instantly his grip tightened—he would not let her go. She gritted her teeth in despair, but lay motionless, afraid to move. She waited for his next assault.

It did not come. He nuzzled her cheek and held her fiercely. He sighed; his breathing grew deep and even. Ceidre was astonished. Could he be asleep? How much had he imbibed? True, males seemed to have a propensity for being able to sleep no matter what the circumstance, and he had consumed a bag of wine. She should have known, she realized grimly. That he would not jest and tease unless he was in his cups, 'twas not his personality. Yet she felt a twinge of something wistful, for he had been almost likable. Then she resolutely turned such traitorous thoughts away. The Norman was detestable, and she would not forget it.

Her predicament suddenly struck her.

Ceidre realized he was sound asleep, Guy was downstairs, and she was free to do as she pleased. Her heart tightened. She would shut the door. Guy would assume her to be with Rolfe, and let him think what he would. She would use a rope or clothing to let herself out the window. She would drug the guards, get a steed, and Morcar would be freed. . . .

Ceidre moved carefully, gingerly extricating herself from the sleeping Norman. Once afoot, she went swiftly toward the door, to close it. If Alice was awake, and Alice had heard them, let her think the worst. Morcar's freedom was more important.

CHAPTER 21

In the solar, Alice paced, furious.

He would cuckold her even as she slept next door—with her own sister! Alice wanted to scream, she wanted to shriek. She would dearly love to kill Ceidre, if only she could. She was being made a fool, for all the world to see, and she could not stand it.

She strode resolutely into the hallway, then paused, losing courage. She desperately wanted to wed Rolfe tomorrow. Dare she put her foot down? Dare she demand he cease his dallying? What if he grew so annoyed he decided to call off the wedding? Oh, if only she had more power!

He wants you because of Aelfgar, she reminded herself. You do have power, 'tis merely untried. If you do not test it, you will never know its true extent.

Determined now, Alice eyed the closed door. There was no sound coming from within, not even grunts and groans. Another thought struck her—what if her sister had killed her groom?

She would not put it beyond Ceidre, who was truly loyal to Edwin and Morcar. Spurred on, Alice pushed open Rolfe's door. To her shock, a snore greeted her.

Ceidre gasped, jumping back from an open trunk.

"What are you doing?" Alice demanded, looking again at at Rolfe, fully clothed in undertunic and hose, sprawled on the bed. They had not been fornicating like animals. She was almost disappointed. A thought struck her. "Have you poisoned him?"

"No, of course not," Ceidre said, calmly closing the trunk. "He is drunk and fell asleep. I merely sought another covering for him."

"You whoring liar! I want you out of here—this instant! I know why you came." Alice was so angry, tears appeared in her eyes. "To seduce him—to seduce him until he freed Morcar!"

" 'Tis not true," Ceidre said quietly. "I came to demand he release Guy from his dotage upon me. Alice—" Her voice lowered. "We must help Morcar."

"You are a fool," Alice cried, and then she raced to the door. "Guy," she shouted. "Guy, come quickly, this witch has poisoned our lord!"

Ceidre froze, stunned.

Guy appeared instantly, looking murderous. On his heels were Beltain, two others, and Athelstan. They pounded to the bed.

"I did not," Ceidre cried out. "He is drunk!"

Guy took Rolfe's shoulders and shook him.

"She poisoned him with her witch's weeds," Alice said. "Guy, I command you, put her in the dungeons with her brother, 'tis treason what she did."

Guy shook Rolfe harder, who groaned and, with great difficulty, sat up, blinking. "What happens here?" he muttered thickly.

"My lord, are you all right?" Guy asked worriedly. "Have you been poisoned?"

Rolfe focused, then he grinned and laughed. "Nay, not poisoned," he murmured, falling back upon the pillows. "Bewitched, Guy, bewitched. . . . Leave me now."

"I think he is in his cups," Guy said, confused. "I have never seen him thus before."

"He drank two good pints of wine with supper,"

Athelstan said. "And I saw the maid bring him another bag after—and then another. Let him sleep it away."

Alice flushed under Athelstan's regard. "I only sought to protect my lord," she said. "What should I have thought, to see him so, with her in his room, rummaging through his chests."

Guy stared at Ceidre. "What did you search for, mistress?"

"A covering." She shrugged. "Look, he lies atop the blankets, and 'tis chill at night so close to the sea."

"I will see to him," Alice announced. "Get out," she said to Ceidre. "And stay out!"

Ceidre, recovered, could only think one thought: All her plans were ruined.

For this night.

The sunlight awoke him, blinding him.

Rolfe groaned. As sleep rapidly fled, he became aware of a splitting headache, one that felt as if a rock were being repeatedly crashed against the back of his skull. Instead of capitulating to the urge to stay abed, he forced himself to sit up.

Last night he had gotten very drunk.

And today, today was his wedding day.

He groaned again, long and loud, and cradled his head in his hands. He could remember everything—or almost everything.

Yesterday at dinner he had begun to imbibe in a grim self-congratulation for Morcar's capture. The wine had touched him strongly after his long, exhausting duel. He could not understand why his mood was so somber, so dark, when he should be rejoicing. He recalled William's promise, that should he bring him Edwin and Morcar he would be awarded Durham too.

Had the king meant it?

Morcar was a worthy foe, he had brooded, draining

another cup of wine. Rolfe had had instant respect for both brothers when he had met them shortly after Hastings. Their reputations as strong leaders preceded them. Rolfe could judge a man for himself, and well, he thought. The moment he had seen them both he had known they were strong, smart, dedicated, and brave. He had also not trusted them.

Morcar was a worthy opponent with a sword as well. His thoughts became darker—he could still hear Ceidre's screams when he had pressed his blade against the Saxon's heart. Now, despite the wine and the hubbub of those eating boisterously at his table, he had a terrible image of her, eyes wide, frantic—desperate. She dearly loved her brother.

She had played at treason.

She unmans me, he thought grimly. He was no fool. She had been summoned to meet her brother, a traitor, and she had gone, defying him, knowing full well the penalty for her act. Yet he had not punished her. He had protected her instead. And by protecting her, by not punishing her, by withholding the fact of her treason from his king, he became culpable too. His standards were high, and strict. Yet for the first time in his life he had violated his own code of ethics. If he was not careful, he would become so unmanned Aelfgar would come careening down about his ears—or worse, he would fail his king.

Because of a woman.

'Twould not happen again. He would keep Ceidre firmly at heel, even if he had to keep her on a leash like a mutt. But she would not defy him and commit treason again, and he would not have to punish her for another betrayal. For, if she undertook another act of treason, he would not let her escape the consequences —he could not.

His thoughts could not get grimmer. Alice had

been, again, overly attentive. She kept his cup filled. Her hand brushed his. She laughed long and false in his ear. She pressed her breast against his arm. He was indifferent—worse, annoyed. Ceidre, of course, would not look at him from her place at the low end of the table. He hoped she realized she was more than lucky to escape so lightly. Damn the ancient gods! He had lost his manhood. That witch had him protecting her when she was trying to destroy him and all he cherished.

His bride whispered something soft and sweet, but Rolfe did not listen. He stared at the bronze-haired woman seated below him and could not help comparing her to his bride. By God, it should be Ceidre he was wedding, not this spiteful little wench!

There was nothing that could be done, yet he could not shove his deepest wishes from his mind.

And then, hours later, just when he had decided to attempt sleep, just when he had stripped to his bare skin, she had appeared at his door, an echo of his basest thoughts. And suddenly the night was no longer grim. Darkness became light. She had answered his silent prayers, she had come to ease his mind, and, he hoped drunkenly, his tortured body.

But here, unfortunately, Rolfe's memory of the day before began to grow hazy.

They had kissed. He had kissed her and she had flared like a hot flame. But then what? He could not remember another thing, his last thought being in Ceidre's arms. He had not bedded the wench—had he? No, surely he would remember such a fortuitous occasion!

There was a knock upon his chamber door. Rolfe was jerked completely back to the present. He grunted a response, and Athelstan appeared, looking quite lighthearted. Rolfe scowled at the aroma of porridge wafting toward him. "Take that out of here," he demanded. "At once!"

"Good morning, my lord," Athelstan said cheerfully. " 'Tis a beautiful day, is it not?"

Rolfe watched him warily. "I know not."

"But 'tis your wedding day," Athelstan said, setting the bowl down upon a chest. "And you have overslept. You must get dressed and be at the chapel in an hour, my lord."

Rolfe held his face in his hands and groaned. "In an hour? 'Tis impossible." His headache had just increased.

CHAPTER 22

It was so very easy.

Preparations for the wedding feast had been underway since yesterday morning. The kitchens were a madhouse, with twice the number of serfs scurrying back and forth from pantry, to hearth, to chapel's courtyard. A wedding was a celebration not just for the nobles, but for the entire village. As such, there had to be enough bread, mutton, and ale for everyone. And this wedding was an even more special event, for their lord was new, and no one wanted to displease him—rather, everyone feared his displeasure.

Ceidre's heart was lodged in her throat, and her stomach had been queasy ever since she had awoken. It was, she knew, nerves, because of what she had to do. She had learned from gossip that the Norman intended to transport Morcar to York immediately after the wedding—thus it was now or never, do or die. But the timing was truly perfect. In this chaos she knew she could succeed. Indeed, she had to.

And she would not think about the penalty she might face. After all, hadn't he shown her leniency once? But a slight shudder swept her, for he had warned her and warned her well.

And she would not think about the nuptials either.

Teddy came running out of the kitchen, trencher and beaker in hand, heading for the back of the manor

—and the entrance to the dungeons below. Ceidre caught up to him. " 'Tis for the guard?"

Teddy didn't stop, he was breathless, sweating. "Aye, it is, an' me arse is gonna get whupped if I don't get back to turn the chickens!"

"Give it to me," Ceidre said, grabbing his wrist.

Teddy halted, panting, but his eyes glimmered with shrewdness. Then the brief look of understanding was gone. He shrugged. "Thank ye, Ceidre." He handed her his burdens and was running back up the hill.

He knew. Ceidre was certain, just as she knew if their deed was discovered, he would plead ignorance—and she herself would take all the blame. Her chest was so very tight. She wished she did not have to deliver the fare, but she could not give this terrible task to an innocent. She was holding bread, cheese, and ale. The same trick would not work, and Ceidre was prepared. She put everything down, then hurriedly opened a small basket she was carrying. Within was a soft goat cheese—made with herbs. She put a few generous slices between the bread, felt a twinge of guilt, threw aside the cheese Teddy had brought, and continued down the path.

Once he digested the cheese, the guard would not be able to control himself. Corncockle was a most efficacious laxative.

The dungeons were actually a dark, dirt-floored hole beneath the manor, entered from a rock latch-door in the ground. Ceidre had ventured inside once, when she was so very young—and she would never forget it. There was barely any air to breathe, and no light, none at all. Rats scurried in the darkness, and slime oozed between her bare toes. Her brothers had encouraged her to go down to explore it, and Ceidre had thought nothing of doing so. But once inside, the overwhelming closeness began to terrify her, and she felt hot and strangled for lack of air. "We are going to close the door so you can see what it is really like," Morcar called.

"No!" Ceidre had shouted, but it was too late, the door banged shut, and she was enveloped in thick blackness.

Something happened. She could not breathe, and she thought her lungs would explode from lack of air. The walls seemed closer, caving in upon her. Ceidre screamed. She screamed and screamed, clawing the walls madly, knowing she was going to die, to be buried alive. . . .

Instantly Ed threw open the door, leapt down, and lifted her in his arms. Ceidre was shaking and panting, weeping uncontrollably, and it wasn't until she was back outside in the bright daylight that she realized what a silly fool she had been. Now she knew why she had always avoided exploring caves with her brothers, and since that day she had never ventured into a tiny, closed space again.

It was a travesty. Morcar, the second son, a prisoner in his own hold. But not, she thought resolutely, for long.

The guard, a burly oaf of a man, eyed her grimly. Ceidre did not smile. She set down the trencher, handing him the bag-beaker.

"I do not want your witch's potions," the guard said.

"Fine," Ceidre said shortly, and she picked the trencher up and the bag of wine. She turned to go.

" 'Tis not poisoned?" he asked.

"Am I stupid? The last time I was lucky, my lord graced me with his mercy. I dare not such a trick again. Look, I will take a bite of everything first if it soothes you."

"Do so," he said.

Ceidre did so, unperturbed. One bit of cheese would not harm her much. The guard watched and was much relieved. She left him eating merrily.

She was late. The procession for the chapel would be starting, and her absence would be conspicuous. Grimly Ceidre picked up her skirt and quickened her pace. For the ceremony she had donned black, for she was mourning this occasion. Already the villagers and Normans had lined the road from manor to church, which was at the edge of the village, a small stone building. Ceidre's place was at the front, and she stood beside Athelstan. His regard was intense and she did not like it. She studied the ground. All around her was the happy laughter and conversation of Aelfgar's people, joyous in anticipation of the festival to come. Rich aromas of bread, stew, and pies hung thickly about them. The sky was daringly blue, the sun warm and bold. Children frolicked, dogs yapped. Ceidre began twisting the cord of her girdle.

"Here they come," shouted someone, and a cry went up.

Ceidre looked.

Alice, dainty and elegant on a blooded white palfrey, came first, led by Guy and Beltain. She wore a magnificent gown, virginal white, encrusted with a thousand pearls, which Ceidre knew she and her maids had been sewing on ever since the Norman's arrival. A veil of lace, glinting with gold thread, hid her face. It could not hide her wide smile. Her dark, rich hair hung free to her waist, a riot of curls. She looked every inch the virginal bride, every inch the lady of Aelfgar. Ceidre almost felt uncontrollably sick.

And then she saw him.

In all truth, he took her breath away.

He sat his mean gray stallion as if he were born to the saddle. The destrier was bedecked with all his gear, including a royal-blue blanket, gold trimmed and beribboned. Blue and gold streamers waved from his mane and tail, from bit and bridle, even from Rolfe's stirrups. The animal pranced, held tightly by his rider to a slow, tortured pace.

Rolfe's tunic was the same rich royal blue, but of the finest weave, so fine it shimmered, reflecting the sunlight, making him appear to dazzle, like a god. In fact, his appearance was greeted by the most absolute hush of reverence and awe. Indeed, he seemed too beautiful to be mortal. His cape, a red velvet lined with gold, waved behind him. His scabbard was encrusted with jewels—with rubies and sapphires and yellow citrines. One of his hands rested casually upon the hilt, and on it flashed a huge signet ring of black pearl. His hose were dark red, garters blue. His spurs were gold, and they gleamed.

He sat straight and still. He did not smile. Ceidre found herself staring, and thought how much she hated him. She hated him for everything—for his usurping of Aelfgar, for this marriage to her sister, for his lust for her, for his unholy beauty. Bitterness welled like bile. He was almost passing her now, and his eyes suddenly riveted upon her. Ceidre hoped he could see just how much she despised him.

If only her heart did not feel as if it were breaking.

The ceremony was, as usual, short. It took place outside, so everyone could be witness, and within a few moments of their arrival, it was over. Rolfe, holding Alice's hand in his, turned to face the crowd. Everyone roared with approval, rice and ribbons were thrown. He was tall and golden, she was petite and dark. And now they were man and wife, the lord and lady of Aelfgar.

CHAPTER 23

The guard had run frantically into the bushes.

Ceidre had left the boisterous feast, unremarked amid all the revelry. She had crouched, waiting, for her chance. A bay mare was bridled, tethered in a copse of trees just beyond her. As the guard ran, Ceidre darted for the latch-door.

No one was about, of course, the entire village being at the wedding celebration. Ceidre threw the bolt and pried open the heavy stone. "Morcar! Morcar!"

She saw him rise and stand directly beneath her. " 'Tis you, Ceidre?"

She flung down the rope ladder. "Hurry! Hurry!"

He had only been in the hold two days, and he scrambled up quickly. But outside he blinked, dazed. "I cannot see."

Ceidre slammed down the door and bolted it. She took his arm and they began to run. " 'Twill pass," she whispered. She noticed his leg was stiff—and bandaged.

In the copse they halted. Morcar, his vision returned, grasped her shoulders. "Bless you," he whispered.

"Your leg, how is it?"

"I am fine. The Norman sent a wench to tend me," he said, untying the mare.

Ceidre saw that his thigh and arm were both neatly

wrapped, and she was stunned that the Norman had had him cared for. Morcar leapt onto the filly's bare back. Ceidre jerked herself out of her reverie. "God go with you," she cried.

"And you, Ceidre," he said, blue eyes flashing. Despite his pallor, he was the Morcar she knew and loved, proud, handsome, nostrils flared now with the scent of escape. "I will be back," he said.

He wheeled the bay and galloped into the woods. Ceidre watched him disappear, and only then did she sink trembling to the ground. She could not help it—she began to release some well-deserved tears.

Rolfe did not smile.

He sat beside his bride beneath an ancient walnut tree as his men and the villagers drank, ate, and danced all around them. He did not drink, nor did he eat. His headache had not lessened, and he still felt overly ill. In truth, he was somewhat dazed. He could not believe it had come to pass. He was finally married. He looked at his bride.

Her face was flushed. She was nibbling daintily, and feeling his regard, she turned to look at him. Her eyes were wide, tremulous, yet excited. She smiled.

Rolfe did not smile back. He turned away, wanting nothing more than a gallop in the fresh air—perhaps that would restore his natural humors. Barring that, he was ready for bed. He was very tired, like a laggard. Had he not slept at all last night? The aftereffects of the wine were worse than he had ever imagined, and now he understood what most men suffered from time to time.

"Are you not hungry, my lord?" Alice asked, for the third time.

"No."

"Does the feast not please you?"

"It pleases me," he said, wishing she would not bother to make aimless conversation. He was most distinctly not in the mood.

"Perhaps some wine?" She held up the bag.

He lifted a hand. "No, Lady, please, my head aches and I am most tired. Eat as you will, but leave me to my preferences."

Alice replaced the bag and restrained herself from scowling.

Rolfe folded his arms and stared, unseeing and bored, out at the crowd.

And so the celebration went on.

It had been endless, but now it was finally over.

Rolfe paced the solar, waiting for word that he could enter his chamber where his bride readied herself. Never had he been so tired, his every joint aching, his head now, thankfully, numb. It was not late, but he longed to lie down and embrace the comfort of sleep. Yet this was his wedding night. He would be, he thought, very lucky if he could find any desire for the wench who was his wife. In truth, he was not just too tired to bed her, he was too tired to deal with this entire new circumstance of wedlock.

Alice was shaking. She could not help it. She had finally attained her heart's desire, to be the Norman's wife. But now, now she was clad in her finest nightgown, all sheer lace, awaiting him in his bed. Now she must pay the price—and she dreaded it.

She recalled very clearly his thick body, overly large with muscle and sinew. He was repulsive. At least her betrothed, Bill, now dead, had been more pleasing to her eye. He had been slim and slender and graceful—not in the least frightening. Nor had he been a boor! Oh, God, how she wished she could close her eyes and sleep through the upcoming ordeal. But she could not. Nor could she cry and scream. Ceidre enjoyed her husband's embraces, so she must prove herself equally receptive. She must bear it, and pretend to be well pleased. Again Alice shuddered.

He entered.

Alice clutched the covers and stared. As usual, he had been rude and withdrawn all day, and now, now he was no different. He did not spare her even a glance! He began to strip, unashamed, right in front of her. Alice got a glimpse of his broad, hard chest and lean flanks and immediately turned her face away. She would not look if she did not have to.

The bed shifted under his weight as he climbed in from the other side. Alice froze, unable to breathe. He groaned and sighed. She waited, perspiring now. He did not touch her. In fact, he was absolutely still. Slowly, carefully, Alice moved her head.

He was lying on his back, one hand flung across his eyes, sound asleep.

Alice stared, shocked.

Her first reaction, relief, fled. On its heels came disbelief—he did not even desire her—then anger. He would brand her sister with his hot looks and his big lance, but her he would ignore! She was his bride, but until he lay with her, they were not truly wed, not in God's eyes or the church's. Alice seethed.

Rolfe awoke gradually, the deep sleep he had entertained leaving slowly. He was aware of the warmth emanating from the other side of the bed, and, groping, his hand touched the soft flesh of another, of a woman.

His first thought was ecstatic—Ceidre. She was here, in his bed, awaiting his pleasure. Then disappointment and remembrance reared itself at once.

'Twas not Ceidre.

He had only to turn his head to see his bride. The lady Alice.

Rolfe sighed, completely awake now. As usual in the mornings, his manhood was throbbing, hard and ready. He remembered all too well that last night he had not consummated the marriage, being impossibly weary. And already, aware now of the identity of the woman who lay next to him, who was his wife, his blood was beginning to slow, his ache to ease. He would consummate this marriage now, quickly, before he lost his desire.

It should be Ceidre here, he thought grimly, reaching for his bride.

She gasped as he pulled her close, rolling on top of her. He kneed her legs apart, pulling her gown up and out of his way. He kept his eyes closed. He focused on the other—that bronze-haired witch who haunted him day and night. His need increased.

Alice let out a sob as he probed her dry flesh.

A horn of alarm sounded.

On top of Alice, but yet to make entry, Rolfe froze, all thoughts of bedding his bride fleeing, and then he was on his feet and lunging for his sword. The sound of alarm was called again. Rolfe threw on his tunic and yanked up his hose. He heard someone pounding up the stairs. He had his chausses on but not gartered when Guy banged upon the door.

"Enter," Rolfe roared as the horn sounded again.

"My lord," Guy shouted, panting upon the threshold. "I am sorry—"

"What passes?" Rolfe demanded.

"The Saxon has escaped!"

Rolfe froze.

"Morcar has escaped," Guy repeated. "He is gone!"

CHAPTER 24

"What happened?" Rolfe demanded.

" 'Twas just discovered when a serf brought his breakfast, my lord. Louis opened the door to hand down the fare—but the prisoner was not there."

Rolfe was already heading out the door.

"My lord," Alice cried, clutching the sheets to her neck.

Rolfe paused, tension rippling visibly through his body. "Not now, Lady."

"You know who had a hand in this," Alice said triumphantly. "You know well it could only be my sister!"

Rolfe scorched her with a look and ran downstairs, followed by Guy. "Divide up the men into four groups to search for a sign. When did Louis begin his guard duty?"

"Last night at midnight."

"Was the prisoner there then?"

"He does not know," Guy said grimly.

"And it was Jean who had duty that day?"

"Yes. They are both awaiting you," Guy said as they entered the hall. "As you can see." The two apprehensive men stood alone in the hall.

"Who was the last to see the prisoner?" Rolfe demanded.

Jean, flushed, stepped forward. "I did, my lord."

"When?"

"When I first took guard, yesterday morning."

"And did you know if the prisoner was there when you left your post?"

Jean hung his head. " 'Twas late. I thought he slept."

"So you"—Rolfe turned to Louis—"did not inspect to see if the prisoner was there either?"

"No, my lord," Louis said, standing straight and tall. "I too thought he was asleep. But—"

"What?"

"He could not have escaped during my watch. I did not close an eye, nor did I take one step from my post. This I swear, and if I speak false, let God smite me as I stand."

Rolfe believed him, and he turned to Jean, who was crimson now. "What have you to say?"

" 'Twas me," he croaked. "I was deathly ill, my lord. All of a sudden I had a severe cramping. I could not hold my bowels."

Rolfe stared. "You deserted your post."

"I was sick, so sick I could not control myself."

Rolfe's face was hard and rigid, but he contained his wrath well. Only his eyes showed his emotions. They blazed. "At what time were you sick?"

"Just after I took my dinner, my lord, during your wedding feast."

"Strip him of his sword," Rolfe said to Guy. He then looked at Jean. "You are relieved of duty until I deem it otherwise."

Guy turned to Rolfe. "Do you think . . . ?"

"I am almost sure of it—he was poisoned. Have there been any other reports of this strange illness?"

"No."

Jean jerked upright. "My lord?"

"What?"

"She brought it to me."

Rolfe thought the hall had become strangely still. "Who?" And he knew.

"The witch—my lady's sister—Ceidre."

For a moment Rolfe didn't breathe, didn't move. Then his heart picked up its beat. His face was devoid of expression, of emotion. "And you were not suspicious—after she poisoned Guy at Kesop?"

"Aye, I was. But she took a bite of everything, my Lord, to prove 'twasn't poisoned. Yet now I think they were small morsels, my lord, very small."

Rolfe's nostrils flared. In his mind was hard, hard anger. She understood well what she had done, and the consequences, but she had done it anyway.

Treason.

And in his body there was sickness, deep, reaching from his heart straight into his soul.

"I knew it," Alice cried from behind them. "She asked me the other night, my lord, to help her plan Morcar's escape. Of course, I told her she was a fool."

Rolfe had been about to tell Alice to be quiet, but now he was all ears. "And you did not inform me?"

"You were sleeping from the effects of the wine, my lord," Alice said with the faintest of smirks. Her eyes glowed. "I commanded Guy to put her in the dungeons for treason, yet he would not!"

Rolfe looked at Guy.

Guy shifted. "The lady Alice thought she had poisoned you, my lord, and thus accused her sister of treason. I determined you were in your cups, so did not lock up the wench. If I have behaved wrongly, I will gladly accept just punishment."

"You did rightly." Rolfe held up a hand, taking a breath, mouth tight. "There is no need to hunt for Morcar—the Saxon is long gone."

Guy nodded.

"Find Ceidre," Rolfe said. "And chain her in the stables, with a guard."

"Yes, my lord," Guy said.

Rolfe turned and walked to the large trestle table, his back to the company. He stood unmoving, and then his arm rose. His fist came smashing down. All his raw power was in the blow. The noise was deafening; the table cracked.

Ceidre shifted and tried to find a more comfortable position upon the straw. Her wrists were tied behind her and from there secured to a post in the stable. Her guard sat upon a bale of hay, ten yards from her, arms folded, watching those who passed by. And the passersby were many.

She no longer flushed as, upon one pretext or another, the villagers strolled by to gawk and stare. She had been sitting here for half the day. She was used to their slack-jawed gaping and even to their pity. Everyone had made a point of coming to see this new attraction, and the whispered word treason abounded.

Alice had come too. Her stride had been hard and purposeful, eyes dark and bright. Ceidre had stiffened instinctively, the movement causing the rope to dig into her flesh and burn. She sensed the worst. "Now you will pay, witch," Alice had hissed. "Now you will pay!"

Her sister had shaken her already shattered nerves as no one else had. Thankfully, she did not pause to stay and taunt, but hurried on. Ceidre blinked back tears, trembling. Her own sister hated her enough to gloat. And Alice was right, now she would pay. She knew the price well, she had been warned.

Oh, sweet Mary, what would he do?

Ceidre was afraid.

She had known the instant she saw Guy approaching

this morning that he had come for her. There had been no point in running—where should she go? She had waited, near the village well, facing him valiantly, head held high. She had been very certain Guy would take her to the Norman. So despite her outward poise, there had been thick unease within her. Her heart had wings and fluttered like a trapped bird. She must not show fear. She must not shiver like a stray in winter. Yet instead she had been escorted to the stables and tied up. And here she had been all morning and all afternoon. With no food, not even a blanket to sit upon. Not that she could eat, she would surely vomit if she tried. An hour past she'd been brought a cup of water to wet her dry, parched throat, and was finally allowed to answer her body's needs.

When would he come?

Fear lurched in her breast again. It was a formidable lump that she could not swallow. With the passing of time it grew, expanding uncontrollably. His rage would be beyond anything she had ever seen before. If only he would come and the confrontation could be gotten over with! This waiting was torture of the worst sort, and she could not stand it another minute! Perspiration had long since gathered under her arms and between her breasts and upon her brow. She knew, with certainty, he kept her waiting like this apurpose, to feed her fear. And it succeeded.

And her worst fears began to rear themselves in the darkest hours of the night.

Would he hang her?

She prayed for mercy.

Ceidre would not beg information from her guard, although she desperately wanted to. She would not beg for audience, or to know her fate. Yet the thought came—if she begged the Norman, if she wept, if she clung to him, perhaps he would show mercy. She imagined him standing there, stone-faced, ruthless, cold-hearted, while she clutched at his tunic, begging for leniency. She knew positively then that he would not spare her this time. Her mind, traitorous to her soul, sped on. What if she tried to use a woman's wiles to gain his mercy? No! She could not! She could not weep, beg, or seduce! No, she would never beg—she would staunchly bear whatever she must, even if it were her own death.

She was going to be hanged.

She had committed treason, her life was forfeit.

She could not sleep. Nor could she cry. Instead, she sat huddled and frozen, her mind conjuring up the worst images of herself—dangling at the end of a rope.

CHAPTER 25

Rolfe's eyes were bloodshot, and they mirrored his frustration. He sat alone in the hall, as he had all night, after ordering everyone out. He had dozed. But his dreams had been nightmares of the worst sort. Ceidre screaming, her back bare and bloody, while his man whipped her with his lash. Rolfe had screamed for a halt, yet the gory flogging had continued. He realized, as he shouted again, that he was opening his mouth, screaming as hard as he could—but no sound was being emitted. And then he woke up, sweating and trembling, to find himself sitting at the table in the hall where he had passed the entire night.

He could not do it.

He had to.

Rolfe rubbed his face and his eyes. He was a commander. His word was law. He controlled his men and the occupied territories because the threat of punishment for a breach or treason was real. His fist was iron; it had to be. He rarely showed mercy. His men rarely disobeyed. Traitors were whipped, if boys or women; male adults hanged. Harsher lessons were dealt in the more difficult territories, as just due to more serious instances of rebellion. At Kesop, the village had been razed for the villagers had harbored a dozen Saxon archers. 'Twas the declared policy. If a policy was declared, it must be the law, with no exceptions. Or soon, very soon, there would be chaos and anarchy.

He could not do it.

"My lord?"

Rolfe had not heard Guy enter. He gestured for him to sit. "I cannot do it."

Guy, ever his closest man, understood. "She has bewitched you from the first, my lord."

"Aye, that is true."

"My lord," Guy said urgently, "there is not a soul in the village who does not know what she has done."

"I know."

"Everyone waits to see what you will do."

Rolfe smiled, without mirth.

"You must punish her."

"If she were my wife," Rolfe said, "I could lock her up and throw away the key and no one would object."

"She is not your wife," Guy said.

Rolfe laughed. He thought of his wife, asleep upstairs, whom he had not even seen since yesterday morning when the news of this treachery had been revealed. "Believe me," he said heavily, "I know well which dame is my wife and which is not." He stood. "Bring her to the courtyard at noon."

Guy was also standing. "Yes, my lord." There was a question in his eyes.

" 'Twill be done," Rolfe said grimly.

Ceidre heard the edict immediately. The village rippled with excitement—she was to be brought to the courtyard at noon for the eaorl's punishment. Ceidre was sick. Rumor and speculation abounded. Would she be whipped, or hanged? Perhaps the lord, who had a hot eye for the witch, would do neither, but toss her into the dungeons for a day or two. This was a big event for Aelfgar, the first instance of the new lord's exercising of his power in discipline, for the most serious offense there was—treason. Everyone was breathless with anticipation, wondering what he would do. Most thought it would be the worst, for the lord was a cold, hard man, and a Norman as well. Ceidre knew that they were right. She was losing what little control she had over her emotions.

She was shaking and ready to weep. She was deathly afraid. She had tested him too many times—and now she would hang. She prayed. She prayed to Jesus, she prayed to the saints. She even prayed to a few old pagan gods she had never beseeched before. She prayed for the strength to bear her fate, to be brave and strong and die a martyr, not a coward. She was so terribly afraid she was going to weep and beg for mercy, clinging to his feet.

It was many hours till noon, and time was merciless, cruel, her pace slow and snide. Ceidre watched the sun—she could not bear its slow, inexorable ascent. And then a shadow fell across the straw at her feet, and Ceidre looked up, startled, for no one had dared to come this close all day. It was Alice.

Alice smiled meanly. "He is enraged, Ceidre. You have cost him a most valuable prisoner, and he will show no mercy."

Ceidre closed her eyes. By the gods, she did not need to hear this! Not now!

Alice hunched down. "You are going to die."

Ceidre opened her eyes, her face amazingly calm. "I will bear whatever I have to."

Alice laughed. "As if you have a choice!"

Thankfully, Alice turned and left. Once she had slipped outside, Ceidre hunched over, retching dryly. Then she crouched panting. So it was true, she would hang—when deep inside, all along, she had clung to the faint hope that he would spare her life.

Then something miraculous began to happen.

She could feel her frightened heart begin to slow. The terrible, gut-wrenching fear quieted. The whole world quieted—the baaing of sheep, the laughter of villagers, the groaning wheel of a passing cart. She was no longer trembling. Her body felt heavy and lethargic; she had become utterly relaxed, as if given a potion to slow her senses. It was almost a feeling of serenity. The sun was not hot, it was warm. The earth was not cold, it was cool. The birdsong above mellowed, the yapping of the hounds dimmed. Only her vision remained sharp, in fact, the world became brighter, more focused. She no longer thought of what would occur. No images haunted her. Instead she sat back, her breathing steady, and waited for them to come for her. And there was peace.

At noon Rolfe stepped out of the manor. He was not surprised that the entire village had turned out, he expected it. In fact, he had just sent Beltain and Louis to rouse anyone who had not come. All of Aelfgar would witness the price to be paid for treason.

His mouth was clamped in a hard, controlled line. His eyes were opaque and showed nothing. His face was expressionless, except for the extreme rigidity there. He stood unmoving on the manor steps. He tried to detach himself completely from any emotions whatsoever, a feat he had long managed with complete success. So far, so good. He could not be unaware of the fluttering of his heart, but he was in control of himself.

Lady Alice stood beside him, head high, her hand on his arm.

The villagers began to whisper excitedly, someone crying "Here they come!"

His stomach lurched. Rolfe clamped down harder

on his jaw and watched Guy and Ceidre approaching. Her hands were still tied behind her back. Her dress was dusty and covered with straw. Her thick braid was scraggly, many strands escaping, and it hung over one breast. Her head was high, shoulders erect. Her chin was in the air. As she came closer, he saw the mask of her expression—one of calm and dignity. His heart lurched with an emotion so strong he was not sure if it was pride or something more.

Guy brought her to him. She turned her purple eyes upon him. Her chin had not lowered. Rolfe saw the utter calm in her gaze—the trust. His own heart tried to leap out of his chest, and he felt a trickle of perspiration begin to descend from his temple. Guy paused with Ceidre in front of him.

Rolfe stared into her eyes. She was proud and serene on the brink of disaster. He could find no fear in her gaze, just acceptance. She was braver than most men, and he admired her greatly in that moment. She would not let her people down by weeping and begging; she would not show him any weakness.

"Ceidre," he said, low. His tone was harsh with pain, yet intimate. He had not meant to address her in such a manner.

She smiled serenely, and then he saw the thinnest filming of tears. "I am ready," she said simply.

He wanted to take her into his embrace—and protect her. "You have committed treason," Rolfe said quietly. "Ten lashes."

She blinked furiously, lucid cognition flashing in her gaze. Ten lashes! That bitch had lied! She would not hang, she would not die, and oh, she was so lucky, for she could survive this!

Rolfe saw her shock and relief. He himself was stunned, in that moment knowing she had been ready to accept a martyr's death, that she had thought her fate to be the hangman. He heard the sigh of relief rippling through the crowd. Beside him, Alice gasped. He did not care. He could not believe she had been so courageous—just as he could not believe she knew him so little to think he would sentence her to death. He wanted to laugh—without mirth. And he wanted to weep for what was to come, yet he had never shed a tear in his life.

"Ten lashes," he repeated, his voice husky and harsh. As anyone who had ever suffered the whip knew, ten lashes was plenty for the delicate skin of a woman. As it was, his heart was now beating frantically. He must use all his strength, all his self-discipline, every reserve he had, or he would not make it through this ordeal. He was a scant instant from reversing his decision, and he knew it. He nodded abruptly to Guy.

Ceidre was led to a post and turned to face it, her back to the crowd. Guy ripped open her dress from shoulder to waist. Her back was long and elegant and graceful, her skin slightly tinged with gold. Rolfe realized he had ceased to breathe. "Louis," he barked, causing the man holding the whip to turn sharply.

"Ne rompe pas la peau," Rolfe commanded harshly. *Do not break her skin.*

Louis paled.

Rolfe was sweating. He saw Ceidre stretched taut, unmoving. "Begin," he said.

The lash snaked through the air and sliced cleanly across Ceidre's back. She jerked but did not cry out. Her skin did not break, but a fat red welt appeared. Rolfe clenched his fists, hard. Beside him, Alice made a sound, something that sounded impossibly like a snicker. Rolfe shot her a quick glance and saw that she was smiling. Furious, he hissed, "Restrain your pleasure, Lady!"

Again, Ceidre spasmed beneath the whip, and Rolfe flinched as well, he who had never flinched in the face of physical hurt before. The whip fell again and again. It was not until the sixth lash that she made a sound, a small cry of anguish. Rolfe took one step off the stairs. The seventh and eighth lashes fell, and a streak of blood appeared among the crisscrossing of welts. Ceidre gasped and moaned, jerking hard against her ropes. Rolfe gripped the hitching post near him with all his strength. He could not remove his eyes from Ceidre, yet he was aware of his wife's guttural pleasure in her sister's pain. The final lash descended. Ceidre sagged, trembling, against the post. Rolfe moved.

He was at her side and cutting her free before Louis had even coiled his whip. He ignored the gasping of the crowd. The last three lashes had cut into her delicate skin, making him sicker than he already was. Had he eaten this day, he would be throwing up. "Ceidre," he managed, supporting her with one arm around her waist.

"Don't touch me," she murmured, gasping, but she did not fight him.

Very gently he lifted her into his arms. *"Je le regrette,"* he whispered.

She whimpered and clung, tightly, her face buried in his neck.

CHAPTER 26

Rolfe carried her inside and up the stairs. His instinct was to carry her into his bedchamber, but reason returned, and he swept her into the solar and upon the bed that had been Alice's before the lady had become his wife. Ever so gently, he laid her down, upon her stomach.

Alice was on his heels. "What are you doing?" she cried, pink-faced. "She must be put in the stocks, then the dungeons! You have already been too lenient—"

Rolf whirled, enraged. "Your conduct is ungracious."

Alice froze.

"Get to our chamber and think on what befits the lady of this manor."

Alice's eyes went wide. "You would confine me to our chamber?"

"Go now," Rolfe roared. "Until I request your presence!"

Taking a deep breath, Alice turned and stalked out.

Rolfe closed his eyes briefly, assailed with the image of his wife as Ceidre writhed in pain beneath the whip. Alice had enjoyed her sister's punishment, and the recollection was hideous. Then he moved, dropping to one knee. His hands ached to touch her, but Ceidre lifted her head to look at him, pain in her gaze—and hatred. "Get away from me," she hissed.

At the very least, Rolfe wanted to tuck back errant strands of hair away from her face. Her tone, and her hate, stopped him; his arms fell to his sides. He rose. "You will be tended to," he said, his tone hoarse even to his own ears. "And you are confined to this room." He wanted her close by, and comfortable, until she healed. And he would not question his own motives.

"What?" Ceidre was sarcastic, drippingly so. Then her voice broke. "You do not listen to your good wife, my sister? You do not toss me into the dungeons? Do you now, belatedly, show mercy?" To her horror, a fat tear escaped to roll slowly down her cheek.

Rolfe hated himself too, so he could understand now how she felt. He watched the path of the tear, wishing he had the courage to reach out and erase it—he who had never lacked courage before. His gaze moved to her back, swollen with welts, and the three long abrasions where, finally, the whip had broken her skin. She would be scarred. Because of him.

Her name was on his lips, and he could not prevent its escaping, low and harsh, urgent and agonized. "Ceidre . . ."

She seared him with contempt and turned her face to the wall.

Rolfe studied her. There was nothing else for him to do but to leave, yet he was loath to. She was so pitiful now in her wounded state, yet so magnificent in her courage. He turned away.

Only when he had closed the door behind him did Ceidre begin to weep.

"There, there," her grandmother soothed. "I know it hurts, just hold still."

Ceidre tried to do as she was told while her granny cleaned her abrasions to prevent an infection. Every little touch stung, and her back burned and throbbed unbearably. More tears seeped from her eyes, tears of pain and self-pity.

"You are a strong one, lass," Granny said in her low murmur. She was as old as the hills, a big-bosomed, plump woman with white hair and Ceidre's own dark purple eyes. "You will be healed in no time."

"You do not chastise me?"

"I know you, Ceidre, you did what you thought was right. A soul can do no more."

"I must help my brothers, I must."

"Shh, do not get in a dither."

Ceidre laid her head back down while the old woman packed a poultice on her wounds. "I hate him, truly," she murmured. "He has no heart, none at all."

"No?" her grandmother asked. "That must be why he ran to you and cut you down and carried you, in his own two arms, with all of Aelfgar watching, into his home."

Ceidre flushed. "Mayhap 'twas guilt, but that would truly be a surprise." Yet she could see his eyes, as he had looked at her before the flogging, with their dark, strained depths, turbulent, roiling. And she could hear his voice, hoarse and pleading, as he called her name—but pleading for what?

"He did his duty, as you did yours," Granny said. " 'Tis a fine coil, this is, with him wed to Alice but with eyes only for you. And now this."

"He is merely randy, like a goat," Ceidre spit out. "He takes any passing wench that amuses him. I amuse him most now, yet I am his wife's sister and he is decent enough to leave me be. But that whets his overly large appetite."

"Ahh," mused her grandmother. " 'Twas for lust that he carried you to your sickbed."

Ceidre was angry, and she snorted. The door opened precisely then, and Ceidre knew, instinctively, that it was the topic of their conversation. She met his steady regard with a hot glare.

"How is she?" Rolfe asked, stepping to the bedside.

"She will be fine, 'tis her peasant stock that makes her strong."

Rolfe did not smile. Ceidre turned her head away but was aware of him gazing at her naked back. Her torn dress had been completely removed. From the hips down she was covered with a thin blanket, and she felt very vulnerable lying bare as she was.

"Will she scar?" Rolfe asked grimly.

"Yes, but not too badly if the salve is applied frequently. With time, who knows? Perhaps the marks will fade so as to nigh be discernible."

"With time," Rolfe echoed, staring.

"There is nothing more for me to do," Granny said, rising heavily.

Rolfe took one last look at Ceidre, her head averted, then stepped with the old woman to the door. "Thank you," he said.

Granny looked at him with a smile. " 'Tis not for you to thank me, my lord."

Rolfe looked at her. "Thank you," he affirmed, and followed her out.

Alice heard him coming.

She was pacing like a caged cat, ire in her every stride, in the tight lines of her face. She froze at the sound of Rolfe's strong steps upon the stairs, then struggled to attain a pleasant façade. It was not easy to do.

It was late, past supper. He had not summoned her for their evening meal, and instead a serf had brought her food and drink as she remained confined in their chamber. All of Aelfgar knew, she was sure, that she was being punished—and it was because of that witch, Ceidre.

Humiliation and fury vied equally, but strongest of all was hate. She hated her husband, and she hated his whore even more.

But she must get a grip on her emotions. He had not touched her since that first morning, when she had awoken beneath him to find him attempting to fornicate with her. She wished now that he had succeeded, that the consummation of their marriage had taken place. But it hadn't. Tonight, however, there was no reason he would not fulfill his duties.

Rolfe entered, barely sparing her a glance. Alice had already changed for sleep. She paused by the hearth in a robe, her eyes huge and riveted upon him. Like a doe, she was poised, waiting to gauge his mood, his actions. He sighed and began stripping off his tunic.

"You look tired, my lord. Please, let me," Alice said, coming to him.

He nodded, no thanks forthcoming, and allowed her to lift off the tunic, then the undergarment. Alice tried not to touch his skin, but failed, and she shuddered. He did not notice.

He bent to release his garters, and Alice hurried to do so for him. He let her, and as she removed them, he stepped out of his chausses and hose. Alice made a show of folding his things neatly, so as not to have to look at his blatant nudity. The man had no modesty, no shame. She remembered how it had felt, his male organ, poking at her, and she felt her tension rising. She fought with herself and managed to maintain a semblance of calm.

He was already in the bed, one arm outflung, eyes closed. Alice approached, blinking. He did not look like a lusty groom, he looked like an exhausted man about to sleep. She slid in beside him and, once under the coverlet, removed her robe. He did not move. An awful realization arose—he was going to sleep! He was not going to touch her!

A part of her rejoiced. Yet her smarter self, her ambitious self, was cool and calm and knew this could not pass. Alice shifted her body so that her knee touched his. There was no response.

She was not a seductress like her sister. How was she going to get his attention? And why, why was he behaving like a monk? He knew his duty! Alice touched his arm. "My lord?"

He wasn't asleep, for his eyes opened immediately, and he gazed at her lucidly.

Alice's mouth trembled. "I am so sorry," she whispered, her lashes fluttering down, "I did not mean to displease you. Can you not forgive me?"

" 'Tis forgotten," he said with a grunt. "Now, go to sleep." He rolled over, facing away from her.

She wanted to take this good fortune and escape his attentions, but she could not. "My lord? Might I have a word with you?"

Rolfe turned back over, sitting up. "What is it you wish, Alice?" His tone was short and rude.

Her temper flared. "You do not wish to consummate this marriage?"

His eyes narrowed. "No, I do not."

She blinked, shocked, not having expected this answer. For a moment she was at a loss. "You do not want to consummate this marriage?" she repeated.

"No."

Alice shrank back against the wall. "I do not understand. I am your wife."

Rolfe's eyes were blue flames, and in a violent action, he jerked out of the bed, pacing away from her. When he turned, she saw that he was very angry. He could not possibly be harboring such rage at her!

"Then I will explain," Rolfe said harshly. "Your behavior today sickens me. I have no desire to touch you. None—as you can see." He gestured crudely at himself.

She went white, then red. A long silence prevailed. Finally Alice broke it, stunned. "You do not wish to be wed to me?"

"You are my wife," Rolfe said. "We are wed."

"Not truly. Not in the eyes of God."

His stare was cold. "Perhaps, when the mood takes me, I will rectify that. But not today. Not tonight."

Alice covered her trembling chest with her hand. She could not believe this. He might consummate the marriage one day, if the "mood" took him. And yet what was she to do? Shout her humiliation to the world? No, she would never be able to hold her head up again, if everyone knew he had not taken her as was his duty—when all knew he lusted openly after her sister. He must know she would say nothing. Tears came to her eyes. "You do not want sons? I can give you many heirs, my lord. I am young and I am healthy."

Rolfe smiled, without mirth. "I have sons—half a dozen scattered from Normandy to Anjou. I have two more bastards in Sussex. Believe me, madame, I do not lack for heirs."

"So 'twill be a marriage in name only," Alice said bitterly—and then she was struck with a thought. She hated the very idea of his touching her, and she always had, yet because she wanted to be his wife, and it was her duty, she had wanted this consummation. But now she was his wife, and if no one knew the truth, then she could be his wife without suffering his touch. . . .

"When the foul memory of your malicious pleasure in your sister's pain recedes, I will most certainly exercise my rights," Rolfe was saying. "But 'twill not be this eve, so you may rest easy, your maidenhead is yet spared. Good night, Lady Alice," he ended firmly, striding back to the bed.

How she detested him.

How very lucky she was.

And of course, she would have to make sure all of Aelfgar assumed their marriage was truly consummated. But that would be a simple task, indeed.

CHAPTER 27

Despite exhaustion, his sleep was not deep, and it was troubled.

Tomorrow he had planned to take Morcar to the king. A messenger had been sent upon the Saxon's capture to inform William of the good news. Rolfe tossed restlessly, imagining the king's reaction when he learned of Morcar's escape. His wrath would be terrible. He would want to know all the details. And of course, some sort of punishment would be forthcoming—to himself, Rolfe, the commander in charge.

Rolfe did not question his urges, he only knew he must protect Ceidre. He would not reveal her identity to William. She had been punished. She was a serf. He would state that a serf, a woman, had carried out the act of treason and had been punished. But it was not so simple. Because it was only partially the truth—because it was equally a lie.

Ceidre was no simple serf but Morcar's half sister. This was important information, which the king would want to know. If William ever found out it had been withheld, he would be furious. Rolfe's omission of the fact was betrayal.

He was betraying his king—to protect *her.*

Surely he was bewitched in the most literal sense of the word.

He could not do it. He could not betray his king. He

was William's first and foremost commander, and as such, he knew his duty, he understood honor and loyalty. He had spent the past ten years serving his liege, and serving him well. To betray his king was to betray himself. Yet how could he rest loyal to William and protect Ceidre as well?

To reveal her real identity was to risk a graver punishment for her than what she had suffered, perhaps even death.

He was torn. This dilemma occupied him thoroughly, grimly, and he sensed disaster lurking not far from the present. For if he continued to protect her, a traitor, where would it finally end? How to draw the line between her acts of treason—and his own?

His own punishment, be what it might, did not even enter into his thoughts.

His wife lay sleeping beside him. He had sensed her relief when she had come to terms with his intention not to consummate the marriage. Rolfe almost snorted in disgust. At himself. A month ago he would have consummated this marriage whether his wife repelled him or not. But now he was not just repulsed every time he thought of her triumph in Ceidre's pain; he was enraged. He was allowing his unfed lust to rule him. It must stop.

He had made a vow that he would not touch Ceidre, and he reaffirmed it now. And if he could not touch her, he must put an end to his sexual hunger for her, as it could not be appeased. But how? Surely it was easier said than done.

Damn the woman, he thought, not for the first time. Didn't she realize her head was in the balance, haughty little chin and all? Didn't she realize that she was interfering in royal affairs, and that if William chose to hang her, there was nothing he could do to save her pretty little neck? Or—and he had a sudden moment of brilliant comprehension—did she sense her power over him, and believe he himself would betray his own king to save her, thus allowing her to act recklessly, stupidly? If she was going to commit treason, the least she could have done was not let the whole damned world know she was the traitor!

And, for the first time in his life, as Rolfe lay in the dark, he felt fear. It curdled in his guts. It was rank, it tasted like bile. Never in his life had he questioned the natural order, never in his life had he cared about a woman's feelings, if she was hurt, or pleasured, and never in his life had his own loyalty to his king been in doubt. He was the king's man. If this fact of his existence ceased to be, then just who the hell was he?

You are Rolfe de Warenne, he told himself firmly, Rolfe the Relentless, eaorl of Aelfgar—and you are King William's most trusted commander. He still could not sleep.

Or maybe he had drifted off. At first, he thought it was his wife who had awakened him with a pitiful, mewling noise. But his senses were keen, and he was as wide awake as before, listening—and Alice lay sleeping soundly. The cry, pitiful, a child frightened or hurt, sounded again. An instant later Rolfe knew it was no child but a woman, the witch of his dreams. He was out of the bed before the realization had firmly anchored itself.

She cried out again, with a sob.

Rolfe was at the door, his body tense, his thoughts filled with dire predictions—she was in pain, fevered, because of him. At the door he stopped short, remembering himself. Ceidre was moaning. He could see into her chamber, and she was thrashing about in the midst of a dream. He was sure she was assailed by the same image that was haunting him—that of her flogging.

He turned and rudely shook Alice, "Wake up," he said. "Alice, wake up."

Alice blinked. "My lord—what is it?"

"Go to your sister."

She sat up. "What?"

"Go to your sister. Awaken her from her dream, see if she is in pain. Now."

Alice's features became pinched in a mask of anger, but she calmly stepped to the floor, pulling her robe closed around her. Rolfe followed her after lighting a lamp, but he paused on the threshold of the chamber, refusing to go any farther. Alice shook Ceidre as rudely as he had shaken her. "Gently," Rolfe said. "She is hurt."

Alice bit her lip but eased her motions. "Ceidre, wake up. Wake up this instant."

Ceidre heard Alice, laughing, as she tensed for another lash. It hurt unbearably, she could not stand it, she was going to cry out, scream, be weak before the Norman—and she did. She knew she was weeping. It hurt so much. She kept seeing him, proud and beautiful and golden, and her heart was a traitor, begging him to come to her, soothe her, take her away. No, someone in her dream shrieked. He is the enemy, he is the one hurting you! She refused to listen. In her bizarre nightmare, he was her savior. She knew the ending of the story already, which was strange, she knew he would come to her, hold her, take her away, stop the pain. And she needed him to hurry, to do it now. "Rolfe, please," she cried. "Rolfe, please."

"Wake up, Ceidre," Alice snapped.

Rolfe froze after the first cry. He had never heard his name on her lips before. His body, already as taut as a coiled spring, became tauter. And then she cried his name again. He moved like a striking panther; one instant at the door, the next at her bed. He told himself it was the dark, the night, his own exhaustion, that was making him put his hands gently, so gently, on her shoulders. He ignored Alice's gasp. She leapt to her feet as he sank down on the bed at Ceidre's hip. "Wake up," he said huskily. "Ceidre."

His hand moved to the nape of her neck, into tendrils of hair that had escaped the coiled braid. She was whimpering and sobbing. He wasn't sure if she was asleep now or awake, but she shifted onto her side to curl against him as he slipped one strong arm beneath her to hold her close to his chest. "Wake up," he murmured, his breath touching her brow. The endearment "sweetheart" was on the tip of his tongue. The urge to brush his lips against her brow, and then to taste her tears with his tongue, was clamoring for fulfillment. Even so, he was acutely aware of his wife standing a few steps from him, livid. Damn Alice.

His chest was bare. Ceidre's small, warm palm slid across its contours and finally anchored on his shoulder. Her face pressed into the broad plane between his nipples, wetting his skin with her tears. Rolfe cupped the back of her head and held her closer. He felt he had reached a pleasure so profound he had never experienced it before.

He forgot about Alice. He nuzzled the top of her hair. He held her tighter. She clung harder. "Forgive me," he said hoarsely, while his inner mind was astounded that he, Rolfe de Warenne, her lord and master, should ask her, or anyone, for forgiveness. He ignored this voice. In the darkness of this night, the rules did not matter: Anything was possible. And he felt the instant of her full awakening.

She became still in his embrace, her lashes fluttering against the flesh of his pectoral muscles like the teasing of butterfly wings. Rolfe, anticipating what was to come, tightened his hold, pressing her head farther against him. He had stopped breathing. So, he thought, had she.

With her awareness, he felt awkward, clumsy, and foolish, yet completely reluctant to let her go. And he felt a soaring thrill, like a victory, that she did not struggle, but now, in fact, snuggled closer with a sigh. He could not believe his good fortune. He rocked her slightly, realizing there was no need for words, for explanations. And then he felt her steady breathing and suddenly realized she was not awake, as he had thought—but asleep.

Vast disappointment claimed him.

"This is obscene," Alice hissed.

Had she been sleeping all along? he thought foolishly. What did it matter? Was he being reduced to a fool? But for a moment, the thought that she had been unresisting in his arms had been exhilarating, like a potent wine. He gently laid her down again. Then he turned to look at Alice.

Before she could speak, he said coldly, "If you had comforted her the way a sister should, I would not have had to do so myself."

Alice's eyes filled with angry tears. "You shame me before all my people!"

"I have not shamed you."

"To take my sister as your leman is not to shame me?"

"She is not my mistress, Alice," Rolfe warned her. He took her arm and led her out of the chamber and into their own. He did not release her. "But it is time I made something very clear. You are my wife. You will be treated as such. But if ever you question my associations with a woman again, I will lock you away. I am a man and I have my rights. You do not question them. I will take any woman who is mine for the taking if she pleases my eye. And when I tell you Ceidre is not my mistress, you do not call me a liar. Ever. Is that clear?"

"Yes," Alice said, chin lifted. "May I speak?"

Rolfe released her and nodded, his thoughts fleeing back to the room across the hall.

"I do not begrudge you your mistresses," Alice said. "It pleases me, you know that—I am a lady and I prefer being spared your attentions. I did not mean to call you a liar. I just know how she flaunts herself—"

"Enough! The topic wearies me. I am going to bed. You may do as you wish."

He turned his back on her and strode back to their bed. Many moments intervened before Alice followed.

CHAPTER 28

"Where are you going, my lord?"
"York."
Alice was surprised, and she did not try to hide it. It was first thing that morning; they were still in their chamber. She watched Rolfe as he gave careful instructions to Guy, who was remaining behind, in charge of his men and the manor. Guy nodded and left. Rolfe quickly packed an extra change of clothes—tunic, undertunic, chausses, and hose. He added a velvet mantle in the richest rust color, the underside aubergine. The mantle he now wore, over his hauberk, was the familiar black over red, both sinister and utilitarian. The brooch boasted a huge, glaring yellow citrine. It was still chill out in the first hour after dawn.
"How long will you be gone?" Alice asked, anticipating his absence with great relish. She would not have to worry about the "mood" to consummate their marriage overtaking him; nor would she have to deal with his impossible arrogance and manners. Freedom. She wanted to sing with her joy.
"No longer than necessary," he said. "A fortnight at most. If something arises to detain me, I will send word."
Alice nodded. She knew better than to ask why he was going. If he wanted her to know, he would tell her.
She watched him stride to the door, his mantle

swinging out around him, his spurs clinking, his hand resting casually on the hilt of his sword. He reminded her, she thought, of her father and her brothers—worldly, lordly, proud, a warrior. She was not sure if this pleased her or displeased her. She supposed it did both. The latter because it put her in a position of continued impotence; she would never have power because he would usurp it all for himself, as the men of her family had. And the former because, as a powerful lord, he ensured her position as the lady of Aelfgar by ensuring his own position. One day, at least, their sons would come into their inheritance. This reminded Alice that truly she must bear him a legitimate heir—if only to keep her own place at Aelfgar.

He paused in the doorway, looking across the hall. Alice felt hatred for both him and her sister well up. She was brutalized by the image of her husband holding her sister last night, so gently it was unbelievable. And with this reminder, her instincts began shrieking renewed warnings. Ceidre was a grave threat to her no matter what Rolfe said. She sensed it. She knew it.

Rolfe grimly gave a lingering look at Ceidre's chamber. Alice could see that Ceidre slept still—and she could also see that her lord was waging an internal battle—which he won. He strode aggressively down the hall, and for a moment Alice remained, listening to the sound of his hard footsteps on the stairs. She seared her sleeping sister with a look, then hurried after her husband to see him off.

A dozen of his men were already mounted in the courtyard. They were all fully armed with sword, lance, mace, and shield. Pennants waved in the breeze from their lances. Their steeds stomped restlessly, blowing. All the soldiers wore leather-padded mail hauberks and chausses and helmuts. Alice shuddered. They were a frightening lot, and Ceidre and her brothers were fools for thinking the Saxons could even hope to win against these mounted soldiers.

Rolfe's horse waited, held by one of his men, kicking out at anyone whose shadow came too close. His ears were laid back, and his massive head bobbed in temper. The man holding him had to dodge his lethal hooves on more than one occasion. Rolfe paused on the steps, his black cape swinging about him. Its red underside reminded Alice of blood.

"My lord, there is something I would like to ask," Alice said softly.

His impatience showed, but he nodded.

" 'Tis time, I think, that Ceidre be wed. Mayhap to one of the villagers, or the reeve."

Other than the tensing of his jaw and the flashing of his eyes, Rolfe's face remained expressionless. Alice hurried on, laying a hand on his sleeve, her voice sympathetic and earnest. " 'Twould truly be better, my lord, for all of us."

"I will think on it," he said shortly.

"God speed you, my lord," Alice said politely.

"And you," Rolfe said. He turned abruptly and mounted the stallion, which even tried to kick out at its master. Rolfe hit the beast's neck hard with his open palm, and the animal quieted. The column moved out, Rolfe's own pennants, in black and red and royal blue, streaming behind him.

Alice lifted her gown and literally ran upstairs. As she had hoped, no maid had yet come to their chamber. She found her eating dagger and did not think twice, but cut her little finger. She dripped the blood onto the sheets. And smiled.

As an afterthought, she smeared blood between her thighs, then called for a bath.

The sheets could not be missed, but better yet, the maid who helped her to bathe would spread the news like a wildfire. The marriage had just been consummated.

Ceidre awoke with a strange feeling of remorse. She remembered the dream as if it were real—she could almost feel, still, his warm, hard body as he held her so tenderly, soothing her in her anguish. She did not want to awaken. She wanted to sleep—and continue to dream.

But she was not asleep in the heavy, velvet embrace of a magical night. She was awake. The sunlight was pouring through her window, and with it came ugly reality. Ceidre shifted onto her side, wincing as she tested newly forming scabs, evidence of that reality. You are a fool, she told herself. He would never be like that. He is an ogre and the enemy and he had you whipped. To dream of him is insane. And, she thought helplessly, unfair.

Because there was something so compelling about the dream.

She was hot. She realized she was sweating slightly and knew she had taken a low fever. You have him to thank for that, she reminded herself. Anything to escape the dream's clutches.

A maid was singing a wicked ditty in the great chamber as she did her duties there. Ceidre sighed and sat up, reaching for the urn of water. It was empty. She was so thirsty, so sore, so hot, and so tired. She fell back onto her stomach, head on her arms, trying to douse the remaining ashes of the dream. It had been so *real.*

She heard someone coming up the stairs but did not pay close attention. She drifted close to sleep again, wondering when her grandmother would come, wondering, foolishly, if *he* would come again. How dare he show his face here, she thought, as the two maids chattered, giggling, across the hall. One of them mentioned the Norman, giggling again, and Ceidre found herself listening despite herself.

" 'Tis a lusty one, he is, I've heard all the stories," Mary said.

"If he's so lusty, how come he hasn't touched none of us, not since he's come?" complained Beth. "Sweet Mary, that day at Kesop, I'll never forget—he was so strong . . ."

Ceidre had a graphic memory assault her, the Norman thrusting into Beth, his face dark and strained, his member red and slick and full.

" 'Twould insult Lady Alice," Mary said. "That's why he doesn't touch any of us now. But he will, in time."

" 'Twas a bigger insult, if you ask me, that he did not take her on their wedding night," Beth said. "If it were me, he would not have slept till dawn!"

Ceidre sat up. She shouldn't be eavesdropping. But she was. She could not believe what she was hearing—it could not be true. And if it were—why was her heart beating so rapidly? Why did she feel lighter? "Beth, Mary, come here," she called.

The two maids entered sheepishly, Mary holding a pile of linens in her arms.

"What are you talking about?"

They looked at the floor. "Nothing," Beth lied, blushing.

"Tell me the truth, 'tis most important—for Aelfgar. He did not bed Alice?"

Beth looked up. "He did not bed her until last night," she said, looking at the pile of linens.

Ceidre didn't really hear. She felt dismay and something else, worse, something sickening, and she stared at the sheets. While she had been in that foolish, soothing dream, he had been with Alice. Mary interpreted the look as a question and held them up, to show the bloodstain. Ceidre looked away. Why did it hurt now, when she didn't care? When she had thought it done with days ago, on their wedding night? She had no right to be hurting! None!

"Please bring me water," she said, lying back on her side. It was the fever, she was sure, why else would she be fighting accursed tears? "And Granny."

"You laggards," Alice said from the doorway. "Get going." She watched them race away, then paused to lean smugly against the wall. "You don't look well, Ceidre."

"Go away, Alice," Ceidre said wearily.

"Now I know why you spread your thighs for him, Ceidre," Alice purred. "It's good, isn't it, having that big thing inside you? Why, he's randy as a bull! I thought I wouldn't like it—but I found I loved it."

Ceidre imagined him rearing over Alice, powerful, his organ massive and ready, and shook away the image. She stared at the floor, her cheek on her arm. "Alice, I am not well. I have a fever. Would you send Granny to me and some water, please?"

"I won't have that witch in my house," Alice said vehemently. "But I will send you some water." She turned and left abruptly.

Ceidre wanted to call out and tell her she needed poultices from her grandmother or she would get an infection, but she did not have the strength. All she could do was shed a few lonely tears. And it was evening before the cup of water came.

CHAPTER 29

The stone of York gleamed diffused shades of tawny white. William was taking no chances; this time the castle would be stone and impenetrable. The wooden palisade surrounding the burned-out shell of the old timbered keep had been replaced with York's glinting pale stone. It was completely finished.

Rolfe and his men rode past the construction site. Most of York's villagers had been summoned to this task. Huge winches and pulleys were used to move the big blocks about on the site, but it was manpower that settled each block into its precise place. Oxen pulled sleds transporting the stone from the quarry. Activity was intense and constant, drays approaching with stone and supplies, serfs working the winches, men beneath the stone blocks, supporting them as they were raised or let down, knots of villagers shimmying blocks into place in the tower itself. Vendors hawked bread and pies, mutton and ale. Those too young to be enlisted in the royal effort ran barefoot, chasing one another, puppies on their heels. The first and ground story of the new tower had been nearly finished as well.

They had not wasted any time, and it was three days since he had left Aelfgar, a bright, hot late June afternoon. They rode through the city, because York, a trade center since the days of the Danes, had a wide thoroughfare. It sprawled right up against the moat and palisade of William's castle. Immediately their arrival began to be communicated by the housewives and aldermen, by the peddlers and beggars, by vendors and pickpockets, through every alley and doorway and window of York. Rolfe heard his own name roll off someone's lips in a hushed, awed excitement, not without a little fear, on more than one occasion.

William resided inside the palisade's walls, of course. The purple pennant bearing his crest was visible from outside those walls, floating high above the village on a pole. They rode across a drawbridge and into the inner bailey.

Rolfe left orders for his men and rode directly to William's tent. A page took his stallion, another announced him. William was closeted with Odo, his half brother and one of his most powerful nobles now that Odo had Dover, and the Bishop of York, a Saxon, Ealdred. It was common knowledge that Odo coveted this bishopric, and Rolfe was certain he would have it—sooner if not later.

William was clad, as usual for him when not in battle or afield, in a long cream-colored tunic and girdle, delicately embroidered in ivy green, a velvet purple mantle draping his broad shoulders. He was delighted to see Rolfe. "Get up, man," he cried when Rolfe went down immediately on one knee. "Up, rise, dispense with the formalities. Where is he? I wish to spit upon that treacherous swine!"

Rolfe rose. His gaze was unflinching. No messenger could have come swifter than he, and in truth, he had not wanted to subject one of his men to William's wrath. *Not when it was his fault.* "Morcar has escaped, Your Grace."

William, stared, just for an instant, and then he bellowed, cursing. He knocked over a table, venting a huge fury. Odo and Ealdred were standing. William turned on them. "Out, out," he shouted, his eyes bulging, his face above his beard red. "No, you stay," he roared at Odo when he too turned to leave. Ealdred ducked hastily outside.

William turned to Rolfe. "Explain yourself."

"He escaped during the wedding feast. By the time it was found out, 'twas too late. He is gone. I am at your disposal." Rolfe, expressionless, dropped again to one knee.

William shouted, cursed, and paced. Odo remained silent in the background. Finally he stopped in front of Rolfe, staring down at his bowed head. "I cannot believe this," he said, under control, his famous temper reined in with an iron hand. "You are my most trusted commander. How could this happen? Was it treason? Was your guard bribed to look the other way?"

Rolfe's insides tightened. He remained on one knee, head bowed. "My guard was taken ill. He left his post because of the malady and has been stripped of his duties. I deemed further chastisement unnecessary."

"Get up so I can look at you," William said, and when Rolfe did, he continued. "He was poisoned?"

"Yes."

"Damn." William punched his fist into his open palm. "These Saxon are a nest of vipers, but I will break them, yes I will!" He pierced Rolfe with his black gaze again. "I take it the perpetrator of this deed of treason has been found?"

Rolfe's heart leapt, then quieted. "Yes, Your Grace."

"I want the details," William said. "Are you reluctant?"

"No. 'Twas a serf. A woman. She gave my man the poison, then freed Morcar. She has been dealt with."

"Dealt with? You had better mean hanged!"

Rolfe met his gaze. He was pierced with something he could not name, something that felt like fear. And it was not for himself. Yet the moment had come, and he could not lie to his king. "She was flogged, Your Grace. She will not commit treason again."

William actually blinked. "Have you taken leave of your senses! This serf cost me the leader of the last rebellion—and she is merely whipped? What is the meaning of this, Rolfe?"

Now was the moment when he should reveal Ceidre's identity to his king. Rolfe stared back at William. There was nothing compromising in his look, or in his tone when he spoke, but nor was there a challenge. "My lord, she is a serf—*my serf.* You have never had cause to question me before. I have punished her. She is in my keeping, under guard. In my judgment hanging would have incited the inhabitants to further treason, therefore I exercised restraint. 'Twould also have incited the brothers, personal vengeance added to political rebellion. I believe I have acted wisely. Yet I know that Morcar's escape is, ultimately, my responsibility. I await whatever you deem just penalty for my failure." Rolfe held William's gaze and again dropped to one knee; then he looked down.

William stared at his bowed head, then paced away. He finally turned back. "Your duties as castellan of York are suspended. My sentence is light—because you I trust more than my own right arm. But know well, Rolfe, were you any other, I would strip you here and now of everything you possess. You may go."

Rolfe rose gracefully. He supposed he had gotten off lightly—but he was angry and using iron discipline not to let it show. He could barely believe what had just happened—that he had been relieved of the castellanship of York—and with it, half of his power. He had expected chastisement, but nothing of this magnitude. And it was all because of that witch, he thought furiously.

Everything was because of that witch.

For he had, in fact, in deed, betrayed his king. Had he also betrayed himself?

"Rolfe." William's smooth voice halted him just before he exited the tent. "Bring me their heads and you will have redeemed yourself."

Edwin paced.

Morcar, usually the volatile one, squatted by the campfire, poking it with a stick. He was not paying attention to what he was doing; he was regarding his brother. Edwin's strides were long, slow, and deliberate. He was deep in thought. Albie stood silently, half in the shadows of the woods, regarding both brothers.

It was a starry night deep in the fens, those wild borderlands between England and Wales. Two dozen men graced their camp, nestled in the crook of a timbered hillside. Many were sleeping, their snores a steady punctuation to the night. One played a flute, the sound lonely, nostalgic, melancholy. Occasionally hoarse laughter broke the low hum of whispered conversation.

Morcar rose, hands in the folds of his mantle. It was chill in the evening. He kicked a twig. Edwin turned to him. "I am going, Morcar," he said, low.

"You cannot! 'Tis too dangerous. By God, man, look what happened to me! My head was almost served up to that Bastard Conqueror on a silver plate!"

"I am going." There was only authority and resolution in Edwin's voice, and something else, something Morcar had never heard until recently, a tone he hated, and feared. Resignation.

"You are the thinker, the logical one. Surely you, of

all of us, know this to be insane!" Morcar protested, blue eyes flashing. He meant every passionate word.

"I cannot stay away," Edwin said wearily. " 'Tis my heart I am separated from."

A silence ensued. Edwin turned away, to stare up at the stars. Morcar watched his brother's back for a long while before he spoke again. "Wait yet a few more days, Ed. You still limp when fatigued or put to the test. If we go, you must be in full strength of limb."

Edwin almost smiled. "We? No, dear brother, I go with Albie, alone."

"No," Morcar said, warning in his voice. "We shall not be separated, nothing will keep me from following, I swear it. The Norman is a dangerous, deadly man, Ed, but the two of us together can prevail—if we must."

"I have no intention of locking horns with Rolfe the Relentless," Edwin said. The darkest of shadows flitted across his face. "Not yet."

"You cannot take him," Morcar said bluntly. "I am better with the sword than you, admit it, and he took me."

"I will take him," Edwin said slowly, his dark gaze steady. "When I must. Anyway"—he sighed—"this time 'tis moot. I go to spy."

"We go to spy."

Edwin gave in with a shrug of his broad shoulders. "It must be done. I must know, for myself, what passes, and if the rumors are true. By God, to think he's moved the village?" Edwin's voice rose in uncharacteristic temper. "He's moved *my* village?"

" 'Tis the Norman way, we've seen it time and again," Albie offered from the shadows of the trees.

"But when 'tis seen in one's own home, one's patrimony . . ." Edwin trailed off.

"What else does our network say, Albie?" Morcar

asked eagerly as the young man entered the glow cast by the firelight. His chausses and mantle were covered with dried mud, testimony to his hard riding earlier and his recent arrival at the camp.

"The marriage is done," Albie said, hesitating. "And he builds new fortifications in the Norman style."

Morcar cursed, Edwin grew grim. "Damn Alice," Morcar said vehemently. "She thinks nothing of betraying us!"

"How is Ceidre?" Edwin cut in.

"My lord, there is a terrible rumor . . ." Albie trailed off.

"Out with it," Edwin demanded.

"She is not hurt?" Morcar gasped.

"There is a rumor she was punished for your escape, Morcar. Flogged."

Morcar cried out in frustration and outrage, Edwin clenched his fists. " 'Tis only a rumor, and you know how a story can change through the telling of two dozen or more different tongues. Mayhap 'tis not true."

"Why did I not take her with me?" Morcar cried in anguish. "I did not think, I never think!"

"Do not blame yourself, we do not know if it is the truth," Edwin said, a hand on his brother's back. But his lips were curled into a feral line. "We need Ceidre where she is."

"There is another rumor," Albie offered. "But not a better one." Edwin's look made him continue. " 'Tis said the Norman openly lusts after Ceidre, his looks are so hot just to watch them is to get burned." Albie shrugged. "So mayhap he did not flog her."

"If he touches her!" Morcar shouted, enraged. Edwin restrained him, absorbing this before continuing. "And news of Hereward?"

"The Wake is planning a rebellion against Roger Montgomery. Near Shrewsbury or not, I do not know."

"Good," Edwin said. "We will go to Aelfgar, and after, we will meet with Hereward the Wake."

"What are you thinking?" Morcar demanded.

For the first time Edwin smiled. The sternness of his face was relieved, revealing handsome features and even white teeth. "I am thinking, brother, that in September we go to war. You, me, and Hereward the Wake."

CHAPTER 30

"Will she die?" Alice asked.

The maid, Mary, stood next to her in the solar as they stared at Ceidre's wet, trembling form on the bed. "I dunno," Mary whispered.

Alice clenched the cord of her girdle as if it were a rosary, worrying it continuously. She had denied Ceidre her grandmother—after all, she was a witch, and Alice was not about to have another witch in her home—and, enjoying her immense, newfound power, she had also denied her any further care. A sennight had passed. No one had been allowed into the room except Alice, not even Mary, who would gossip. Ceidre had shriveled up before her eyes, wasting away with fever. She had lost her temptress's beauty. She was a gaunt skeleton of her old self.

"Do you think she will die?" Alice demanded again impatiently.

Mary shifted nervously. "I think so," she squeaked. She had never been asked by her mistress for her opinion before and was afraid to give it.

Alice had always hoped Ceidre would die. In the beginning, a week ago, when she had locked Ceidre in with a bare minimum of water and nothing else, she had felt triumph. The witch would learn her place, she would suffer; and when Alice had realized a day later that her sister was ill, she had hoped that she would die. But now there was no feeling of triumph, just anxiety.

If Ceidre died, would she be blamed?

She thought of the Norman and tried to imagine what he would do. Her anxiety made her want to vomit. She had no doubts he would lock her in some shed and throw away the key—forever. After whipping her, of course. Alice vividly imagined herself under the lash, she could even feel its excruciating pain as it sliced open her delicate skin. She shuddered. Tears came to her eyes. It wasn't fair. Ceidre would die if left unattended, and it was what she deserved. But Alice would pay a price she could not afford and was afraid to face. Therefore, she would have to try to save her wretched sister. But what if she died anyway?

"Send for that old witch, Mary, and now. No." Alice grabbed her arm. "You get her yourself, tell her Ceidre is dying, make her bring all her potions. Quickly. Go!" Alice pushed her hard out the door.

She walked forward to stand over her shaking, fevered sister. She wished the Norman could see her now. He would feel no lust, only revulsion. It was a wonderful fantasy, but reality intruded. Lord Rolfe would punish her, Alice, if he saw Ceidre now, so Alice realized she had better pray that Ceidre make a fast recovery before he returned. There were other ways to get rid of her bastard sister; hadn't he said he would consider marrying her off? Maybe he would marry her to a Scot to secure his northern borders, and that would be the end of Ceidre. What a perfect idea!

Alice decided to go to the chapel. The whole village would know that she was praying for her sister's health. And she would make sure to pray every day.

Ceidre saw Death.

Death was not a leering, grotesque old man. Nor

was he the devil. Instead, she was sweet and beautiful and seductive, an enchantress offering peace ever after. The woman floated above her, around her, her ghostly flesh sweet and fragrant, her hair long and honey blond. She was perfectly formed too, and very beautiful. She smiled, and with her finger she beckoned.

Yes, Ceidre thought, I will go. I must, I cannot stay another moment in this living hell.

She hurt. Her entire body was in agony, as if crushed beneath stones. She was on fire. Throbbing. She needed water, but had none. A thought occurred —maybe she had died—maybe this was hell. Then she heard her sister's voice, asking if she would die, and she knew she was still alive.

She thought of the Norman, and anger raised its head. Death still beckoned, smiling serenely. "No," Ceidre tried to shout. "I cannot go yet. Go away!"

But she came closer, still smiling, so enchanting Ceidre wondered if she was a witch. Then she gasped, shocked. She realized that the woman beckoning her, floating so close, Death, was herself.

It could not be.

Ceidre reached out, to touch the womanly spirit in her exact image as it hovered nearby. Her other self, or Death, or whoever it was, reached for her, palm open, fingers spread. With horror, Ceidre realized Death wanted to touch her, to take her hand and lead her away from her earthly self. In confusion, she wondered if she were looking at her soul, about to depart this life.

"Come," Death crooned, her voice sweet and soft. "Come with me now."

Ceidre was panting and afraid. If her soul had left, then she was truly dead. An image of the Norman reared itself before her, his eyes hot and bright, his face hard and unyielding. "No," she shouted, dropping her hand, no longer tempted to touch the ghostly apparition. "Go away, I will not come, not yet. 'Tis too soon."

Death came closer.

Ceidre shrank away. But there was nowhere to go, and still the woman, her mirror image, approached. Ceidre knew she had lost, and she wept. When Death had put her face to hers, Ceidre closed her eyes for the end of all earthly time. Nothing happened. When she opened them, the eerie reflection of herself had gone.

And her grandmother smiled at her through thick tears. "Don't cry now, sweeting, 'twill be all right. You have come back, Ceidre, you have come back."

Ceidre fell back against the pillows, exhausted. She closed her eyes but gripped the flesh-and-blood hand of her granny, refusing to give it up. Had it been a dream? Or had she seen her own soul?

True to his word, Rolfe returned to Aelfgar within a fortnight of his departure.

The past sennight since he had faced William's wrath had cooled him down—barely. He could not forget that it was because of Ceidre he had lost York, it was because of Ceidre he had lied to his king and betrayed him. This doubled his repressed ire. 'Twould not happen again. If she had to be kept under constant guard, drain though it might his resources, as every manjack was valuable to him, 'twould be done. And he was determined to recoup his losses. He would bring King William Morcar, alive or dead. And in so doing, he would banish his own betrayal of his liege lord from all existence. He would rectify the great wrong he had committed.

The sight of his domain lifted his spirits and brought with it a rush of exhilaration. Work had continued on the new fortifications. The tower was finished, the village rebuilt, the walls of the bailey just begun. In another fortnight his fortifications would be completed and the transition to stone could be begun. He did not intend to waste a moment.

And if that witch knew where her brothers were hiding, he would find out.

He couldn't help it; he thought of her often, too often. It did not take much to make his manhood lift hard and high, just a thought, and this added to his temper. It was, he told himself, because he had not bedded a wench in a very long time, not since he had relieved himself with the peasant at Kesop. That was about to change too. His lack of desire around other women was ridiculous and annoying; if he had to force a different disposition upon himself, he would.

Lady Alice was waiting to greet him in the courtyard, making the foulness of his mood soar. He dismounted, turning to Guy. "Any problems?"

"No, my lord, and as you can see, everything has gone well."

"Well done," Rolfe said, placing his hand on Guy's shoulder. The younger man could not contain a grin. Rolfe turned to Alice. "My lady, you fare well?"

She curtseyed. "Yes, my lord. I have already ordered a bath and wine. Are you tired?" Her gaze searched his face.

"No, but I am in desperate need of a bath." He wondered where that witch was.

Rolfe followed Alice inside, glancing around. No sign of Ceidre. Good, she had better stay well out of his sight. In his chamber he stripped methodically with his wife's help. The steaming water felt good. A knock on the door did not raise his attention. Alice ordered in the maid, bearing cheese and bread and wine.

Rolfe stared at the maid. He had seen her around

before, of course, and vaguely recollected that he had fucked her at Kesop, but he had never really paid attention or looked at her closely. She was dark, plump, big-breasted, and comely. He eyed her wide hips. She caught his regard and threw him a sultry glance. Rolfe ignored it. So she was amenable, not that it mattered.

"This bread is stale," Alice said. "I will fetch more." She looked at Beth, who was gathering Rolfe's filthy garments. "Launder those immediately."

Beth murmured an affirmative, Alice skittered out. Rolfe was aware of her hasty departure, wondering why she was newly afraid of him. He could smell her unease, and the excuse to leave was poor—Alice was bossy enough to send the maid for more bread. The maid. She was slow to collect his things. He eyed her buttocks as she bent to retrieve his hose, big buttocks, fleshy and round. "Come here," he said.

She straightened and turned. She was smiling.

Rolfe was leaning back in the tub, waiting. She did not have to be asked twice, but strutted over, hips swinging, still carrying his clothes. Rolfe looked at the clothes and looked at the floor. She understood and dropped them. He handed her a sponge. She knelt beside him, glanced at him briefly, and began to soap his shoulder.

Rolfe's gaze was devoid of expression, but he looked at her full breasts. "Are you nursing?"

"Yes," she breathed.

Casually he reached out to cup her, her flesh full and heavy with her babe's milk. She went still. He leaned forward and took her nipple, through her tunic, in his mouth. He began to suck.

Beth gasped. She clutched his wet shoulders, shoving her bosom against his face. Rolfe released her, slightly disappointed. He was mildly aroused, he supposed, but only half hard, surely not capable of performing. Yet. The woman, he noticed, smelled sour, and it was unappealing. He refused to compare her to another—one who smelled of violets. "Tonight bathe as I am doing. Meet me in the stable after I sup."

Beth smiled, her face flushed, her gown wet, nipple distended. "Yes, my lord, gladly," she murmured. "Shall I finish your bath?"

He waved her away. Later would be soon enough.

CHAPTER 31

Something inside him quickened as he descended to take his supper, but he refused to pay it attention. It most certainly was not eagerness, nor anticipation. Still, he knew damn well she would be at his table, and he paused on the threshold of the hall, his gaze sweeping it and all its occupants.

Ceidre. She was already seated at the table's foot, where she normally dined. Her back was to him. His gut was so tight it ached, just from the real-life, flesh-and-blood presence of her, and he was angered at his response. At all of his responses, for now there was the tightening in his sac, the heavy weight, which had eluded him earlier with the maid. He strode to his place, Alice upon his heels, resolved to ignore her, and took his chair.

Everyone commenced eating at once. Rolfe had been ravenous, now he could barely get down his food. He found he could not fight himself; he looked down the table at her. Even from this distance, he noticed her pallor. In fact, he thought she looked smaller, defenseless, vulnerable. She did not look at him. Not once.

Of course, he thought, feeling ugly, like a bitten dog. She had hated him when he was merely the Norman enemy, now she would hate him more for the punishment he had inflicted upon her. He attacked his food. When he was done, but far from replete, Alice laid a hand on his arm.

Rolfe jerked his gaze to her, and at the look of contained wrath upon his face, Alice quickly let her palm slide to the table. "I am sorry," she said.

" 'Tis not you," he managed gruffly. He swore to himself that tonight, once and for all, he would get Ceidre out of his system, out of his thoughts, out of his damn life.

"My lord?"

He grunted, draining a cup of wine.

"Have you given any thought to the subject we discussed?"

He tossed a bone at the dogs. They descended upon it, snarling and fighting among themselves. "Which subject?"

"Marrying my sister," Alice said in her tiniest, most tentative voice.

The thought worsened his mood. "No." He closed the subject with his tone. In truth, he hadn't thought about it, not once. But now, now the idea taunted him. It was distasteful, repugnant. It was a solution.

He would not do it, and that was that. The decision made, he felt better, relieved. He would exorcise his lust for her in the usual way, with the maid, with any wench he happened to want. But marry her to another he would not do. Besides, she was dangerous, she needed to be kept close by, under his watchful eye. This last satisified him with its logic.

He rose abruptly. "Send Ceidre to me," he told Alice.

Her eyes widened. "You have something to discuss with her?"

He thought of her brothers and smiled grimly. "Aye." He walked over to the hearth and stared into its flames.

He felt her approach. Her presence was tangible, sweet. Exciting. His body was alive, wired. His breath was more rapid, even shallow. He was perspiring. From the heat of the fire, he told himself, and laughed. His cock had already reared itself up. He turned to face her.

He gasped.

For a moment he thought it was not her, but some haggard older relation. And then he realized it was her.

She colored at his horror, looking away. Her hands, thin and almost translucent now, clutched the folds of her gown.

Rolfe recovered. He touched her chin, gently, afraid that this shadow of the woman he had left behind might break, and turned her face up. She had lost a stone. Her face was gaunt, huge dark shadows beneath her violet eyes. He looked into their depths and was moved, for they were haunted, scarred, a tableau of pain and suffering. And still so very beautiful. She was thinner, she was pale, even her hair had lost its luster, but she was still beautiful, and this amazed him. "What happened?" he managed. His voice sounded raw.

"I was ill."

Guilt, horrific, incriminating guilt, overwhelmed him. He did not have to ask, but he did. "From the flogging?"

Her gaze, defiant, proud, alive, held his. "Yes."

"How are you now?"

"Fine. I know I do not look it, but I am." Her chin was raised. She dared him to say otherwise. Yet he could see that she was trembling.

"Are you with fever?"

She shook her head.

"You are shaking," he said, touching her shoulder.

She drew away from his touch, and he heard the sound of her suspended breath.

"I—I am fine."

She was afraid of him, or, at the least, as wary and apprehensive as a pup that had been kicked. But should it be otherwise? He was grim. Self-hatred welled. "I want you to rest. I want you to eat. I want you to eat six times a day. I want you to gain back your weight."

"Is that an order?" Despite the sarcasm, her voice quavered.

He would not, could not, be angry now. "Yes. In a sennight, Ceidre, I expect you to look as you did before I left. Is that clear?"

"Mayhap 'tis better now," Ceidre said frankly. Her gaze was steady. "You will not chase me now, and I do not have to run."

He smiled slightly, and let his glance dip to her bosom, which she had barely lost, if at all. On her slender frame it was more voluptuous than ever. "Shall we put this theory to the test?"

She folded her arms and backed away. "You would lust after a sick woman?"

His smile was fuller now. "You said you were not ill."

"You can see for yourself that I lied."

"So now we add liar to the label of traitor?"

"Why not? Husbands are also adulterers."

"Are you implying something?"

"Me? I speak only the truth."

"When it suits you, you speak the truth; when it suits, you lie. You are not constant, Ceidre," Rolfe purred.

"And when it suits, you bed your wife, and when it suits, you chase after me!" Ceidre flung back, her cheeks stained pink. Her eyes widened—at her audacity and bravery.

He closed his hand over her arm, but her courage thrilled him. "Stop. You are getting overwrought. You will be ill again."

"Do you care?" She was instantly horrified at her telltale bitter tone.

His jaw tightened. For a long moment he did not answer. Then he said abruptly, "The health and well-being of every serf on Aelfgar is my responsibility. As is yours. Where are you sleeping?"

"Lady Alice let me move in with my grandmother."

"I want you under this roof."

"The better to chase me?"

His gaze pinned her, and she shrank. "The better to guard you, Ceidre. You are a traitor, and my responsibility. I do not trust you, not as far as I can spit." And he thought of his loss of York—and his betrayal of his king.

The hall was empty, as he had ordered, except for Guy. Through the open front door Rolfe could see the comings and goings of his men and his serfs. It was a glorious day, hot, bright, the first of July. There did not seem to be a cloud in the sky. Inside, it was overly warm, and a thin film of sweat covered his skin beneath the lightest-weight undertunic he possessed.

Guy was aghast. Rolfe had informed him of his meeting with William and the punishment that had been meted out for Morcar's escape. " 'Tis unfair," he cried. "You have no cause to be treated like any other. You are his best man and he knows it!"

"William has never been one to play his favorites too heavily," Rolfe said, staring out the door again. He was waiting for Ceidre, whom he had summoned. Last night, in his distress, he had lost all his intention and desire to interrogate her. But that must be rectified. "I want her watched carefully now that she is up and about," he said.

Guy did not have to be told who "she" was. He hesitated.

"Spit it out," Rolfe said.

"My lord, I do not trust her. Mayhap she should be kept confined."

The thought was frankly distasteful. "She will not betray me again," he said, with confidence he did not feel. "Besides, I need her." He smiled at Guy's confusion. "If anyone will be in touch with her whoreson traitor brothers, 'twill be her."

Guy's eyes lighted with understanding.

Ceidre appeared in the doorway, the sun behind her, creating a halo, dimming her. Rolfe gestured her inside, away from the sunlight, and she came, warily. His chest tightened again at the mere sight of her, and from his physical response, he was reminded of yet another thing—how he had failed to exorcise his lust for her last night. In his agitation he had completely forgotten to rendezvous with the maid. Now she even holds me faithful, he thought, unamused.

Guy moved to leave. "Stay," Rolfe ordered, and smiled at Ceidre. Her eyes widened. He gestured at Alice's chair. "Sit."

She came forward, apprehensive now, and sat. He towered over her. "Where are your brothers, Ceidre?"

She blinked. "I don't know."

"Do not lie. I am your lord, and I am demanding this information. Where are they?"

"I do not know," she said, lips set mulishly.

He reached out and touched her cheek, the stroke soft, gentle—frightening. "Because of your treachery I have lost York. And because of you I will regain it.

Nothing will stop me from finding Morcar and returning him to the king. Do you understand?"

She was angry, her eyes were almost black, burning. "If you think I will help you, you are wrong!"

"I am considering a marriage for you," Rolfe said expressionlessly.

She gasped.

It was a lie, but he knew she would cherish her independence, and he would lie now to get what he wanted. "If you please me, I might reconsider. If you do not please me, I will choose you a groom—today. And he will not be averse to beating the truth out of you, as I am. He will most likely be a common sort, eager to please his new lord, and he will not let his wife defy him. Do you understand?"

"You wouldn't."

"Oh, I would," he said softly.

Ceidre gazed at her hands, folded in her lap. "I truly do not know where they are, except that they are in the fens," she said at last, looking up. Tears glimmered, hanging heavily on her lashes.

Rolfe knew she told the truth; he could see it in her eyes. He felt remorse for his bullying, yet swept it away. "Very well," he said. She had told him nothing he did not already know.

"Please, my lord," Ceidre said hesitantly.

He waited.

"Do not make me marry."

"I will think on it," he said gruffly. Summoning Guy, he turned and walked out.

CHAPTER 32

Ceidre stared hard at the royal messenger.

A week had passed since that abrupt interview. Every morning Ceidre had awakened with dread that Rolfe would summon her to him again, this time divulging the identity of a groom and stating his intention to see her wed. She knew, if he chose to do so, there was nothing she could do to prevent it. She was afraid.

Yet the summons did not come. Instead, life crept lazily along. Most of the inhabitants of the manor were moved into the new keep, herself included. The manor, now enclosed in the bailey, served as another hall where the excess of Rolfe's men and servants could sleep. The Norman tower was hot and airless, and Ceidre hated it. The ground floor was used for storage, the first as the hall. On the top story were the lord and lady's chamber, as well as a solar and antechamber. Ceidre slept in the great hall, below Rolfe and Alice, with Guy ever present and nearby.

She had been given nothing to do since Rolfe's return. She spent most of her time with her grandmother, in the village, away from him and his new, monstrously ugly building. She gained back all the weight she had lost, maybe a touch more. She felt strong again, and her near brush with death was almost, but not quite, reduced to the memory of a bad dream.

Ceidre just happened to be in the great hall fetching a clean undertunic from her pallet, carefully rolled up and shoved into a far corner. It was dark in the cavernous hall, darker still in its corners, and she froze when Rolfe and another man, dressed for travel, entered. Blinking in the dim light, it took her only a second to see that he was a royal messenger.

She stared at him.

Rolfe shouted for wine and refreshments and the two men sat carelessly at the long trestle table. Rolfe leaned back in his chair, unaware of her presence, as Mary came in with bread, cheese, pies, ale, and wine. The messenger began to eat ravenously, draining first one cup of wine, then another.

Ceidre hunched closer into herself.

"I am in no rush," Rolfe said. "There is no need to act the wolf."

"I rode hard, my lord," the messenger responded, mouth full. "The king's orders." With a greasy hand, the messenger extracted a scroll and shoved it at Rolfe.

Rolfe took it but did not open it. He toyed with the string without untying it. "What news at York?"

"Two Danish vessels were spotted just off the coast," the messenger mumbled. "Another invasion was feared. Yet they went right past. 'Twas most strange."

Rolfe said nothing.

"The king is pleased with the rebuilding of the castle and has named Odo's bastard, Jean, castellan. Scots raided Lareby and burned the village to the ground. Odo took a royal force and repelled them, chasing them far into Cumbria. That is all," he finished, reaching for a pie.

Ceidre's heart was pounding. The missive, the missive, she prayed. If only they would discuss it. She was afraid to move. She had already spied for too long; it was too late to make herself known. If she was caught now, she would truly be in jeopardy.

"Where are the Danes now?" Rolfe asked.

"Gone south."

Lazily Rolfe poured himself a cup of wine and sipped it.

"Oh, William has stated that he intends to crush these rebels by this winter. He will not pass Christmas at York, he intends to be at Westminster."

Rolfe smiled slightly, a mere curling up of the corners of his mouth.

At this precise moment, something furry and alive scampered across Ceidre's bare foot. Ceidre was not afraid of rats, just cautious, for their bites were poison. But she was listening so intently that she was taken by surprise, and she gasped.

Rolfe was standing, piercing her with his gaze.

Blushing, Ceidre got to her feet, clutching the clean undertunic. She could not look away from him.

Now he truly smiled. "Come here, Ceidre," he said quite amiably.

"I just came to get another tunic," she mumbled hastily. "I—I did not want to disturb you."

He was still smiling. "Come, Ceidre." His gesture was expansive.

She came forward, out of the gloom of the corner, until she was an arm's length from him. Her heart beat wildly, he was unruffled and calm. "Sit," he said.

Her gaze widened. He pulled out Alice's chair, and with a hand on her shoulder, she found herself sitting beside him. He casually draped his big frame back in his own chair. The messenger finished his pie, rubbed his hands together, and burped. "My lady," he said.

"She is not my lady," Rolfe drawled. "She is Lady Alice's sister." Then he proceeded to ask the messenger about his journey, about the villages he had passed through, the attitude of the villagers, the state of their harvest, the conditions of the road. Ceidre stared at the scroll, so near Rolfe's hand. They discussed the weather. They discussed Hugh of Bramber, who was wedding a Saxon heiress. They discussed everything but the royal missive.

Ceidre sat very still, so as not to draw attention to herself, wondering what he was doing, why he had told her to sit, and trying not to look at the scroll. Her gaze kept wandering back to it, and Rolfe's hand, relaxed on the table, a centimeter from the missive.

"I do not begrudge Hugh Bramber," Rolfe finally said. "He is a good man, and he will secure his fiefdom well."

"Yes, my lord," the messenger said agreeably.

Rolfe reached for the scroll. He finally glanced at Ceidre, who felt herself flush. Then, to the messenger, he said, "You may go."

The man bowed and left, swaggering away. The effect was ruined when he broke wind, loudly. Rolfe toyed with the scroll, and Ceidre tore her gaze from it again, with increasing difficulty. She was perspiring. He was playing with her, wasn't he? She lifted her eyes to his. He was regarding her steadily, casually. Was there the hint of amusement in that cool blue gaze?

"Do you read, Ceidre?"

She could not believe her good fortune; she almost choked on it. "Y-yes."

His head inclined slightly. " 'Tis most unusual for a man, much less a woman."

"Yes."

"But then, you are most unusual, are you not?"

She stared into his gaze. Was he referring to her evil

eye? What did he want? He smiled, once, and began unrolling the scroll. Her heart sank when he held it up and perused it. Then he lowered it. "I do not read. Read it to me."

Her heart stopped, then began racing again. Her hands trembled as she took the scroll. She dared not look at him. "First," she said huskily, and coughed to clear her throat, "there are greetings from William. It says"—and her heart sank—"that a spy has been caught, a spy of—of my brothers."

"Continue."

"Another rebellion is planned, but the spy did not know when, or where. Maybe it will be soon. This is an alert." She rerolled the scroll nervously. Her mind was racing. Who had been caught? Was Edwin truly planning another uprising—this soon? It was too soon! The Normans would be waiting now. She had to warn them!

She realized he was watching her intently. She blushed again, handing him his missive. He stuck it into the flame of a candle, setting it on fire. Rolfe held the scroll aloft, studying it as it burned. His face was impassive. But his mind was not.

The bait had been taken; the trap was set.

Teddy's father was her uncle, her mother's brother, Feldric. He was a dozen years older than Ceidre, and widowed. Teddy was his youngest, at fourteen. It was a few minutes later, and Ceidre was no longer feigning nonchalance, as she had when she strolled into the village with one of Rolfe's men trailing after her. Feldric was stacking bushels of wood. "I cannot," he said.

"Oh, you must, I beg you! Think about Annie!" Ceidre cried, referring to her mother.

"That is not fair," Feldric said, pausing, a hand in his gray hair.

"What has happened to my brothers is not fair," she shot back. "Feldric, we must warn them that the Normans are aware of their plans! We must! I know you can find them. Look," she said urgently. "I would go if I could, but that brute outside guards me every minute of every day. Tonight you can slip away, Feldric. Once you are in the fens, as a Saxon, you will find them instantly. Please."

He sighed. "All right," he said. "I will do my best. But if I cannot find them in a fortnight, I am returning, and that is that."

"Thank you," Ceidre said, meaning it. "Thank you."

That night Feldric left, on foot.

Beltain followed.

CHAPTER 33

Ceidre awoke the next morning with a strange, eerie feeling of anticipation. Mingled with this was worry, over what she had discovered the day before, and elation—she had sent her own messenger to find her brothers. She was finally doing something to aid Edwin and Morcar, and the taste of her activity was sweet. It was also heightened by a personal victory—she had fooled the Norman. She had actually succeeded in outwitting him!

His eyes stroked her lazily during the noonday meal. Ceidre felt as if her guilt showed, as if he could read it —she could not meet his gaze. Then she chastised herself, for there was no guilt to feel—it was her duty to abet her brothers, her duty to fight the Norman. But it was guilt she felt, or something suspiciously like it.

Beth nearly dropped a trencher on her lap, in the process whispering in Ceidre's ear to meet her in the kitchens as soon as she could. Ceidre was surprised, but hid it. She knew Beth, of course, but she was not exactly a friend. That Beth would relay such a message thoroughly aroused her curiosity, and her hopes.

She sought her out after the meal, when the Norman and his men had ridden out hunting. An ever-present shadow followed her—one of the Normans whose name she did not even know. The shadow occupied herself with ogling Beth and smirking a stone's throw from them. "What is this about?"

Beth's face was flushed with excitement. "I have seen Morcar," she whispered, looking hastily around.

Ceidre's heart stopped, then sped on. Now she understood Beth's flush, for Morcar had tumbled her many times and Beth, like all women, was half in love with the rake. "Where?"

"Your grandmother's."

Ceidre could not believe it. She gaped, and then she turned to go, only to realize her shadow awaited her. "Damn!"

"I will take care of him," Beth assured her. "Oh, Ceidre, if only they would throw this Norman out on his knees!"

So much, Ceidre thought, for Beth's attraction to her lord. Ceidre paced the kitchen impatiently while Beth strutted over to her man, apparently named Roger, and began a blatant seduction. Roger was no fool, but he was also not equal to withstanding Beth's unfair tactics. Bluntly she delved into his trousers. He gasped. As Ceidre hurried past, Beth lowered her head to his full, naked organ.

I owe her, Ceidre thought, glancing around her, trying to be casual. She wanted to run, she wanted to shriek—with joy, and anger. He is a fool, she thought, furious, for coming again. Only Morcar would dare to come into the village, right under the Norman's nose! Ceidre rehearsed a vehement speech and flung open the door to her granny's. The old lady sat at the table with not one man, but two.

Ceidre closed the door and stared.

Edwin stood, with a slight smile.

He was so handsome. So strong, and tears of joy came to her eyes. He opened his arms, she rushed into them. He held her and rocked her. Ceidre clung, sniffing. Since her father had died, Edwin had taken that place, if possible, because he was the exact image of Aelfgar, within and without. "I cannot believe you have come, all the way to the village!"

"Hush," he said, a finger on her lips. "Do you not greet your wild brother?"

Ceidre smiled and turned to embrace Morcar. He held her apart. "Are you all right? Is it true? I heard—"

A gesture from Edwin interrupted his worried questions. "We have time." He looked at Ceidre. "Truly, I did not intend to come this far, but when the Norman rode out with half his men, I could not resist."

"He is hunting. He will not be back until late today, maybe tonight."

Edwin's gaze searched her. "Are you all right, Ceidre?"

"Yes." She suddenly remembered everything. "Ed, I just sent Feldric to find you!" And she quickly filled him in on the royal missive of the day before.

Edwin paced thoughtfully, Morcar fretted. "It must be John," he said. "He has not been seen in a sennight."

Ceidre spoke up. "Mayhap I should know where you are, to be able to—"

"No," Edwin said, his tone a whip's lash. "What you did was right. A true Saxon can find us, just as the Normans can't. It will take Feldric time, but he would, eventually, passing through many tests, reach us. I do not want you endangered, Ceidre."

She nodded, thinking of the Norman's threat to find her a husband if she displeased him. "You will postpone whatever you are planning now?"

Edwin looked at her, then shook his head.

"Oh, Ed, please! 'Tis too dangerous!"

"We are not afraid," Morcar spat out.

"The timing will be right, Ceidre," Edwin said. "Trust me." He smiled, becoming incredibly handsome. "As you trusted Father."

"I do," she said softly.

Morcar, as ever, was impatient. "Ceidre, were you hurt after I escaped? And is it true that the Norman lusts after you?"

Ceidre flushed at the last question. "I am fine."

"Is that an answer?" Edwin asked.

She could not lie. Never, to her brothers. "He had me flogged. But 'tis finished now."

"Damn him!" Morcar cried furiously. "I'll kill him!"

"You are very brave, are you not?" Edwin said quietly, watching her.

Tears came to her eyes. "You would have been proud. I did not beg for mercy, I did not cry out."

"I am proud," Edwin said. "Will you help me, Ceidre? At great risk to yourself?"

"You know I will."

"Good." He smiled. "Continue to spy. What you've done is good. But now that I am planning a new rebellion, I need information. I cannot wait for it to fall into your lap, or mine. I must have it."

Ceidre waited expectantly.

"Has he touched you, Ceidre?"

It took her a second to understand this abrupt change of topic, and when she did, she flushed and looked away.

"I see he has," Edwin said. Morcar leapt up, swearing to castrate him. Edwin told him to be quiet. He lifted her chin, gazing into her eyes. "Are you still a maiden, Ceidre?"

She was beet-red. "Yes."

"He does not fear you like the others. Is this true?"

"Yes."

"The gossip is he wants you badly."

It was a question. "I—I think so."

He released her chin to pace away, then turned back. "He is very handsome."

Ceidre's eyes went wide. An inkling began, and it horrified her. "Ed?"

"Ceidre, you can have power over him if you are careful and certain. The power of a woman over a man."

Morcar gasped, Ceidre stared.

Edwin's voice was low, steady. "I do not ask this of you lightly. If you cannot bear his touch, or will not, I understand. But I have thought long and hard, Ceidre. What is one maidenhead in the course of this war?"

She was stunned, she was devastated. Tears came to her eyes. He was asking her to give herself to the Norman, to be a sacrifice. Edwin, her brother, her god.

"If you become his leman, Ceidre, willingly, cleverly, you can have access to his innermost secrets."

"I can't believe you'd ask this of her," Morcar said furiously.

When Edwin looked at him, it was with resignation and something else, something tortured in the window of his soul. "I did not order it and I do not ask it lightly, and if I could give what she could, if the Norman wanted me . . ." He trailed off. Then his voice was strong. "For Aelfgar I would sacrifice my body."

Edwin was asking her to give herself to the Norman. To let him use her body, to become his mistress. The thought was an echo, laced with despair and hurt. Ceidre tried not to cry. Why was she so crushed? This was war. Her life, her virginity, was insignificant. What was significant was Aelfgar, her brother's patrimony, the liberation of Mercia, the defeat of the Normans. Oh, Sweet Saint Cuthbert, she had no choice. "I will do it, Ed."

He did not smile. "I knew you would."

Her mouth trembled, tears spilled onto her lower lashes. "But, Ed," she said, "what if he really doesn't want me?"

"Then you will lose nothing," he said.

CHAPTER 34

Where did one begin a seduction of one's enemy?

Ceidre was curled up on her pallet, unable to sleep, debating this topic, when Rolfe and his men returned from their afternoon's sport. Periodically, her eyes would burn and tear, and her heart would swell with pain. She shoved such despondency down, the best she could. She trusted Edwin, she always had. She wanted to help him. She was being a silly goose to overreact to his suggestion this way.

She felt betrayed.

And nothing would make the sick feeling go away.

Rolfe's men were a noisy lot, but Ceidre attempted to ignore them as they stomped in, demanding food and wine. Rolfe's own voice could be heard, and he sounded well pleased. Ceidre rolled onto her side to face the crew, attempting to find the bane of her thoughts, the target of her new ambitions. He was warming himself by the hearth. His profile was to her, proud, perfectly molded. Ed was right—he was handsome. His hair glimmered molten gold in the firelight. Alice handed him a cup of wine, which he drained effortlessly. Then she said something, and Rolfe smiled one of his rare smiles. It was like a sunburst. As if suddenly feeling her gaze, he turned to look directly at her.

She could not begin now, it was too soon. Ceidre

abruptly dropped her regard and rolled onto her other side, her back to him. Despair welled again. Despair, and hurt.

She was not a seductress. She did not even know where to start. Hadn't she failed miserably with the first royal messenger? And although, prior to Edwin's proposal, she had known the Norman wanted her, now she was filled with doubt and dread. What if it was just a game? What if his lust for her was a figment of her imagination? What if, at the last moment, he was suddenly repelled by her eye as most other men were? What if he rejected her?

And she had the horrifying thought that if her plans did succeed, if he came to her bed and took her, she would weep as he used her body, betraying them all.

Her sleep was riddled with a melange of half-waking dreams.

She was the seductress. She walked past him in a thin undertunic. They were in a meadow, his gaze smoldered and burned. Ceidre felt powerful; she laughed. She danced for him. Whirling and whirling, her skirt lifting about her legs. And all the while he watched. . . .

She had taken off her clothes. Stark naked, she walked to him. He waited with that hot gaze. Ceidre did not feel fear, and she did not feel despondency. She felt exhilaration.

She was very close when he started laughing.

He laughed and laughed. Ceidre froze, confused. Then she understood—he was laughing *at her.* He did not want her, and she had been a fool to think he did. No man wanted her. Alice appeared, also laughing. "Witch," she shrilled. "Witch! He is mine!" Alice embraced Rolfe, who was still laughing. Ceidre wanted to disappear, to die. This couldn't be happening. . . .

"Witches are whipped," Rolfe said.

"A hundred lashes," Alice said, sneering.

Ceidre tried to beg for mercy but she found, to her horror, that she had no voice. And then she felt the lash, the brutal pain of the whip, and she screamed. She sobbed. Alice's taunts echoed. Rolfe was still laughing, because he thought she was funny—he did not want her.

Then someone held her, soothing her, the flogging over. It was incongruous, it didn't make sense, but she knew it was Rolfe. "Shh," he said, like a father to a babe. "Shh."

Ceidre woke up, her face still wet with tears. The men were all rousing, the dogs yapping. She lay very still, her heart pounding. She could remember every vivid detail of the dream. It was worse than her worst nightmare, the one she'd had recently, of the flogging. This one . . . She shuddered. She was a fool. It was only a dream. But it had been so real.

'Twas only a dream, she told herself sternly. And you know he wants you. And if he doesn't, if he rejects you, you have suffered rejection before, 'twill be no worse than the other times—and you will be spared,

She could not delay what must be inevitable.

No fool, Ceidre, knew she must be subtle, maybe resist him a little even as she flaunted herself. Details of the dream reared themselves again, and angry, she swept them away from her mind. She must be strong, and brave. She got up and hurried outside to wash her face and throat, her arms and chest. An idea struck her, owing to the persistence of her shadow, this one a very young man, really a boy, named Wilfred.

Usually, when free to do as she pleased, Ceidre performed her ablutions in a nook of the creek that ran through the village, one just outside town and shielded by the forest. This had no longer been possible, not since the Norman's possession of Aelfgar, for she was afraid of his men. She would beg Rolfe to let her bathe without her guard. He, of course, would refuse—and she would very subtly suggest that he be the one to accompany her. Ceidre felt a touch of fear-laced excitement. She would order him to turn his back, then she would strip completely. In no time, she was sure, she would be his mistress. 'Tis better to get this over with, she told herself, her heart pounding. It would be a while before he trusted her enough to start revealing information to her, as it was.

The only thing she worried about was if her plan lacked subtlety. Well, she supposed, she would soon find out.

But sooner would have to be later, Ceidre discovered as she approached the keep, for the Norman was already mounting up with a handful of his men. He twisted abruptly, and Ceidre realized she was staring. Just in time she caught herself from a reflexive response to look away and held his gaze boldly.

His eyes widened, surprise crossed his face. Ceidre held his gaze and watched the surprise gleam and transform itself into something bright, burning. Her stomach actually did somersaults. In fact, beneath his now openly smoldering regard, her entire body tightened and she felt breathless. I am not being subtle, she managed to think, and she tore her gaze away.

She was blushing, and she thought to escape within the keep. She was almost at the outside stairs when he rode her down, his big horse practically brushing her back. Ceidre leapt and backed away nervously, but he moved the stallion in closer, until her spine was at the wall. He leaned down, smiling ruthlessly, with those hot blue eyes. "An invitation like that must be answered," he murmured.

Her heart was leaping into her throat. " 'Twas not

an invitation," she squeaked, only too late realizing she should be thinking, planning, seducing, but most definitely not denying his words.

"No?" He grinned, still boxing her in. His knee almost touched her breast. "Be careful with those looks, Ceidre. This thing between us is no game."

"I—I was only . . ." She trailed off. His leg was disconcerting her as it pressed into the fullness of her breast. He was disconcerting her, with his handsome face, his predatory smile, his bright, bold eyes.

"Yes?" His grinned openly, apparently enjoying himself. "Perhaps you were admiring my form," he suggested.

She saw the opening and seized it. "You know," she flung back, feeling in control now, "that the women eye you often. You like it."

"I like it when *you* eye me," he corrected lazily. His horse shifted. By accident? His knee caressed her breast. Her nipples were hard and tight, and Ceidre looked down to see that they were quite evident. She felt color rising.

"I am human, remember," she mumbled, "no witch, as you know, just flesh-and-blood woman."

"You do not have to remind me," he said softly, leaning down again. His finger touched her cheek. It trailed to her throat. His gaze dipped lower, blatantly assessing her bosom. Ceidre was almost strangled with something nameless, or something she refused to name. She knew well, from memory, how his hands felt on her breasts, and she wondered if he would touch her there now. She wanted him to.

Of course he wouldn't, they were in public, surrounded by his men. He shifted his horse backward, putting distance between them. His smile was twisted now, like the dog denied the bone. His glance now was just as derisive, and insolent. He turned abruptly and with an arm raised, to command his men to follow, he rode down the motte and through the raised portcullis.

Ceidre folded her arms tightly about her. Slowly, as the fog of wanting that his presence had generated lifted, coherent thought returned. He wanted her, it was no wish, but clear and true. She would be able to carry out this seduction easily, very easily. Why, then, was there this choking feeling in her heart?

She turned to go up the steps into the keep. It was then that she saw Alice, on the top step, staring down at her, her face flushed and pinched. Alice. A factor she had not considered. In fact, she had forgotten completely about her.

CHAPTER 35

What game, he mused, was this?

Rolfe leaned back in his chair, replete with his noonday meal, staring at the bronze-haired wench below him. Throughout the meal she had cast brazen glances at him. Brazen, that is, for Ceidre. Because there was a vulnerability contained in them, an element of shyness, that, no matter how hard she tried to be bold, she fell short of the mark. If he were not so hot for her he would be amused. But he was hot. Uncomfortably so, his groin swollen and thick. He had adjusted his hose many times. Why, now, after all the fear, the wariness, and the anger, was she attempting to be so bold?

What did she want?

Should he test her, see how far she would go?

Or was he wrong? Mayhap it wasn't a game. He knew she fought her desire for him. Perhaps finally, she was as smitten as he, the urges unbearable, and she was succumbing to them. Perhaps now, with the passage of time, she had forgiven him all his trespasses and saw him only as a man. He struggled not to give in to heady elation, to be cautious, wary, and cynical. It was impossible not to be thrilled.

He had not forgotten his vows. If she continued, with mere looks, half shy, half bold, to provoke him, he would become undone, forsaking his vows, and enter a near-incestuous relationship. Rolfe's mouth pursed grimly.

He tore his gaze away from her, and to distract himself, he tuned in to the conversation between Guy and Athelstan. They were discussing the Scots, ever a problem in these far northern lands. William may have chased a clan of Campbells far into Cumbria, but reports had come in of raids upon his own lands, near the lonely village of Eoshire on the coast. Campbells again, Rolfe thought, from Tantalon.

"A few sheep today, a dozen tomorrow," Guy said vehemently. "But they do not know my lord. He will chase them into their rotten sea!"

Athelstan smiled, as Rolfe would have if not so agonized, at Guy's passion. "The Scots are wily, the Campbells the most of all. The best way is to make an alliance. Although they can't be trusted to hold the peace for long, 'tis a respite."

Alice's voice surprised everyone into absolute attention, even Rolfe. "Mayhap," she said slowly, "if it were the right alliance, things would not become undone so quickly."

Rolfe was amused. "What do you know of these things, my lady?"

She regarded him levelly, her big brown eyes wide, innocent. "I have lived in these harsh lands my entire life. Did you not know my father, the old eoarl, actually considered marrying me to one of them? To a Scot?" Her pitch was higher. "For peace, you understand. But I begged him to reconsider, and he did."

"Marriage is the best and surest way to cement relations," Guy said earnestly.

Rolfe chuckled. "What know you of marriage, Guy?"

The young man colored. "I know facts, my lord. Had William not changed his mind and married his daughter Isolda to Edwin of Mercia, you think there wouldn't be harmonious, aye, sweet relations betwixst Saxon and Norman now?"

"William would have been twice the fool to give that man so much power," Rolfe answered. "Even though, I recall, Isolda dared to beg him not to change his mind."

"Well," Alice said, "in this case the participants lie closer to home. Do you know the Scot my father approached rejected me?"

Rolfe looked at her, wondering what she was leading up to and not doubting that she was angling purposefully somewhere. Otherwise she would not flaunt a rejection, and never before had he heard her profess the least interest in politics or warfare. He raised a brow, to show interest.

Alice smiled, gazing at him squarely, despite the lie she was making. "He wanted Ceidre, and of course"—she could not keep bitterness out of her tone—"my father would not even consider it."

Rolfe smiled, without pleasure; now he understood. "You think, Lady, he might still want your sister?" His tone was impassive.

"Yes," Alice said, too quickly.

"My lord," Guy said, "excuse me, but what a grand match for our sakes!"

Anger, furious and boiling, bubbled up in him. But all he said, so coolly, was "Perhaps."

And he thought, I am a fool. I should marry her off to a Scot, secure my borders, maybe, and never lay eyes on the witch again. He imagined, graphically, some big redheaded Scot driving himself into Ceidre, and knew he would not do it.

Alice sat back, turning her face down to hide her smile. Rolfe did not miss it. He abruptly launched himself out of his chair and through the hall. A soft hand on his elbow, behind him, stopped him. "My lord?" Ceidre asked.

He was stunned that she had touched him. She clasped her hands now, twisting them, trying to meet his gaze and failing. He had heard the note of nervousness. "You wish a word with me?" he asked, trying to contain feelings, ripe ones, suspiciously heartfelt ones.

"Please, yes." She bravely glanced at him again.

Was this a game or not? he wondered, and he, usually so decisive, could not decide. He gestured her to walk with him, and they strolled outside and down the broad wooden steps into the inner bailey. "Well?"

Ceidre flung a glance behind her. At first Rolfe thought it was to see who was nearby, then he realized she was making him aware of Wilfred, her guard. He began to understand; in fact, he suddenly knew why she had been so bold all day. She wanted him to cease his constant vigil of her. Rolfe smiled tightly.

"My lord, I beg a boon," she said, confirming his suspicions.

He folded his arms and waited.

"Ever since I was a little girl," Ceidre said, "there is this place I go." She peeked at him. "To bathe."

He said nothing, confused but infinitely patient, waiting for her to reveal herself.

"In the creek," she blurted. "In a hidden spot. But since you have come, I have been afraid to do so, because of your men. I am most dirty. I want to go there, but how can I with this oaf you have set on me, day and night? Please, free me for an hour. What harm can I do in an hour?"

He imagined her naked, hip deep in the creek, her breasts full and gleaming. "You are a traitor, Ceidre," he said quietly. "You have what you deserve."

She swallowed. "If I go, with him"—she pointed at Wilfred—"he will rape me!"

"Come here, Will," Rolfe said. When the young man had, he said, "Ceidre is going to bathe in the creek. You are to guard her, as usual, but you will turn your back. You are not to look. She has ten minutes to do what she may. If you touch her, the penalty is death, by my own sword" He looked at Ceidre. "You have nothing to fear." Still, he waited.

Her face paled. "You—you are sure?" she croaked.

"Very sure. Of course," he said coolly, "you can order a bath in the antechamber upstairs, if you wish."

Her nostrils flared, her purple eyes darkened. "I want to bathe in the creek," she said angrily. "I want to swim and frolic, I want to have fun."

So now she wanted to swim, which was entirely different from bathing. "Ten minutes," Rolfe said. "You may frolic to your heart's contentment for ten minutes."

A silence ensued. She was upset, he could see it. Why?

He seriously doubted this was about a swim or a bath in the creek. She was up to more mischief, or she was testing him, he wasn't sure which. He had let her send Feldric to her brothers, because he wanted to be led to their lair, to locate it so he could capture them. Yet he was determined to prevent *her* from committing treason again, at all costs. For what punishment would he have to administer this time? Therefore, the guard remained. Did she hope to go to the creek to rendezvous with some Saxon traitor? Or did she think to entice him, seduce him, with this "bath" of hers? Was this a ploy to get him to follow her—right into the jaws of a trap?

"I do not trust him," Ceidre finally said, referring to Wilfred.

How far would she go? If she truly wanted to bathe, and only to bathe, she would give it up. "Then do not swim, or bathe, or whichever it is you want to do."

Surprisingly, a moistness entered her eyes. "You—you do not—you do not want to . . ."

"I do not want what?"

There was actually a tear on her lash. He had the urge to take it away with his fingertip. "You I would trust," she said, so low he thought he had misheard.

"What?"

"You I would trust." She wasn't looking at him, she was regarding her hands, worrying the folds of her gown.

She wanted him to go with her to the creek, where she would bathe. His ears were actually ringing. Seduction or entrapment? "You want me to guard you while you shed your clothes and bathe naked?"

"N-no, I mean, y-yes."

He caught her chin in his calloused grip, lifting it. "What game is this?" he demanded, even as he knew he should test her by playing the game to the end. He should follow her to the creek. His temple throbbed visibly. Would she dare to commit treason again? Would she?

"No game," she whimpered, shrinking.

He was hurting her, hurting her because he wanted to go with her, wanted to watch her, wanted to take her . . . while she was most likely playing at treason again. "Do you think to seduce me?" he growled, easing his grip.

"N-no."

"Do you want me, Ceidre?" he purred, dangerously.

"No! Yes! Stop!" Tears spilled onto her cheeks.

"Which is it?"

"Let me alone, leave me be!" she cried.

He released her. His heart was pounding. She was up to something, he doubted she merely lusted for him, knew he could not be so lucky. He was furious. Enraged because of her invitation, her probable motivation. "Go," he choked. "Go now. Will is your guard. Bathe or not, I do not care." He strode away. Later he would find out what she had done. He would not follow her into the jaws of a trap and thus catch her at treason, again.

Ceidre tried not to cry, because Will was just a few paces behind her. Under the shade of an apple tree in the orchard, she regained her shattered composure. The plan had been awful, and she, she was the worst seductress in the world. She was humiliated. She was hurt. And . . . if he truly wanted her, wouldn't he have agreed to go with her?

It was a hot, airless day. Ceidre stared up at the sun, a burning ball, oblivious to Will, who was uncomfortable and looking everywhere but at her. She hated the Norman. She hated Edwin. She had failed—she hated herself.

She would swim, she decided abruptly. It was hot, she was hot, and more important, she was angry. Now it would not be a seduction, she could enjoy herself, and if her guard dared look at her, she would kill him with the biggest rock she could find. Ceidre got up and marched through the orchard. She stopped so abruptly Will bumped into her, and she whirled on him. "I am going swimming," she shouted at him. "And not for ten minutes, for the entire godforsaken day. And if you look, or if you try to touch me, I'll curse you, your mother, your father, your brothers, I'll give you the pox, and you will die!"

Will recoiled, white-faced.

It had felt good to yell, but now she was ashamed at

having taken out her anger on the poor soldier. She strode on, ignoring him. She would pretend he wasn't present. He would not ruin her swim, and she would pretend she was truly free.

And she would not think of how she had failed.

CHAPTER 36

He had to know, and that night, at supper, he singled Wilfred out as everyone ate. "Did she go to the creek?"

"Yes," Will said, growing pale. "I did not touch her, my lord."

"I do not doubt it," he said, his heart beating thickly. She had gone. Had she been honest, then? Had she really only wanted a swim? If so, did she really trust him to be able to stand guard over her while she bathed? The relief he felt was vast, yet he could not shed all of his suspicion. He turned his gaze to her. She was eating, with gusto. Her hair, coiled in a braid, gleamed from its fresh wash. His breathing was constricted.

Dare he trust her?

The next day Will sought him out as he watched his men drilling against each other. Every day they honed their skills as knights, with lance and shield, mace and sword. At the sight of Will, Rolfe grew agitated. Something had occurred or Will would not leave his post. "What has happened?" He was afraid she had relapsed into the sickness that had almost claimed her life. A dozen other equally fateful possibilities tore through his mind.

Will was panting from his run across the field. "She is at the creek. You did not give permission for her to go again, and I explained this, but she would not listen. Indeed, she laughed and asked if I would stop her. What shall I do?"

"You are not to leave her unguarded for a second," Rolfe said, hard. "Your orders stand, Will. Go to her now." He was furious that the boy had left her alone. Tomorrow he would set him to an unpleasant task for failing in his duty, maybe demoting him to stable duty, or those of a page. Will jogged off, and Rolfe watched him, watched him the whole way, seeing exactly where he disappeared into the trees. He memorized the spot.

He could not concentrate on his men. He kept glancing to the east, to the place where Will had disappeared, to where she bathed. So it was not a trap. She had not intended to commit treason. She had, truly, unbelievably, only wanted to swim in the creek. Was she naked? He pictured her thus. Beltain forced Guy to drop his lance in a furious charge, and he whooped.

"If you do not do better, Guy," Rolfe said, "you will find your head on a Saxon's pike."

Guy scowled, angry. Rolfe barely watched as two of his best knights rode at each other for another exchange of blows. He glanced again at the woods where his nymph frolicked. With a growl, he raised his own lance. Guy and Beltain had just separated. Neither was unlanced this time.

"Beltain," Rolfe called, slipping on his helmut with one hand. He picked up his shield. Beltain had readied himself, and Guy had moved aside. Rolfe nodded once and let Beltain begin. When the knight was racing toward him, Rolfe spurred his destrier into an answering gallop. He relished the feel of the powerful brute beneath him. He relished the sight of the terrain speeding in front of him. He relished the sight of Beltain on his huge bay, approaching head on. Rolfe smiled. His lance ripped into Beltain's. Beltain's own weapon barely glanced off the edge of Rolfe's shield. Rolfe savagely reined in his stallion, whipped him around, and was attacking again before Beltain could recover. This time, his charge was so powerful Beltain was unhorsed. His men laughed and shouted. Rolfe sat panting, looking again toward the woods. His gaze pierced Guy. "Your turn."

He called out a dozen of his men, one by one, and unhorsed half of them, broke Roger's lance, and cracked Beau's shield. Charles suffered a sprained ankle from his fall. The men no longer shouted and laughed. 'Twas not unusual for Rolfe to participate in their drills; in fact, it was expected. What was unusual was that he would drive himself remorselessly, taking on a dozen, instead of two or three or even four. His savage mood was all too visible.

Rolfe threw down his lance and then his helmut. His blood was bursting in his body, he was panting heavily. Sweat plastered his curls to his scalp. He looked, again, at the woods, then gave his steed his spurs.

At the edge of the line of trees he dismounted and proceeded on foot. He was no longer winded, but breathing easily, so he could hear the bell-like sounds of the running creek, and he could also hear splashing. And was she singing? He saw Will first. The boy had his back to the creek, his face to Rolfe, and he gaped. Rolfe made a motion for him to be silent and another for him to leave. And then he looked.

She was not naked. He was disappointed. She was waist deep in the creek in a thin undertunic. It was opaque, hinting at the warm tones of her flesh beneath. Her hair was loose, a glorious mass of bronze and gold, only the ends wet. She was laughing, splashing about, and was beauty immortalized. Lightly, unconsciously, Rolfe touched the tumescent protrusion that was his manhood.

She ducked beneath the water and came up sputtering. Her tunic molded her body, leaving nothing unrevealed. Her full breasts, her slim waist, and as she climbed onto a rock, he glimpsed the lushness of her hips and buttocks. Her nipples, he saw, were hard and tight. She dove in again.

His breathing was already harsh and uneven, and he cursed himself for coming. He reminded himself that she was his wife's sister. He reminded himself of his vows to God. He was so hard he hurt. He touched himself again, through tunic and hose, and almost groaned. Never had he been so hard, this near to bursting. She surfaced. She moved thick, wet strands out of her face. Then she hopped onto a boulder, lifting her face to the sun, eyes closed, her body arched, breasts thrust up like an offering to the gods.

He was shaking. He reached into his hose, gripped the length of his cock, squeezed. She shoved thick strands of hair from her face, shaking her head like a wet puppy. The innocence of her action only heightened his need. His blood roared in his ears. His eyes slipped to what her parted legs offered to his view. His hand slid up. I should leave, he thought, and knew he would not.

She turned abruptly onto her stomach, and he was lost. He wanted to hold her lush buttocks, squeeze them, knead them, as he was kneading himself. He groaned, heard it, and knew from the way she had stiffened that she had heard it too. He didn't care. He couldn't. His hand was sweeping up and down his turgid length, no longer languid, but quickly now, he was so close, and God's blood, he needed this, he needed her now. . . .

She whipped upright, looked around, saw him, saw what he was doing. For one instant their gazes locked. When he closed his eyes, he still saw her, shocked, gasping. He released himself, then jerked faster, faster, and he cried out, coming violently, again and again.

His heart had not slowed when he opened his eyes, sure she was gone. She wasn't. She stood now on the far side of the creek, eyes wide, mouth parted, quivering, arms folded across her breasts. Staring. He pulled his hose up. "Would you still trust me to guard your bath?" he asked harshly.

She shook her head wildly.

He wiped his hand on the tree near him, never removing his gaze from her. The next time, he wondered, would he be able to resist what he truly wanted? The question did not have to be answered. He had lost control of the situation. Therefore, the situation had to be changed.

"What?" Alice gasped.

"Beth told me, Lady," Mary said eagerly, correctly assessing her mistress's surprise as interest.

"They were here," Alice cried, still stunned. "Are you sure? If this is a mistake, I will have you flogged and thrown in the dungeons!"

Mary shrank, her pretty mouth trembling. " 'Tis the truth. Beth only saw Morcar, but he said Edwin had come too. She was sent to fetch Ceidre so they could meet." Mary eyed her. "Are you not pleased with me?"

"Oh," Alice breathed, her heart pounding. "I am pleased!" Absently she extracted a gold coin from her girdle, then pushed Mary toward the door. "Leave me, I must think!"

When Mary had left, Alice sank, trembling, upon the bed. She had known it would come to pass! Ceidre was playing at treason again. Only this time she had not been caught. What punishment, she wondered, would

Rolfe inflict this time? Surely he would not let her get away with this! Meeting her own brothers right under his nose! Alice knew exactly what she would mete out, and she clapped her hands, smiling. This was her chance to get rid of her sister, finally.

She knew precisely how to proceed. Hurriedly she rose and ran downstairs to find her lord. He was just coming inside, looking quite relaxed, without his customary grimness, and Alice thought that this was most fortuitous. The gaze he turned upon her, at her greeting, was level and even, not annoyed. "I must speak with you," Alice said huskily.

He smiled slightly. Indeed, his mood was good. His gesture was expansive. "A chair, my lady."

"There must be no ears to overhear us," she said. "Can we adjourn to our chamber, my lord?"

His look was bemused, but he allowed her to precede him upstairs. Trying not to be dramatic, Alice closed the heavy rosewood door behind them. She turned to find Rolfe seated on the bed, indolently lounging there. "My lord, I have spies about, my own spies."

He looked at her. "Indeed?"

"Yes. And I have just learned something of great import that affects us both."

"So it seems. Continue."

"The afternoon you were hunting, Ceidre met with both Edwin and Morcar."

Rolfe stared.

" 'Tis true. They came right into the village once you had left. She is planning treason again, my lord!"

"This is a serious accusation. Do you have proof?"

"Yes! The maid, Beth, relayed a message betwixt Morcar and Ceidre. She may lie and deny it, for she is most fond of Morcar—indeed, 'tis said one of her brats is his—but if you beat her she will tell the truth."

Rolfe stood and paced to the dark, unlighted hearth, his back to Alice. He turned slowly. "You are quick to wish your sister ill, Alice. Rightly, I think, I am suspicious of this accusation."

Alice went to him, and brazenly touched his sleeve. "My lord, I am lady of Aelfgar. I intend to continue to remain so. If treason against you rears itself, I will fight it—for treason against you is treason against me. I have, for the first time in my life, what I want. I will not willingly give it up. Your interests are mine, thus I protect us, not just you. True, we are not close, but you must know I am loyal. *Me* you can trust."

"A pretty speech," he murmured.

"A true one."

He did not respond.

"What will you do?" Alice asked boldly.

His glance skewered her, but she was too intent, and she did not falter. Seeing this, he almost smiled—bitterly. "I see you are eager to impart your thoughts. Please continue."

She smiled, a quick, lightning smile. "She will be your downfall, my lord—our downfall. She is here among us, yet she is a spy—she is too dangerous. You have few choices. Truly, if she were a man, she would already have hanged. As you can see, this guard you have set upon her has failed you. Therefore, you must lock her away, forever."

"Or?"

"Or you can marry her to a Scot. Or a Frenchman, an Irishman. But she must be far, far away, where she can do you, and us, no harm!"

"My thoughts," Rolfe said, "exactly." And his mask disappeared, his eyes blazed with fury.

CHAPTER 37

Rolfe was livid.

He was enraged, and not because the two Saxons had dared to sneak into Aelfgar under his own nose. That showed their daring—in fact, he respected it, and would remember well their unpredictability for the future. This was cause for concern and reflection, not rage. His anger was centered on Ceidre.

She had again betrayed him. She was risking her neck. She knew what she did. Did she truly think he would be so lenient with her again? Lenient! Rolfe remembered the ten lashes, the eternity he had stood there and watched her suffer, and knew he could not endure to observe a like punishment again. She must sense this! How else would she dare to continue to play the traitor?

She did not know that he had, in truth, protected her the last time from his own king and had, in so doing, violated his own strict code of ethics, himself committing a breach through omission that bordered on treason. This could not happen again. He would not let it happen again.

He paced the chamber. Alice had been sent out. He understood his wife now, and believed her. Like himself, Alice was ambitious. They both coveted the power Aelfgar gave them. He had not seen her as an ally before, just as a nuisance. Now he realized she was his ally, and a valuable one. Her ambitions could rest fulfilled only as long as his did. He had told her not to do anything regarding the matter they had discussed and to keep her spy's ears open and mouth shut. This was exactly the kind of spy Rolfe needed to protect himself and his position at Aelfgar. It was an unexpected boon, an unexpected gift from his wife.

What was he going to do with that witch? He wanted to punch the wall, but recalled too vividly the pain he had endured the last time she had aroused him so, when he had slammed his fist into the trestle table downstairs. He managed to restrain himself.

Alice had assessed the situation shrewdly—he was impressed. Ceidre *was* dangerous. She was worse than a spy, because she hated him personally. He knew this, had always known it. His guarding of her had failed once, it would fail again. In truth, there were two options, as Alice had pointed out—lock her away, or marry her off and send her away.

He cursed savagely. He could not do the latter. He refused to analyze why he could not exile her through a marriage. The first choice was distasteful too. Yet he could not keep the situation as it was. Hadn't he reached this conclusion this afternoon at the creek? Now, understanding how Alice would truly serve him well as a wife, there was added incentive to rid himself of the other. Either that or protect her now, and protect her again, and again. Until he, Rolfe de Warenne, ceased to function as the king's man.

This time would be easy. He could make up an excuse to Alice, that Ceidre would lead him to some goal, perhaps to her brothers, and this was the reason he was pretending he did not know of her last act of treason. Such a lie. He would harbor and protect a traitor? For the second time? It was incomprehensible, unbearable!

He was Rolfe de Warenne, the eaorl of Aelfgar. He had followed William to Normandy for everything he now had. Because of Ceidre, he had already lost half of his holdings, the castellanship of York. Alice was right —she would be his complete downfall if something were not done. He had realized this for some time, yet now he must confront the situation.

He could not continue to protect her as he harbored her in their midst. He could not. It violated his every ethic. He was ceasing to be an effective commander, ceasing to be a leader, losing his values, his courage, his resolution. Always, in his life, he had known what was right and what was wrong, and always he had acted accordingly. Now nothing was clear.

No, he thought, as his mind shrewdly grasped another straw, one thing was clear. If *he* did not protect her, someone else had to.

Rolfe suddenly smiled at the solution that presented itself. He strode to the door, flung it open, and bellowed for Guy.

"What?" Guy gasped, paling.

Rolfe smiled again, the smile cool, ruthless. "You will marry Ceidre," he said softly.

Guy gaped.

"The banns will be posted tomorrow," he continued relentlessly. "You will wed the day after. Do not worry about dispensation. I grant it now."

Guy somehow recovered, but there was no mistaking his abhorrence. "Yes, my lord."

"I will provide the dowry, of course." This time Rolfe's smile was genuine. "The parcel that is Dumstanbrough—with the village, of course. We will ride over your borders tomorrow. As for services—I need you now, Guy, as you well know. This year you will give me three hundred of your days. You know I am fair. If Aelfgar is secure next year, we will reduce it accordingly."

Guy was now flushed with pleasure. Like most knights, this was his dream come true. It did not matter that Dumstanbrough was a tiny hamlet of a dozen huts, at most. What mattered was that now he had his own honor, small as it was. He would have his own men, eventually, when he could afford them. For now, to have Dumstanbrough was enough. His page would be his number-one man, and he would be promoted and given his spurs. "Thank you." Guy gasped, going down on one knee and taking Rolfe's hand. He kissed it.

"Up, up," Rolfe said, pleased. "Now we must talk, seriously."

Guy nodded, all attentiveness.

"Ceidre will bear watching, Guy."

"I know," Guy said quickly. "Do not fear, my lord, she will not betray you, or me, again."

Rolfe nodded. He knew Guy would not hurt Ceidre, just as he doubted Guy could curb her activities. Of course, if he kept her pregnant she might mellow considerably. He hated that thought, so he shoved it away.

Guy left shortly after, and Rolfe ordered a passing serf to bring him wine. It was almost a celebration. He had nearly solved his problem—nearly. His priority was to protect Ceidre, and this he had done. As Guy's wife, should she commit treason again, she would not hang but be locked away indefinitely. Marrying her to one of his Norman nobles was the smartest thing he could have done other than locking her away himself, or sending her away to marry a foreigner—and never seeing her again.

He was instantly angry at himself. It did not matter if he ever saw her again. She could not be his. Ever. He had just given her to one of his finest men. He was saving her ungrateful neck. And Guy was just and good. He did not have a temper, he would not abuse her. Rolfe could not stand men who hurt those weaker than themselves, and he could not stand the thought of Ceidre being hurt—by anybody.

Something hard and unpalatable, however, was wedged in his chest. He knew well what it was. It was jealousy. Facing this, his mind was suddenly filled with the image of Guy taking his bride on his wedding night, on succeeding nights. Guy was young, lusty, and virile. Rolfe knew this well, they had taken many wenches together. He would satisfy Ceidre, pleasure her, make her moan in ecstasy.

It was no longer, he told himself, his affair.

Ceidre did not know why she had been summoned. She did not like Alice's smug, satisfied glance, which followed her as she climbed the stairs to the upper floor. Dread threaded her being. The door to the great chamber was open. Rolfe was within, his broad back to her. At the sound of her footsteps, he turned.

She blushed. She couldn't help it; she could not look at him now without recalling, vividly, his performing a very intimate act upon himself, his hand full with his own sex. She had been stunned to find him there, invading her privacy—and in such a manner. Stunned, and something else. At first she could not move, she was mesmerized by him and what he was doing. Something hot and aching pierced her, making her tremble wildly. When he had finished she had scrambled to the other side of the creek, breathless, still shocked. She knew what she had witnessed. She just could not believe it.

He was regarding her steadily now, and her color deepened. She found herself looking at his right hand, remembering. At his groin, now clad and completely hidden. Catching herself, she looked up, wanting to flee, to be anywhere but here. He was almost smiling, and she knew, unfortunately, that he was aware of her thoughts. She tensed for some biting remark, preparing for a verbal battle.

"You will marry Guy Le Chante."

She gasped.

"The banns will be posted tomorrow. The wedding will be the day after." His gaze was level. "Consider yourself lucky."

She stepped forward, shocked. "No! I mean, this cannot be! How—what do you mean?"

"Exactly as I have said. You will marry Guy. I have given him a small fief as dowry." He did not smile. "You will be lady of Dumstanbrough, Ceidre."

She did not care, she was too stunned and too upset. "Please, I do not understand. This must be a trick!"

He lost his patience. " 'Tis no trick. You are to be wed. That is all. Leave me." He turned away.

She could not fathom it. If he wanted her, why was he marrying her to another? She was supposed to seduce him, become his mistress. Yet she was to be Guy's wife. She felt the hot burning of tears just behind her eyes. So he did not want her. "I will not," she said, quavering.

He turned, looking deadly, displeased. "Do not think to defy me on this," he said, so softly she quaked. "My resolve is like a boulder. 'Twill not budge."

"You are punishing me!" she cried. "Why—I told you my brothers are in the fens! 'Tis all I know! Please, my lord, don't do this!"

His nostrils flared, his eyes blazed. That she should beg, near tears, almost undid his resolve and increased his ire. " 'Tis no punishment, woman. You are not thinking. You have just been given your own manor. Do not be ungrateful. Do not test my will." He gave her his back rudely, ordering her out.

Ceidre hesitated, choking on a sob wedged deep in her chest. This could not be happening! If, in truth, he didn't want her, had it all been a sadistic game? Had his looks been a mere mockery, some form of cruel torture? And what of this afternoon? Tears welled.

She desperately grasped logic. Even if he lusted after her, 'twas unimportant. He did lust after her, but what was lust to a man like him, or to any man in the greater scheme of things? He had everything he needed. He had both Aelfgar and Alice. If he really wanted her, he would not be wedding her to another, he would keep her as his mistress. What he was doing was proof of the depth of his interest in her—and it wasn't very flattering. She tried to swallow down the thwarting of her plans to help her brothers. What should she do? Submit docilely? Did she have another course? She stared at his rigid spine, almost blindly.

She took swift steps to him and laid her trembling palm on his sinewed flesh. "Please," she breathed. "Please, I beg you."

He shuddered beneath her touch and twisted to face her.

Ceidre did not remove her hand, the result being a caress as he moved, and now she touched his chest. She could feel his heart, strong and powerful, its beat accelerating. Their gazes locked. "I will—I will do anything," she whispered. Tears blurred her vision. "But do not make me marry Guy."

"Anything?"

"Y-yes."

"Are you offering yourself to me, Ceidre?"

She forced herself to hold his gaze. "Y-yes."

His hand came up and closed over hers, and for an instant she thought she had achieved what she was aiming for. Then he squeezed her palm, almost crushing her, and she whimpered. He was angry. "Do not think to tempt me, witch," he said with a growl. "Do not think to tease me. And cease your tears—they will not work."

"I am not," she said, trying to free her hand, and when the pressure increased, she ceased abruptly.

"You will wed Guy," he said savagely. "Nothing will change my mind, not even the offer of your lush body. Now get out of here. I do not want to lay eyes on you again until your wedding. Be gone!"

It was a roar. He shoved her away, and she stumbled. Then she fled.

CHAPTER 38

She could run away.

It wasn't too late.

This was Ceidre's last thought the following evening before sleep claimed her, and it was her first waking thought the morning of her wedding.

The time since the Norman had informed her of her marriage had passed in a blur. She was aware of panic and fear. She was about to be married to a man she barely knew, a Norman, her enemy, and one day, maybe soon, she would be leaving Aelfgar—forever. Panic and fear swelled, strong and nauseating. This was happening too fast. She could not let her fate be decided like this!

She was aware of failure. She had a mission to fulfill, for Ed and Morcar. Even now they probably thought her warming the Norman's bed, his mistress. Yet she was no closer to this goal than she had been when she had agreed to do her brother's bidding; in fact, she had never been farther from it. She was not about to become his mistress, she was about to be married to one of his men.

Hurt. It was there, raising its awful, multifanged head. She fought it, denied it. But it was there. She hurt inside, like a wounded cub. *He did not want her.* He had rejected her. He had married her sister. Alice warmed his bed every night. She, she was nothing but an amusing diversion, a light dalliance. This was now proven—because he had rejected her overtures of the past few days and was now, in the crowning rejection of them all, marrying her to his own best man.

Ceidre cried. She did not want him, she told herself furiously. She hated him, she always had. But the rejection was foul and bitter. She, who had been rejected so many times, was rejected again. Why was she not used to it? Why was she not immune to these crushing feelings? Why did she feel as crushed as she had the time her father lied, telling her the suitor he had approached was not good enough for her, that he had changed his mind, when in truth she knew she had been rejected again?

She told herself she cried because she had failed Ed and Morcar. Not because the one man who had ever dared to treat her as a woman had only been amusing himself, and had now cast her off, finding a better use for her, while he slept with her sister.

It was not too late. She could run away. Yet where would she go? To Ed, wearing her failure like a banner upon her arm? Should she hide in the woods, like a wild animal? She would be hunted, this she knew, and she even supposed he would eventually find her. She did not doubt his prowess over her. Ultimately the end result would be the same—the altar.

Ceidre stared at the ceiling of the great hall. Everyone had long since risen and left, but she did not care. Depression was vast, weighing her down. The best she could do, she decided, was marry Guy and spy upon him as well as the Norman. At least, that way, she would still be fighting for Aelfgar.

It was no consolation.

Ceidre's best gown was a bright, sun-gold yellow. She had always loved it. Today she hated it. Alice watched while Ceidre allowed Mary and Beth to help her don it. Alice abruptly cried out for them to halt.

"Take it off," She said.

Ceidre barely looked at her, not really caring what she was up to. Alice turned and ran across the hall into her and Rolfe's chamber. Ceidre was being dressed in the solar. The ceremony was to take place shortly thereafter at the chapel. A small feast, nowhere as elaborate as the one given upon Rolfe's wedding day, had been prepared. Rolfe had given Guy his old chamber in the original manor, now in the bailey. Ceidre felt sick.

Alice returned, carrying something. "Take off that wretched undertunic," she ordered Ceidre. " 'Tis most unseemly for a bride."

Ceidre did not care. Her undertunic was plain wool, ivory, worn in places, a simple shift. Mary helped her draw it off, and Alice handed her a tunic of her own. "You want to look your best for your groom, Ceidre," she purred.

The tunic was virginal white, almost new, the finest weave, so fine it was sheer. Ceidre hated it. Mary slipped it over her head. Alice was much smaller than she was, so it fit like a glove. " 'Tis too small," she noted listlessly.

With a needle and thread, Mary let out the bust and hips. It still fit like a second skin, but at least this time it would not tear at the seams. The brilliant yellow gown followed, with a purple girdle. Beth began brushing Ceidre's long, flowing tresses, murmuring all the while about how she was the most beautiful bride ever to be. "And all this hair! Incredible, so long, and so thick! Guy will be a lusty one, he will, when he sees you! Like a goddess, you are—"

"Shut up, Beth," Alice snapped.

Mary wove yellow carnations into her hair. They

formed a wreath around the crown of her head, then trailed down through the loose mass. Ceidre refused to look at herself in the proffered looking glass.

Rolfe was waiting for them downstairs, outside on the steps of the keep. He regarded her without expression. Ceidre, seeing him, felt an awful stabbing, and humiliation followed the hurt. She allowed herself a moment's anger, seeking it, relishing it, and she glared, wishing she could smite him dead on the spot. He was completely indifferent, gesturing to the white palfrey awaiting her, the same one Alice had ridden to her wedding. Her feeling of being sick increased.

Guy was waiting at the chapel. Rolfe, as her lord and master, would give her away. He held the palfrey's bridle and they descended down the motte and through the portcullis. The chapel was in the bailey, and everyone from Aelfgar had turned out for this event.

Ceidre did not look at anyone. She stared, instead, somewhat blindly at her palfrey's dainty ears. Her gaze wandered to the squared shoulders of the man leading her mount. He was dressed for the occasion, in a royal-blue tunic and red mantle. She had a flashing image of how he had looked as he rode his stallion to his own wedding, godlike, pagan, beautiful, and ruthless. Recollections started to tumble, one after the other, through her mind—Rolfe stroking his own sex, Rolfe carrying her inside after the flogging; Rolfe drunk, smiling, cajoling a kiss from her; Rolfe as he sat his steed, ordering the razing of Kesop. As if feeling her regard, he abruptly glanced at her. Ceidre hoped her hatred showed. He looked away.

Guy was standing nervously in front of the chapel with Father Green, who, if in his cups, was hiding it well. Guy had also dressed for the occasion, in a fine green velvet mantle and tunic, with red hose. He blushed, not looking at her but once.

Rolfe helped her dismount, his touch impersonal, and led her to Guy. He stepped back. Father Green raised his voice, coughing once. To Guy, he said, "Hast thou will to have this women as thy wedded wife?"

"Yes, sir."

"May thou well find at thy best to love her and hold ye to her and to no other to thy lives end."

"Yes, sir," Guy said.

"Then take her by your hand and say after me I, Guy Le Chante, take thee, Ceidre, in form of holy church, to my wedded wife, forsaking all other, holding me holiest to thee, in sickness and health, in riches and poverty, in well and in woe, till death do us depart, and there to I plight ye my troth."

Guy repeated the words, and it was done.

Ceidre had married Guy Le Chante.

Ceidre paced her chamber. She looked around. It was truly a bridal chamber, with garlands strewn across the bed, wine and food laid out. She was supposed to be readying herself to receive her new lord, but she would not. She was still clad in her yellow gown. At least, she decided, she could get rid of these flowers. She began removing them abruptly.

The wedding feast had lasted hours. All around them was drunken boisterous laughter and dancing. As the newlywed couple, they had graced the raised dais under the walnut tree. Guy had eaten and drunk merrily, in no rush to leave the festivities. Ceidre had not taken one bite of food or one sip of wine. At first, he had offered her, as a groom should, the choicest morsels of what he picked for himself. She had refused everything ungraciously. Then he had ceased offering anything to her. He had not attempted conversation after, which had suited her just fine. She had sat still as a stone, ignoring everything and everyone.

Except for Rolfe. She could not ignore him, not when she was so keenly aware of him, not when he sat on her right. Like her, he did not seem inclined to conversation, yet he made an effort to quip with Guy. She was aware that he gazed at her from time to time. She refused to acknowledge him. She did not look at him. She was in a strange state, her wedding almost felt like a dream. And this state was infinitely preferable to the pain she had felt upon awaking, that same pain she had harbored the past few days.

There was a knock upon her door.

Ceidre clenched her fists. "Enter."

Guy appeared, closing the heavy door behind him. Then, noting her state of dress, he looked unsure. "I am sorry, I am too quick. I will come back." He started to leave.

"No!" Her abrupt command halted him. "I am not readying myself for you," she said, her tone hard.

His eyes widened.

"I did not want this marriage," she said furiously. "And I do not want you!"

His face changed, grew hard, making him seem older, making her remember that he was a Norman knight and one of Rolfe's best men. "But I want this marriage," he stated.

"You want Dumstanbrough—not me!"

He flushed. " 'Tis true. But Dumstanbrough comes with you, 'tis your dowry. I will not give it up—or you."

"You may have Dumstanbrough," Ceidre spat. "I care not. But you will not have me."

He stared. "You deny me my husbandly rights?"

"If you touch me," Ceidre hissed, "I will kill you!"

He blinked.

"I will curse you, do not doubt it. Your manhood will shrivel up. Your teeth will fall out. You will lose your hair. You do not think I can do this?" She laughed, slightly hysterical. "I have potions! You will be an old man before your time! I warn you!"

Guy crossed himself nervously. "Do not do anything rash," he said. "I would not hurt you!"

Ceidre relaxed slightly. "Look," she said, "I will be your wife—I am your wife. You did not want me before this wedding. I know it. You have never looked at me the way a man looks at a woman." Bitterness touched her tone. "Men do not look at me that way, not once they know of my eye. I am used to it. No one needs know what passes between us. Just because we are married, you do not need to come to my bed, when you do not want me, when you are afraid of me. Seek out your lemans, I care not. Can we agree on this?"

"But what about children? I need heirs."

"Then take a mistress," Ceidre said frankly. "Make sure she is a virgin and is faithful to you. Adopt her get. 'Tis simple enough."

"In truth, I do not want you," Guy said. His words stabbed at her. Ludicrously she thought of Rolfe. "But not because I am afraid of you."

"Of course not."

" 'Tis most unnatural not to consummate a marriage."

"No one will know. Besides, you have not married a natural woman. Do you really want to bed one with the eye?"

Guy grimaced. "No, I do not. Not when the world is full of fair wenches. I have just never shied from my duty before."

"Guy, what about your duty to God?"

He suddenly smiled. "You are right. You are not

natural, not godly. My first duty is to God. Why did I not think of that? We have a bargain, then. But no one must know the truth, Ceidre. No one."

"Believe me," she said, overwhelmingly relieved. "I will not tell a soul."

They stared at each other, then Guy shrugged. He strode to the trencher on the chest and picked up a pastry. "Are you hungry?"

Ceidre smiled. She was suddenly starved. She opened her mouth to reply, but her words were cut off. There was a violent pounding upon the door.

Ceidre froze. Guy leapt forward, hand upon the hilt of his sword. "Who is it!"

"'Tis your lord, open up," Rolfe demanded harshly.

Guy threw open the door anxiously. "What is it! Are we attacked?"

Rolfe stared at Guy, his blue eyes brilliant. "I have come to claim my rights."

Guy was taken aback. "Of course," he said instantly. "What rights, my lord?"

Rolfe's diamond-hard gaze swung to Ceidre. "*Le droit du seigneur.*"

CHAPTER 39

A stunned silence ensued.

Ceidre's stare was locked with Rolfe's. The meaning of his words shocked her—he had come to bed his vassal's bride. Her heart was banging wildly, uncontrollably. His gaze did not waver from hers. In it she saw both anger and fierce, unyielding determination.

Neither was aware of Guy, who recovered first, glancing from one to the other. "Of course, my lord," he murmured, backing out, and then the heavy door swung shut behind him, with a bang as loud and ominous as a clap of thunder.

Ceidre jumped; Rolfe moved. He suddenly unclasped the brooch holding his black mantle together and let the heavy cloth fall to the floor. Ceidre's eyes widened, she took a step back. He was unbuckling his sword belt. Total comprehension set in. He would take her now. Now, after rejecting her, after giving her so casually to another. Now, at his convenience—not hers. "You can't mean this!" She gasped.

For the first and only time, he removed his glance from her, to lay his sword carefully aside. Then she was pierced again by bold, brilliant blue eyes. "Oh, I do meant it," he said harshly. There was nothing smug in his tone.

He was shrugging off his tunic in one quick movement and tossing it aside. In the flickering candlelight his naked torso rippled and gleamed like bronze.

She was still stunned by what was happening, by the impossibility of it, the arrogance. "You have given me to Guy!"

His stare was hard, blazing like his tone. Was there a trace of bitterness there? "You think I do not know this, and know it too damn well?"

She clutched the bedpost. "And Alice!" she cried desperately. "Alice is my sister—your wife!"

"I am lord of Aelfgar!" he shouted furiously. It was the wrath of gods. "I am lord here!"

Ceidre reacted in real terror. She whirled and raced around to the other side of the bed. Rolfe ran after her. Even as she moved, she knew, with a huge, terrible fear, that there was nowhere for her to run to, that she could not escape. His mind was made up, and his will was steel. His iron hand closed on her wrist, dragging her forcefully up against his body. "No!" she screamed, struggling like a madwoman.

With his leg, he caught hers deftly, knocking her feet out from under her. She went down, as he had intended, and was on her back in a trice, writhing and bucking, while he straddled her, a knee on each side of her hips. He seized her wrists. His thighs were rock-hard, pinning her in place as she twisted desperately, futilely. He released her and, in one violent movement, ripped her gown and undertunic open, from throat to waist.

With a vicious cry, Ceidre raked his cheek with her nails, drawing blood and flesh.

His response was immediate; he grabbed both of her wrists with one hand, wrenching them up over her head and holding them down on the hard floor. She froze in the face of his overwhelming power. For one moment they stared at each other, his expression savage, determined, hers panicked.

"Do not fight me," he commanded. "You cannot win."

"I will always fight you," she cried, bucking again, hopelessly trying to dislodge him. "Norman!"

He kneed her thighs far apart, throwing her skirt up to her waist. There was one instant in which she was aware of the large, wet tip of his penis suddenly free and naked against her inner thigh. Ceidre fought to close her legs but it was useless. He impaled her.

Ceidre gasped from the lightning lancing of pain. She turned her head aside and closed her eyes. Her heart was pounding furiously. He drove himself into her roughly, quickly, deeply. She could feel him, every inch of him, all the slickness and power. His rhythm was harsh, fast and deep, the pace increasing, increasing . . . And then he collapsed with a raw cry on top of her.

So it was over, she thought, as a tear trickled down her cheeks. It had come to pass. No seduction, but a rape. At least it had been mercifully quick. She lay very still, her heart thundering, hoping he would revive quickly and leave her.

He made no attempt to roll off her. Ceidre could not help but be aware of many things. His face was buried in her neck. She could feel his beard, slightly rough, and his breath, warm and rapid against her flesh. His hard chest crushed her naked breasts, and his heart was thudding as fiercely as hers. His legs were between hers, tight, not relaxed, holding her thighs apart. And the semisoft maleness of him was still inside her, reminding her of the heat and hardness she had just experienced, reminding her of the slickness and power . . . He was throbbing within her, demanding her sensual response.

His arms, around her, tightened. Ceidre hoped he would get up now. There was a new nagging feeling raising itself, one she did not care for. Her breasts ached when he shifted slightly, her nipples hard and tight—she could not mistake that the feeling was pleasant, and worse, where she held him inside her she was aching as well. Then she felt something else. His mouth, open on her neck.

Ceidre tried to twist away, but pinned beneath him, in his embrace, she could not. His lips nibbled so gently, and a fierce stabbing of pleasure swept her. Again she shifted uneasily. She felt his mouth on her throat. One of his hands teased the side of her breast, causing her breath to choke inside her. And within her, she felt him hardening. Helplessly her body contracted around him, and she could feel it, and was stunned at the heat and length and fullness she housed. He groaned, pushed deeper into her, and raised himself slightly to look into her eyes.

Ceidre met his gaze, but she could barely think. She certainly could not breathe. Her body was throbbing madly, fevered with desire. She arched her pelvis, trying to pull him into her more fully, even deeper. He smiled slightly, and bent and claimed her lips.

She opened to him, unsurely.

His hand caught a hank of her hair. He played ever so softly with her mouth, gently inserting his tongue. She opened wider, straining against him. He probed deeper, rocking his huge shaft as far as he could into her. Ceidre gasped into his mouth, the sound a startled plea. She kissed him back, demandingly now, and her mouth caught his, nipping insistently.

It was an explosion. He anchored her head, kissing her wildly, forcefully, their tongues battling, their teeth grating. He lifted his head and thrust into her, again and again. Ceidre rocked madly against him, eyes closed, head thrown back. She was clinging to his massive shoulders. As he drove into her, she felt his mouth on her nipple, felt his teeth. It was the end, for her world exploded in sensations the likes of which were unimaginable, and she was lost, lost to this existence, climaxing again and again.

She opened her eyes slowly, stunned. He was braced on his hands over her, still hard and throbbing within her, not moving, watching her with a brilliant gaze. What had happened? she thought frantically. Remembrance came floooding back. This was the Norman. The man she hated. He had raped her violently, and moments later she had attained the fiercest of desire, and the most agonizing of ecstasy, in his arms. She blushed, with shame and fury. She pushed at his shoulders. "Get off," she hissed.

But he was already ducking his head. Ceidre remained rigid for one more moment as his tongue swept her nipple, teasing and taunting, and then she gave in to the hot, agonizing pleasure he had induced. She clutched his head to her breast, his hair caught in her fingers, uncaring. He laughed hoarsely, the sound full of triumph. He began nipping and licking her breasts until she was moaning in complete abandonment, pumping her hips against him wildly, frantically, panting, gasping, and then he allowed himself, finally, to join her, thrusting fiercely, roughly, deeply, and this time their cries of pleasure came together.

Ceidre had just become cognizant of her surroundings again when Rolfe rolled off her. "I don't want to leave you," he murmured. She had to look at him. He was on his knees beside her, broad-shouldered, narrow-waisted, so powerfully and beautifully made. His hose was open; his manhood hung thick, flaccid, wet. Her gaze found his face.

He was also studying her openly, and his hand swept

over her full, lush breasts, down to her small waist, and across the softness of her belly. His touch was, it seemed, reverent. She could not read his expression, as contained as it was, yet when his gaze lifted, Ceidre saw the smoldering, uncontainable glow in his eyes. Before she could react, he was lifting her and carrying her to the bed. So it was not yet over, she thought, and realized, dumbly, that the surging in her heart was gladness.

He climbed in next to her, stretching his full, long length out beside her, his hand again on her belly, propped up on one elbow. He was caressing her languidly, with obvious enjoyment and with clear carnal intent. She watched his hand, so large, like all of him, on the pale skin of her abdomen; she watched his expression as it became strained. She could feel his manhood thickening against her thigh. Ceidre heard her own sigh, knew her eyes had drifted closed, felt herself arch sensually beneath his touch. His response was a guttural sound. And then he threaded his fingers through the dense curls guarding her femininity, and she gasped, half pleasure, half protest.

He groaned, sliding his hand completely over her, one finger parting the wet folds of her, and he held her like that. All thought of protest died. Ceidre pushed herself further into his grip. "Please," she thought she heard herself say.

His mouth caught her nipple, tugging it. His fingers slid slickly into a deep cleft. Ceidre moaned loudly, lost to everything but what he was doing, and with urgency, she thrust herself at him. With his own cry, he rolled on top of her, entering her.

Rolfe cradled her as she lay asleep in his arms.

He could not sleep; he would not sleep. He had taken her many times, he himself had finished thrice, but he was not tired. He was alive, the kind of alertness that he had experienced only after a battle, every nerve ending tingling, blood pumping, mind working. He lay on his side, one strong leg flung over hers, his arms around her. He pulled her closer, if possible, into his embrace.

The candles had long since burned down, but he had interrupted their continuous lovemaking to light more. He had wanted to see her, watch her every wild response, as he moved thickly inside her, over her. Hadn't he guessed it would be like this? That she would drive him relentlessly, past all human boundaries and limitations? Hadn't he guessed that she would be ecstasy as none other could be, as he had not dreamed could exist?

Her face was against his chest, and he smiled when she nuzzled her cheek more fully into his hard planes. Unthinkingly, he dropped a light kiss upon her head. Distracted by her magnificent hair, he began stroking it, from crown to nape. His hand trembled.

He was thick with desire again.

Incredible, but he would not question it. He had already overused her, he thought, although she had met him as frantically as he had taken her, each and every time. If she was bruised, let her heal tomorrow. Tonight was theirs. Tomorrow belonged to another.

Anger swept him, hard.

But being a disciplined man, he willed it away, instead concentrating on the path of his hand. From her nape he explored her shoulder, broad for a woman, yet not overly so. He ran his palm down her arm, then twined his fingers with hers. In her sleep, she gripped him tightly.

It would be dawn soon and he would have to leave. The night had sped too quickly. He touched her waist, stroking it, then reached to lift one full white breast.

Long nipples, he thought, watching them harden as he merely held her, nipples to nurse a babe—or a man. He lowered his head and tongued her.

Still asleep, she shifted herself so that her breast was more accommodating. As the darkness in their chamber lightened with the graying of the sky outside, Rolfe began to suck her more fiercely. He slid his hand between her legs, his finger toying with her. He knew the instant she was awake, before she gasped. Then, languidly, she spread her legs wide, arching for him, her long white throat exposed as she tossed her head back.

The sky outside the Saxon windows was now a pinkish gray. He felt the panic, like a knife in his stomach, as he shifted between her eagerly parted thighs. He caught her mouth with his as he thrust abruptly into her, pinning her lips to her teeth. She cried out; he clasped her buttocks and drove deep, deeper, into her. As he thrust, her eyes flew open, her gaze sleep-fogged, passion-glazed, but unwavering upon his. He bent to kiss her again. She must have felt what he was feeling, must have seen the dawn, for her nails raked his back as her mouth attacked his. "Please," she cried, "please!"

It might have been the same plea as his—to hold onto the night, deny the dawn, or it might have been the plea for instant gratification. Rolfe ceased to care. In Ceidre's arms, inside her tight, hot sheath, he was lost. Lost. She matched him thrust for thrust, kiss for kiss. He felt her nails again, and they drove him insane, making him wild to go deeper, until he was *one* with her. Together, violently, they rose and fell, bucked and writhed, drenched with sweat, panting, gasping, until as one they cycloned out of all earthly existence.

Ceidre was still waiting for her heart to cease its violent thundering when she felt him leave her. She knew it was dawn, she had seen its rosy tendrils of light when he had awakened her with his passion. There was a constricted feeling in her chest, one suggesting imminent tears. She felt the bed tilt and did not have to look as he left it.

She closed her eyes, afraid to open them, afraid to face the dawn and him. She heard him dressing. The lump inside her grew, until she thought she might strangle. Should she open her eyes? Or feign sleep? Say something? He had not said a word to her all night, not since he had carried her to the bed. The lump persisted, unbearably. She heard the clink of his scabbard and knew he was donning his sword belt.

Ceidre opened her eyes.

He was standing in the middle of the room, wrapping his cloak around him, but his gaze was upon her. She refused to allow herself to cry. There was no expression on his face, although it seemed taut with willful control. His eyes were opaque, windowless, shadowed. He held her gaze, then let it slide to her bare torso, her breasts and waist. She had forgotten to pull the covers up, but she was past blushing. He glanced at her briefly again, then turned. In three long strides he reached the door, opened it, and was gone.

She sat up. She stared at the closed door, at the empty room, hugging herself. The door grew blurry, the room grew vague. Tears spoiled her vision. She would not cry, she told herself. Then she pulled her knees in, dropped her head, and began to weep, rocking.

CHAPTER 40

Ceidre had pulled herself together by noon.

She had not seen a soul since Rolfe had left her. Guy, of course, would be with the other Normans, drilling in the field, or carrying out whatever tasks Rolfe had given him. Ceidre had no maids to wait on her; she never had. Servants were using the manor's kitchens, to feed the excess of men, but other than the carrying sound of their voices, she had no truck with them. She was very, very grateful for the privacy.

She could not hide forever, and she knew it.

After the tears, she felt sufficiently numb to get dressed and attend the noonday dinner, as always. Sooner or later she would have to face the leering looks of everyone. Sooner or later she would have to face *him.*

However, when she realized she had no clothes, just the ripped yellow gown, she started to cry again. She had no choice, so she donned it, holding it together the best she could, managing to conceal her bare flesh. The moment she entered the kitchens, all the serfs' chatter stopped, and they stared, wide-eyed, at her.

This was a different kitchen staff, of course, the original one, including Tildie and Teddy, now working at the keep. Her gaze sought out Lettie, who was close to her own age and who was regarding her with sympathetic blue eyes. "Could you run up to the manor and fetch my rust gown and an undertunic?" Ceidre asked.

Lettie shoved wet strands of red hair out of her face. "Tore it right off of you, did he?" Her tone was sympathetic. "I'll just be a minute," she promised kindly.

Ceidre was horrified, she felt like weeping again. She returned to the manor but could not enter the bridal chamber. Instead she paced the hall below, alone. Lettie was true to her word, and returned with her things instantly, slightly out of breath. Ceidre thanked her.

" 'Tis all right," Lettie said, smiling. "If we don't stick together, those brutes will destroy us, now, won't they?"

Ceidre was somewhat surprised at Lettie's philosophy, because she made herself available to just about any man around and it was no secret. In fact, since the Normans had come she was continuously at their disposal. Ceidre began to change.

"Hurt you, did he?" Lettie asked, pointedly eyeing her bruised wrists.

Ceidre recalled the way he'd wrenched them back after she'd drawn blood on his cheek. Surprisingly, she felt the urge to defend him. "No. He didn't."

Lettie dropped the topic. "Why don't you stay abed today? No one will care."

Ceidre looked at her. "I am going to the keep to dine, as usual."

Lettie shrugged. Then she grinned mischievously. "So tell me, is it true? Is he as big as a bull and as tough?"

Ceidre flooded with color. She wouldn't answer, she couldn't.

* * *

Rolfe paused before seating himself at the table, surveying the room. She hadn't come yet, and he was overwhelmed with disappointment.

He got a grip on himself. 'Twas over. He'd had her, sated himself, exorcised his lust. He had tried his best not to think a single thought about her since he'd left her, and he'd succeeded. Now was no time to fall back into old ways. He did not care if she came to eat or not, did not care that she was married to another, did not care that tonight she would lie in another's arms. He sat down abruptly.

He was aware of Alice filling his cup. He hadn't seen her since last night at the wedding feast. He spared her a curt glance now. Her face was carved in white stone. Her hand, pouring the wine, was steady. She did not look at him.

Nor did he care. He was the lord here, and if he chose to exercise *le droit du seigneur* with every bride that graced his fief, he would, and she would not say one word about it. He began to eat, quickly and quietly. Still Ceidre did not come. He refused to think about her, yet he was suddenly worried. She did not have the strength he had, and she had matched him all night long. Perhaps she was sick, or hurt from his attentions. Perhaps she was so bruised she could not get out of bed. Or perhaps she was merely defying him, refusing to come to his table.

'Twas not her day.

Ceidre was late, and she was aware of it, but she did not hurry. She made her way slowly toward the portcullis, staring at the ground. Dread filled her, and that nameless, breathless, quivering lump had risen to choke her again. Why was she so near tears? She should be relieved. She had survived the worst, and now it was over. Indeed, she was now another man's wife. This would not only protect her from the Norman, but it gave her her own status, and she had even made the bargain to keep Guy out of her bed. She *should* be happy.

"Ceidre, Ceidre!"

Surprised, Ceidre turned to see Feldric huffing up the hill after her. She turned and started down to meet him, her body tightening with anxiety. "What is it?"

She knew he was back; she had noticed him yesterday at her wedding. He paused to catch his breath, then said, "My boy is sick. Can you come?"

"Of course," Ceidre said, as two knights passed them. She followed him down the hill and over the outerbridge, knowing well that his boy was not sick, he had been trying to tell her something. Had he a message from her that he hadn't been able to give her yesterday? She felt a flaring of interest. Once they had left the castle's walls and were in the village, she demanded the truth.

" 'Tis Albie. He wants to speak with you."

Ceidre hurried her pace. Albie was waiting at the mill; no one else was about. He lounged in deep shadows, careless but watchful, disguised as a serf. "Is it bad news?" Ceidre asked immediately. "Are they all right?"

"Yes, they are fine, do not worry so," Albie soothed.

"Thank God," Ceidre said, relieved.

"Ed is most impatient. You have news for him?"

Ceidre froze, then she blanched. "No, I do not."

His eyes were soft. "You did not take the Norman to your bed yet, Ceidre?"

So Albie was privy to everything. Now she blushed, to her chagrin. "Ed sent you because he thought I might have learned something? 'Tis too soon!"

"We run quickly out of time," Albie remarked. "In

seven weeks we rebel, Ceidre. You have learned nothing? You have not lured the Norman to your bed? Tell me something!"

She was hotly red. And more miserable than ever. "Albie, I'm afraid I only have bed news. The Norman has married me to one of his men!" To her horror, she felt tears escaping.

Albie stared, then muttered an inaudible curse.

Ceidre wiped her eyes. Albie laid a rough hand on her shoulders. "I am sorry, Ceidre," he said.

" 'Tis not the whole truth," she said, sniffing. "There is some ancient pagan custom they keep, and he claimed me on my wedding night."

Albie turned startled eyes on her. "What? Why, that is good news!"

She recoiled. "I did not learn anything." It was good news that she had been raped? She was suddenly furious, with Albie, with her brothers.

"Don't you see? You can still become his mistress, if you are careful and cunning. All is not lost with this plan. You must do so, Ceidre. We need you privy to his innermost thoughts if we are to take back Aelfgar and chase him to the sea!"

She wanted to tell him that she did not want to be privy to that barbarian's innermost thoughts, nor did she want to share his miserable bed. She said neither, the feeling of hurt she had been harboring all day increasing to overwhelm her. No one cared what she had been through. She had been raped; then she had experienced utter ecstasy in her enemy's arms, which was worse than rape. He had left her as coldly as he had first taken her. No one cared what she felt. No one. The Norman had used her, her brothers were using her. Ceidre hugged herself. She was so utterly alone. Damn them all.

"I had better go," Albie said. "At least I can report some progress. God be with you, Ceidre."

She was too angry to call out a like farewell. Too angry, too hurt. But she knew one thing. She was not going to become the Norman's leman, oh no. Never would she share his bed again. Even fortified by this resolution, she didn't feel better. Not at all.

He knew the instant she entered the hall.

He and his men were more than halfway through with their meal. Like a magnet, his eyes were drawn to her as she made her way quickly and gracefully to the table. Her head was high, chin in the air. His breath seemed to get stuck in his chest. She did not look his way, and then she took her seat.

Rolfe became aware of many things at once. Alice's rigidity as she sat beside him and the utter, absolute silence of his men. And that he himself was staring. He resumed eating. He no longer was hungry, but he ate rhythmically, as if entertaining the same gusto as before. Conversation slowly resumed. Rolfe did not look down the table again. He did not have to look. Her presence filled his senses.

Ceidre was shaking inside. The instant she had entered the hall, the talk had ceased, and every eye had been riveted upon her. She had attempted to show no feelings, to remain like a marble statue. It had not been easy to do, with her heart winging frantically, with his hawklike gaze upon her.

She could not eat, but realized, suddenly, that she had made a mistake. She was sitting at the lowest end of the table while Guy, her husband, sat on Rolfe's right. A quick glance confirmed that Guy was aware of this too, for he was coming to her. Ceidre felt herself flushing. He paused beside her. Someone snickered not far from her. Guy lifted a furious glance at the culprit, one of his own cohorts. "Lady, please, 'tis unseemly you dine below the salts now that you are my wife." His hand was on her elbow, urging her to rise. His gentleness and kind tone made Ceidre unbearably grateful.

"But is she yet your wife, Guy?" Beltain chortled from the other end of the table. "Mayhap you should take her to bed and rectify that immediately!"

Laughter greeted this reference to Rolfe's having bedded her in place of the groom. Ceidre went hot red. Guy froze next to her. Ceidre wanted to shrink away, with everyone joking at her expense. The one responsible for this entire mess, of course, said nothing, just sat there listening indifferently. Ceidre realized she was glaring at Rolfe, but he was not looking at her. Nor was he amused.

"I demand satisfaction for such coarse comments," Guy said stiffly, flushed. He pulled Ceidre to the other end of the table, where she dreaded going. Athelstan slid over to make a place for her, and she quickly sank down upon the bench, wanting to sink, instead, through the floor. Rolfe was oblivious to her, as if she were invisible, and she wished, desperately, that she were anywhere but here.

"The good knight is malhumored." Beltain laughed. "But I know how his good humor can be restored!" He chuckled again, lewdly, and more laughter rose.

Before Guy could retort, Rolfe interjected, "Enough."

At least, she thought miserably, beet-red, he had the decency to end Beltain's crude insinuations. She stared at her hands, folded in her lap, a silence ensuing. Rolfe rose abruptly from the table. "There will be no quarrel among my men," Rolfe stated. "If Guy's wife is offended"—and still he did not spare her a glance—"Beltain will apologize." With that, he strolled out.

Guy's wife, Ceidre thought, shrinking up inside. He had called her Guy's wife.

"She is most offended," Guy said into an interested silence. "Apologize, Beltain. Do not make me defy our lord."

"I am most sorry," Beltain said to Ceidre, who finally lifted her eyes. " 'Twas only a jest. I meant no harm."

Ceidre mumbled an appropriate reply. She was sorry she had come to this meal, sorrier still that she had laid eyes on the Norman, that cold, unfeeling animal. He cared not an ounce that they had shared a night; he had no feelings at all. He had finally gotten what he wanted, and he had clearly forgotten everything that had passed between them.

If only she could forget as well.

CHAPTER 41

He had succeeded; he hadn't thought of her all afternoon.

But his success was short-lived. Supper was over, and his men had long since adjourned for the evening. Rolfe found himself in his chamber, alone, pacing like a wild caged lion. Now, now he could not stop his thoughts; he had not the willpower. Ceidre taunted him as twilight deepened the sky to jet-black. Ceidre—with Guy.

Now, at this very moment, was she writhing beneath him in ecstasy?

Rolfe cried out, slamming his fist against the mantle, the same fist he had bruised not so long ago on the table in the hall. Pain was fierce and instantaneous, he welcomed it. But it did not provide the distraction he sought.

He was going mad, he thought, for he could barely contain feelings he had no right to. Feelings of fury, feelings of jealousy. The desire to hurt, to punish, to kill.

He tried to calm himself with logic. Ceidre was only a woman. There were women in this world aplenty. For some reason, he was still entranced by her, but it would pass. There were more timely matters to reflect upon than a mere woman. Matters of state, of treason. Treason. He had given her to Guy to protect her from the ultimate, irreversible fate that awaited traitors to the crown. God, he groaned, was Guy taking her now? Worse, was Ceidre truly welcoming him? Ceidre would make any man insatiable, he knew this first-hand. He could not contain his wrath, his rage—he was strangling with it, and he wanted to strangle his own best man and good friend.

He could barely stop himself from leaving the keep, striding down to the manor, pulling Guy off Ceidre with his own bare hands, then slamming him into the wall for touching her. . . .

I am truly mad, he thought. She is his wife!

There was an untimely knock upon his door. Rolfe strode to it and flung it open. Alice, seeing his blazing expression, took a step back. She was dressed in her finest bedclothes. "What do you want?" he said with a snarl.

"I . . ." What could she say? She had come in desperation, hoping he would receive her as a husband should, praying that he would get her with child. She had never seen him so livid, and she was justifiably frightened. But she was also desperate. She sensed, with all her shrewd intuition, that her position had never been more precarious. The fact that he had chosen to bed Guy's bride sharpened this awareness. She would ignore the humiliation she had suffered the best she could. Alice knew she must conceive his child quickly, to distract him from that witch.

For she was aware of a horrifying possibility, one that could bring her ruin. What if Ceidre bore his child?

"My lord, I've brought you some hot wine. Perhaps 'twill calm you."

"I do not want it," Rolfe said through gritted teeth.

Bravely Alice stepped past him, aware of his incredulous expression and, too late, aware of his rage at her forwardness. She placed the wine on the chest, trembling. She turned to him, knowing that as she stood directly in the firelight he could see through her finely woven nightclothes. Would he rape her? she wondered, with a frisson of something almost like excitement. He had ripped Ceidre's clothes from her—this was common gossip. She shivered. Would he rip hers off too? Would he strike her?

"I do not want any wine," Rolfe said harshly.

"My lord," Alice said softly, trembling, suddenly short of breath, "mayhap I can ease your need now—your loneliness."

"Get out!" he roared.

Alice jumped.

"Get out—and do not dare to enter here until I demand your presence!"

Rolfe watched her flee. He kicked the door viciously shut in her wake, so hard it shuddered and groaned. Then he continued pacing, tormented with his own thoughts.

The sun was high in the sky. Rolfe urged his tired mount forward. The gray was docile, his flanks heaving, and his coat was wet with sweat. No wetter than Rolfe's own skin. His tunic, beneath the hauberk, clung damply to his frame. "Again," he told the four dozen men he had been drilling, and been drilling with, all day.

Someone groaned, and Rolfe swung his head furiously to find the culprit, but he could not discern who had dared to object. "Guy!" he called out. "You stay at the end of the line, to face me again."

Guy's face was red and damp from exertion. He nodded, his expression quizzical. The men had divided into two lines, one on each side of the field. Rolfe cantered to his own line, replacing his helmut.

His adrenaline was flowing thickly. He stared at Guy from his position opposite him.

He had pushed his men remorselessly, relentlessly, all day. But not harder than he had pushed himself. And now, as he faced Guy again for the sixth time, a sickening image crossed his mind. Guy impaling Ceidre. Tonight, he thought grimly, Guy would be too tired to walk, much less fuck.

He called out, and the two lines charged at each other.

Rolfe rode at Guy with a cool smile. His lance struck Guy's shield squarely, again causing the young man to lose his balance, but not unhorsing him. He had unhorsed him twice—the first two times they had made a pass at each other. Guy had quickly discovered that this was no easy jousting, that he was going to be pushed to his limit. Since then, with sheer determination, he had met Rolfe fearlessly, grimly. His own lance missed Rolfe completely this time.

Had Guy fucked Ceidre as soundly as he had?

They charged again. Rolfe's lance caught Guy's shield squarely another time, almost unseating the knight. Guy's own lance grazed Rolfe's shield. Rolfe moved his steed back to the line and gave another order to commence.

It was almost suppertime when he finally allowed his men to quit the field. He watched them walking their tired mounts to the bailey. No one spoke, heads hung, lances pointed at the ground. They were the best, Rolfe thought, with sudden fierce pride. He had pushed them beyond human endurance, and they had not failed him. When the time came for battle, they would be undefeatable.

He saw that Guy was waiting for him, and he scowled. He knew he should not have pushed the young man so hard, that he was taking out his frustration upon him personally. Of course, Guy could take it, or he would not be his second in command at such a young age. Still, Rolfe did not want to look at him, did not want to talk to him. To see him reminded him of what the other man had, what he still wanted. Nevertheless, he walked his steed to him, and together they headed back to the keep.

" 'Twas a long day," Guy said, glancing at him, "but the men proved they are worthy of you, my lord. Not one complaint, not one laggard."

"They did well," Rolfe agreed. He paused. "You did well."

"You tested me overmuch, I think," Guy said. Then he grinned. "The day will soon come when I will unhorse you!"

Rolfe had to smile. "I await it—but I do not hold my breath." Guy laughed. The problem was, Rolfe thought, that he liked Guy, he could not hate him, as jealous as he was.

Jealous—was he actually jealous?

"So," Rolfe said, before he could stop himself, "how do you find married life? 'Tis blissful?"

Guy hesitated, and Rolfe saw it, with a shrinking feeling. As comrades-in-arms, they had wenched together profusely. Guy had bragged on many an occasion of a sweet tumble, had openly discussed the charms he had enjoyed—graphically, as men were wont to do. Rolfe himself had never been one to discuss his own experiences, for, until Ceidre, a toss in the hay was a toss in the hay, one barely distinguishable from another. Guy's enthusiastic descriptions of this redhead and that blonde amused him; why, he could rarely recall the hair color of a wench he had bedded! Now, however, he was disappointed, for Guy was not eager to share the pleasure he had found in Ceidre's arms. It was, Rolfe supposed grimly, because he felt respect for a wife that he did not feel for a dairymaid.

" 'Tis agreeable," Guy finally said, with some unease.

Rolfe felt himself flushing. He knew himself just how agreeable Ceidre was. He was positive, in that moment, that Guy would not share graphic details with him as he had used to because he was so smitten by the woman in question. Because he had tasted her passion, and was protective of it. Because it had been passion that had enthralled them last night—while he paced his chamber like a madman.

Rolfe urged his steed on ahead, his face dark, thunderous.

Alice was about to settle in front of the hearth in the hall after supper with her embroidery and her lapdogs. She felt him approaching, and every fiber of her being tensed. Rolfe paused in front of her. His gaze was direct, although his voice was moderated so as not to be overheard. "Make yourself ready for me," he said. "I will be awaiting you in my chamber."

Alice's eyes opened wide, but he had already turned and was going up the stairs. She started to tremble. Finally, finally this mockery of a marriage would be consummated. She was so nervous, and so afraid, her stomach hurt. She was keenly aware of his ugly mood these past few days—since he had bedded Ceidre on her wedding night. Unbidden, graphic images flashed—images that had been haunting Alice. Rolfe ripping off Ceidre's gown and knocking her down, throwing himself upon her while she wept, impaling her with his huge manhood. Hurting her.

Alice shuddered. She had not been able to get this particular fantasy out of her mind, not since Mary had told her the gossip, even showing her Ceidre's torn yellow gown. She wondered if he would take her that way. She shuddered again, breathless.

In his chamber, Rolfe sipped a cup of wine. His thoughts were not on his wife, about to come to him a virgin, but on another man's wife—on Ceidre. At night his thoughts became intolerable, his mood equally so. He knew damn well Guy was with her now, touching her, fucking her. Anger and jealousy engulfed him, made him throb from his head to his toes. His pumping blood even filled his groin. He was so frustrated he felt he might jump out of his skin.

A knock on the door interrupted his thoughts, and grimly, realizing who it was, he called for his wife to enter. There would be no delaying, he thought resolutely, what should have been done a long time ago. Instead of dwelling upon another man's house, he would put his own in order.

Alice saw that he was in the same grim mood, and that he was drinking, although apparently sober. Again, his gaze was level. " 'Tis time to consummate this marriage."

"I will not resist," she told him, her voice frail. "I want your sons, you know this."

"Then I will do my best to give them to you." He gestured at the bed.

Alice climbed in, rigid with fear, with excitement. The room became utterly dark as he doused the lamps, and she heard him stripping off his tunic and hose. She recalled his big, ugly body, so powerful, strong enough to break a woman like her. He climbed in beside her and, for a moment, lay still, making no move toward her. Alice felt the first touch of disappointment. According to Mary, he had taken Ceidre on the floor—that was where her blood had been. He had ripped off her clothes, thrown her on the floor . . . She shifted uncomfortably.

He made a sound, almost of disgust, but surely she had heard it wrongly, and rolled toward her, shoving her gown up to her hips. His hand stroked over her thighs, then delved between her legs. Shock reared, and she tried to shift away.

"Be still," he said. "I need to touch you or I will not be able to take you."

Disappointment loomed. Alice was no fool, and she knew what he was saying. She could feel his sex organ against her outer thigh, and it was not rock-hard like a stud stallion's. Not rock-hard as it had been when he had raped her sister. He was touching her to arouse himself, and to be touched so intimately was disgusting. He finished fingering her, then heaved himself on top of her. He reached down and positioned himself. Alice kept imagining how it had been with her sister. She could not believe this was the same man. He thrust into her.

The pain was overwhelming, and she screamed.

Rolfe stopped, not because of her cry, but because despite the power of his thrust, she was so small and narrow he was momentarily deterred. Rolfe impaled her again; again she screamed, as if he were ripping her apart. Having had many women, he knew she was unnaturally small and that he would hurt her until he finished, owing to his own uncommon largeness. There was no way to avoid it.

Alice knew he was killing her. "Stop," she begged, weeping from the raw pain. "Stop, you'll tear me in two! Please!"

He paused, still within her. "I am sorry," he said indifferently. "You are too small for me, but 'twill get better, in time, I assure you." And he began moving rhythmically, steadily, harshly.

Alice wept, the burning, tearing pain unbearable, trying to push him off with her fists. His movements did not cease. And then, just when she thought she would faint from the excruciating agony, she was swept into a violent series of tremors and contractions, crying out with pleasure, gasping into his neck.

Her orgasm surprised Rolfe. He had not even been completely aroused, not as he knew he could be, and because she was not made for a man like him, he was glad, otherwise he might, truly, kill her. He was surprised at her response because he had not been pleasuring her but hurting her. Her climax, however, brought his blood to the level he needed, and he began thrusting more rapidly, seeking release. She moaned, in pain, he knew, but he was almost finished, and he was determined to spill his seed in her.

She whimpered again.

Rolfe felt himself swelling further, hardening further, as he buried himself as deep as he could. She screamed. Her nails dug into his shoulders. "Harder," she cried. "Oh, harder, yes!"

He came as she sobbed and keened beneath him.

He rolled off of her immediately, separating their bodies while still in the fog of his aftermath. His mind cleared instantly. He almost laughed in the night. His malicious little wife liked pain. He supposed it should have been a surprise, but somehow, it wasn't.

CHAPTER 42

"My lady, you must come at once." Mary gasped, panting.

Ceidre was in the corridor between the kitchens and the manor, instructing two boys on their duties for the day. "What is it?"

" 'Tis the lord. He is hurt and will allow no one to touch him but you!"

Almost a week had passed since her wedding night. Ceidre had not seen Rolfe since the horrendous noonday meal the day after. She had kept to the manor, overseeing its servants, and she had kept to the village —anywhere that would keep her as far as possible from him. Once, when she was cutting through the orchard on her way back to the manor, she had heard the sounds of his men in their mock battles, and she had glimpsed him, from a distance, on his huge gray steed. She had not paused to watch, but had hurried on. He hadn't seen her.

Two days ago he had taken a dozen men hunting for large game, including Guy. Ceidre was well aware that the hunting party had just returned, for she had heard first the watch's horn and then the large cavalcade passing through the bailey, the sound of so many horses' hooves echoing thunderously. She had been replacing the rushes in the manor with Lettie, and she had ignored their advent. Lettie had not. She had cried out gleefully and run to the doorway to watch, waving at her favorites.

Ceidre had forgotten, the best she could, her wedding night. The truth was that it had become almost like a dream and, like a dream, haunted her mostly after dark. She tried not to think about the Norman, and when his golden image invaded her mind, she was quick to tell herself how she hated him. The hurt at his casual indifference to her was gone, numbed now with the passing of some time, into her own attitude of indifference. Therefore, it was a surprise that her blood should start racing madly at Mary's words. "I will fetch my potions," she said. He was hurt!

Her feet had sudden wings, and she returned in a flash. Mary was crying, wringing her hands, urging her to hurry. "What happened?" Ceidre asked, somehow getting the words past the lump that was trying to choke her.

" 'Twas a boar! He has been gored, Ceidre." And she started to weep.

He had been gored. The maid was hysterical, so Ceidre ignored her, running now. She was aware that her throat had tightened at the ominous words, that her heart was palpitating unsteadily. She was flying across the bailey and through the inner portcullis. She was not aware of bounding up the steps of the keep, or throwing open its huge door. Most of the Norman's men stood huddled and quiet in the great hall. Oh God, it was like a burial! They parted as she swept through their midst.

In the doorway of his chamber she came to an abrupt halt. Nothing could have prepared her for the sight of him. Alice and Beth were hovering by his side, as were Athelstan and Guy. She could only see his shoulders and head and neck; he appeared naked. He was *not* lying in agony, as she had feared, but sitting straight and tall, his face in that hard, contained mask she knew so well. Her heart froze at the sight of him. He was golden and handsome, he was sexually magnetic, and she had forgotten this in the past week.

He saw her, and their gazes locked. Ceidre realized she had stopped breathing, so she took a long breath. Anger reared. He was not badly hurt, this she could clearly see, because he looked her over carefully, the way only a man who has been intimate with her could, in a way that suggested he would be intimate with her again. She blushed.

"Come here," he said, his voice strong, in a command. "I am hurt."

If he was hurt, she was a witch, Ceidre thought caustically. She came forward, lips tight. Her heart was thudding so hard it was painful. The men moved aside. She noticed that Alice did not, and that her delicate white hand was clasped possessively upon his shoulder. The sight almost stopped her in her tracks. It certainly brought a sudden nausea to her. He beckoned her forward.

Then she saw that he was hurt, and a cry escaped her lips.

He was completely naked. His right thigh, nearer to her, was gashed from hip to knee, raw and bloody. "Get water and linens," Ceidre ordered, kneeling by his side, at Alice's feet. She was aware of his gaze relentlessly upon her, as she gently touched the unmarred flesh near the wound. It was already hot. His leg tightened beneath her fingertips. "It hurts when I touch you?" she asked, with real worry.

"No," he said harshly. "Your touch does not *hurt* me, Ceidre."

His tone made her look up. His gaze was both so bold and so intimate that for moment she forgot his wound and the presence of everyone in the room. She recovered, however, when Alice shifted angrily, her skirts swishing. She noted, then, the tight curve of his mouth, and knew he was in some pain. "How hurt are you?"

"I've suffered much worse."

"Do not play the hero with me," she snapped.

His tone was low, almost a purr. "I want only to be a hero in your eyes, Ceidre."

A flashing recollection of her wedding night pierced her. "Then you have gravely erred in judgment, my lord."

"I realize that." His laugh was bitter.

"My lord," Alice cut in, her voice high, "you look uncomfortable. Here, lean back, I—"

"I am fine," Rolfe said curtly. "Do not hover over me, I am not a boy."

Alice removed her hand from his back, taking a small step back. Ceidre quickly dropped her gaze to his torn flesh, but not before receiving the full brunt of Alice's glare. Alice's movement, as well, crowded her unreasonably, but she said nothing and began a careful inspection of the wound. It was not deep, not deep at all, and she was relieved. But it would require a few stitches after being more thoroughly cleaned. Beth returned with the items she had requested, and Ceidre placed everything upon the floor where she knelt, within easy reach. Alice's skirt billowed near the urn of water. Ceidre looked up at her sister and said politely. "Would you move, Alice? I need room."

"I will not," Alice said, her face pinched.

"Lady Alice, take yourself to the hearth," Rolfe ordered, and that was that. Alice obeyed, mouth pursed.

Ceidre couldn't help feeling sorry for her sister, to be spoken to with such obvious dislike. She wanted to ask the Norman exactly how he felt about his wife, and if he disliked her so, she wondered how he could bed her, night after night. She reminded herself that liking had nothing to do with lust—as she knew firsthand. And of course she could not voice these questions, even if they were alone in the room, 'twas not her affair. She picked up a clean rag. " 'Twill hurt."

"I suffer gladly," he murmured, holding her gaze.

She broke the contact, thoroughly unsettled now, and began cleaning the wound. He made not a sound, although she was aware of his big leg cramping beneath her gentle touch. She became thoroughly immersed in what she must do. When the wound was cleaned to her satisfaction, she picked up needle and thread. She did not hesitate. Her stitches were small and neat and very fast. Rolfe was so still he might have been carved of stone. She was keenly aware, however, that his breathing was harsher than usual.

To distract him, she conversed. "Was the hunt successful, other than this?"

"Yes, very. We took three deer, one with a sixteen-point spread. A wolf, and of course, the boar."

"Of course. Am I to assume 'twas your lance that slew it?"

"Yes," he said.

She finished with a sigh and looked up. For the first time his stark nakedness struck her, as she glimpsed his groin, its member flaccid now, the soft curve of his belly as he sat, the narrowness of his hips and the breadth of his chest. Flushed, she put aside the needle, preparing a poultice. "However did you manage to get gored?"

"It happens easily, the boar is mean and unpredictable."

"They are too deadly to be hunted," she replied, placing the herbs packed in linen upon his thigh. " 'Tis foolish for men to seek such sport." She was careful to look only at what she was doing, but now she was keenly aware of his hard leg beneath her fingers.

" 'Tis the danger that draws us," he said.

She could feel his gaze on the top of her bent head. " 'Tis a boyish need to prove a tardy manhood," Ceidre retorted with feeling.

"You cannot accuse my manhood of being tardy," he said softly.

His sensual tone brought a hot blush and she swiftly raised her gaze to his—only to glimpse the swelling of his organ. She faltered completely, at a loss. He smiled slightly, a smug, satisfied look in his bold gaze. "You are clearly not suffering," she managed. She rose and turned, but he grabbed her hand.

"Do not leave me."

"I am finished." She was forced to meet his regard.

"Do not leave," he repeated. "I am in pain."

"The pain you are in is quite clear," she retorted, angry now.

"You can ease it—if you would."

"Your wife can ease it!"

"You think so?" He cocked a brow. "She cannot, only you can."

"Do not say such things," she hissed. "Let me go."

"Only if you promise to return. I will allow no one else to tend me. The poultice must be changed, must it not?"

"Yes, but anyone—"

"You must tend me."

"All right." She surrendered.

"When will you come again?"

She hesitated. "Tomorrow."

"Tonight. You will come tonight. Mayhap I will catch a fever." He smiled.

There was, of course, that possibility, although

Ceidre though it was indistinct. "I will come when I have finished my duties at the manor," she said.

His face grew suddenly dark, blue eyes stormy. "Yes, of course, your duties. To your husband? Does he command your presence every night?" His tone raised. "Does he? Have you missed him these past two nights? *Have you?*"

She was stunned by his anger.

"Tonight," he said through gritted teeth, "you have duty to me, your overlord. Do not," he purred, "forget who I am. I gave you to Guy," he warned, "and I can take you away."

Ceidre shook with fury at his presumptive autocracy. The fact that he was right—that on Aelfgar his will was law, that he could order a divorce and Guy would willingly oblige him, that he could dispose of her, despite her husband, as he saw fit—increased her rage. "I am finished here. May I go?"

"You may go," he said silkily. "But do not think that you are finished here." He smiled, a tight, ruthless smile. "Do not think that we are finished."

CHAPTER 43

His leg throbbed, but Rolfe heaved himself up from the bed to limp to the fireplace and stare into its flames.

It was evening now, and his ears were attuned to the sounds outside his door, purposefully left ajar. He listened intently for movement, but there was no sound. Ceidre had not come.

He was angry—with himself. He had taunted her with sexual innuendo. He had not meant to. In truth, he never talked to any woman the way he spoke with her. Her bronze-haired, purple-eyed presence seemed to be his undoing. How could he have taunted her as he had? Mayhap it had to do with the fact that he hadn't set eyes upon her in a sennight. Mayhap it was her touch, so gentle, so tender—and ultimately, despite the superficial tear in his flesh, so arousing.

But to taunt her sexually with his wife and her husband in the same room?

He could not control his physical arousal, but he certainly could control his words. There was no excuse. They had both heard, he had seen it on Alice's tight-lipped white face and in Guy's searching gaze. He was surprised, if not confused, with the young man's response. Guy had not been angered, or, if he had been, he had hidden it well. Rolfe knew that if he were Guy and another man made such suggestive remarks to his wife, if she were Ceidre, he would kill. Of course, he was Guy's liege lord, and Guy, he knew, worshiped him.

He regretted ordering her presence this night, just as he was disappointed that she had not come. She was probably, he thought with sudden depression, in Guy's arms this very minute. And then he heard her.

His head whipped around, listening to the light footfalls approaching, waiting, watching as his door swung open. She appeared there then, in all her golden and bronze glory, a mutinous expression on her face, her lush lips tight, her eyes flashing purple fire. Rolfe realized he was smiling with his pleasure at seeing her.

"I see you have not succumbed to the fever," Ceidre said curtly. "Therefore, may I leave, my lord?"

His smile widened. He hobbled to the bed and sat. "Come check my leg."

She huffed her disdain, but obeyed. He was wearing only a tunic that came to midthigh. She did not pause or hesitate, but lifted it to reveal his thigh and the rest of his naked body. Damn, he thought, he was truly well, for he was rousing instantly into thick tumescence.

"This is a farce," she cried, jumping away from him.

"I cannot help my response to you."

"I refuse to cuckold my husband!"

His anger was instant. "Think you I called you here to commit adultery? To cuckold my best man?"

She flinched slightly under his icy stare. "Think? Oh, no, my lord, I know it!"

He grabbed her wrist and yanked her hard, right onto his bed, almost across his bad thigh. She struggled once and went still. "You flatter yourself, Ceidre," he said roughly.

"You are a beast!"

"I do not cuckold my best man."

"Then let me up—let me go."

His other hand captured her chin, forcing her gaze to his. "You are so unwilling. You love him?"

"What?" She struggled anew now, but it was futile.

"Do you love him so soon?" His tone was harsh. "A few tumbles, and you are so loyal? Answer me!"

She shook, she said nothing. He saw tears well in her eyes.

"Does he please you so, Ceidre?" Rolfe said in a dangerous tone.

" 'Tis not your affair," she cried in a small voice.

"Answer me!"

"Yes," she shouted, then wept. She would never let him know the truth, that her own husband found her repulsive and preferred the comfort of Lettie and Beth to herself. Never would she share this secret, this humiliation, with this man.

"I am not going to hurt you, I am not going to touch you, I am not going to rape you—cease your tears," he said, his tone filled with loathing. He pushed her violently away off the bed. She stumbled and almost fell. She looked at him and saw the glittering fury. It was so strong, she thought it was hatred, and she shrank.

"Get out," he said, low. "I have changed my mind, I do not need you—as you can see."

Ceidre wiped her eyes and stood, squaring her shoulders. She could not look away from his dark, violent gaze.

"Go to your husband," he said softly, ugly. "Go to him, charm him. But stay the hell away from me."

For some reason, the urge to go to him and take away the controlled loathing in his tone swept her, and she did not move, unable to do so.

"Why do you wait? Do you now play the seductress? Do you think to cast a spell, standing there honey-haired, beautiful, trembling as if with hurt? What you have I have seen before many times. You are only a woman, like any other, and my response to you is the same as with all the others."

His cruel words struck her with the force of a blow, and she turned, numbly.

"Tell Alice to come to me," he called to her departing back. "Tell her to come to me, I have need of her now."

Ceidre escaped.

CHAPTER 44

A week later, Rolfe and Guy rode out to inspect Guy's holdings at Dumstanbrough thoroughly. Rolfe's leg was slightly stiff, which he deemed the riding would ease. They took with them a dozen men, in case of a run-in with Scots reivers, leaving Aelfgar well defended and under Beltain's authority. They reached this outermost village belonging to Rolfe in a day and a half and had completed their inspection by that nightfall.

As his men lounged around the campfire, preparatory to sleep, Rolfe stood and stretched. His leg ached slightly. The village was quiet now, after the initial uproar that their arrival had caused. Apparently, being so far north, they saw little of their lord and master, and apparently cared just as little whether that lord be Saxon or not. Ample fare and atrocious ale had been provided for his men. Guy had already chosen a site for his manor. As soon as Rolfe could spare him, he knew Guy would be returning to see to its construction. This made him envision a day in the future that surely must come—Ceidre living here as the lady of Dumstanbrough.

Not that he cared. Let her have Dumstanbrough and the husband she already loved so well! Maybe Guy would bring her with him when he returned, and leave her here when he left to resume his services at Aelfgar. If it weren't for Ceidre, Rolfe would be thoroughly pleased with the turn of events. Guy was a fierce knight, and having him on this northernmost border would be a boon to his defenses. Rolfe had already decided to take on more men, and some of these he would garrison here as well.

Ceidre. Did she pine for her husband? He felt the ugliness rising within him, and stalked away from the campfire, as if to outdistance his emotions.

She loved Guy. Fickle was the first word that raised itself, she was fickle. But how could that be? He snorted, feeling derision, directed at himself. A rape did not win her heart. But hadn't they shared more after? And what did he care about her heart! Love was for fools—for women and boys. In truth, it did not exist, it was merely a polite excuse for lust. Could she have truly found such passion and such ecstasy in Guy's arms? He reiterated to himself that he did not care, he had his choice of wenches, and in the dark one could barely tell them apart.

He stopped, realizing he had reached the village, about to turn around to return to the camp. There was a feeling of potency in the velvet night cocooning him. He was keenly aware of it; almost as if he was pierced with something, poignant and intense, like a need, but a need of what? As he started back to the camp, a husky laugh caught his attention. Despite the sexual note, he instantly recognized the tone as belonging to Guy, and pausing, his gaze scanned the environs.

In the darkness, he finally made out an embracing couple beneath an oak tree, the rays of the moon drenching them. His curiosity was not idle; he *had* to know if it was really Guy, and he approached until he was certain. It was Guy. He had the woman on his lap, her skirts tossed up, his hips rocking her rhythmically as he fucked her. Rolfe felt anger sweep over him.

He did not move, and presently they finished, the woman rising, shaking out her skirts, laughing, Guy adjusting his hose and patting her behind. He started when he saw Rolfe. The wench also noticed him, and she gave him a sly look, but Rolfe ignored her. She left, disappointed.

"You are looking for me, my lord?"

"No, I just happened upon you." They started walking back to the camp together.

Rolfe looked bluntly at Guy. "You are not faithful to your wife." It was, of course, a statement, yet it was also an opening, a question.

It was dark, but from Guy's tone, Rolfe knew he was blushing. "No. Of course not. I am too young to grow old with one woman, and a witch at that."

He felt the anger again. "She is no witch, Guy."

"I am sorry, I forgot you believe otherwise." Guy was nervous and it showed.

"I am surprised," Rolfe said carelessly, "that after being in her arms, you would find the energy, or desire, for another." His glance skewered the younger man again.

Guy was silent, with unease. Rolfe knew it, and wondered if it was his blunt reference to having been the first to bed his wife, or something more. Finally Guy shrugged. "I am young." Head down, he trudged on.

Rolfe knew that if he were married to Ceidre he would not have the energy or desire for another. He stared at Guy thoughtfully. And he wondered how Ceidre would feel if she knew her husband was so eager to seek out other women.

"Arrest her," Alice said.

Ceidre froze in the midst of lighting two tapers in

the hall of the manor. Two Normans rushed forward, one of them taking her arm. Beltain stood with Alice, his face dark. "What is going on?" Ceidre cried.

Alice smirked, her face ugly with malicious intent. "You have committed treason one time too many, Ceidre, and in my lord's absence I must protect him and what is his! Arrest her!"

"Treason?" Ceidre gasped. "I have not—"

Beltain interrupted her, waving a parchment that he was holding. He was grim. "A maid found this in your chamber, Lady."

Ceidre looked at the paper. "I know not what it is."

"It addresses you. 'Tis from your brother Edwin."

Her heart stopped, then renewed its beat. " 'Tis a lie! That is not mine! I have never seen it! I did not receive it! I did not!"

Beltain was very somber. "It addresses you, 'twas found in your chamber, and it is from your brother. Someone passed this on to you. Who?"

"No one, I tell you," she cried, truly furious at this deceit. "This is all false, 'tis a trap!"

"You have committed treason before," Beltain said. "The whole world knows this. Before your marriage, my lord had you guarded night and day because he did not trust you. Nor do I trust you, and the evidence is clear." He paused.

"She is very shrewd, Beltain," Alice remarked. "And she is a witch. If you do not throw her in the dungeons she could well escape—and my lord would be enraged."

Ceidre froze.

"She will not escape," Beltain said heavily. "She is Guy's wife, I cannot throw her in the dungeons. But I, personally, will guard her."

Ceidre closed her eyes briefly in relief.

"No!" Alice cried. "She will cast a spell and you, like the others, will be impotent to fight it! Believe me, I know!"

Ceidre could not believe this was happening, and she turned a cold, angry gaze upon Alice. "You did this, did you not? Tell me, as I know you cannot write yourself, who wrote this note, this forgery?"

Alice ignored her. "I warn you," she said to Beltain. "I warn you! Remember Morcar's escape!"

Beltain turned heavily to Ceidre. "I am sorry, but Lady Alice is right. Put her in the dungeons," he said to the two knights.

"Wait!" Ceidre cried, frantic now. "Let me see that note!"

Beltain shrugged and handed it to her. Ceidre glanced at it, then lifted a desperate gaze. "This is not Ed's writing!"

"It matters not whether he wrote it himself," Beltain said. "He probably cannot write and had a friar write it for him. Take her down now."

"No, please!" Ceidre grabbed Beltain's sleeve. "Please, I beg you!"

She was propelled forward, Beltain regarding her with pity and disgust. She twisted to look at her sister. "Do not do this," she pleaded wildly. "Alice, what will you gain? When the Norman returns—"

"He will have you hanged!" Alice cried.

With a thud, the rock door closed above her, immersing her in total blackness.

Ceidre did not move. She stood completely still, barely breathing, clutching herself. Her heart was thundering so hard she was afraid it might explode. She tried to take a deep breath and failed, choking. The air was thick and closed and foul with human excrement. Because it was summer, she had been barefoot, and now wet, slimy mud oozed through her toes. It was damp and cool in the dungeons, but that was not why she was trembling. Her tremors increased.

She was not alone, and she knew it. She could hear movement, slight, scuffling movement—rats. Tears came to her eyes. As much as she hated the Norman, she started praying frantically for his return. She was sure he would have her released the instant he returned, but even if they only stopped for a day at Dumstanbrough, that would still be two days away. At the earliest. She would not survive.

She moaned, a long, low sound. The shaking of her body became violent, her breathing became fast and shallow. And still she could not get air into her lungs.

Gasping for air, desperate to fill her constricted lungs, she started to cry. She had to get out of here! Somehow, she had to! She could not breathe—she could feel the walls caving in on her! She would suffocate, she was suffocating, she would be buried alive! With a scream, half a sob, Ceidre leapt for the trapdoor. It was way above her head, taller than two men, but she sobbed and leapt, tears streaming down her face, again and again, gasping for air, her heart speeding out of her chest. She had to get out, she had to! Somehow she had found the wall, the dirt hard and dry, and she began frantically, hysterically, to claw at it. "Let me out," she screamed. "Let me out," she sobbed. She clawed and clawed, ripping her nails, weeping, trying to climb up to the door. She would get a foot off the floor, only to slide helplessly back down. Finally she fell sobbing and panting onto the ground.

Something warm and alive touched her foot.

Ceidre screamed again, jumping up. She attacked

the wall with all of her strength. Her nails ripped, warm blood oozing down her fingers, but she was oblivious. She renewed her efforts. They were superhuman—or those of a madwoman.

CHAPTER 45

The advent of dawn carried with it the same potency Rolfe had felt the night before, except the intangible feeling had increased. Rolfe awakened with his instincts keen, as if alerted to and sensing out danger. 'Twas almost as if they were foretelling an ambush. Urgency crackled in the air. "We will not dwell," he told Guy, and ordered his men to depart.

The feeling of urgency grew. Rolfe pushed his men at a faster pace than they had come, although not carelessly, his gaze attuned to every sight around them, his ears to every sound. He was expecting *something* ominous. But when they finally made camp, way after dusk, no event had arrived to shatter their tranquility. Rolfe could not sleep, tense with foreboding and filled with this urgent need to return to Aelfgar.

They arrived before noon the next day. Rolfe had half expected to find Aelfgar under attack or razed to the ground. The sight of his keep and the village, both intact, relieved him, but, annoyingly, he could not shake the dread apprehension clinging to his soul. Alice, ever dutiful, greeted him in the courtyard, telling him she had already ordered a bath. Rolfe nodded, waving her away, turning to Beltain. He instantly remarked the knight's somber countenance. "What has passed? What has happened in my absence?"

"Everything has been fine." He hesitated. "Except that a missive was found in Lady Ceidre's chamber."

Guy, a few paces away, straightened and turned at this. "What missive?" Rolfe demanded.

" 'Twas from her brother," Beltain said.

Rolfe felt his anger, hard and boiling, filling him. "That wench will not learn," he muttered. "Send her to me, and bring me the missive," he snapped. She had commited treason again. Dread welled to join the anger. It filled every fiber of his being.

"Release her from the dungeons," Beltain was ordering.

Rolfe whipped around. "You put her in the dungeons?"

"As your wife pointed out, 'twas the only way to ensure she would not escape." Beltain met Rolfe's gaze frankly. "I was hesitant, but decided 'twas better to do so and guarantee she would be an imprisoned prisoner when you arrived, rather than an escaped traitor."

Rolfe did not question his own motivations. He was already striding down the hill, all anger in abeyance, the sense of urgency overwhelming. He was barely aware of Guy on his heels, grim, and Beltain, sober. He raced through the portcullis, almost running now, his strides eating up the ground. As soon as the manor with its dungeon was in sight, he was calling to the guard to open the trapdoor. The man threw the bolt, then lifted the door up. Rolfe reached his side and, without breaking stride, knelt and swung himself lithely down into the black pit.

He blinked, trying to adjust to the darkness. "Ceidre? Ceidre?"

There was no sound, no indication that anyone inhabited this dark, dank hell, and for an instant he thought she had somehow escaped. Then he heard a low moan. His head whipped toward the sound, and he made out a vague form crouched upon the ground. "Ceidre!"

He reached her in an instant and was unprepared for a hoarse, shrill scream. He bent for her and was met by a feeble attack. Her fingers harmlessly grazed his face as she tried to claw him. Ignoring this, he lifted her into his arms. She was covered with mud and muck and she stank. For a second, as he moved beneath the open trapdoor, she was inert, and then she twisted and clawed at him again.

" 'Tis me, Rolfe, stop it," he said, calling for the ladder.

She did not stop her feeble, very feeble, contortions, trying to wrench away, trying to rake his face. Her breathing was hoarse, ragged, and very shallow. His gut was tight with fear. " 'Tis me, Rolfe," he repeated in a low, firm tone.

"Let me out," she rasped, her voice a pitiful raw whisper, barely audible. "Let me out!"

"I am taking you out," he said softly, something sick twisting inside him. "Do not fight me, I am taking you out."

He slung her over his shoulder, realizing she was too weak to climb up the rope ladder herself, and he caught it with one hand. He balanced a foot on the lowest rung, then, sure of himself, he rapidly climbed up. The guard took Ceidre from him when he was high enough to do so, and Rolfe quickly made his way to the top, hoisting himself easily out of the dungeon.

He froze, then cried out in horror.

Ceidre was covered with mud as she crouched panting and shaking where the guard had deposited her. Her hands and forearms were streaked with blood—there was even blood on her face. His gaze flew back to her hands, to see that they were raw, the nails torn, some missing. But worse, much worse, was the wild, crazed look in her eyes, as she huddled blinking in the light—like a frightened, maddened animal.

He approached her instantly; she recoiled. Something huge and incredibly tender rose up in him, and very slowly, he dropped to his knees beside her. "Ceidre, 'tis Rolfe, you are freed now . . . everything will be fine."

She looked at him, blinking rapidly, wary and afraid, reminding him of a trapped fox, tensed and ready to bite. He had the urge to weep. With a slow, trembling hand he reached out to her, not touching her. "Ceidre?"

He saw the moment of flaring recognition. She dropped her head with a sob. She was panting harshly, head hanging, fingers embedded in the ground. Rolfe touched her shoulder and felt her shudder. But there was no shrinking, no resistance. He gently took her into his arms.

She clung.

His embrace tightened as he rose to his full height. His expression was a rigid mask, to hide the real agony he was feeling. She buried her filthy face in his neck, and he felt the wetness of tears. He was keenly aware of her thundering heart, her harsh, rapid breathing, and it worried him. And he felt her hold tightening, tightening, until she was almost strangling him. His answering grip was nearly as fierce and, somehow, impossibly tender.

He recollected his men and turned a livid blue gaze on Beltain. His knight, he saw, was stricken with horror. "I am sorry." He gasped. "I had no idea . . ." Beltain turned to Guy. "I am sorry. I am sorry!"

Guy nodded. "She lost her mind," he said matter-of-factly. "You could not know she would do so. I've seen it before, grown men made crazy when imprisoned beneath the ground." He turned to Rolfe. "Shall I take her, my lord?"

"No," Rolfe managed, not trusting himself to speak to Beltain, whom he could murder easily if he let himself. With long strides, he carried Ceidre to the keep and into the hall and up the stairs. He gently laid her down upon his bed. She clung to him like a monkey, weeping, refusing to release his neck. Rolfe found himself sitting, holding her, stroking her tangled, mud-encrusted hair. She sobbed into his tunic front, still trembling violently. He ran big, firm, yet soothing hands over her back, again and again, stroking her, caressing her. "Shhh," he intoned. "Hush now, sweeting, hush now, *chérie,* I am here, and all will be well."

She began to babble. She began to tell him of how she had almost died, how she could not breathe, how the ground had tried to swallow her up. How she had screamed and begged to be freed but no one had answered, how she had tried to climb up the walls, until her nails were torn and ripped raw, how she had tried to tunnel out, until she fainted. Her voice was a bare whisper, practically inaudible from all the screaming she had vainly done.

"Do not talk now, sweetheart," he whispered back, his large hand cradling her head. "Do not talk, you must let your voice heal."

She went still and quiet for the first time, her face still buried against his chest. He began kneading the back of her skull. Her breathing was slower now, though not yet normal, and her trembling was a shadow of what it had been. Relief overwhelmed him, and with it, he became distinctly aware of a murderous fury.

And he became aware of something else, someone's presence. He turned his head without moving, still stroking her, soothing her, and saw his wife. Her face was glazed with hatred and malicious triumph, but at the sight of his blazing blue wrath, the expression was instantly replaced with fear. She stepped back.

Rolfe was so enraged that his voice, when he spoke, was low and calm and even. "Get out," he said. "Await me in the solar, and do not move from it until I come."

Alice did not need to be told twice. She fled.

He was shaking. He got a grip on himself and looked down at Ceidre's head. Covered with mud and muck, like an animal. He trembled again. Then, very gently, he shifted apart, because he wanted to talk to her, he wanted to look at her, he needed reassurance that she was sane again. But she whimpered in protest and went with him, clutching him desperately. Firmly but so gently, Rolfe slid his hand from the back of her head to her chin, his thumb stroking along her jaw in little wisps of movement. He felt her relax anew and lifted her face up so he could look into her eyes.

They were full of pain, but lucid. He knew it was not physical agony, but emotional, and it hurt him even more. Her gaze, though, was wide and grateful—and trusting? And so vulnerable. Not even seeing her dirt not even smelling her stink, Rolfe's own lashes fluttered down and he gently touched his mouth to hers.

Her lips were soft and passive, but not unyielding. Rolfe felt choked with tenderness and despair, with pity and paternal protectiveness. His mouth plied gently, his tongue touched her lips and retreated. Bolder now, he increased the pressure, parting her, touching her teeth. And he retreated again.

His lust had arisen, so immense, he thought he might explode in his hose.

Shaken by the overwhelming need to bury himself in her, to comfort her this way, and with the giving to take his own comfort, to reassure himself with her responses that she was still Ceidre, still his, he rose separating himself from her. This time she did not make a sound of protest, but her gaze was glued to him. She lay exhausted and still. He noted, gladly, that she was breathing normally at last.

He walked to the door and bellowed for the hot water for his bath. He paused there, afraid to go near her again, seeking control, afraid of the terrible depth of need he had just experienced. He felt her riveted gaze and turned to see her staring with the same wide-eyed look. There was apprehension mingled with the trust, and he saw that her fists were clenched upon the bedcovers.

"I am not leaving, do not worry," he said huskily, correctly understanding why she was anxious. He noted that her palms relaxed, some of the tension left her gaze.

He came back to her. "Are you all right now, Ceidre?" She did not answer. "Talk to me. Please."

She looked at the floor. "I was so afraid."

His hand found her hair. "I know."

She choked on her fear, an unshed sob. "I prayed," she whispered. "I prayed you would come."

He swept her back into his arms. "I did come, I did come, but not soon enough, and I am sorry." She clung, and he almost didn't hear the knock upon his door.

He watched the servants bring in the hot water, filling the tub. When they had finished he ordered them out. He returned to sit next to Ceidre, pulling her upright. His hands were already loosening her girdle. She did not protest. "You will feel better once you bathe," he said.

He tugged her onto her feet, between his thighs. She was weak and she clutched his shoulders. He stripped her of her gown, then her undertunic. He tried not to look at her naked body, at her small waist and full, shimmering breasts, at her lush hips, at her femininity. He carried her to the tub and gently placed her in it. She sighed, closing her eyes.

Rolfe knelt beside her. He watched her immerse herself under the water, watched her come up with a sputter. She floated loosely and turned her head to stare at him.

The water did not cover her big, beautiful breasts, and her long nipples were hard and pointed. He was undone, throbbing and needing release, needing to bury himself inside her. But her gaze was still dark with her phobia of the dungeon and wide with her childlike trust of him. He picked up the soap and handed it to her. His hand trembled; his entire body shook.

"No," she said, closing her eyes. "I am too tired. Tomorrow. . . ."

So he washed her hair himself. There was no question of calling a maid. Then he washed her feet and legs, only as far as they were covered with mud, to just past her knees. When he picked up her raw hands she whimpered, when he gently soaped them she wept without fighting him. He did not touch the rest of her body—she trusted him, but he did not trust himself.

He wrapped her in clean linen and carried her to his bed. As he placed her in it, she said, "Do not leave me," in her raw, tortured voice.

"I will not," he promised.

"Hold me."

He hesitated, then was lying beside her, and before he could embrace her, she was crawling into his arms. She fell instantly asleep. He did not.

CHAPTER 46

Rolfe left Ceidre sleeping soundly on his bed, curled up in a tight ball, like a child.

His strides were hard and determined as he crossed the hall and swung open the door to the solar, with such force that it clapped like thunder against the wall. Alice, seated in bed, watched him approach with wide, frightened eyes.

He did not pause. As soon as he was close enough, he hit her, hard, across the face, the blow making her scream and fall back onto the pillows. He had used enough force that the slap would leave an ugly mark, but not enough to crack her jaw. Shrinking from him, she whimpered. He stood over her, panting with his rage.

"Your ill will toward your sister has gone too far, Alice. You are confined indefinitely to this chamber. You are not to leave it under any circumstances, do you understand me?"

She looked at him, crouched on her hands and knees now, her small bosom rising and falling rapidly, eyes wide.

"Do you understand me?" he ground out.

Her mouth opened. "My lord," she said, and her tone was thick and husky. Her gaze was on his mouth, and then it moved to his groin. "My lord," she breathed, and the tone ended on a low, sexual moan.

He recalled her begging him to thrust harder and hurt her in his bed, and he was overwhelmed with disgust and revulsion. He turned abruptly, leaving. He heard her chasing after him and was so stunned when she threw herself at his back that he froze. She groaned, pressing herself against his buttocks. He twisted around and shook her off, too late realizing, as she gasped, moaning from the floor, that he was arousing her, not frightening her. He left, slamming the door behind him.

A quick glance into his own chamber showed him the Ceidre was still soundly asleep, untortured by dreams. The sight of her was enough to make him linger, that odd swelling feeling bubbling again in his heart. He forced himself to turn and go downstairs.

The hall was empty save for Guy, Beltain, and Athelstan. Although it was the latter who asked how Ceidre was, Rolfe saw the agonized look in Beltain's eyes—and the steady one in Guy's. "She will be fine," he said grimly. His look was utterly cool as it lanced Ceidre's husband. "You do not inquire after your wife?"

Guy flushed. "Of course I do."

"She is asleep—in my bed."

Guy said nothing.

His anger was impossible to swallow. "Do you want to wake your wife, after her ordeal, and remove her to your own chambers? She is welcome to stay where she is. I will take a pallet in the hall."

Guy shifted uneasily. "I do not want to disturb your comfort, my lord."

"You do not disturb me," Rolfe said quickly. "Fine, she may stay." His tone dismissed Guy, and he turned his gaze upon Beltain.

His captain immediately dropped to one knee, unsheathing his sword and laying it at Rolfe's feet. "I am at your command," he said levelly.

"Sheath your sword," Rolfe said. "If I had not seen, twice now, the sincere regret in your eyes, I would strip you of your command. The dungeon is no place for a lady. Yet that you considered her cunning does not escape me. You could not conceive of her fear of the pit. Therefore, take up your sword, rise, and learn from your mistakes."

Beltain stood lithely, his expression level. "Thank you, my lord, for your clemency."

Rolfe dismissed him with his hand. Beltain did not know how close he had come to being murdered just a few hours ago. He realized he was alone with Athelstan, and he frowned, anxious to go back upstairs. His gaze wandered where his thoughts had gone, and Athelstan followed it.

"You had best send the lady Ceidre to Dumstanbrough as soon as she is well."

Rolfe gave him a look.

"You cannot bear this situation, my lord, and you know it well. Guy is not jealous, which is good, and he trusts you, which is better, or you would lose a fine captain and a truly loyal soul."

"You think I do no know this? And what do you suddenly care for my dilemmas?"

"You are a just man, a good leader," Athelstan said softly. "It is a shame that 'tis war, not peace, which brings you to us."

"Dwelling on what should be is for fools and poets."

"Send her with her husband to Dumstanbrough," Athelstan urged. "If you lose your best man, you will come to hate her."

"I am Rolfe de Warenne," Rolfe said softly. "I am Rolfe the Relentless, the king's best man. You think I cannot control a mere passing fancy? Think again. Yes, the witch is enchanting, but never will I forget she belongs to another. Now go to bed, old man."

"Gladly," Athelstan said, turning. He paused. "Passing fancy or obsession, my lord?"

"To bed!"

"And which bed will you go to?"

Rolfe did not reply, watching him leave. The old Saxon had more nerve than most men. Obsession? 'Twas not an obsession. He would not allow it to be such.

Ceidre awoke and was instantly aware of whose bed she was in.

Her memories were harsh—and tender.

The awful nightmare of her imprisonment for a day and a half, which had seemed like eternity, was abrasive but fading. More potent, it seemed, were the events since her rescue and her recollections of her rescuer.

Had his hands really been so gentle, as if she were a chick that might be crushed by mistake? Had his tone been so soothing, as if she were a newborn, motherless babe? No, 'twas impossible—it had to have been a dream!

She was stunned to find that it was way past noon, that she had slept for almost an entire day. Ceidre could not stop wondering, as she roused herself, if he had really been a gentle savior. Certainly the recollection of his carrying her here, to his bed, was true. She was wrapped in linen towels, naked beneath them, and this fresh discovery kindled a vague remembrance of being bathed—but she was sure she was imagining that Rolfe had done so. In all likelihood, being out of her mind from the choking fear, she had been delirious and hallucinating, thinking one of the maids to be the Norman. Yet she was tortured with the need to know what was real and what was not.

Her hands were bandaged, and as she dressed, they

were stiff and sore. Ceidre shuddered, reminded forcefully of her endless attempts first to climb the walls of the dungeon, then to tunnel out. Once dressed, she returned to the manor where she shared the chamber with Guy, without passing anyone.

Her husband returned before supper, as was his custom, for he bathed each second day, and recently, due to the Norman's overzealous demands on the mock-battlefield, every day. Ceidre, as usual, had his hot water ready and clean garments waiting, along with wine and a few spiced cakes. His glance swept her. "Are you all right, my lady?" There was compassion in his tone.

She blushed, feeling like a fool for having behaved like a crazed woman. "Yes, thank you. Here, let me." She helped him disrobe.

"I would have awakened you for dinner, but Lord Rolfe thought you should sleep until you woke yourself," Guy said, letting her pull his tunic over his head.

For some reason, this comment deepened her color. "Yes, well, I was certainly a laggard today. Did all go well at Dumstanbrough?"

"Yes, the land is rich, if rocky, but the villagers barely till it. They are shepherds, but that will change. I will show them the benefits of the harvest." His tone was rich with excitement as Ceidre bent to ungarter his hose. "And there is a perfect site for a keep, a natural hill. There is no water for a moat, but a deep ditch will keep all invaders out."

Ceidre straightened, smiling slightly. "I am glad you are pleased, my lord." She meant it. Guy had proved to be a good husband. He never had a harsh word, never raised his hand. True, he did not love her, true, he was out late most nights, and Ceidre knew he wenched excessively, but this, of course, relieved her. Now he stood naked before her, a finely made, lean man. His nakedness discomfitted neither of them. Ceidre found herself comparing him to the Norman, not for the first time. There was no comparison, the other taller, broader, his muscles so thoroughly hewn, as if by a master whittler. And of course, the Norman would never stand naked unaroused before her for long.

Guy was unaware of her scrutiny. "Ceidre?"

It was the first time he had called her by name, so intimately, and her gaze flew to his face.

"Did you receive the missive from your brother?"

"No! 'Twas a lie!"

Relief swept Guy's face. "I believe you. I have not known you long, not even a fortnight as your husband, but I begin to understand many things." He looked at her. "I am no longer afraid of you, Ceidre."

She felt her tension in her trembling knees. "No?"

"I believe, still, that you are a witch, but I also believe you are a good witch. I am right, am I not? You do not seek to harm, only to heal."

Ceidre was afraid. If he no longer feared her, would he want to assume his husbandly rights? She did not find Guy distasteful, not at all, yet she had no desire to share his bed—indeed, she felt an urgency to keep their relationship chaste.

He did not wait for her answer. "I also believe you are no liar—although I know you are loyal to your brothers. I am glad you did not commit so foolish an act. Ceidre, I will not allow my wife to betray my lord. Do you understand?"

"Yes."

He sighed and climbed into the steaming tub. "Will you wash my back?"

"Of course."

"Afterward, I will go tell Rolfe that you did not receive any missive from your brothers. Anyway, you do not need to fear further punishment. Our lord believes you have already suffered enough in the dungeon, regardless of the missive." He settled back in the tub.

It had not occurred to Ceidre that further punishment would be awaiting her, not because she had suffered enough, but because she was innocent. Now she was relieved her husband believed the truth and would even defend her if need be, although apparently 'twas unnecessary.

As she helped him bathe, her thoughts immediately hurled themselves to the more imminent crisis—she wanted desperately to know if he had changed his mind regarding their relationship, but was afraid to bring up the topic, reluctant to give him ideas. She was relieved that under her touch he did not become aroused, and thought that this was a hopeful sign. But she found herself anticipating the night with worry and dread. If he had changed his mind, she realized there was no way she could stop him from consummating their marriage. Oh, she might hold him off for a night or two, owing to her recent ordeal, but ultimately she would be forced to capitulate.

Ceidre knew she was a fool. Guy was a good man and, although Norman, not half the enemy their lord was. He was kind. He now had his own fief. One day he would be a powerful northern lord in his own right, and she was his wife. She should accept it, she should warm his bed, bear his children. They were already becoming friends, and this friendship would grow. Not so long ago the suitor her father had approached had rejected her, and all her hopes of every marrying had been dashed. Yet fate had intervened. She had been gifted with a husband, both a fierce warrior and a gentle soul. What woman could be luckier? She was a fool if she continued to keep him at a distance.

Her mind discovered this quickly and was sure it was the truth. Yet she could not find the determination in her heart to change her relationship. She hoped it was *not* because a golden pagan image kept invading her thoughts.

CHAPTER 47

Ceidre was surprised by the courtesy she received from the Norman's men at supper. Not only did those seated near her inquire politely after her, Beltain openly apologized. Ceidre was pink with embarrassment. "Since I was a child," she told him, "I have had an unnatural fear of that dungeon. You could not have known."

She was seated next to her husband, who was on the Norman's right. Alice had not come to take her place, and Ceidre wondered why. She avoided looking at Rolfe, although she was impossibly aware of his presence, of his every gesture, his every word and movement. Memories of his tender comforting of her assailed her, and whether real or not, they felt real. When he addressed her openly, she had no choice but to lift her gaze to his.

"How do you fare today, Lady Ceidre?"

Lady Ceidre, not Ceidre. She looked at him. His poise was relaxed, yet there was a bold tension in his blue eyes. He appeared to be casual, yet she could feel his intensity. He toyed with his eating dagger, yet his regard seared her. He was so handsome her breath was stolen away. "I am quite well, thank you."

He nodded and turned to Athelstan, and began discussing the breeding of a wolfhound.

Once having gazed upon him, Ceidre found her

glance constantly flitting to where he sat. He had the presence of royalty—the powerful presence of royalty. Seeing him reminded her that by now her brothers were awaiting information. Albie had told her to send Feldric again as soon as she had worthy news to impart. Of course she had no news; she had not become his mistress and was unable to gain his trust and his ear. She found it difficult to remember, now, why she had so furiously decided never to become his leman. She felt no anger toward him, none at all. As if sensing her regard, he shot her a look.

Their glances held and burned.

Ceidre tore her gaze away and continued to eat. Worry raised itself frankly now. She had been so involved with her own problems, with being married to Guy, with being taken on her wedding night by the Norman, with being imprisoned in the dungeon, she had forgotten the very serious predicament she was in. Her brothers were planning a rebellion by the end of August. They were intending to overthrow Rolfe, and, she assumed, to drive William the Conqueror south, and out of Mercia. They were expecting her to provide them with information. She knew they had other spies, but none so well placed here at Aelfgar. She had promised them she would become the Norman's mistress and obtain information. They were depending upon her. They knew her nature, and knew she would not fail them.

Which, of course, she could not.

Now that she was no longer angry, she could think clearly, logically, and knew she had to fulfill her duties to her brothers first and foremost. She eyed the Norman. She was a terrible seductress, this was proven. She had tried to seduce him and he had married her to his vassal. Even now she felt the pinpricking of hurt. Yet it was nothing compared to what she had felt before. She was not sure, in truth, if he still wanted her, as he had on her wedding night, and even if she did attempt a seduction, would he forget his loyalty to Guy? On the other hand, he was their liege lord, and if he really wanted her, he would be arrogant enough to take her and justify it because of his overlordship.

Her stomach was in knots. Now that her own problems had faded into insignificance, she felt the great weight of responsibility that her brothers had placed upon her. Gazing upon the Norman, she knew to do nothing was to fail. She must, at least, try something.

He looked at her again, his gaze sharp.

For a brief instant, Ceidre was mesmerized by those smoking eyes. Glancing away, she knew what she must do.

Because he had not been able to sleep the past night, tossing and turning, his mind filled with the horror of finding Ceidre in the dungeons, crazed with fear, he should have been tired. No, Rolfe thought, he was tired, bone weary, but he doubted he would be able to sleep on this eve as well. Why had she kept looking at him during supper?

He was in the great hall, wine in hand, gazing into the hearth. He was loath to go upstairs. Most of his men were already asleep, their snores strangely soothing. Other than the dying fire, the hall was cast in shadows of the night.

He tried to turn his thoughts away from her, and failed. She had seemed fine at supper, as fine as ever—as radiant as ever. Thank God the ordeal she had endured had been brief—he wished it had been briefer, if not nonexistent. He hoped Guy would not take her this night, that he would allow her to rest. Such speculation brought an instant stiffening to his spine, a tightening to his gut. Yes, he decided, Athelstan was right, he would send them both to Dumstanbrough. He was a fool if he did not.

He drained his cup, left it on the table, and trudged up the stairs. He took an oil lamp from a wall sconce and pushed open the door to his chamber. He set the light down, moved his hands to the clasp of his sword belt. His gaze raced to the bed, which was cast in dark shadows. Nevertheless, there was no mistaking that it was occupied.

He was not angry, he was disgusted. "Get yourself out of my bed, Lady Alice, and hie yourself to your own. I have no wish to consort with you tonight. And you push me greatly, to defy my orders. You are still confined to your chamber, and now I will think twice before lifting your punishment."

Ceidre sat up, the covers dropping to her waist. She was magnificently naked, her full breasts gleaming ivory, her long bronze tresses swirling about them, yet parting for her erect nipples. Rolfe thought he was dreaming. "What are you doing?" he croaked.

Her breasts shimmered, rising and falling too rapidly. "I want you," she said simply, her violet eyes holding his. And Ceidre realized she had spoken the truth.

Rolfe stared into her gaze and saw everything he wished to see there. He was at her side, her arms were open. He came into her embrace like a ship finding its safe harbor. She held him. He moaned again and lifted his face from her neck to find her mouth with his.

There were no thoughts in his head other than her name, her being, her presence, her willing gift of herself to him, of what was about to pass. He pushed her down, kissing her hard, and she opened, responding as fiercely, clutching his hair so hard it hurt his scalp. He did not care. With his knee he spread her thighs, rocked his thick penis into her groin, lifted his head and nipped her throat, then caught her nipple to bite it gently. She whimpered and arched, wrapping her long legs around his hips, pressing her plump, wet flesh against his rock hardness. Rolfe captured her mouth again and thrust his tongue deep into her. He was aware of her hands wildly stroking his back, urging him on, then grabbing his hard buttocks. "Ceidre," he cried. Her tongue entwined frantically with his, pulling him furiously deeper, and any further words were cut off.

He gasped when her hands moved from his backside to his groin, one palm closing around his massive length, hard. He bucked, rearing; she ripped his hose off his hips. "Yes," he cried as she jerked him roughly to her entrance. Clasping her bottom, he thrust deeply into her.

They moved together, hard and fast, panting, gasping, moaning. Her nails tore his back, his hands bruised her buttocks. He knew he was about to erupt, about to spill his seed into her. "Ceidre," he cried, shaking violently as he paused, trying to restrain himself.

"Do not stop!" She caught his face and kissed him, urging him with her hips. He was lost, he plunged into her, again and again, and then she grabbed his arms, as if he were an anchor, and she keened, head flung back, arching convulsively. He saw her face, dark and strained with passion, and miraculously thrust again, bringing her to another orgasm, watching her, relishing his power, and again and again. She was sobbing now from the pleasure he had given her. Like a ripe plum, he burst within her.

CHAPTER 48

Sanity returned.

Rolfe's heart was thudding thickly. He was still on top of Ceidre, and within her, and he had her wrapped tightly in her arms—as if to hold on to her forever. He could barely believe what had happened. She had come to him. She had wanted him. She had responded to his passion as fiercely as he had given it. Ceidre—Guy's wife.

He rolled off her, grim now, and stared up at the ceiling. He felt her touch, a soft caress on his bicep, and he jerked his head to her. Anger—at himself, at the both of them—faded, to be instantly replaced with warmth. She was radiant and gorgeous, and mostly it was her eyes that held his, shining with pleasure—with joy.

He looked at her hand on his arm. Naturally, she stroked him, as if enjoying the feel of his skin, his flesh, his muscle and bone. Unbelievably, he could feel his desire renewing itself. He stopped her hand abruptly.

"Where is Guy?"

She met him steadily. "He is out wenching. Have no fear, he will not miss me this night."

The words came out before he could stop them. "He is a fool."

She said nothing.

He moved closer to her so that he was looking down upon her, into her eyes. "Did I hurt you, Ceidre?" His tone was thick. He still held her hand.

"No." She smiled, a smile of contentment, and something else, something more, something that choked him with pleasure.

"After your imprisonment, maybe 'tis not good—"

" 'Tis fine." She squeezed his hand reassuringly.

What was he going to do? He was only a man, and much weaker than he had thought himself to be. He groaned and fell back on the pillows, staring again at the ceiling.

"Do not torture yourself," she whispered, raising up to do so. Her breasts flattened against his arm. Her face was near his.

"Do you read my mind?" he asked gruffly.

"I do not have to read it," she answered. "Your thoughts are written on your face, and besides, I know you well enough."

He shifted onto his side, his palm spreading on her taut back. It slipped to her hip. Her flesh curved perfectly into his hand. "I should never have given you to Guy," he said roughly.

"It matters not. You are our liege lord. You may take what you want."

"Guy most likely will feel differently."

"No, he would deny you nothing."

"You are so sure?"

"I am sure, but if it bothers you, he need not know."

"What are you suggesting, wench?" His grip tightened. "I am not a liar. I do not cuckold my best man. Yet I am doing both!"

Her palm grazed his face. "We need each other, my lord," she said simply.

Her touch was going to undo him. He groaned,

fighting with himself, telling himself to get out of the bed and leave, now. Yet he knew, all along, that he would not. He could not. "You are a witch," he rasped. "Because I am under your spell, of that there is no doubt."

Her hand slid from his jaw to his neck, paused, then slipped to his shoulder. She began rubbing his thick chest muscle. Rolfe's head went back, his eyes closed, he arched himself into her hand. He heard her whisper "You are so powerful, my lord, so big, so strong . . ."

He groaned, lifting her on top of him, nuzzling her breasts. A simple touch, a few words, and he was lost. He prodded her with his throbbing organ. "Can you ride me, Ceidre?"

"I don't know." She gasped, surprised, as he lazily rubbed his swollen tip against her derriere, tonguing a nipple at the same time.

"Ride me," he commanded, holding her in place, then swiftly thrusting up into her. She cried out as he filled her, instinctively shifting to lessen the vast pressure. He held her immobile. "Don't move, I will be gentle, you will get used to it in a moment. Relax."

She trembled on top of him. "You might split me asunder."

"No, no, I will not, trust me. . . ."

He watched her relax, and as she moved, slightly, he saw her gasp with pleasure as she grew accustomed to him. "Ride me," he said thickly.

She needed no urging. Head flung back, breasts thrust forward, she rode him hard.

"How long have you been with William?"

They lay entwined together in the middle of the bed, Ceidre's face resting against his shoulder, his hand drifting in her hair. "A dozen years."

She looked up. "But how is that possible? Are you an old man?"

He smiled slightly. "I am almost twenty-nine. I joined William when I was seventeen. Why?"

"I know nothing about you."

He smiled genuinely now. "You know more than all other women." His eyes glinted. He wrapped his hand in her hair and pulled her head back, turning her face up to his. "You know how to please me."

She blushed. "I imagine you are easy enough to please."

"Release is easy, yes," he agreed, "But that is not the kind of pleasure I am talking about."

She smiled and nuzzled her face against his chest.

He stared down at her. This second time they had loved passionately, fiercely, for hours, yet he did not feel sated—there was an urgency still within him, not as intense, but distinct nonetheless. He wasn't sure it was entirely physical either, but if not, then what was it? He wondered if Ceidre really understood what he meant—that she had taken him to heights of ecstasy so high they were unbearable, and now, lying here in his arms, she was bringing him equal pleasure, although completely different, soothing and calm and replete, except for that elusive niggling sense of urgency he could not shake. Never had he experienced this last kind of pleasure before. When had he, in fact, ever dallied abed with a woman after fucking? The answer was an unqualified never.

He wanted to tell her all this, but did not know how.

"Is your brother as big as you are?"

"What!"

She looked up innocently, saw his expression and grinned. "Do not be lewd! I meant is he as tall, as broad of shoulder—is he as fine of face?"

"What is this interest in my brother?" He was absurdly pleased with her compliments, and his tone was rough to hide this. "How do you even know I have a brother?"

"I have my witch's ways." She smiled; he smiled. "Is he not here in England?"

"Yes, in the south, and if you must know, he is almost as tall, but slimmer. Height runs in my family, but not the breadth. I do not know where I got these shoulders from. Mayhap some Viking ancestor."

"Your shoulders are very fine," she said, touching one. "Will you ever go back to Normandy?"

"There is nothing for me there."

"But do you not have family there? Parents? Other brothers, sisters, cousins?"

He smiled. "Yes, of course. Ceidre," he explained patiently, "I am the fourth and youngest son. I followed William to Normandy for the promise of my own land, a patrimony for my sons. You understand the way of the world. There was nothing for me in Normandy, and there is still nothing for me there. My life is here now. Aelfgar is my life."

She looked at him, rising up. " 'Tis not fair," she said, eyes flashing.

"I do not want to fight."

She instantly softened. "Nor do I."

He looked at her breasts. "Your tits are magnificent, do you know that?"

"So I have been told."

He had been caressing one, now he froze. "Who in hell told you such?"

She laughed. "I wanted to see your reaction. No one, my lord."

"Guy does not tell you how beautiful you are?"

Ceidre hesitated. She looked away, thinking frantically, trying to decide if she should tell him the truth.

"Ceidre?" There was a hint of warning in his tone.

She gazed at him. "Guy has never seen my breasts, my lord."

He stared. "I do not believe this—he beds you in the dark or with your clothes on?" Rolfe sat up. There was distinct jealousy in his tone.

"He does not bed me."

"What are you saying?" he demanded.

"He has never touched me. He is afraid of me because I am a witch and does not wish to consort with the devil's own. He is my husband, yes, but he takes his pleasure elsewhere. We have an understanding and it suits us both."

Rolfe could not believe it; he gripped her shoulders. " 'Tis the truth?"

"Yes," she breathed.

"He has not bedded you, not once?"

"No."

He hauled her up against him, kissing her with hard, brutal passion. She resisted his onslaught instinctively, hands pressed against his shoulders, whimpering when he drove her roughly against the wall. He instantly lessened the pressure, his mouth becoming gentle, soft.

"Do not fight me," he said hoarsely. "You are mine, Ceidre, mine."

As he kissed her she could feel him controlling a fierce, brutal passion, she could feel it in the shaking of his big body. And the contradiction, the tenderness, the sensual stroking of his mouth, when he was so desperately ready, brought something forth in Ceidre, something shimmering and bright, more than just an answering passion. She clung to him, returning his kisses. He had already spread her thighs, and now he thrust abruptly into her. She was wet and ready, fueled by his explosive need. Moments later they cried out, one after the other, in the throes of hot, heady pleasure.

He held her tightly afterward. "You are mine, Ceidre, do you understand?"

She looked at him. She saw the ruthless, uncompromising look upon his face; his gaze was brilliantly hard, like diamonds. "Do you understand?"

She was frightened by his tone. "I am still Guy's wife."

"No one will touch you," he said. "I will take care of Guy." His gaze was piercing. "I am truly warning you, Ceidre; 'tis good you are afraid. If a man touches you, I will slice off his hands with my sword—do you understand?"

She nodded, breathless and trembling.

"And if another fucks you, I will kill him with my own hand—while you watch. Do you understand?"

"Yes."

"Good." He smiled a hard smile. "I do not share what belongs to me, and from this day forward you are mine."

She was appalled, she was also exhilarated. Unthinking, she touched his cheek gently. The hard brilliant look in his eyes—the look of a ruthless conqueror—began to soften. "I do not want another, my lord," she said.

The melting in his gaze was rapid. "You speak the truth?"

"I swear it."

There was no hardness left in his regard, none at all. His smile was unrestrained. "You unman me, Ceidre."

"You are not unmanned to feel happy, my lord."

"No? What is happiness? A commander has no place in his life for such emotions."

"Wrongly said, my lord." She touched his cheek again, cupping his face. "A man has room for all emotions."

"A man who caters to all humors ceases to be a man, Ceidre. He cannot function as he should."

"You are happy with me, yet you function well." She smiled lasciviously. "More than well—superlatively."

He laughed, a warm, rich, bold sound that shook her with surprise. " 'Tis not that kind of functioning I am talking about, and you know it." His arm, which was holding her, squeezed her in what was almost a hug.

"Oh, my lord, 'tis good to hear you laugh," Ceidre breathed, hugging him back, hard.

His mirth died as he gazed at her. "I have never laughed with a woman before," he said.

She smiled impishly. "No? I am most flattered. Mayhap I can make you laugh again?"

His mouth quirked. "There are other humors I would rather feel."

She snorted. "Of course, if I catered to you as you would, there is only one humor you would cherish, only one you would have *me* feel, and it is hanging there between your legs."

"You may feel that humor anytime, Ceidre, even now." He pulled her hand toward his belly, she jerked it away.

"That humor does not need more humoring this night."

"But you said you would humor me." He was grinning.

"I am humoring you, fool. And here is more humor." She grinned and quickly tickled him under his arms.

With exaggerated annoyance, he slapped her hands

away. She laughed and dove for his ribs. He caught her wrists, holding them triumphantly. "You cannot win!" But he was smiling.

"I think I already have, my lord," Ceidre said.

CHAPTER 49

Rolfe paused in the doorway of the stable, trying to peer into the darkness within. He held up a lamp and saw her. Ceidre sat upon a bale of hay, her hair loose and streaming to her hips, waiting for him. He smiled.

She smiled back.

He came forward, aware of the need to rush. He urgently enveloped her in his arms; she protested. "My lord, you will set us ablaze!"

He laughed ruefully and went outside to douse the oil lamp. He returned, impatience overwhelming, yet because he could not see, his steps were measured. She called out to him, like a siren, guiding him to her, luring him on. He crushed her to him, seeking her mouth fiercely, possessively, demanding a response. She gave it with equal fervor. It was a long time later before they came up for air.

"It feels as if we have not seen each other for days," Ceidre managed, stroking her hand down his neck.

"From dawn to dusk is long enough," Rolfe said roughly. "I cannot wait another moment, Ceidre." Holding her buttocks and anchoring her, he pressed himself crudely against her groin.

"Nor can I," she returned, running her hands over his arousal boldly.

Their mating was quick and fierce, there in the straw, and afterward they lay panting, curled up together. Rolfe began undressing her. "I want to feel you naked against me."

"Yes," she murmured, helping him to remove her garments. She snuggled against him.

"Guy leaves for Dumstanbrough tomorrow," Rolfe told her. "To build his keep and see to his demesne. I have given him a fortnight's leave."

"I know, I saw him, he told me."

"What else did he say?" Rolfe asked.

"Nothing."

"He did not query your whereabouts last night?"

"No," she said hesitantly. "I feel guilty, my lord, even though I know he was himself with Lettie."

"When he returns," Rolfe said, stroking his arm, "I will take care of this situation, I promise you."

Ceidre wanted to ask how, but was afraid to know what he intended. And indeed, what could he do? He might ask Guy to agree to seek to annul their marriage, or he might ask him to maintain their relations as chastely as they were. He certainly would not divorce his own wife and marry her. When Ceidre realized the direction her thoughts had taken, she was stunned. She certainly would never agree to marry the Norman, even if they were both free. He was the enemy! He might arouse her passions, but she was only his mistress to aid her brothers—and she must not forget it for a second. "Did"—she paused—"did Alice remark upon last night? Did she know we were together?"

"I do not know," Rolfe said. "Alice is confined to her chamber for what she did to you, Ceidre. I am sorely tried by her malicious will. I have warned her to cease her rude maneuverings and plottings. Hopefully she realized I am being very lenient."

"You do this for me?" Ceidre breathed.

"Who else?" he said gruffly. "She almost killed you!"

"But—but you confined her before I came to your bed last night."

"Her treatment of you had nothing to do with our relationship, and my punishment of her was independent as well." He smiled into her hair. "Now 'twould be worse, for I have marked you mine in my mind and my heart, and I am possessive and territorial, Ceidre. Anyone who harms you now harms me."

"I do not want Alice to know I have become your mistress," she whispered. "Please."

"Do you think I am so crude as to toss it in her face?" He stiffened.

"She will find out," Ceidre said miserably. "Although no one saw me leave this morning, eventually what we do will become common knowledge. Secrets cannot be kept on a manor."

"It matters not. I am lord here, and no one will dare speak out against you for fear of my wrath." Suddenly he smiled. "Only you dare to oppose me, Ceidre."

"Witches are not afraid of mere mortals." She sniffed.

He laughed, a loud roar.

"Hush," she cried, clapping her hand on his mouth. "You will bring the whole world down upon us!"

"Witch," he said affectionately, still chuckling. "The whole world is asleep, there is no one to hear us, no one but the mice and the horses, that is."

"Is that what pressed against my thigh a moment ago? I thought it was you, but it was suspiciously small."

He grinned again, rolling onto his back and pulling her astride him "If 'twas small, you know it could not have been me." He placed her hand on his rising member.

"Arrogant," she breathed. "Your lance is not so huge."

"Huge enough to make you beg for mercy, weep with pleasure, and cry my name!"

"Did I do those things, my lord?"

"Each and every one," he said smugly.

"And you think 'twas because of this?" She grabbed him.

The smug tone disappeared. He gasped. "I know—I know 'twas because of this."

"Conceited too," she said, sliding her palm down his length.

"You are speaking about," he managed, "your lord. Have you . . . no respect?"

Ceidre slid down his body and rubbed his penis between her breasts and against her nipples. Rolfe gasped. "Is this respectful enough for you, my lord?" There was smugness in her own breathy tone.

"You learn overly fast, witch," he said, flipping her and impaling her in one movement. "Now who is in control?"

"You." She gasped as he moved with tremendous restraint over her. "You."

Rolfe was distracted.

He sat his gray in the field, knowing Beltain questioned him, yet his gaze followed Ceidre as she moved down the path and then veered off it, into the orchard. It was the next day, after noon. Where was the wench going?

"My lord, shall we commence?" Beltain repeated.

"Yes, yes," Rolfe said impatiently. Ceidre had disappeared from his view among the trees and thigh-high grass. "You are in charge," he told Beltain, then spurred his destrier into a canter, toward the orchard.

Once inside, he reined in, looking around. Ceidre

was nowhere to be seen. What is she up to? He wondered, not with suspicion, with curiosity. There was no sign of her, yet he knew she had to be there. He urged his mount forward, his gaze roaming left and right repeatedly. "Ceidre?"

No answer.

He felt a touch of worry then. The woman could not just vanish. A terrible thought occurred. Had she purposefully hidden herself, mayhap to meet with a spy? Or had she tripped and fallen, hitting her head? His tone was sharper. "Ceidre? Ceidre!"

No answer. He urged his mount into a faster walk, almost nearing the end of the orchard. He could see the forest across the road. Unless she had been running, she could not have crossed the orchard and disappeared into the forest so quickly. Maybe she had started to run once she had escaped common view. He felt a dread. If she was up to no good . . .

A laugh sounded.

It was soft and fairylike and it was hers, he would know that musical, magical sound anywhere. Relief swept him. And with it, something else. He whipped his head around. "Ceidre? God's blood, wench, are you playing a game? Where are you?"

Another fey laugh, and then something hit his head, smack in the middle. It didn't hurt, but it didn't quite tickle either; it was an apple. Amazed, he jerked his gaze up to the treetop above him.

Ceidre smiled down at him. "Have you followed me, my lord?" she asked serenely.

She was a breathtaking vision of honey and gold up in that tree, and for a moment he couldn't answer. He feigned annoyance. "What are you doing up there, Ceidre?"

"Picking apples, of course," she said sweetly. "Would you care for another?" Before he could answer, she tossed one at him. He ducked, so it missed his shoulder in the nick of time.

Incredulous, he stared at her. "What in the hell are you doing?"

"Picking apples," she insisted, grinning. "Why have you followed me?"

"Why do you think, siren?" he muttered. "You lead, I follow!"

She laughed, pleased with his remark.

"Do not let it go to your head, and do not throw another apple at mine!"

"All right," she agreed.

He eyed one bare calf, exposed because her skirts were tangled around her. "Come down here," he said, softly now.

She raised a brow. "But I am not finished."

"Come down here," he repeated, his tone sensually coaxing.

"If you want me, you will have to come up and get me," she called, and she shimmied higher into the tree.

"Are you mad?" he said. "That tree cannot hold up weight!"

"If you want me," she said, and she gave him an utterly bold, provocative look, one that held his gaze then raked him thoroughly, "then you will have to come and get me, my lord!"

His breath caught at such seduction. Then, smiling with purpose, he reached up and hoisted himself into the tree. It groaned and swayed beneath his weight. The branch he was on cracked. Undeterred, he moved higher, reaching for her pretty little ankle. She eluded him deftly and, with the speed of a squirrel, shimmied down past him, dropping easily the last bit of the way to the ground. She was laughing at his amazement, and she paused beneath him, hands on her hips. "You look silly in that tree, my lord, and it is about to break in two!"

She took off at a run just as he jumped to the ground. He darted after her. He lunged for her; she dodged, a tree between them. He reached right, she dodged left, he reached left, she dodged right, all the while laughing. Rolfe was grinning. He feinted left and waited for her to go right. She did, and he caught her with a cry of triumph.

"Put me down," she cried as he lifted her high in his arms and spun her in the air.

"But you like heights," he said innocently. "Is this not high enough for you?"

"You'll drop me," she cried, but she was laughing.

"Never," he replied, but nonetheless he clutched her to his chest. She wrapped her arms around his neck. "What kind of game was that, Ceidre?" he asked huskily.

Her violet eyes stroked the depths of his. "An amusing one," she said simply. "Were you not amused?"

He grunted, secretly having enjoyed such silly nonsense as thoroughly as if he were a boy of six. "This amuses me," he said, and he bit her chin, then claimed her mouth with hard, checked passion.

"Will you take me here?" Ceidre gasped as he knelt, pushing her onto the ground.

"Here, now, in the dirt," he said roughly, "as I have longed to do from the instant I first saw you."

Ceidre looked at him.

He lay on his back, his head propped up with their clothes and straw, gazing absently ahead. She was draped partly over him, her chin on his chest, her legs entwined with his. He had a hand on the small of her back, and it drifted lazily, stroking her flesh right down to the full curve of one buttock.

It was that night, and they had met in the stable. Rolfe was completely relaxed, and the hard line of his mouth was softer now, hinting at contentment. He was so unbearably beautiful, she thought, and her heart was so swollen it positively ached. He glanced at her, and his blue eyes were so uncharacteristically soft that Ceidre almost choked with the ripe, bursting sensations filling her.

"Why do you stare?" he asked, his hand moving up to tangle in the thick tresses of her hair.

" 'Tis easy to stare at you, my lord," she said boldly. "You are a sight that takes a woman's breath away. Of course, you know this."

He smiled. "You think me handsome, do you?"

"You know I do. 'Tis a most unfair distraction."

"Good," he said, caressing the hair of her head. He toyed with her ear. "Then we are even, because I have long since ceased to think straight around you."

His words brought her pleasure, and to hide it, she ducked her head, rubbing her nose into the thick hair of his chest. How could she be so contented? In the back of her mind, what was always there, nagging, niggling, annoying, and now wrenching, surged forward. This is not real, her inner voice said. You have seduced him for a purpose—and do not forget it!

She wanted to forget it, she realized, aching now in her entire being, her entire soul. Even if it was only to forget it until the day came when she must be a spy. When she had agreed with her brothers to become his mistress, she had never dreamed it would be like this; had never dreamed he would be like this. Oh, yes, he was arrogant, he was autocratic, he could be harsh and demanding, but he could also be infinitely gentle. She knew she no longer hated him. In fact, she could barely think about anything other than him when they were apart, she quickened at mere thoughts of him, much less the sight of him, and since she had come unbidden to his bed, she had discovered that she longed to be there, in his embrace, more than anywhere else.

She would not think of the future, she decided, and for now, she would pretend that this thing between them was real, unfettered by politics and treachery.

She was inadvertently caressing his arm, enjoying the many textures, the slightly coarse hair, the hard, hard bone, the nearly as hard muscle, the silky skin. She propped her chin up. "My lord? Do you not grow bored?"

He smiled slightly. "Bored?" He grinned. "Have I acted bored this night? Are you not pleased? If not, that can be remedied instantly." His hand swept from her head to her buttocks and delved immediately lower.

She wiggled and caught his hand, stilling it. "I am most satisfied, my lord. Be serious."

"Serious? But you would have me spend all my time playing games," he said, and he nipped her ear. "With you."

She pushed his jaw away. "I do not want to play games now. In all truth, you are not bored?"

He sat up, bringing her with him. "What is this about?"

"You do not want," she said cautiously, heart pumping, "me to send for another? Mayhap Lettie, or Beth?" She looked at him.

"You wish to make a threesome?"

She punched his bicep softly. "You know I do not! Please"—and her tone was tinged with anxiety—"tell me the truth."

His smile faded. "I am not bored, Ceidre, not with you. I do not want Lettie, or Beth, or another. I want you."

Her heart leapt. She was exhilarated and she could not contain her feelings. She was beaming.

"This pleases you?" he asked softly, his thumb tracing her jaw.

She lowered her eyes. "Yes."

He shifted her abruptly, so she was on her knees astride his lap, one on each side of his thighs. "I like pleasing you, Ceidre," he said, low. "I like the way you have been looking at me this night."

Her thoughts had started to spin away, for his shaft was tumescent again, and the tip was poised against her femininity. "Again?" She gasped.

"I wish to prove, beyond any doubt, that I am not bored," he said.

CHAPTER 50

"My lord? I beg a word with you," Alice said, poised in the doorway of the solar, where she was confined.

It was still pitch-black out, but soon dawn would lighten the sky. Rolfe was just returning from the stable, but he was unperturbed to be caught coming in at this hour. "What is it you wish, Lady? You are up early this morn." His tone was pleasant.

Alice stared at him. His mood was good, because he had been rutting away the night with her bastard sister. Did he think she would not know? Or did he even care? Did he even care that all the serfs were gossiping about him and that witch—and about her, his true wife? They had even been fornicating like two animals in the dirt in the orchard in the middle of the day—Mary's husband's brother had seen them. She knew that to show her hatred would undermine her cause, but for the life of her she did not know how she could keep her emotions out of her eyes. Yet he, the fool, was so besotted he apparently did not notice. He leaned relaxed against the wall, waiting with unusual patience. She thought she saw the hint of a satisfied smile in the corners of his mouth.

"My lord, I beg you to tell me, when will you lift my punishment?"

"You could have killed your sister," he said, pushing off the wall, all signs of pleasantness fading. "A few days' confinement is nothing. You have yet, I presume, to consider what you have done, yet to understand how you have defied me and displeased me. I am not ready to lift your penance, Lady, by any means." His gaze pinned her.

"I did not know," Alice flung bravely, "that she was your leman, or I would have treated her otherwise. She was only a traitor to my knowledge, and I treated her as such. I was looking out for your interests, my lord—for *our* interests."

"Do you truly think me a fool? You despise your sister, and your jealousy has proven dangerous. Were you a man, I would do more than confine you to your chamber with your servants at your beck and call. Do not test my charity," he warned.

"Does Guy know you are cuckolding him?" Alice snapped.

"Is your pride hurt? I am sorry, but I never intended fidelity when I married you. I do not give fidelity to any woman. If you expected such, then you were sorely deluded. Good night, Lady."

"But with her! With that witch! With my sister!"

He turned back, livid. "I owe you no explanations. I will fuck where I will; return to your chamber."

Alice did, slamming the door hard, then shivering, waiting with tensed expectation for him to intrude with his fury, to punish her for her insolence, beat her, rape her. . . . He did not come.

She had lost all her power.

She was nothing, a prisoner, with only a few servants to obey her commands. Ceidre had pushed her into this position, and Ceidre would usurp her place entirely if she did not do something to prevent it.

"If only she had died in the dungeon," Alice muttered, fists clenched. "If only there was a way to rid myself of her once and for all!"

* * *

Ceidre was aware of a new deference the instant she entered the great hall for the noonday meal. She was careful not to look at Rolfe, just as she knew he did not look at her. Yet his men ceased their conversation at her appearance, parted so she could make her way through them, and one, whom she did not know, held her elbow as she seated herself. Beltain, on her right, offered her wine with a smile. She flushed hotly, despairing that everyone had learned that she was sleeping with the Norman.

She was happy to see, however, that Alice's chair was still vacant.

Now that Guy was gone, she was on Rolfe's right. It was disturbing. She kept her eyes down and concentrated on eating, yet once, when she reached for bread, he did too, and their hands met. Her startled gaze flew to his, as his did to hers. For a brief instant they looked at each other, and then she quickly averted her glance. Rolfe tore off a piece of bread and handed it to her politely. "After you, Lady," he said causally.

"Thank you," she managed, just as polite. Her ears were burning.

Ceidre knew, if everyone in the hall was aware she was the Norman's mistress, her sister knew it as well.

She felt guilty. Alice had wanted to marry the Norman, and Ceidre knew she cherished being his wife. She was sure that she would be faithful and would willingly bear him sons. They had shared marital relations as well. Ceidre knew, with despair, that Alice had enjoyed it, for the Norman was a superb lover. She felt she owed Alice something—an explanation. But she dreaded it—Alice would only be angry. Indeed, Ceidre thought, if our roles were reversed, I'd want to kill her! If he were my husband, I would not let another woman touch him, not if I could help it!

Ceidre's thoughts were distracted throughout the meal. Afterward, when the men were dispersing, she decided she must go and try to explain to her sister. She debated asking the Norman's permission, then decided against it. He might forbid her from seeing Alice, either because of her punishment, or because they were wife and mistress. Ceidre was about to go outside to wait for an opportune moment to sneak upstairs, when a messenger from William was announced.

Rolfe returned to the table with the messenger, ordering everyone else out. Ceidre lingered as his men, already in the process of departing, continued to do so. Her heart was thumping. She felt a sick knot in her stomach. Would he ask her to read a missive again? Yet she did not see a scroll.

Rolfe lifted his gaze and looked at her sharply, then, seeing it was she who remained, a softness appeared in his eyes and upon his face. Ceidre bit her lip, knowing her color was high. They were alone in the hall, except for the messenger. "I will speak with you later," he said, his tone softer than she had ever heard him use before. It was a dismissal.

Ceidre left.

"What do you want?" Alice cried, furious.

It was several hours later, and Ceidre had found the opportunity to steal unnoticed upstairs. She quietly closed the door behind her. "Alice, we must talk."

"Talk! I don't want to even look at you, much less talk!"

"I know you are upset, and I am here to explain."

"Explain?" Alice laughed. "Oh, I understand, Ceidre, believe me. You cannot resist that big cock, can you? You think I do not know myself, firsthand, how much pleasure it brings?" She sneered. But there were tears in her eyes.

Ceidre could not help imagining Alice in the Norman's arms, and it hurt. She momentarily could not speak.

"He is truly insatiable, is he not?" Alice continued, voice high. "Do you know that this morning, when he returned before dawn, we had a fight and then he took me—in the hall, on the floor?"

Ceidre stared. "I do not believe you," she said. The problem was, it was just the Norman's style to do exactly what Alice had described. Yet could he have still had the stamina to do so after being with her all night?

"What, are you upset? You think he will rest exclusively unto you? Hah! You know he is not a man to be faithful to any woman, and certainly not to his whore!"

Alice wanted to hurt her, and Ceidre was aware of it. This did not stop her from succeeding. Alice was right. The truth hurt. It hurt so much she had to ignore it. With resolve, Ceidre folded her arms tightly. "I did not want to become his mistress," she said stiffly. "You know me well, Alice, you know I would never give myself willingly to the Norman—to the man who has stolen Aelfgar from Ed."

"He raped you?" Alice sneered skeptically, but her eyes were bright with sharp interest.

It was not in Ceidre's nature to lie, but she wanted to somehow spare her sister further pain. Instead of recalling all the pleasure she received in the Norman's arms, she tried to focus on that first night, the first time, when he had raped her on her wedding night. "Yes."

"You liar!" Alice shrilled. "Mary's brother-in-law

saw the two of you in the orchard—and it wasn't rape! You were hot, he was hot! You liar!"

Ceidre paled. They had been seen? Embarrassment turned her pink. "I don't know what he saw," she mumbled, dismayed, realizing her attempts to explain were failing miserably. "It must—it must have been the Norman with another."

"Liar, liar, liar! Witch liar!" Alice screamed, fists clenched. "You enjoy it, you are a whore like your mother, Ceidre. Just like your mother, only a whore, a damn whore!"

"It's not true," Ceidre cried, as an awful doubt raised itself. "Ed asked me to become the Norman's mistress! Ed asked me so that I might keep a better eye on him! It was not my choice, it was my duty!"

Alice blinked. For a moment, a silence stretched between them, Alice's face filled with growing comprehension, Ceidre horrified at what she had inadvertently revealed. "You sleep with him to spy?" Alice gasped.

"Not to spy," Ceidre said quickly, too quickly. "Just to be aware of what he does. There is a difference! The Norman would never tell me his secrets, he is too clever." Her words were rushed, her heart speeding on wings. "You know the Norman would never tell me anything, Alice!"

Alice was stunned, and so excited she could barely contain herself. How could Ceidre be so stupid—to tell her this! She was a spy! She was using the Norman!

Ceidre wanted only to escape. "I do not ask your forgiveness," she whispered, "but I had to explain. He really did rape me, and I really had no choice!"

Alice said nothing. Ceidre hurried to the door and left. Clearly she was shaken. Smiling, Alice clapped her hands excitedly. She could not wait to tell her husband that his whore was using him to spy for his archenemies. She could not wait!

"Ceidre, I must go."

Ceidre, naked and snuggling against Rolfe's side, jerked upright. They were in the stable, and it was still hours before dawn. "What? So soon? Why?"

He smiled and touched her quivering breasts. "In truth, I am not ready to leave you," he said, lifting her voluptuousness. "But I must." He released her and stood. "I go to York at dawn."

"To York?" She echoed. "At dawn!"

He began to dress.

Ceidre was aware of many turbulent emotions, the first being an overwhelming disappointment. "For how long? When will you be back?"

He paused, clad in hose and tunic, then knelt before her, cupping her face. "You will miss me?"

She trembled. " 'Tis too soon," she said bitterly. "Will—will Guy return before you do?"

"Mayhap," he said evenly. His thumb caught a tear. "Do not cry, sweeting. When I return we will have many more moments like this night."

Was she crying? Was she that upset that he was leaving her? She had been upset ever since the confrontation with Alice that afternoon. And what about the messenger? Why was he going to York? Damn Ed! Although maybe it was better that Rolfe would go now, for a while, because of what she had so stupidly told Alice. Yet she clutched his hands. "Take me with you," she breathed, her face close to his.

"I cannot." He started to rise, but she would not release him, and he pulled her up with him.

He was mostly dressed, she was stark naked. One candle, carefully placed so as not to cause a fire, illuminated them, casting most of its light upon her naked form. Ceidre was aware of it. She was aware that he was affected, eyeing her breasts, her belly, the coarse auburn hair between her legs, her curved thighs. Deliberately she leaned slightly forward, so her nipples brushed his chest, tightening. "Take me with you," she begged. "We have had so little time together."

"Ceidre . . ."

The agitated rise and fall of her chest was causing her nipples to stroke his skin repeatedly. He was not oblivious; Ceidre was very much aware of the smoldering of his gaze. She shifted slightly, so one thigh touched the bone of his hip, so her groin pressed against his other leg, riding it. She felt him hard and aroused against her navel. "Guy will return while you are gone," she said breathlessly. "And I have not told you, but he is no longer afraid of me, he said so before I came to you the first time. He still thinks I am a witch." She was rushing on, pleading without shame. "He said so, but a good one, one who will not harm, only heal. Now my threats to curse him if he touches me are idle, useless. Now it is only a matter of time until he decides to make me his wife truly. I saw how he has looked at me," she lied desperately. "He will return and he will bed me, rape me!" She sobbed. "Please take me with you! We have had so little time together!"

He cursed, gripping her arms so tightly she winced. "You have learned your power over me too well, little one," he said. "I cannot resist your lush body when you press and tremble against me, as you know damn well. I cannot resist your tears, and mostly, I cannot bear the thought of you with another—you know this too!" He cursed again. With his hard leg, he pushed her against the wall, forcing her thigh to ride up to his waist.

"Will you take me with you?" Ceidre cried.

"Yes," he growled, pulling down his hose and plunging into her so smoothly she was against the wall, thighs locked around his waist, clinging, before she even knew it. "Yes." He groaned. "God's blood, yes."

CHAPTER 51

They arrived in York two days later. William's royal garrison, Ceidre saw, was teeming with activity. She had managed to avoid anxiety during their journey, riding alongside Rolfe, sharing conversation and warm looks, even making him laugh upon occasion, much to his men's amazement. Rolfe gave no explanation to anyone as to why she was accompanying him, and of course, no one dared to question her presence. After initial pink embarrassment at the knights' surprise, Ceidre recovered and was soon truly enjoying herself. How could she not, after all? She was astride a beautiful blooded palfrey in the full bloom of summer, seated next to her handsome, golden lover—it was as if they were amusing themselves with a pleasant, innocent outing. There had been no incidents to hinder them, and they made good time. Yet now, seeing the comings and goings of William's soldiers, including his messengers, Ceidre felt dread ballooning deep in the pit of her being.

The question loomed: Why had Rolfe been sent for? And now, seeing what were clearly travel preparations for a large number of troops, she feared the worst. An armed force would be leaving York, and it could only be related to the rebels.

Rolfe left her at his tent, which was quickly raised within the inner bailey, but did not restrict her to it.

He went to see William. Ceidre felt as if a fairy tale had ended. She could not rest happily at York in the face of what she was seeing. She had to find out what was occurring, and why. She prayed that the Normans were going to ride out after Scot reivers and not after Saxon rebels.

She spent the rest of the day wandering in the village, where gossip ran rampant and all the village women were eager to share it with her, another Saxon. The Danes were going to invade again, one bakerwoman said. William was going to ride to the coast to meet them head on. A fisherwoman told Ceidre that William was furious over an ambush a sennight past, in which he had lost a top captain. He intended to scour the borderlands until he found the rebels responsible, and hang each and every one. An alewife told her that Hereward the Wake was reportedly close by, and this was the target of the Bastard Conqueror; another woman told her that her brothers' whereabouts had been discovered and that William would rout them and capture them, once and for all.

This last made Ceidre sick with fear.

She purchased meat and pigeon pastries from a vendor, along with a few exceedingly plump plums, and headed back to the castle's walls. They had been completed in wood and partially built in stone since their destruction during the last uprising. She was allowed into the outer bailey when, being questioned by the guard, she stated she had arrived with Rolfe de Warenne. She ignored a few lewd comments and a wink. After passing over the next drawbridge, she incurred the same questions, and this time had to wait until Beltain appeared to vouch for her. The heavy, spiked portcullis slammed shut after she was let in.

Rolfe had not returned to his tent. Ceidre paid a

young boy to fetch water, and she washed every inch of her body by hand and sponge. She donned fresh garments, nibbled on the food she had bought, and paced restlessly. Dark shadows fell, the night grew black. He had obviously stayed to dine in the keep with William, she thought, chagrined. He had forgotten her presence or was careless of it. Then she told herself she was a fool for feeling jilted. She did not want to sup in William's hall, and if she had, how would Rolfe explain her presence to his own liege lord? He would certainly have to, for William could question him about anything and everything. Her appearance at his side would at the least cause a scandal, at the most a royal uproar!

It was close to midnight when he made his entrance. His face, harsh in the light of the torch he held, softened upon seeing her as he drew the flap closed behind him. "I am sorry, sweetheart," he said, and she melted.

He had not ensconced the torchlight when she was hugging him fiercely, seeking his lips. A startled sound escaped him, then he met her demanding mouth with equal fervor. "I like this greeting," he said huskily sometime later.

Tears came to her eyes. "Take me now," she said harshly. And she caught his face in her hands and kissed him, forcing his mouth open, plunging her tongue aggressively within.

He took her quickly, roughly, right there on the pallet, and although Ceidre found physical release, she was not sated. Her fear and anxiety were choking her. She draped herself over him and around him, and could not burrow close enough. He caressed her lazily, then laughed. "I see you missed me," he teased.

She did not look at him, she felt like crying again. "I

always miss you when we are apart, my lord," she said breathlessly.

He was silent, but she felt his heart beneath her palm, and it had jumped in response to her words. He stroked her hair. "Is it true?" he asked, nuzzling the top of her head.

"Yes," she said, and realized, stunned, that she was not lying.

"I thought of you this day too," he admitted. He wrapped both of his powerful arms around her and held her more firmly against him. "Have you eaten, sweeting? Are you hungry? I will call for food and wine."

"I have eaten," Ceidre said, kissing his neck quickly.

He stroked his palm down her naked back, to explore the full curve of her bottom. Ceidre felt him hardening again. She felt a wild, uncontrollable need to be with him again, to have him inside her again, as if she could exorcise reality, or at least hold it back for a while. She slipped onto her side, her breasts provocatively crushed atop his chest, and reached down to fondle him. He tensed, then sighed with pleasure, his own fingers seeking her nipples and finding them.

She looked at him. His burning gaze met hers, then he threw his head back, revealing his thick, strong throat, arching his tumescent penis into her hand. His mouth opened, his breathing became ragged. Ceidre watched his face become strained as she continued to arouse him, kneading, squeezing, sliding up and down the smooth, hard length. He groaned, thrusting into her hand. "Ah, Ceidre . . ."

She slid onto her knees and nuzzled his full shaft with her face. He gasped, grabbing her head. Her tongue flicked out, to touch the ripe tip, to taste his seed. "Don't stop," he cried.

She kissed him, she licked him, she took him in her mouth.

Moments later he yanked her beneath him and plunged into her, again and again, his hands everywhere, until she was shaking and screaming in ecstasy. He followed instantly, collapsing on top of her.

They cuddled in silence for a long while. Ceidre stroked his chest, then said, her mouth against his heart, "How long do we have, my lord? Before you must leave?"

He paused, as he had been caressing her waist, then resumed. "And you are so sure we leave—witch?" His tone was light, teasing.

He has learned to play so well, she thought, and the sadness was overwhelming. Her soul felt on the verge of shattering. "I am not blind. I see all the preparations. You and your men ride out—for war." She sat up abruptly, her eyes filling with tears.

"Why do you cry?" he asked harshly, sitting also.

She shook her head, the tears falling unfettered.

"Do not fear," he said, his tone both rough and gentle, "we do not ride after your brothers."

Her relief was immense. Yet there was guilt now, and the sadness induced by the hateful reality that she had been forced this day to face, so she cried harder.

"Why do you cry?" He touched her cheek.

What should she say? That she cried because she was a spy, not a simple lover? "I am afraid, afraid of all this," she managed.

"Dare I hope," he breathed, capturing her chin, "that some of your fear is for me?"

She looked at him mutely and nodded.

He smiled, leaned forward, and kissed her mouth softly. "Do not fear for me. I will return to you, Ceidre. Nothing can stop me."

"Will there be fighting?" she asked, touching his jaw.

He hesitated, searching her eyes. "Hopefully, yes."

"I hope you do not find the Wake!" Ceidre cried, meaning it.

"We know where he is, Ceidre," he said, still regarding her. His look was strange, searching, but she was too distraught to really mark it.

"How do you know? You cannot be certain!"

"We have many spies—and they are everywhere." His gaze never left her.

"So you go to destroy him," she said.

"Of course. He has been planning another rebellion."

She felt guilty beneath his steady regard, but he could not know her innermost thoughts. She leaned forward and hugged him, hard. She was aware that for a moment he did not respond, but finally, slowly, his arms went around her. She clung. "When do you leave, my lord?"

There was something lacking in his touch, in his embrace. "As soon as Roger of Shrewsbury arrives—in two days."

She thought: oh, my God, Roger Montgomery too! The Wake had not a chance against such a force! And with a part of her mind she was aware of the strange emptiness of his caress, and the way he was waiting for her response. "At least with such a strong force, I can rest easy knowing you will not be harmed," she managed, into his shoulder.

She looked up and saw a dark thundercloud upon his face. "Do you care?" he demanded harshly. "Do you care, Ceidre?"

"Yes!" she cried, and it was the truth. But there were so many lies, and tears filled her gaze again.

He crushed her to him, twisting her beneath him.

His mouth, upon hers, made up for all the passion his touch had lacked a moment ago; it was so fierce he cut her lip. Ceidre did not care. She welcomed his brutal touch, she welcomed him.

CHAPTER 52

Rolfe did not leave her the next day until noon, to take his dinner with his lord. Ceidre had been sick with dread all morning, and trying, unsuccessfully, she thought, not to show it. He had appeared, somehow, oblivious to her anxiety. This increased her worry. She truly did not believe she was such a good actress, and she also knew he was very clever. Yet he was really unaware of her agitated state of mind.

The instant he left, Ceidre hurried to the village. She was cautious, unlike the day before, but no one followed her. The guards called out a greeting to her as she left the castle, and waved. Yesterday, before he had gone to see William, Rolfe had given her some coin, and today she asked him for more. He had gladly supplied it, without question, impatient, in fact, to be gone. Ceidre used the coin to pay the smith's son to take a message to Hereward the Wake. Last night she had managed to find out from Rolfe that the Wake was hiding in the fens near the Welsh village of Cavlidockk. "Do you go far?" She had asked. "Not farther than Cavlidockk," he had said. His gaze was level. "I trust you, Ceidre," he added bluntly, shocking her. She had managed a smile, and turned her face away before he could see the damning blush.

She had no choice. She had to warn Hereward of the danger he faced. Otherwise, it could be a slaughter.

* * *

The next morning at dawn Rolfe held her slightly apart, gripping her arms, staring down into her face. It was chill out, without the summer sun, but that was not the whole reason Ceidre shivered, wrapped hastily in a mantle and quite naked beneath. He was fully dressed for battle, in chain-mail hauberk and chausses, his sinister black cloak hanging from his shoulders, the citrine brooch at his chest winking. His hands on her tightened.

"God speed you, my lord," she said softly. She could not look away from his bright blue gaze.

A muscle in his jaw ticked. "Can you not, this once, call me by my name?"

She wet her lips. "God keep you—Rolfe."

His nostrils flared, his eyes flamed, and he crushed her in his arms. She clung to him. "God keep you, Ceidre," he whispered, then he claimed her mouth passionately.

He drew apart, gave her a last look, and turned on heel and was gone. Ceidre did not go out to watch him ride away; she couldn't. Miserably she sought her pallet and refused to leave it until the sun was high in the sky.

She felt listless. There was nothing she wanted to do. She bathed, she dressed, she ate. She supposed she could drift through the days until he returned—he had said he would be back within a sennight. Or she could pull herself together, somehow, and shed this cloying fear. Fear for him, for her brothers, for Hereward, for all the rebels, for them.

Oh, God, she thought. I care for him, I care for the Norman, and this cannot be! I cannot let it be! He is the enemy, he is the usurper of Aelfgar, he is my sister's husband! I am only his leman, and my duty lies to my brothers!

Frantic, she left the castle, striding into the village, wanting to outdistance these impossible feelings, these awful realizations. In an orchard, blackened grotesquely, the trees mere stumps, she paused to weep. She was about to pull herself together when a girl she vaguely recognized approached. Ceidre sat up, brushing her eyes.

The girl was shy, a pretty thing, almost a woman, blushing a fiery red. "I am sorry, Lady," she said, flustered. "I must speak with you, but I shall come another time." She turned to leave.

"No, stop, 'tis all right, I am being silly." Ceidre managed a smile. "Your name is Maude, is it not?"

"Yes." She blushed again. Then she glanced furtively around. "Your brother Morcar wants to see you."

Ceidre gasped. "What?"

Maude smiled with pride. "I am his friend," she said, and another blush swept her. "So I am glad to help him fight these Norman pigs! When you first came I sent him word that you were here. He expects me to keep him informed of all I see here at York," she explained patiently. "I am to use my judgment," she added proudly. "He has sent word back. His man Albie awaits you ten kilometers north of here, by the river Wade at the crossing. He will take you to them."

Ceidre was ecstatic. She clutched Maude. "You are a good woman," she said, then eyed her. "How old are you?"

"Fourteen next month," Maude said defensively.

Ceidre intended to give Morcar a piece of her mind. He had a hundred women to choose from, but he had to bed a babe, even if she was pretty and pleasingly curved! "Thank you," Ceidre said. "I will not forget this."

Maude smiled. "Send Morcar my love." She blushed again.

"Please, Ed, change your plans!"

Edwin regarded her sadly. "I cannot, Ceidre."

"This time you will be killed! The Normans have spies everywhere—he told me himself! Look—they have discovered Hereward's whereabouts! They could discover yours!"

"I have spies everywhere too, Ceidre."

" 'Tis too soon! Can you not at least delay? You will be defeated, maybe killed! Ed, please, reconsider what you do!"

Morcar was regarding her with folded arms. "What is this, Ceidre? Why are you so overwrought? Has he told you to come and beg us to cease?"

"No!"

"If he has," Morcar continued, " 'tis because he would like nothing more than to have us hand him Aelfgar on a pewter platter!"

"He has not sent me here," she protested.

"Has he hurt you?" Edwin asked, regarding her steadily.

She flushed. "No, he has not."

"You have done well, sister," Edwin said. "He must trust you completely to have been so foolish to tell you his plans and Hereward's whereabouts."

"So—he did not lie? Hereward is really near Cavlidockk?"

"Yes."

Ceidre had, in the back of her mind, feared the Norman had dissembled, discovering her game. But he had not lied, which meant he did trust her, and oh, how she hated herself and this entire damn war!

Edwin took her shoulders. "You care for him?" His tone was quiet.

She shook her head to deny it, even as tears escaped.

"Of course she does not care for that Norman pig!" Morcar roared, blue eyes blazing.

"In war," Edwin said, ignoring his brother's outburst, "we all do what we find distasteful. War is not a happy time."

Ceidre choked back her sobs. "I know, Ed," she said, hugging him.

"And to love the enemy is perhaps the worst of all," he said heavily.

She blinked up at him. "I do not love him."

"Have you seen Isolda?"

She jerked. Isolda was William's daughter, the one he had promised to Edwin after Hastings, then married to one of his own vassals. "No, I have not."

"I heard she was at York, with her husband. I heard she is with child—again." It was a question.

Ceidre had known Edwin was furious when William had reneged on his promise of his daughter as a bride, but never had she suspected he might actually have wanted Isolda for more than a royal alliance. Rumor had it, of course, that she was beautiful, tall and blonde and regal. "I will find out," she promised him.

"It matters not," he said, turning away. "Once it mattered, but that has long since passed." He looked at her. "All that matters is Aelfgar. I can never give up until I have taken back what is mine. I need you, Ceidre."

Her heart split precisely in two. "Do not fear. I will never deny you."

"This I know." He hesitated. "Ceidre—be careful. The Norman is shrewd. Do not let him catch you at these games."

Ceidre felt suddenly strangled. "What if . . ." She drifted off, unwilling to voice her fears. What if he guessed that she had been involved in warning Hereward away? There would be no proof, yet . . . She would not entertain it. Nor would she alert Ed to her thoughts. She was afraid he would fear for her and order her to remain with him and his men. Ceidre realized she did not just have to return to York and the Norman—she desperately wanted to.

A hundred Normans rode in double file, still ten kilometers south of Cavlidockk, deep in the forested hills known as the fens. Rolfe rode with his men in the lead, William in the middle, Roger at the back. There had been no sign of rebels so far. In another hour they would stop, scout out the Wake's camp, then surround and attack. Rolfe smile grimly. Soon another nest of vipers would be wiped out—if all went well.

Someone screamed a death cry.

Rolfe was aware of the ambush at that same instant and was shouting to his men to wheel and fight. Arrows flew from the trees above them, and Beltain, at his side, gasped when one pierced his shoulder. Rolfe was already riding at an archer in a tree, sword raised, and with one blow he hacked off the branch holding the man. The archer fell, and Rolfe effortlessly cleaved him in two.

A full-scale battle ensued. Wielding his sword ceaselessly, Rolfe slew half a dozen Saxons methodically, efficiently, without pause. And then the glade fell into a hoarse, panting silence.

Rolfe saw that the last of the Saxons had fled, and he called for a halt.

With horror, he stared at the ground before him. It was littered with a score of rebels, all dead or dying and dismembered. But another dozen of the dead and dying were his own men, who, in the forefront of the cavalcade, had taken the brunt of the attack.

"We were betrayed," William shouted, galloping up. "I saw Hereward myself, even exchanged blows with the traitor! I have lost three men, Roger one. How have you fared, Rolfe?"

Sickness choked him. "Much, much worse," he said. A dozen of his men, the best in the land . . . He spotted Beltain, his shoulder and torso drenched with blood, and spurred his mount to him. "How badly are you hurt?"

"I will live, I think," Beltain said, although he was ghostly white.

Rolfe called for aid as he vaulted from his stallion. He helped his captain down, stanching the flow of blood with a quickly placed tournicot. Beltain mercifully fainted from the loss of blood.

He was bandaged before he revived. Rolfe grimly did so himself, concentrating wholly on his task, his hands efficient and dexterous. Yet his mind, his mind was spinning—a dozen of his best men . . . ambush . . . Litters were made, the wounded tended to, the dead lashed onto the sleds to be brought to York for a Christian burial. William paused by his side. "I am sorry for your losses," he said sincerely.

"Shall we go on?" Rolfe asked harshly.

"We will burn Cavlidockk to the ground for harboring these rebels, though they have long since gone," William said. "Roger, as my marshal in Shrewsbury, will do this. You and I will return to York—to lick our wounds."

Rolfe said nothing. He stared at his dead men, bloody and gored, young William decapitated. Twelve of his men—the best fighters in the world—dead . . . betrayed. . . .

"These damned Saxons have spies everywhere," William gritted.

"Everywhere," Rolfe echoed. Betrayed.

He was so sick, he thought, in that moment, he would heave up his guts like a boy after his first battle. And suddenly, he did.

CHAPTER 53

He had returned!

The garrison was alive with talk of the return of William and his men, spotted as they entered the village. Ceidre wanted to run out into the outer bailey and launch herself into his arms. Of course she could not do this. Instead, she retreated to his tent, pacing nervously, excitedly. Oh, she could not deny it—she had missed him! At the same time, she dreaded his return, certain her guilt would show. And—what had happened? Had Hereward managed to elude his attackers? More important, was Rolfe all right?

The tent door swung open.

Rolfe stood there, backlighted by the sun, and Ceidre could only make out his imposing bulk. "My lord?" she breathed, her eagerness etched upon her face.

He stepped in, dropping the flap closed behind him. His face was stone. His eyes were ice-cold shards. Ceidre shrank inside. "What—what happened?"

He stared at her, his mouth a firm, hard line. "What happened? We were ambushed just south of Cavlidockk."

Her eyes widened. "Ambushed!"

His jaw clenched. "At least," he said harshly, "I know you did not know of that!"

Her hand covered her palpitating heart. She took a step back. "What do you mean!"

He stepped forward, crowding her. "Do you not know what I mean, Ceidre?"

"No," she squeaked, so afraid now.

"The truth! Tell me the truth, damn you, Ceidre!"

"I do not know . . ." She faltered, tears filling her eyes.

He grabbed her and shook her, hard. "Did you betray me? Did you? You knew we were going to Cavlidockk! Was I a fool to trust you? Answer me!"

Tears welled and spilled. She shook her head to lie, to deny it, but no words came out. She was sick with guilt, sick at heart, and it must have shown, for suddenly he released her with such force she flew onto her back on the pallet. She lay there, panting.

" 'Twas you!" he roared. "I see it in your eyes! Answer me!" he shouted, more furious than she had ever seen him, his face red, the cords standing out in his neck. His hands, clenched into fists, shook. His eyes were crackling blue flames.

Her own hand covered her mouth, trembling, and then she wept, reaching up to grab his palm. "I had to," she said, sobbing. "Please understand, I had to!"

He threw her off, staring, stunned.

She saw then, too late, that he had refused to believe what he had thought, that maybe she could have convinced him she was innocent, but now there was no taking back her confession. She lifted her tearstained face. "But you are all right," she said. "There was no harm done, no—"

"No harm done! A dozen of my men dead—because of you!"

She gasped, horrified.

He knelt, his expression twisted with bitterness and revulsion, and drew her forward by her shoulders. She winced but welcomed the pain. "You are a lying, conniving woman. You take me in your arms and play the inflamed lover, all the while shrewdly planning to betray me, waiting for an opportune time!"

She opened her mouth to protest, but could not find any words, for the indictment was true.

He yanked her roughly to her feet and dragged her out of the tent. "Where are we going?" She gasped.

He did not answer. She saw his face, filled with ice-cold resolve and red-hot fury. She was afraid.

When she saw that he was taking her to the keep, she dug her heels in. "What do you intend?" she cried.

He turned on her, livid, hand raised in fury to strike her. Ceidre cried out. The blow did not come. His grip was so tight she thought she might faint. "You may be dragged on your belly, 'tis of no import to me, or you may walk." And he yanked her forward again.

She stumbled to keep up. He could not, she prayed, fighting the tears down, he could not be doing what she thought. . . .

The great hall was filled with men. Most sat at the table, three times the size of that at Aelfgar and with William at its head. Rolfe did not pause. He propelled Ceidre forward, to the dais where William sat, then pushed her abruptly to her knees on the floor. His hand anchored in her hair, holding her facedown, her nose against the stone. "Here is the spy, Your Grace."

Silence swept the room.

William stared at Rolfe. "Your mistress?"

"Yes."

William rose. "Everyone out!" His gaze locked with Rolfe's, as he waited for his men to leave. When they had, he spoke. "You are sure?"

"She has confessed," Rolfe said coldly.

William looked down at her. "Raise up my prisoner," he said.

Rolfe yanked her to her feet, ignoring her whimper.

Ceidre lifted her gaze to the king's.

"You sent a spy to warn Hereward of our advent?"

Although she wanted to cry, she lifted her chin a notch. Her voice trembled. "Yes."

"And how did you learn of our plans?"

Ceidre hesitated. She had betrayed Rolfe, but now she would protect him from his liege lord. "I eavesdropped around the garrison."

"She lies," Rolfe stated. "I trusted this witch because she warmed my bed so eagerly. I told her where we were going, to allay her fears for her brothers. More the fool, I."

William ignored this and kept a steady regard upon Ceidre. "She is most charming of appearance. She resembles that scoundrel Morcar somewhat. You are lucky, wench, that Lord Warenne saw you married to Sir Guy. I have spies everywhere and I am well aware that this is the second time you have committed treason to me. I knew that you freed Morcar. Clearly you are unrepentant. Your sentence is imprisonment for life." He turned and called for his guards.

Ceidre froze, unable to move, to breathe, to think. The two men entered and approached. William told them to lock her up below. She whipped a frantic regard at Rolfe—he would not let this happen! He would not let this sentence stand—would not let them throw her into the dungeons! Surely he would not!

He ignored her. As the two men grabbed her, she closed her eyes. She knew her fate. It was over. She was to be imprisoned for life. And first tossed into the dungeons. She would not weep, would not beg—she would resign herself to death, for to be closed up below would surely kill her. With a deep breath, she managed to walk out between the two guards. Her shoulders were squared, hard, but her hands at her sides trembled.

When she was gone, William turned to Rolfe, who dropped down on one knee, head bowed. "Whatever you decide, 'tis not less than I deserve."

"You are right, of course," William said, walking away. He picked up a cup of wine, sipped it, and turned to gaze at Rolfe, who was still kneeling in deference. "Get up, Rolfe."

Rolfe rose gracefully.

"This is most strange. First you chose not to tell me that the serf who helped Morcar escape from Aelfgar was this wench, his bastard sister."

Rolfe was too bitter to be startled. "Again, I am a fool."

William ignored him. "But I let it go, trusting your judgment. 'Tis strange that you then wed her to Guy. 'Tis stranger still you allowed her in your bed. In one blow you cuckold wife and good friend. Is it true—that she has the eye?"

"Yes, but she is no witch."

"Mayhap she did give you a potion," William said. "Because you are not a man to behave as you have, nor are you one to spill our secrets—in bed, good God! It matters not how comely the wench is!"

Rolfe said nothing. But his eyes blazed.

"You are angry. I am glad to see it. You have been punished enough. You did not mean to abet her, and the result was you lost a dozen of your men. I will not add to what you are already suffering."

"Thank you, Your Grace," Rolfe said without gratitude. His jaws were clamped together.

William sighed. "In truth, despite the betrayal, we weakened their numbers and drove them from their lair, as we intended. Although our losses were heavy, we still succeeded in our plans."

"Yes."

"I place the wench in your custody. My dungeons are overfull already; besides, 'tis fitting, I think. Yet do not mistake me—she is a royal prisoner."

Rolfe smiled, cruelly, coldly. "I gladly accept," he said.

CHAPTER 54

"Your confinement is ended," Rolfe said coldly at the door to the chamber.

Alice rose from the bed, staring. Then she swept forward, dropped to her knees, and took his hand. "Thank you, my lord," she said humbly. "I beg your forgiveness." She lifted her face, her mouth quivering.

He ignored her, gesturing for her to rise, and turned grimly to examine the heavy door and inner bolt. A man stood at his heels. "This must be removed," he told the carpenter. "I want it placed on the outside. It must be unbreakable. Do you understand?"

"Yes, my lord," the carpenter said, inspecting the door.

Rolfe crossed the room with hard strides, to peer out an arrow slit. Not even a child could slip through, he noted with satisfaction. There was only one way out of the solar, and that was through the door. "The bolt shall be wood for now, but made of iron immediately. Inform the smith," he stated.

Alice, wide-eyed, wet her lips nervously. "What passes, my lord?"

His disdainful gaze swept her, surprised she was still there. "You will move back into my chamber," he told her shortly. "Your sister will be imprisoned here."

"Ceidre!"

Rolfe started to leave the room, and Alice hurried after, catching his sleeve. "My lord, what has happened!"

He did not break stride until he was in their own chamber. He ripped off his hauberk. "I need a bath now."

Alice scrambled to call for one.

"Your sister has committed treason one time too many," Rolfe said carelessly, yet with such an ice-cold attitude that Alice shivered. He pulled off his padded leather undertunic. "She is the king's prisoner, and her sentence is for life. William has placed her in my custody. She will never leave the solar until the day she dies."

Alice bit her lip to keep from smiling, unable to believe her good fortune. She wanted to know details, but she would find them out soon enough. "I wanted to warn you," she said carefully, "before you left for York."

Rolfe pierced her with a cold gaze, clad only in his hose. "Did you?" His tone was mocking.

Alice flushed. "She came to me the day before you left, my lord."

"If there is something you want me to know, then spit it out."

He was rude and crude and she hated him. Yet she remembered the feel of his huge lance inside her, the pain and the pleasure, and imagined him taking her again, roughly, hurting her, making her hate him, making her weep, making her keen. The carpenter's blows as he nailed the new bolt in place on the solar door began ringing out. She lifted her chin. "She came to apologize for bedding you, my lord. She wanted to explain that 'twas her duty—to her brothers."

Rolfe stared, expressionless.

"They had asked her to seduce you and gain your

trust—to spy. 'Twas the only reason she shared your bed, she said. She thought to ease my mind." Alice laughed lightly. But she was watching him, and she rejoiced silently when she saw the hot, red anger flooding his face and the hard, cold hatred filling his eyes. He turned away from her, and she smiled quickly, unable to contain herself.

When the tub was filled, Rolfe eased himself in. His heart was thudding thickly, too thickly, and he kept remembering how he had come to this room and found the witch naked in his bed. It had been a plan, a scheme of her brothers—seduce him and spy. And he, the fool, had been led by his eager cock. Well, he thought, a cold laugh passing his lips, 'twould never happen again.

His anger choked him. It had been choking him since she had actually confessed—he could not escape it. And with it came the hate.

She was a traitor, and she was his prisoner, and she would rot in that chamber until the day she died.

Ceidre was led by a guard into the solar. He released her and left, slamming the thick wooden door closed behind him. She heard the bolt falling, the sound ominous, final.

She hugged herself, hard, and looked around.

This was where Alice had been confined, yet the chamber no longer resembled that room. The bed had been removed—a straw pallet and blanket took its place. One candle had been provided, with a cup of water and a chamberpot. Being so bare, the room seemed vast, even though it was half the size of the chamber across the hall.

Ceidre walked to the arrow slit and looked out, tears filming her gaze. She had been imprisoned in the dungeon at York for half a day. That dungeon had been nothing like the one at Aelfgar, fortunately. It was large, taking up the entire space beneath the keep, and airy in comparison, not pitch-dark, with cells and many prisoners. She had been able to breathe despite the cloying fear in her chest. True, her breathing had been shallow, she had felt as if she was going to suffocate, but somehow the awful madness that had seized her in the other dungeon had not overwhelmed her. Maybe it was because of the other prisoners, maybe it was because the place was so large. She had had her own cell, half the size of this chamber. She had huddled in a corner, ignoring the other prisoners, perspiring and panting, but she hadn't tried to claw her way out in a futile hysteria.

She had wept.

The pain in her heart overshadowed all else, and she did not care that she might be swallowed up by the ground or choke to death from the lack of air. She wept, hopelessly, endlessly, grievously. She had betrayed him, and Ceidre knew what kind of man he was. She knew he would never forgive her. She wept until she had not another tear to shed, because she loved him.

The realization came much too late.

And even if it had come sooner, what difference did it make? She loved her brothers too. She would have been torn between the two irreconcilable sides. She would have, however, refused to spy, but brooding upon what might have been did not change anything. He would never forgive her.

The ride back to Aelfgar had taken two days. Ceidre had only seen Rolfe's back upon occasion. He had cut her out of his existence with one brutal blow. She knew this, was not surprised, just as she knew there would never be any going back to what they had once shared. Fortunately, she had no tears left. Her heart ached with its broken love. And whenever she saw his broad shoulders, or heard his voice, she could not tear her gaze from him. Yet he did not once look her way.

Not once.

It was growing dark. Ceidre wondered if she would be brought another candle once this one was finished. She decided not to light it. She was uncertain how her confinement would be styled. Right now, she feared the utmost deprivation. In truth, she was surprised she hadn't been sent to the black pits beneath Aelfgar.

She heard the bolt being removed and assumed it was bread and ale, the fare she had subsisted on since her imprisonment. She leaned her cheek against the wall, not bothering to look. Yet when the door was open, she knew who had come. She could feel his presence—it was overwhelming, vibrating with force, seething with hostility—and she jerked around, eyes wide.

Rolfe stood framed in the doorway in the last dimming light of the afternoon.

Ceidre said nothing, but her heart was leaping wildly—with hope. Why had he come? Oh, God, please let him forgive me, 'tis all I want!

Rolfe looked around, then smiled with cruel satisfaction. His gaze pinned her. Ceidre saw the contempt, undisguised, and the hatred, and all her hopes died. She slumped, beaten. He hated her. "I had no choice," she whispered, the words unbidden. "You must believe me!"

He smiled, another cruel twisting of his lips. "You think I care about your choices, Ceidre?"

"Have you never been forced by circumstance to act against your will?"

"Pretty words." He laughed roughly. "Pretty words from a pretty whore. Proof lies in the deed, and you have indeed proven yourself."

She gulped air. "Please listen, please!" She heard herself begging. "I had no choice! I sought only to protect Hereward, not to harm you! Never to harm you! I—"

He reached her in three strides, twisting her arm up behind her back and forcing her against the wall. "Stop!" he shouted. "Stop with your lies! Words spill from your lips like honey, but 'tis poisoned honey—like the honey that spills from here!" He grabbed her crotch.

She whimpered. "I love you."

He released her and laughed. "More honeyed words!"

" 'Tis the truth."

His face was filled with revulsion. His eyes were brilliant. "Do you love me, Ceidre?" A cold purr.

"Yes."

"Show me," he said. "Show me, prove it. Deeds—not words."

Ceidre froze, her heart pounding, unsure of what to do. How to convince him? Was she really being given this chance? How to soften his heart, heal it? Take away the ugly hatred?

He laughed, the sound bitter, and turned to leave.

She catapulted against him, her cheek on his back, her whole length pressed to him, clinging. He froze. "Do not go," she cried, choking on thick tears. "Let me show you, let me, I will!"

He did not move.

Her hands were shaking as she ran them over his shoulders frantically. She kissed his shoulder blades, his spine. She wrapped her arms around his waist and nuzzled his side. She curved her groin against his buttocks and held him, as hard as she could.

"I love you," she whispered, and she slid her palm up to his heart, to feel its fast, hard beat. She slipped her fingers down, into his hose, to touch the silken flesh near his navel. She was instantly rewarded with the big tip of his aroused sex springing against her hand, and she felt a tremendous relief—he still desired her, at least! "Let me love you, my lord." She gasped, her heart racing wildly. "I will show you—"

She was suddenly wrenched free of him and thrown backward, against the wall. She stumbled but did not fall. He was enraged.

"Save your whore's tricks for a farm boy," he rasped, blue eyes blazing, and then he was gone.

CHAPTER 55

The lying whore sought to seduce him again.

Did she think he was a fool? Rolfe paced his chamber in a fury. He had been enraged since supper, nothing would quell the flames within him. He hated how his body had responded to the slut. He told himself he would respond like a man to any woman, ugly or fair, not just to the witch who was imprisoned in the chamber just beyond his door. God curse her! Maybe he should have let her work her wiles, see how far she would have gone to prove her "love"! Maybe he should have taken her and fucked her until she could not walk! He was a hair's breadth from doing it now!

"Will you come to bed, my lord?" Alice breathed.

He looked at his wife with disdain, eyes blazing. He understood her husky tone. She wanted a fucking. Well, it would be no problem, because his groin was thick and swollen with his anger. He stripped methodically. He climbed into the bed and pulled her beneath him, impaling her instantly.

Alice gasped from the suddenness of his entry, and whimpered.

Rolfe moved hard and steadily, eyes closed, imagining it was Ceidre beneath him, crying out in pain, trying to push him off as his wife was doing. He plunged deeper, harder, wanting to hurt her, the bitch! Alice sobbed and writhed, clawing his chest. He caught her wrists, yanked them out of his way, driving himself mercilessly into her—the traitorous witch. The woman beneath him keened wildly in orgasm. Rolfe was still filled with the need to hurt Ceidre in the most basic, primitive way, and his angry, brutal thrusting did not cease.

Ceidre did not see Rolfe alone again, and two days after his hurtful, hate-filled visit, he rode out with a dozen men. She watched him leaving from the arrow slit, the pain in her heart as vivid and agonizing and heavy as ever. He was unbearably handsome as he sat his big gray, his face tight and closed—the way he had been that first day she had ever seen him at Kesop. It was hard to believe that this man was the same lover who had played with her in the orchard, teased her in the dark of the barn. He had learned to laugh and love so well, she thought, unbearably sad, and now he had learned to hate with the same fervor.

Mary was the only one to come to her chamber, bringing bread, cheese, and ale, once in midmorning and once at dusk. She was left with minimal amounts of water, and had not yet used the candle to test her captor's generosity—as she suspected he had none and would not bring her another candle. Her chamberpot was emptied every other day, thankfully. She was denied a bath—told, in fact, that if she wanted to wash she should use what was given her to drink. So she became dirty, and did not care.

Mary was deep in Alice's graces, and Ceidre knew this. Apparently the Norman knew it as well, and for this reason had chosen her to tend her. Mary, however, was a gossip. She was not malicious, just talkative, although Ceidre suspected Alice supplied her with the painful information she provided.

Mary was happy to tell her how the Norman had

kept Alice awake all through the night with his big shaft, until she was begging—happily—for mercy. God, it hurt. He hated her, and she knew he would go to other women, had never even hoped he would be faithful to her, a mere mistress, but it hurt more than she could bear. She hid her feelings carefully though, sure that Mary would be questioned quite thoroughly by Alice for her reaction.

Ceidre learned that the Norman had ridden out to fortify a position on his northeastern border with Wales. He would be gone at least a fortnight, maybe two, building a lonely keep in the midst of the barren wilderness. When Beltain was well, she was told, he would be given this small outpost. She was also told that her husband, Guy, had returned shortly after the Norman had left.

The days passed. Monotony at first was relieved by reliving every moment since he had entered her life that June day in Kesop. This proved too painful, and Ceidre tried to stop her memories, but it was impossible. There was nothing else to do except stare at the four walls. She worried as well for her brothers, knowing as each day passed the rebellion they were planning was coming closer and closer—and praying they would survive once again. Ceidre knew she should not bother to keep count of the days, yet she did, telling herself she was not marking the time for *his* return. She wished with all her being she could strike him from her heart. It was not to be.

A week after the Norman had left she realized that her monthly course was late. Not only was it late, her breasts were sore and she was nauseous in the mornings. There was a distinct possibility that she was pregnant, for Ceidre had been regular since she was thirteen. Her blood did not flow, and after another week passed, she knew she was pregnant with the Norman's child.

It was a gift from God.

She hugged her belly and wept with thanks, for now she had a part of him to cherish and love, a part of him that would grow to be strong and proud and every inch the man his father was, or, a woman blessed with the best traits of both parents. She loved the tiny soul growing within her body, she loved it with all the passion she had given Rolfe, and even more, because she loved him so and this child was created by that love. All her emotions went to this new baby, and nurtured by this event, she became serene, content. She was sure that the babe had been conceived on her wedding night to Guy, six weeks ago, because her breasts were already swollen and she already had the morning sickness. That she had conceived the first magical night she had lain with Rolfe filled her with pleasure.

Her fare, although boring, was enough to sustain her—but not enough to sustain them both. She begged Mary for more, but the maid was afraid of her mistress and balked.

"I can't, Ceidre," she wailed. "I'd be whipped good if I did!"

Ceidre knew she had to have more food for her baby's sake. "Mary, please!"

Mary was panicky. "I can't! You know Lady Alice will have my hide!" She turned to leave.

"Wait!" Ceidre called desperately. Mary paused reluctantly. "Mary." She hesitated. Then abruptly she decided that more nourishment was the priority, the baby was the priority. Alice would learn of her pregnancy eventually anyway, when it was visible, so what difference did it make if she found out now, from the maid, when Ceidre was so desperate for the proper food?

"Mary, I am pregnant—you must bring me more fare!"

Mary's eyes widened, her mouth made a big O, and then she exclaimed that it was no wonder Ceidre was blossoming like a rose in spring, despite her confinement. The maid acceded to Ceidre's wishes, and promised she would be given extra bread and cheese and enough water to bathe twice a week. Ceidre was content. She was going to have Rolfe's baby, and nothing could take that away, nor her joy.

It was not a surprise when the day after this confession, Alice appeared. She was livid. The chamber was cast in dim light because the only sunlight came through the two small slits. Ceidre sat up, having been napping, and although prepared, her body became rigid with tension.

Alice stared at her. "Mary said you have become more beautiful with each day, and I did not believe it! I said it's not possible—she said it's true! Then the little brat said you're with child—are you? Are you?" she demanded.

Ceidre was overwhelmed with pity for Alice, for her jealousy and malice were so evident, making her seem small and vindictive and unhappy, as she was. "I am pregnant, Alice," she said softly, smiling.

"The babe is Guy's!" Alice cried, flushing thoroughly.

Ceidre smiled again. "I am having the Norman's son, Alice."

"No! Once again you lie! Do you think to deceive me, to deceive him?"

Ceidre was amazingly calm, for the truth was the truth, and Alice could not change it. "No—Guy never touched me. Rolfe is the father. Oh, we will have a beautiful golden boy, I just know it!"

Alice was breathing harshly, incredulous. Fury contorted her features. "You witch!" she screamed. "I must have his seed, damn you, you cannot have his baby! You cannot!"

Alice moved so swiftly, Ceidre, lethargic as always in the afternoon, did not react. Alice's hands closed with superhuman strength around her neck. Instinctively Ceidre fought to free herself. Alice had the strength of a madwoman, but Ceidre was bigger and stronger and she broke Alice's grip, coughing. She saw the blow coming too late—Alice slammed the clay water urn on her head. Stars exploded, but Ceidre, fighting for her baby, did not black out. Dizziness assailed her. Alice was dragging her by the arm, across the room, and out the door. Ceidre shook her head, trying to clear away the ballooning spots, stumbling as Alice pulled her into the master chamber. She heard Mary exclaiming in surprise.

Her head cleared just as Alice forced her to sit, hard, on a stone ledge. Ceidre was poised on the edge of the open window, and Alice shoved her, hard.

Ceidre's palm, supporting her weight, slipped, and she saw the three stories to the ground that she would fall if Alice succeeded in forcing her out the window. She heard Mary screaming. She was still seeing a few spots. Alice yanked up Ceidre's other hand, and Ceidre's chin hit the edge of the outside of the window ledge, as she sprawled across it on her belly. Alice shoved her buttocks with all her maddened power.

Her jaw hit the side of the stone castle as she was shoved out, her hands clawing the walls within the window, fighting for a hold. There was nothing to grab on to in the smooth stone, and her breast passed the ledge, the ground looming beneath her dizzily. Alice shrieked.

And large hands caught in her hair, yanking her back into the room.

"No!" Alice was screaming. "No! No! No! Let me kill the witch! Let me!" she howled.

Gasping, her heart beating so hard she thought she might faint, Ceidre clung to the male body holding her.

There was the sound of a sharp slap. Alice's insane screams ceased. Ceidre looked past the man's shoulder and saw that Beltain had delivered the blow to Alice's cheek. Athelstan held Alice as she panted and struggled. Ceidre turned her gaze to her husband's. "Thank you," she whispered. "Oh, thank you!"

"You are all right now," Guy said, soothing her with his hand.

Ceidre began to shake, her face buried in his neck. "She—she tried—tried—to throw me—out—the window!" A sob rose, unchecked.

"You are fine now, Ceidre." Still holding her, Guy spoke to Beltain. "She has gone mad. She must be locked up until Lord Rolfe returns and decides what to do."

"I will have the carpenter board the window. I think we should lock her in here. I will post a guard within to make sure she does not hurt herself."

"I am not mad," Alice hissed. "I am perfectly sane! I hate her 'tis all!"

Beltain and Guy, shifting uncomfortably, did not look at her. Athelstan regarded her with pity.

"Is she all right?" Beltain asked Guy.

"Yes." With his arm around her shoulder, Guy walked her out of the chamber. "Come, Ceidre, you should lie down. Mary, bring wine now."

The maid, whose screams had alerted the men, fled to obey.

Ceidre leaned heavily against Guy, trembling. Alice had tried to kill her. Her baby had almost died. She sank onto the pallet, clinging to her husband's hand.

He knelt beside her. " 'Tis all right now," he soothed. "I am sorry I must bring you back here after such an ordeal, but nothing changes."

"Oh, Guy." Ceidre gasped, gripping his hand. "She almost killed my baby!"

Guy froze.

Ceidre started to cry.

Guy sat beside her and held her gently. "You are having his child, Ceidre?"

She nodded, violet eyes wide and wet, unable to speak.

"Does he know this?"

She shook her head, then grabbed his arm. "Promise me you will not tell him!"

"Ceidre," he protested.

"Promise! Guy, I love him!" she begged. "I love him and he hates me. I will tell him of the child when the time is right—please! I cannot keep it hidden, this you know!"

"He might think it is mine," Guy said thoughtfully.

"No, I told him how it was between us." At his look, she said softly. "He is very proud, and, for a time, I think he loved me a little. He is not a man to share."

"No, he is not," Guy said. Then: "Have you enough to eat? Ceidre! You must tell him at once to improve your conditions!"

"I have more than enough now. Mary is bringing me extra rations, bless her soul."

Guy suddenly eyed her. "Mayhap," he said. "You have put on a bit of weight, your hair has uncommon luster, as does your skin. Your breasts are fuller. I will make sure the kitchen knows to send you extra portions."

"Do not tell him," Ceidre urged again. She blushed. "I know he hates me, but I do not want his gratitude for this. I—I don't know what I want, but not that."

"You are foolish, Ceidre. Rolfe is not a man to love a woman, and he is a hard man with strict ideas of duty and loyalty. He will not forgive you your betrayal. I know him well."

"I know," she said, yet it was as if she had been hoping secretly, still, deep in her heart for forgiveness, for now her spirits crashed heavily.

"And 'tis doubly foolish not to tell him he will be a father, for the baby's sake. Of course"—Guy stood—"I do not want to be cruel, but he already has many bastards."

"I am not surprised," Ceidre said with calm she did not feel. She had not considered this, and it was another numbing blow. "Where—where are they?"

"Three in Normandy, one in Anjou, and two in Sussex, I believe. They are with their mothers, of course. All six are sons," Guy added.

All six were sons. Ceidre almost laughed hysterically. So she would now give him a seventh! Dear Saint Edward! She choked on a sob.

"I am sorry," Guy said, "but these are facts. He will treat you with courtesy for bearing him yet another bastard, but do not expect more."

CHAPTER 56

"We go the last day of September."

Both Morcar and Hereward protested vigorously at Edwin's quiet statement. " 'Tis too soon," Morcar said. " 'Tis in two weeks."

"My men are still recovering from Cavlidockk," Hereward agreed. He was short and slim, dark, a few years older than both brothers.

They stood apart from the camp, almost out of the circle of firelight, speaking in low voices for fear of spies. "How many men can you muster?" Edwin asked calmly.

"Two dozen."

"Good," Edwin said, smiling for the first time. "Because I have three. We will outnumber de Warenne. He lost a dozen of his best at Cavlidockk, thanks to Ceidre."

"You wish to take him by surprise?" Hereward asked.

"Yes. I fear to wait longer as well, because of spies. No one can be trusted these days. And he has yet to replace the dozen lost in the fens. We are the stronger now, it is the time to attack."

"We will attack Aelfgar, then, my lord, not York?" Albie spoke up for the first time. He stood slightly apart, even deeper in shadow.

"Aelfgar." Edwin's tone was hard. "It is as strong as

York now that he has rebuilt the fortifications. If we take it, we can hold off further attacks by William and he will have to sue us, eventually, for peace."

"But as it is fortified so well, how will we take it?" Hereward asked.

"Through surprise, and treachery. One of the maids will open a secret back door, placed in the wall for the inhabitants' escape in event of siege." Edwin looked at Morcar, smiled slightly. "His wenching has been proving useful. Can we count on Beth?"

Morcar grinned. "Absolutely."

"We go the thirtieth, then," Ed stated, and with that, he turned away to stare out into the starless night.

Morcar approached as Albie and Hereward drifted back to the others. "Ed? I am upset with the news Hereward brought of Ceidre. That she was imprisoned as a spy in York, but sent to Aelfgar with de Warenne. I worry for her safety."

"She is safe," Edwin said. "She was not condemned to death but to life imprisonment. Had she not been Guy Le Chante's wife, she would have swung at the end of a rope, I have no doubt. In that respect, we owe the Norman."

"I fear for her because of his rage."

"We will take Aelfgar and then you need not worry any more," Edwin said.

Rolfe learned of the attempt upon Ceidre's life the instant he returned, before he had set foot within the Great Hall. "Was she harmed?" he demanded.

"No," Guy said. "Shaken, of course, but it quickly passed."

"And what was done with Alice?" His heart was thudding. Alice had almost succeeded in pushing Ceidre out of the window and to her death!

"We locked her in her chamber with a guard, my

lord," Guy's voice lowered. "She is sane now, but truly, she was insane to do such a thing. I saw her. She was howling like a madwoman, screaming how she wanted to kill Ceidre. Beltain and Athelstan saw it too."

Rolfe left Guy and strode up the stairs, controlling his temper with vast will and great difficulty. Alice had gone too far. He would not stand it any longer. At the top of the stairs he paused and looked at the bolted door behind which Ceidre was imprisoned. It had been over a month since he had seen her, and he had the urge to throw open the lock and go within—to make sure Guy told the truth, that she was unharmed, that she lived. He struggled with himself and won. He turned to his own chamber, entered, and dismissed the guard.

Alice stood, hands clasped, eyes wide. "They are all lying," she said huskily. " 'Twas a mere spat. I did not intend to push her to her death. I swear it."

"You are leaving Aelfgar in the morning," Rolfe said relentlessly. "Pack everything you wish to take with you."

"Where are you sending me?" Alice cried.

"You are going to France, my lady," Rolfe said coldly. "To the Convent of the Sisters of Saint John."

"I—for how long?" She gasped.

"In the convent you may repent your deeds, if you wish. If not—" He shrugged. "There, at least, you will not be able to harm your sister, or anyone else."

"For how long?"

"Until you are old and gray, my lady," Rolfe said.

"You cannot mean it!" Alice shrieked. "You cannot do this!"

"No? I do mean it, and I can do it. You are not the first wife to be exiled to religious seclusion. You were warned, yet you failed to take me seriously. Were you one of my men you would have been dismissed forth-right, long since. Prepare what you need, Alice, for an extended stay."

Rolfe paced his chamber. He had removed Alice, under guard, to the old manor, never wanting to set eyes upon her again. He was still angry, furious at her attempt to murder Ceidre. This realization made him livid with himself. He still harbored some kind of feelings for that deceitful whore.

She was so close, behind the door across the hall. He paused in his pacing and imagined her asleep on the pallet, her beauty unsurpassed, a seductress's unnatural beauty. He hated her with every fiber of his being. He did not care that Alice had almost murdered her, he told himself, he cared only that Alice had defied him and nearly killed the royal prisoner who was his responsibility. His frustration and wrath increased.

He needed a woman. There had been no one in the past month since his own wife, bedded with rage and frustration just before he had left for his northeastern borders. All his men had gone celibate, for there were no villages and no wenches about in that far, savage clime. He did not think he had ever gone so long without a woman since he was a bare-faced boy. He thought of Ceidre, just across the hall. He could easily fuck her brains out this night.

He hated her, and he would not.

Why not?

She was a whore. He desired her. She had been his whore. She was now his prisoner. She could not deny him, and if she did, he would take her anyway. He was so hard just thinking about it he thought he might explode. With no thoughts now beyond that of instant gratification with the woman who had betrayed him, he stalked to her door, threw the bolt, and flung it open.

She was asleep. The sight of her curled up on her side—a sight he had seen many times before—halted him in his tracks. For a moment his resolve wavered, and then, with renewed fury, he pushed it aside. He reached her and shook her roughly. "Wake up," he said with a snarl.

She blinked awake in confusion. Rolfe squatted, taking her chin in his hand, pushing his face near hers. "Are you awake, witch?"

She gasped with recognition.

"Good." He smiled and stood, hands already pushing down his hose to free his straining, angry member. Ceidre gasped again, eyes widening. "I have need of a whore," Rolfe said coolly. "Spread yourself for me."

She did not move.

He pushed her down on her back, hard, hoping to hurt her, reaching for her thighs to spread them. He was unprepared for her arms, which went fiercely around his neck, her face buried there. "Take me, my lord," she breathed. "I will never deny you."

Her words, her acceptance, her serenity inflamed him. "You cannot deny me, whore," he spat, already on top of her. He thrust into her and she whimpered. Unlike the night he had raped her on her wedding day, she was dry and tight and he knew he had hurt her. He told himself he did not care. Yet he froze just the same, unable to continue ruthlessly.

She stroked the curls at the nape of his neck tenderly, kissing his jaw. "Your whore's games will not work," he shouted, thrusting fiercely into her. She met his rhythm fervently, gasping now with pleasure—he recognized the sound too well. He did not want to pleasure her. He only wanted to use her. He intended to spill his seed quickly, as quickly as possible. In the past, he had had to fight himself from finishing, wanting to give her ecstasy; now he welcomed his unbearable arousal, encouraged it. He reminded himself of every lie she had told, every instance of treason, and the final act—the one resulting in the loss of a dozen of his men. She had probably lied about Guy too, had probably shared his bed many times. After all, why not spy in two beds, or even more? He came violently.

He stood, smiling coldly, adjusting his hose. He could see that she had not been assuaged, her eyes were black with passion and desire. He was pleased to have found release—and even more pleased to have excited her and then denied her hers. "From now on you are not just my prisoner," he said, raking her contemptuously. His gaze lingered on her femininity, damp and exposed with her gown still up around her waist. She did not try to cover herself. "You are my whore. When I feel the need, I will take you. I think this suits you very well, Ceidre."

Her eyes were wide and violet, and he saw the shimmer of tears. "I will never hate you, my lord," she whispered.

"Then I will hate strongly enough for the two of us," he stated, and he turned abruptly and walked out.

It was four days later.

Rolfe cautiously looked around the woods. He was six kilometers from the village, near a huge fallen tree that crossed the racing creek like a bridge. This was most definitely the place for the rendezvous.

He was mounted on his gray, alone. At least, he appeared to be alone. In truth, his men were hidden in the forest, not far—in case this was a trap. His hand rested lightly upon the hilt of his sword.

He heard him before he saw him. Staring across the river, Rolfe watched the rider appear through the trees until he had reined in on the creek's rocky bank. As one, Rolfe and the rider dismounted, moving to the fallen tree. Rolfe leapt nimbly up and walked carefully to the middle, as did the other man. All around them the creek gurgled happily, the sound innocent and bell-like and loud enough to drown out their words—should anyone try and listen.

"Aelfgar will be attacked. There will be five dozen men. The maid Beth will let them in through the secret door in the wall. Edwin and Morcar and Hereward lead."

"When?"

"The thirtieth—in ten days."

"You have done well," Rolfe said. "If you speak the truth, as William has promised, your reward is the fief of Lindley in Sussex."

"Oh, I speak the truth," Albie said.

CHAPTER 57

The Saxon camp was nestled in a hidden dale, within twenty kilometers of Aelfgar.

It was the twenty-ninth of September. The night was pitch-black and moonless, promising a gray, cloudy morning. The camp was completely hushed. There was no whispered conversation. No fires burned. Few were sleeping, however, on the eve of battle.

"Even the weather favors us," Morcar said, low.

Edwin said nothing. The brothers sat side by side on a log. The night sounds were all around them—crickets, an owl, a lonely wolf.

"We will win, Ed," Morcar said, barely suppressing his voice in his excitement. "The time has come to take back what is ours! I can feel it!"

Ed smiled slightly.

"Beth knows what she must do," Morcar whispered. "Just before dawn she will open the door. With me and my men in the lead, no one will know what has hit them! I think we will be within the keep before an alarm is even sounded."

Edwin touched his brother's shoulder, then clasped it firmly. "This time," he said, "it does appear that the gods have favored us."

Ceidre was waiting.

He had not come to her again, not since the one

night when he had tried to use her cruelly and coldly, yet every night Ceidre waited, hoping. If he still desired her there was a chance for them, a slim chance, true, but she would gladly take it. In his arms she would show him how she felt—how she repented her betrayal, how she loved him.

It had hurt unbearably to be treated as a whore, but in a way she welcomed punishment, for she deserved it. Yet, in truth, even though he hated her, she still loved him, and being in his arms could not be a punishment no matter how cruel he tried to be. She sensed the raw, gaping wound she had left, the one he hid with anger and hate. She ached unbearably with love and hurt for him—she had not lied when she had said she could never hate him.

She knew she should hate him. To love one who hated her so thoroughly was hopeless. Yet she could not—just as she could not deny him. If only he would come to her again!

Something was amiss this night. It was already very late. Ceidre was tense in her vigil, for the keep was hushed, and she sensed that something dire was about to happen, was happening. She hugged her knees, staring through the candlelit room at the door. Rolfe, where are you? Come to me!

When Rolfe suddenly entered, approaching her with hard, quick strides, Ceidre felt both dread and joy. His face was so closed, his eyes like ice, and what if she failed? What if he came to seek release and hurt her and she could not thaw the freeze in his heart? She was already standing, trembling. "My lord," she managed. "I am glad you have come." She prayed her heart's deepest feelings shone in her eyes.

Something flickered in his gaze. "Do you think I care?" He laughed, yanking her to him. "I am bored with the pallet, whore. Show me some new tricks."

Tears came to her eyes. "Which kind would you prefer?"

"Any kind," he snapped.

Ceidre lowered her lashes to hold back the tears, knowing she was a fool—she would never penetrate his hate and disperse it. Never. But how to give up her hopes, her dreams?

He made a sound, of disgust, and wrenched her hand down until her palm covered his manhood. It was rock-hard and straining to his navel already. She stroked it blindly, despair filling her. She could not continue like this—but hadn't she prayed for the chance for them to be together? Why did her heart have to feel as if it were breaking? She must be strong and filled with resolve! And then, as she felt him coming under her power, under her spell, she heard him utter a short, hard sound, and she looked up. His eyes were closed, his face dark and strained with arousal. The stabbing of desire was like lightning—her own body grew tense and eager. For she loved him. "Rolfe," she whispered.

He heard her, she saw the flitting of something undefinable across his face, but he did not open his eyes. She leaned against the wall and lifted one thigh to wrap it around his waist. He needed no encouragement, soon he was plunging into her, her legs anchored on his hips, back against the wall. To her surprise, he kissed her, fiercely, the first time he had done so since her treachery. With a cry she kissed him back, claiming his mouth as he possessed hers. They kissed and kissed as their hips thrust, tongues entwining in a desperate dance. She loved him. She loved him so much. "Rolfe," she cried when her orgasm spun her away. "Rolfe, Rolfe!"

He slid her to her feet, stared at her, and she saw something in his eyes, something that had nothing to do with hatred and anger. He suddenly lifted her in his arms and laid her on the pallet. Ceidre's heart clenched. "I want to see your witch's body," he said, and his tone was unsteady instead of mocking.

"What is it?" she said, worry gripping her, all her intuition coming into play. Something was amiss, something was happening! He ignored her, pulling off her gown. For a moment he just stared at her breasts, at her belly, at her long legs. His hand swept over her. "What is it? What happens?" There was fear in her tone.

He did not answer, his eyes on her swollen bosom, his hands testing their weight and feel. Ceidre froze. He can tell, she thought, panicked, that I am with babe. He had not undressed her and seen her naked body in six weeks, not since Cavlidockk.

He groaned and sought her nipple with the eagerness of a nursing infant. Ceidre relaxed. Soon she was gripping his head, and then he was entering her, leisurely this time—gently. She wanted to weep at the beauty of his coming to her. His mouth found her throat, her jaw, her cheeks and ear. His hands played her like a viol. He touched her everywhere, even pausing, magnificently still and full within her, on his knees, reaching down to stroke her wet flesh where they joined.

Ceidre looked at his face. He was watching his own hands upon her woman's flesh, but then he looked up and their eyes met. The blazing passion in his brought her to a rapid, writhing climax.

He was no longer her warden, her torturer, but her lover. He did not finish, but wrapped her in his arms, moving steadily within her, his mouth on hers. Again and again he brought her to a shuddering climax, and finally, with a hoarse gasp, he spewed himself into her.

Ceidre held him, stroking his sweat-drenched back.

Tears were in her eyes. He had loved her as if Cavlidockk had never happened. Dare she hope that this meant something? Dare she?

He rolled free of her and lay on his back, one hand across his eyes, panting.

She studied him openly, her heart near to bursting with hope and gladness. He was tall, golden with muscle, impossibly handsome. Her hopes started to crumble when he got up without looking at her. In the course of their passion he had shed his clothes with her help. Now he dressed efficiently, not sparing her a glance. "My lord?" Ceidre tried.

When he turned to her, a hard, cynical expression, one she had hoped never to see again, was firmly in place. His eyes were narrowed. His fine nostrils were flared with disdain. She felt her hope collapsing like a landslide, and she hugged her hands to her heart. "My lord?" Her tone quavered.

"If you have something to say," he said coldly, "say it."

He still hated her. He would never forgive her. Guy's words echoed—he has strict ideas of duty and loyalty. He will never forgive you your betrayal, Ceidre. And hadn't Guy also said that he was not the kind of man who was capable of loving a woman? She was a fool to love him, a naive fool! She swallowed. "Is something happening? Why is the tower so hushed?"

His smile was ugly. "Think you to betray me again? Do you think"—and he laughed—"because I have shared your whore's passion that now I share my command's secrets? Think again!"

Tears blurred her vision as he marched to the door. Her heart pounded loudly, hurtfully, so much so that she bearely heard him when he paused. "Do not think to leave this chamber tomorrow regardless of what passes," he said.

She was crying, her face turned away, so she did not understand what he had said. And she missed the rest of his words entirely, when he added, low, "You will be safe, Ceidre."

She was only aware of her heart's agony, and the ironic, insane thought—how was it possible to have your heart broken twice?

CHAPTER 58

At the edge of the woods, the Saxons paused. Across the moat lay the wall with the hidden door. Although more than fifty men, they blended with ease into the forest, not moving, not making a sound. It was black out in the pitch of night just before dawn. Morcar crouched next to Edwin.

" 'Tis time to go," Edwin said firmly.

Morcar smiled, nostrils flared with excitement. He turned to his brother and was embraced in a massive, long hug. When Edwin released him, Morcar grinned. "Soon," he whispered. "Where's Albie?"

"Here" came a voice, and Albie stepped through some bushes.

Edwin slapped them both on the back. "God speed you," he whispered.

Morcar gripped his hand. "To victory," he said, then he was gone, racing across the open with Albie on his heels, lost in the engulfing blackness of the night.

At the moat Albie waited, handing Morcar the one end of a rope bridge. Morcar waded in, grinned once at the icy cold, a flashing of white teeth, then plunged on and swam for the far side. When he had reached it he tied the end of the rope bridge to a plank in the wall. Twenty minutes later a dozen men had crossed, with the rest waiting their turn.

When half their number had joined them beneath

the keep's wall, the sky was just faintly lightening, dark now, but not ebony. Morcar gathered his dozen men around him. "Where is Albie?" he asked, looking for his second-in-command.

No one knew where he was, and Morcar felt both worry that something had befallen him and a frisson of nameless fear. He could not wait. They must be within the walls before dawn. "We go," he said, raising his sword.

The door was open, and Morcar smiled briefly, intending to thank Beth in the way he knew best. He slipped through, his men on his heels. He was four steps into the bailey when he saw a glinting of steel, but it was too late.

He turned to meet the attack, sword lifted, when he felt the blade piercing his side. There was a deafening roar all around him as Normans materialized from the shadows, engaging his men. He felt his own sword slicing flesh as the word sliced through his mind—betrayed. We have been betrayed.

Edwin was in the thick of battle in the inner bailey. His heart was sick with the disaster surrounding him. Saxons lay slain everywhere, yet still a dozen fought, as he did. He knew they had been betrayed.

He thrust his blade into the heart of his opponent, only to feel a blade enter his hip. Whirling, he met this new attack, his face grim, determined. He instantly recognized his foe, who also recognized him. 'Twas Le Chante—Ceidre's husband.

Edwin met parry for parry furiously, with determination and skill. Guy, like himself, was covered with blood. Their blades clashed. Guy was tired, Edwin saw, and, like himself, wounded, bleeding from the shoulder. Another blow from Edwin's sword forced the younger man against the wall, off balance. Edwin did not hesitate. He skewered him.

He paused, panting, not watching as Guy sank to the ground with a moan. They had lost. He would weep later. He saw no sign of his brother. He knew he must escape—as long as he remained alive, there was hope of another rebellion, hope of victory. Yet he was also on the keep's steps—and his sister was within.

He was a fool if he tried to free her. His duty was to Aelfgar.

Rolfe paused, panting, his sword in hand. It dripped blood. He himself was unscathed. The battle was all but over, he thought, surveying the bailey grimly. His men were in control, driving the last of the Saxons to the wall. The rebels lay slaughtered, a few of his own men among the corpses. Yet he saw at a glance that he had suffered very few losses. There was no rejoicing. He was too pumped up with the battle, still alert, rigid with tension.

Where were the leaders, Edwin and Morcar?

Unable to stop himself, his glance strayed upward, toward the tower chamber where Ceidre was. She, of course, was safe, for no Saxon had penetrated the keep. He thought he could discern her by the arrow slit, and resolutely he pulled his glance away. Gripping his sword with renewed determination, he turned the corner of the keep and began a thorough search for the rebel leaders.

His gaze scanned everywhere, passing over the dead and dying and the few pairs of soldiers still engaged in combat. Then, like a pendulum, his glance swung backward over the path it had traveled, backward, over blood and gore, dirt and stone, the inert and the active, backward—to Guy.

Rolfe cried out.

Guy lay unmoving, and his mail hauberk was crimson with blood.

Rolfe ran to him and dropped to his knees. "Guy! Guy!" And before his hands even cupped his face, he knew he was dead.

He held his best friend's face, blinking back the hot rush of tears. "Guy," he croaked. "Aahhh." He hesitated, then abruptly pulled him up against his chest. Still he fought the goddamn urge to weep.

"My friend," he said hoarsely. "God keeps you now."

Ceidre stayed near the arrow slit, watching, horrified. What remained of the fighting was on the other side of the tower, and she could barely see the last of the battle, just a few men thrusting swords and swinging maces, a few dead, mutilated bodies on the ground. But she had seen Rolfe earlier, wielding his sword methodically, fatally. He had decapitated a Saxon in one slicing blow, then turned to meet another Saxon about to stab him from behind, easily turning this new opponent back, then dismembering him, finally piercing his heart. Ceidre had watched because she was afraid—afraid for her brothers, who were out there somewhere, and afraid for Rolfe.

When she had seen the Saxon coming up behind him as he was engaged, she had screamed in warning. She doubted he had heard. When he had killed his attacker, she had wept in relief.

He was no longer in sight, yet below her a few men still fought, and she watched, praying.

Her door swung open; she whirled.

"Edwin!"

He was bleeding, limping, bloody sword in hand, but he was alive. "We must go, come with me!" he shouted.

She, who had always obeyed her brother unquestioningly, hesitated. Her mind was full with one thought—Rolfe.

"Come," he cried, grabbing her arm.

Edwin was authority, the Norman hated her, and she could not decide—she went with him. Together they ran down the stairs. The hall was empty, but outside could be heard the shouts of men, the moans of pain, the ringing of swords.

Edwin had her hand. There was no time to talk, not even to ask him how badly he was hurt. He hustled her into the inner bailey, down the steps, and across the courtyard. Men lay dead and dying around them; men fought in isolated pairs around them. He suddenly froze at an open door, one Ceidre had not known existed. She was frightened and her blood coursed with the primitive need to flee and escape. She did not understand why he had stopped. "Go," he suddenly shouted, shoving her through. "I will follow. Go with the fleeing men across the bridge and into the woods. Go!"

"Why do you wait?" she screamed from the other side.

"Go!" Ed shouted, shoving her. "Go!"

Ceidre's hand was grabbed by a Saxon she recognized, and she was pulled down the hill and to the rope bridge that was swinging precariously as the Saxons fled over it, beneath a hail of arrows from the archers on the walls. She tried to look over her shoulder, but Edwin was gone.

Edwin dropped to his knees beside the utterly still body of his brother. His heart had stopped, as had his mind. There were no thoughts, other than please God. Gently he rolled him over to his back.

Morcar groaned.

"God!" Ed shouted in relief. And then he saw the gushing torrent of blood spewing from his brother's chest, and, crazed, he jammed both hands down hard on the wound to dam the flow.

"Ed." Morcar choked weakly.

"Don't speak," Ed cried. "Save your strength—*don't speak!*"

"Can't." Morcar panted.

Furiously, desperately, Ed put all his power into his hands as he pressed them on Morcar's chest. "You will be all right," he said, panting. *"You will not die!"*

Morcar opened his mouth to speak, but no sound came out. He choked on the torrent of his own blood.

Weeping, Ed put more effort into stanching the flow.

"Betrayed," Morcar said, and for an instant, his blue eyes blazed. "We have been betrayed, Ed," he whispered hoarsely.

Edwin started to protest, to tell his brother not to talk, when he met his sightless stare. Vacant, when a moment ago it had burned with intensity. Lifeless.

"God, no!" Edwin shouted to the heavens above, fist raised, and then he lifted his brother into his arms and rocked him, sobbing.

He knew, as he wept, that he must get up and flee or be captured. Yet his grief was so unbearable he could not find the will to leave Morcar. He tried to look at his beloved, handsome face through his hot, thick tears. Morcar was angry and grim in death—not the laughing, handsome rogue he truly was. Oh, God, Edwin thought, the pain unbearable, ballooning in his heart, hurting, hurting . . . he had been slaughtered not moments after he had bravely led his men into their enemy's stronghold.

Betrayal.

Edwin's tears stopped with this comprehension—

and the knowledge that the rest of his life would be dedicated to finding the man responsible for his brother's death.

He rose, Morcar in his arms. He could not leave him, just as he could not have left Ceidre. He took one step, when the cold voice of Rolfe de Warenne halted him in his tracks.

"Halt," the Norman ordered, sword raised. "You are my prisoner."

Edwin stared into the cold blue gaze of his worst enemy.

Then he looked at the Normans surrounding him as he cradled his dead brother to his chest. His arms tightened protectively around Morcar, and he fought the fresh urge to weep. It was over.

He had lost; Aelfgar was lost. It was over.

CHAPTER 59

"Can ye come, my lady?" the old woman asked anxiously.

Ceidre wrapped her cloak more tightly around her. It was early January, and here in Wales in the tiny village of Llefewellyn, there had been a dusting of snow one night past. She barely understood the native tongue of the villagers, but this phrase had become familiar. Once her skill with herbs, her ability to heal, had been revealed, she had received many requests like this one. "Of course," she said softly.

The woman, gray and thin, looked at the beautiful Saxon and wondered, as they all did, at the sadness that never left her eyes. 'Twas a shame, they all agreed, for one so comely to grieve so endlessly. They knew little of her story, only that their native son, Hereward, had brought her here and left her in his cousin's cottage, the cousin long since deceased, then ridden out again to fight his endless wars. She was clearly pregnant, her belly and breasts straining her garments. Her eye made them all fearful and wary, but with time she had shown that she was good and kind. Hereward was something of a hero to the villagers, so his woman, pregnant with his babe, was received without too much consternation, despite the eye, and with a degree of hospitality. Mayhap, the villager thought, if her man would come home for a while the sadness would leave her.

Ceidre walked with the woman to her cottage and tended her husband, ailing from a chronic cough. She accepted a loaf of fresh bread and some smoked tongue in return for her services, then started home.

Home. A lump gathered in her throat as she saw the tiny hut she now called home. She hugged her mantle more tightly to her breasts, sore now in her seventh month of pregnancy. Would she ever see home again?

She knew she wouldn't.

She had learned from Hereward the night after the battle what had happened: Morcar dead. Edwin captured. Albie the traitor. She had wept for days for Morcar, beautiful, blue-eyed, bold Morcar. Life was so unfair, to take the best she offered. Later, more news had reached them—that Edwin had been taken to York, his sentence imprisonment for life. He would be transferred to London when William and his troops left Westminster after Christmas. At least he still lived.

Rolfe had been given back the castellanship of York.

Ceidre wondered if she would ever see him again.

She knew she could never go back. To return meant giving up her freedom, sharing the same fate that had befallen her brother—imprisonment for life. Only a fool would agree to such, yet there were times when she missed Rolfe so terribly she was ready to pack up and leave, return to Aelfgar, accept her confinement—just to be with him.

He hated her. If he had loved her, nothing would have kept her away. She would return to Aelfgar, surrender herself, and accept her imprisonment. Even if she would see Rolfe only from time to time, those few shared moments would be worth it. But he had never loved her. As Guy had said, as even she had known, he was not a man who could love a woman, and he would never love her now, after her treachery. So she would not return—she could never go back.

One day, when she was old, her son full grown, she would send him his son, a final parting gift from her, proof of her everlasting love.

Rolfe reined in on the hill above Llefewellyn, looking down upon the dozen scattered huts. Smoke rose from the roofs, the sky was gray, foretelling rain or snow. His heart was thudding so thickly he could barely breathe.

He had been looking for her for months.

And now, at last, he had found her.

Immediately after Aelfgar was secured, he had gone to her chamber. His first priority was to make sure she was unharmed, as he fully expected her to be. But most of all, he just needed to be with her. Never had he needed her before as he did then. Only Ceidre could help chase away the pain of Guy's death. He needed to hold her—and be held.

His disbelief to find her gone was overwhelming.

He stormed through the keep, shouting for her, but she was nowhere to be seen. 'Twas finally the prisoner who coldly informed him of her escape. Rolfe and Edwin stared at each other, Rolfe so enraged he could not speak. Then he thought of how he had treated her, as a whore, and knew he could not blame her for running away. His shoulders sank. She was gone. She probably hated him.

Her words came back to him, haunting him. "I love you," she had said. Was it true? Was there any possible way it could be true, after he had abused her so badly? He knew, in that instant, that he desperately needed not just her body, but her love—that he could not live without it. He wondered if he loved her.

It was a shocking question. The answer was elusive.

He had never thought love anything more than an excuse for lust, or the humor of the weak and foolish. He was not weak, he was no fool, yet he could not live without her. If this was love, so be it, then he had been struck.

His resolve became obsession. She was his. He wanted her back, and he would find her, and she would never leave him again. He would not keep her a prisoner, although in fact she would be such. He would keep her so pleasured and pleased that she would not think to leave him. He knew he could do it—he was a man who did what he intended. But first, he had to find her and convince her to return, for he would not force her. He would beg her for forgiveness. He, who had never begged anything from anyone.

He would find her when he found the rebels, and slowly, methodically, he encouraged a network of spies until he got a message to Hereward. The Wake was understandably reluctant to meet him, but Rolfe offered him peace on his northeastern borders. Hereward agreed. Then there was the problem of getting him to reveal Ceidre's whereabouts.

"You want her back as a prisoner, Norman, or a mistress?" Hereward asked bluntly.

"She is mine," Rolfe said. "She will be treated well, do not fear this. Yes, she is still William's prisoner, but I will see that she does not lack for any comfort." His gaze flashed. "Nothing will stop me from finding her."

They made a deal. Rolfe released one of Hereward's best men, whom he had taken prisoner during the battle for Aelfgar, and Hereward told him where she was.

Rolfe signaled to his men to wait for him there on the hill, and he spurred his gray down to the rutted road. He saw her instantly as she crossed the path ahead of him. She was walking in the same direction as he rode, her back to him, her hair in one thick braid, glinting like bronze fire. He could barely control himself; he wanted to sweep her into his arms and hold her, kiss her. He merely moved his mount into a faster walk and came up behind her.

She glanced casually over her shoulder to see who was passing and stiffened, eyes wide. It could not be!

"My lady," Rolfe said politely, "I would have a word with you?" It was a question, not a demand.

Ceidre stared, her hand on her racing heart, wondering if she might faint. Oh, he was here, sitting like a king on that stallion, devastatingly handsome, golden and pagan, like one of the lost gods. She blinked the sudden rush of tears.

"Lady?" he asked unsteadily. His gaze slipped to her swollen belly and breasts, then back up to hold her eyes.

"Have—" She swallowed, "Have you come to take me prisoner, my lord?" Tears blurred her vision.

Rolfe slid off his gray, holding the reins awkwardly. " 'Tis I who am a prisoner," he said roughly. His gaze locked on hers. "You have imprisoned my heart, Ceidre."

She stared, hands clasped tightly. "What do you say?"

"I want you back," he said hoarsely. He looked at her belly again. "Ceidre—you carry my child!"

"Who else's?" she quavered, half smiling, half crying.

"My child." He gulped. He took an unsteady breath. Elation and joy warred with anxiety and fear and need. "I will not force you to return. Ceidre . . . can you forgive me? Can you forgive me and return to Aelfgar with me?"

"You are asking my forgiveness?" She gasped.

He slipped easily to one knee. "Yes."

She could not believe it, this was a dream. He was here, bowing before her, asking her forgiveness. "There is nothing to forgive, my lord," she said softly, tears of joy falling.

He rose. "Your generosity has always overwhelmed me," he said huskily.

She touched his face. "I love you."

He closed his eyes, a ragged sound escaping, then pulled her slowly into his embrace. He held her tightly for a long, long time. "I cannot live without you," he finally said against her ear. "I cannot. If this is love, then I have been smitten."

She leaned back in his embrace to look up at him and saw tears glimmering in his eyes. She knew better than to comment upon them, however, and she smiled though her own vision was quite blurred. "If you do not know how to love, then I will gladly teach you," she whispered.

He smiled too, shakily. "You are a good teacher, you could teach me anything. Ceidre"—his tone lowered —"teach me love. Teach me—now."

She took his beautiful face in her hands and kissed him, with all the tender love she felt. Yet, 'twas impossible, they were lusty souls, and the kiss turned deep and hard and frantic. When he pulled her against him she felt his sex, thick and hard, and she laughed, weeping at the same time.

" 'Tis a sign of my love," he told her, kissing her again.

They separated to walk hand in hand, with urgency and many sidelong, burning glances, to her cottage. He embraced her instantly, seeking her mouth with hot, hard lips. Ceidre clung, shaking. She could not bear to be apart from him for another moment.

He laid her on the pallet and undressed her, running his hands over her reverently, over her face, her neck, her breasts, and her hips. He stroked her swollen belly. "You are so beautiful, Ceidre," he told her. "Yet your beauty is not just of the flesh." He looked at her. " 'Tis of the soul."

"What a wonderful thing to say," she whispered.

His eyes were shining suspiciously. "You grow my babe," he muttered thickly, his hand exploring her stomach's contours. Then he corrected, "Our babe."

She laughed, a joyous sound.

He bent and kissed one full breast, then her navel, her belly. She gasped when he kissed the triangle of hair between her thighs. "What are you doing, my lord?"

"Rolfe," he corrected. He spread her thighs and kissed her again, this time his tongue flicking deeply into her. She gasped. "I love you," he said. He froze, then looked up. Their gazes met.

She smiled slightly. He would learn, he was already learning. Then her smile abruptly faded, because he lowered his head and was licking her with his tongue, lifting the bud of her flesh, gently drawing it into his mouth. She came in a violent, arching climax, and when she was through, he slid into her, his gaze hot and brilliant. "You will never want to leave me," he whispered in her ear, stroking steadily.

"I never wanted to leave you," she told him frankly, and then there were no words, just touches, kisses, and their bodies fused and pushing rhythmically together, until their world shattered brilliantly, as one.

"Will you return with me?" he asked, many hours later.

Ceidre was stirring a stew, and she turned. She saw the anxiety in his gaze, and her heart went out to this strong, proud man who had learned to ask, not demand, who beneath his warrior's armor was flesh and blood, heart and soul. "Yes. I love you, Rolfe."

He smiled with genuine pleasure and came to her, wrapping her in a hug. "I need your love, sweeting," he said. "I cannot live without it."

She turned to face him. "Does this mean you forgive me for Cavlidockk?"

"Yes," he said. "You are a patriot, as am I."

Their gazes held. Many unspoken thoughts and worries flew between them. "We must talk," Rolfe said heavily, and taking her hand, he guided her to the table.

"I am sorry," he said slowly, "that I am Norman and you are Saxon. Yet you do love me."

She heard the question. She would reassure him forever if she must. "I do."

He smiled slightly, then continued. "I am sorry Morcar is dead, truly. Your brother is imprisoned. At least he is alive. Can you accept me as lord of Aelfgar, Ceidre?" His tone was blunt.

"I do." She was sad and joyous at once. "There are things we cannot control, I cannot control. I have grieved endlessly for Morcar, and I grieve for Ed. But I love you. Rolfe, I will never betray you again."

"I know." He hesitated. "Ceidre, there is something you must know. When you return, you will still be the king's prisoner. I cannot change that. I can attempt to talk to William, and I will, but he does not forgive treason readily, and the truth is, I doubt he will lift your sentence. To return"—he took a breath—"is to put yourself back in my custody."

"I understand," she said levelly.

"I will never hurt you," he said fiercely. "I will protect you with my life. No one shall take you from me, I swear this. I will not allow it. You are mine—and this means you have all that is mine, and that you have my protection until I die. Do you understand this?"

"Yes." She took a breath. "I am going home with you, Rolfe. Even had you not said this, I would go. I cannot live apart from you either."

He smiled, taking her hand, holding her gaze.

"I would I could marry you," he said suddenly.

Those simple words meant more to her than anything he could possibly have said. She looked at the floor, willing herself not to cry. Alice was still in a convent in France. "I am flattered," she said softly.

"You know it cannot be," he said, lifting her chin so he could gaze into her eyes.

"I know."

"But in my heart," he said, his blue eyes locked with hers, "you are my wife."

No words could have made her happier.

"Alice was never my wife in my heart," he said. "You know the man I am. When I pledge you my heart, it will never be taken back. You are my wife in my heart: You will always have my protection, my loyalty, my fidelity, and—" He hesitated, and then he flushed.

She was so happy she was crying. She gripped his hand. " 'Tis only words," she encouraged softly. "Only words. A man like you is afraid of a few small words?" she teased through her tears.

He smiled slightly. "You also have my love. We are married in our hearts and, I hope, in the eyes of God."

She left her chair to sit in his lap, holding him. He let her, tucking his head in her bosom. She kissed him, trembling with love, stroking his hair. He could not remain submissive for long, and he shifted so he was holding her. She did not care, she laughed, she wept. Never had she been so happy. She knew the man he was, this husband of her heart. He was Rolfe de Warenne, he was Rolfe the Relentless, proud, strong, a man of honor above all else. He had just given her everything she wished for, all that he could. He had given her his heart, his love.

"I gladly accept, my lord," she whispered, and he crushed her to him again.

EPILOGUE

On December 24, 1072, Alice hanged herself in her chamber in the Convent of the Sisters of Saint John.

On December 24, 1073, Ceidre was married to Rolfe de Warenne. The wedding took place at York. Edwin was released temporarily from confinement to give away the bride. Their three children, two boys and an infant daughter, attended the ceremony, as did King William, Roger of Shrewsbury, Bishop Odo, William fitz Osbern, Walter de Lacy, and many others. The bride was radiant and beaming, the groom grinning and proud; everyone agreed there had never been a more lovestruck couple. The king's wedding present to the couple was the suspension of Ceidre's life sentence; and he was named godfather of their infant daughter. Most of the female congregation wept throughout the service, and a few of the men had shiny eyes as well.

Ever generous when the mood struck him, King William remanded Edwin into Rolfe's custody. He also agreed to the engagement of his widowed daughter Isolda to Edwin. They were married early the following spring, and Edwin promptly claimed Isolda's two-year-old daughter as his own. It is rumored that she had visited him in his confinement at Westminster as early as January of 1070.

AUTHOR'S NOTE

Rolfe de Warenne and Ceidre are fictional characters

Edwin and Morcar were powerful Saxon lords prio
to William of Normandy's invasion and the Battle o
Hastings in October 1066. They were the sons of th
eaorl of Aelfgar, who was good, kindly, nobly con
nected, and powerful. Morcar was the younger son
renowned for his handsome looks. They did have
sister, but she was married to a Welsh lord.

Prior to 1066, Edwin and Morcar were weakened b
an attack from the king of Norway, and they did no
fight at Hastings, which was apparently fortunate fo
William. After that battle, both Ed and Morcar swor
fealty to William. William in turn promised Ed hi
daughter, whom I took the liberty of naming Isolda
and gave him control of all of the north, making hi
eaorl of Mercia. His own Norman lords, who had fol
lowed him from Normandy, as Rolfe did, to gain land
and power, were justifiably upset that so much powe
was being given to Ed. William finally reneged on hi
promise to give Ed his daughter, and Ed and Morcar
who had gone to Normandy with William after Has
tings, returned home furious.

In 1068, while there was the threat of a Danish inva
sion, Ed and Morcar staged their first rebellion in th
north. William had secured the south of England b
granting feudal fiefs to his followers at strategic loca
tions, as I have described in this novel. He took hi

army north and crushed the rebels, building castles and leaving royal garrisons everywhere in Mercia, including at York. Both brothers swore fealty to him again and were forgiven. However, there were now royal garrisons and Norman castles in their territories, to keep them in check.

The brothers staged a second rebellion in 1069, killing the earl of Durham (a Norman) and attacking York. York was besieged and demolished. Apparently at the same time, the Danes invaded and were repulsed at Norwich. It is not clear if this was a coincidence. William and his troops crushed the Danes, relieved York, and sent the rebels fleeing. Construction of a second castle at York was begun, with William remaining there to oversee it personally. Meanwhile, his policy to destroy the rebels began in all earnestness—an iron fist. He would burn and destroy every rebel lair and village, even if he burned down most of the north. Historians have referred to this phase as "the harrying of the north." In my opinion this is too light a term for such a ruthless policy. This is where the story of Rolfe and Ceidre begins. Rolfe is William's most trusted commander in charge of securing the north, crushing the Saxons, and carrying out this policy of burning out every inch of every rebel nest.

It worked. One year later, in 1070, there was a last uprising in the fens, led by Edwin, Morcar, and Hereward the Wake. Because of treachery from within, the rebellion failed. Morcar was killed, Ed captured and imprisoned for life. Hereward's fate is unknown.

Because of the fast pacing of this novel, I took the liberty of moving up this last rebellion so that it occurred September 30, 1069. I also gave Edwin a fictional happy ending with his true-love marriage, finally, to Isolda. His final fate is unknown.